D1706623

FOUR LEAF

By Jeremy Russell

FOUR LEAF

by Jeremy Russell

ISBN: 9798809877602

Editing and Design by Rosalyn Newhouse

Published in the United States of America

E3

Dedicated to Jessica, Dolly and Johnny
who think I am a storyteller.

I'd like to acknowledge the following friends that truly helped me with writing this, my first book:

Michael Wisner for spending so much sweat, time and care to help me, both on this, and on anything I've ever needed help on.

Chris Watson for being my writing partner, like a blood brother. Zero chance I could have done this without you.

Jessica Russell for tolerance, encouragement and love. What a team!

Brent Wisner for telling me to do it, giving me a place to stay, and for inspiring the theme of the story.

Thank you to the following friends for being a very important part of the journey and making a major contribution (alphabetical order):

Alexandra Duparc for inspiration
Arwen Dayton for first rate direction and advice
Cartney Wearn for tips that made all the difference
Christina Moss for guidance and belief
Cody Seymour for help on edits and encouragement
Drea Doven for backup and support
Emily Varga for helpful feedback
Helen Wisner for belief and encouragement
Joyce Gaines for insight and expertise
Kris Russell for free rent when I started this book
Liisa Cushing for friendliness and a place to stay and write
Mario Padilla for astute instruction and critique
Rosalyn Newhouse for finalizing the work
Stephen King for his book on writing
Tere Jones for loving, insightful assistance

Chapter 1
Wade Maley, the Aussie

*B*loody hell. Wade Maley, how are you going to get out of this alive?

In the ceiling of a posh conference room, I lie across beams and nibble on Cadbury chocolate lollies to keep my energy up and my mind keen. Marble floor. Big table of fine parquetry. A TV screen and a bar with crystal decanters and glasses. Fancy paintings. A row of windows. Three floors up. It's been hours. Where is this bloke?

Bulletproof battledress and an armor-plated vest, and the backpack slung on my shoulders weighs thirty-five pounds. It's 22:14 and dark. I hear voices, and stiffen to silence myself. The door flies open. The lights come on. My night vision goes bright and I remove the goggles.

Alistair Watson, my hit, and two girls, dazzlers, thirty to forty years younger, frolic in. I look at the photo in my hand. Even though I studied the man for months, it's smart to reconfirm in real-time that I have the right guy. An eager mind sees what it wants. It looks like him. He seems goofier than in studied footage. Must be on the piss.

All three wear satin robes and drink red wine out of crystal. These smoking hot sheilas would probably have 2M likes on Tik Tok. One's blonde and looks no older than seventeen. The brunette is early twenties.

I remind myself that this sick fuck kidnaps 150,000 people a year, mostly to sell for sex, and likely selects custom

1

"merchandise" to his own specifications for personal use. The chocolate lollies bubble in my stomach at the thought.

The three giggle and merry-make. The girls put on a convincing show, feign tickled pleasure flirting with this dirty geezer. Alistair relaxes into a plush conference room chair. I train my .357 semi-automatic with its silencer on the old guy's right temple. The ladies disrobe. A seductive stripper dance. He woohs. It looks like one is about to pull open his robe and give him a wristy. Something I don't care to see.

He needs to be put down. He deserves to die. This is for you, Peyton. I pull the trigger.

The hollow point hits the right side of his head and the left side explodes like a watermelon, spattering bits onto the blonde woman, the wall and exquisite paintings. The naked ladies shriek and run. The clock now ticks... *getting out of here is going to be impossible.*

SEVEN DAYS EARLIER
QUADFILLIUM, WAR ROOM

We're at a conference table with the founder of QuadFilium, Jean Jacques Girard, at the head. Present are the tacticians, trainers, pilot, science guy, hacker and weapons lady. The boss, Jean-Jacques, sharp-looking bloke in his fifties, addresses us about Alistair's compound, with his French accent.

"Alistair Watson runs the largest human trafficking operation in the world. At its core, he kidnaps kids and sells them for sex. Slaves. He is also heir to and CEO of his father's company, Bio-Gen, worth billions. It makes fuel out of living or dead things rather than crude oil. It can take any organic thing, alive or once alive — trees, animals, corn, even feces — and melt it down into black sludge, then process it into high-level fuel, even rocket fuel.

"Bio-Gen is praised for its legacy of recycling, using crop surpluses, and reduction of fossil fuels. It's received environmental and sustainability awards on four continents. Alistair inherited the legacy and hides under the cloak of his father's brilliance and stellar reputation. People think he's got a fucking cape on. They don't know he's obsessed with pedophilia. He makes more money commercializing sex than in bio-fuel and makes Jeffrey Epstein look like a shoplifter.

"He brings in bodies of dead or worn-out slaves, no longer 'useful,' or whose organs have been grabbed. He melts these down at Bio-Gen, making money at both ends, and eliminates the evidence. One human body produces about one liter of fuel. He sells the fuel for three-dollars a liter. Unconscionable. It's time to take this monster out. Ashkay, tell us about the compound."

Ashkay, genius from Pakistan, the lead hacker, says, "As you can see on the screen, the blueprints show the protection and security measures built into the property. Forty-foot-high barbed wire walls surround the forty-acre estate. There are a hundred active guards at all times."

Kris Connelly, key strategist, a short, bald, fat guy from Brooklyn, leans in and adds, "I've been in there. These guards aren't your typical rent-a-cops. Well-paid, seasoned assassins with continuing advanced training to keep 'em on their toes. They can shoot, fly copters, drive anything. Most of 'em have killed people."

Kris Connelly used to be a legit mobster, smuggler and underground mastermind, working with cartel leaders, traffickers, mob bosses... lived that whole crazy-ass life before coming here to QuadFilium. Most practical strategist we have...

with some badass stories and a badass New York accent.

Kris adds, "Your chances of getting in undetected and getting out alive are less than a percent. Don't fuck up even the slightest thing."

"Thanks, mate. Cheers to you, too," I reply.

Ashkay continues, "There's a sophisticated security system to keep people out, but also, and more importantly, to keep intruders locked down if they make it inside. If the intruder alarm is tripped, every room becomes a prison cell. The doors get mag-locked closed, unopenable to anything but a 500-pound battering ram, unless Security Central unlocks it. Gates drop down in front of all windows."

Jean Jacques gets meaningful and serious, "Wade, this is the most dangerous mission ever undertaken in the twenty-four-year history of QuadFilium. I want to let you know that on behalf of all officers and crew, if you don't make it back, we will always remember and celebrate you as a hero. Mazel Tov."

"That's reassuring, boss... She'll be awright." I reply with my signature Aussie phrase.

PRESENT
WATSON COMPOUND, CONFERENCE ROOM

The naked, screaming young women run down the hall outside the conference room door as I drop down from the ceiling. Moments later, the intruder alarm blares. I grab a chair and run toward the window and jam it in to catch the dropping gate before it locks me in. Gates above every window drop. My chair holds one up.

Guards bang on the mag-locked door. I hear them call Security Central on their radios to deactivate the lock.

I squeeze in around the chair, push open the window and

climb out onto the sill. I tie a rappel line to the gate just as the guards enter. They see the chair in the window and fire in my direction. I kick the chair into the room and jump backwards. A bullet glances off my plated vest. The gate slams against the sill and my rappel line goes taut. I slide down to a balcony. The gate stops them and I hear them alert others by radio.

I run towards the balcony edge and see a lawn, twenty feet down. All according to plan.

I think of my trainer's warnings, retired Navy Seal, John Crutcher. *It's the little things that kill you. Death is rarely explosive. It's the quiet, small, unimportant details that fuck you.* If I jump down twenty feet, hit a sprinkler and twist my ankle, I'm immobilized and dead. I look. I'm clear, so I jump. Grass makes for an easy landing.

Sergeant Crutcher talks live into my audio feed. He has real-time satellite view. "Two hostiles coming around the corner on your three... helmets and vests."

Option one: shoot both moving targets in the mouth, the only unarmored part of their bodies, at fifteen feet, while dodging their machine gun bullets. Bad odds.

I go with option two. Drop a grenade and run.

As I listen for the guards to turn the corner, I count down the four seconds to detonation and at three-point-five I drop forward flat on the grass twenty-five feet away, legs crossed, toes pointed down. I hold my hands over my ears and open my mouth to prevent the concussive pressure exploding my lungs.

Boom! A small piece of shrapnel glances off the top of my left heel. A body part splats next to me. One of those bastards must've been right on the grenade. No time to waste.

The forty-foot, barbed wire-topped wall, bubbling out like the foam on a beer. Three feet thick. My next obstacle. I hear the sounds of the next batch of guards and dogs on their way. Crutcher updates into my audio: "Eight hostiles with canines at your six. Nine hostiles at ten o'clock, 125 yards out, estimated safe time is eleven seconds. Over."

My only way out is over, under, or through this wall. Now I'm keen on why Jean Jacques said "good bye" so... meaningfully. He is Jewish... always says "Mazel Tov."

TWO WEEKS EARLIER
QUADFILIUM, EXTERNAL GROUNDS

"Gizmo-man. How ya goin'?" I ask Dimitri, head engineer. Russian as fuck.

"Fine, Wade. Now let me show how can get your body over big wall." Thick accent. His brittle hair doesn't move in the wind. Dark circles under his eyes. Unshaven. But perfect teeth - like all of us.

"Take look at device." Dimitri hands me a black metal shoebox that weighs about thirty pounds.

"What the fuck is this? Am I squatting with this to up my hops game?" I ask.

"You are funny man. Let me show how works," Dimitri says.

He places the box on the grass and pushes a button. Stakes shoot down from the corners into the ground to stabilize it. He turns a couple of knobs to tilt the top in one direction.

"Help me pick this up," Dimitri says as he points at a 170-pound human dummy. We sit its butt on top of the device. He pulls out an antenna-like rod from the back side of the box, extends it upwards and clips it onto a spot at the center of the back of the dummy's vest, holding the body straight.

"This rod very, very important. Must fix to back to keep

straight. Or else projectile flip, or shoot sideways. Now, stand back," warns Dimitri.

He flicks a trigger, and the lid of the box shoots upwards like a jack-in-the-box. The dummy arcs through the air a good fifty-feet up and lands on the tarmac thirty-feet from us. What's left of the device is a six-foot pole with the dummy's seat at the end. The pole looks like a fat antenna or a telescope with cylinders that were collapsed into each other, now extended.

"Bloody Oath! Rippa! You made a fucking catapult out of a shoebox! How in fuck's name?" I exclaim.

"The cylinders of extending pole are under great deal of air pressure. They are flatten into one another like closed telescope and held until spring loose with switch. Extends six feet, shoot projectile into air," explains Dimitri.

"Nice piece of work, Gizmo man. I noticed the dummy's face smacked into the tarmac from fifty feet up, is that part of the deal?" I ask.

"I have solution. Vest has airbag. Make sure body flat, face-down when land. Make sure rod is on back to keep you straight when trigger. If not, flip through air like pinwheel. Rod keep you straight. No flip." says Dimitri.

I point at the top of his head, "Few kangaroos loose in the top paddock?" I ask.

"I don't understand, maybe my English..." Dimitri says.

"It's fine, mate. So, let me get this straight, to get out of the compound, I have to rig up this gizmo, sit on it, like Bozo the clown shot from a canon, fly over the barbed-wire wall, position myself mid-air like Superman and land face down to belly flop on the ground, cushioned by an airbag that deploys at the last second?" I ask.

"Da."

"For fuck's sake."

PRESENT
WATSON COMPOUND, THE WALL

Guards fire at seventy yards and closing. Shooting while running is rarely accurate, especially with a handgun. Also, it's dark. But with enough volleys, they'll get lucky and hit me. Bullets thump into the grass around me. I have seconds.

I pull the metal box out of my pack and fix it to the ground with the spring-action stakes. I adjust the angle, sit on it and attempt to attach the rod to my back. A bullet whizzes past my ear. The footsteps and yelling get louder. Dogs are faster and getting close. The rod clip to my back isn't working. If I don't attach this, and try to catapult myself, my body will spin through the air maybe twenty feet up, and crash back into the ground on this side of the wall for the firing squad to make pulp out of me. I try again and I can't get the clip to connect. Voices, gunshots and barks are louder. I have maybe one more second before the first dog reaches me and the guards are within accurate firing range. *I'm bloody rooted.*

It's the little things that kill you... No shit, Sergeant Crutcher.

Fuck it. I do my best to guess the alignment of the platform to my spine. If I am off by one half a degree, I'm dead. I trigger it and shoot up into the air.

As I launch, I remember why I got recruited into QuadFilium, a word which is Latin for "Four Leaf." A four-leaf clover. Good luck. I have it.

Against the odds, my alignment was perfect. My body clears the wall a few feet above the cloud of barbed wire. At the apex of trajectory, I feel weightless then start my fifty-foot plunge. It's dark, I can't see where I'm going or what is in front of me as the ground approaches and I accelerate at thirty-two feet per second per second. As Gizmo man told me, I'll be going twenty-eight miles per hour when I hit, like jumping out of a car into a brick wall. The airbag will deploy when a sensor on my chest detects the ground coming near.

I sense my body's relative position to the ground, and use leg and arm jerks to level myself with the horizon to land chest down. I hear muted barks and yells from over the wall, the hostiles probably baffled by the contraption.

Bang! The airbag deploys, punches me in the face and knocks the wind out of me. Decelerating from 28 mph to zero in a one-foot span, every organ slammed into my ribs. Nose is bleeding. I can't breathe. I see stars. I pass out.

I come to. I don't think it's been long. These stars will pass. But in moments, the perimeter guards will come. I catch my breath and get to my feet, wipe the blood off, and look out across a large area of virgin terrain before me.

SEVEN DAYS EARLIER
QUADFILIUM, WAR ROOM

Teska Lando sits to my left, intense and focused. She's the helicopter pilot from Texas. And what a beauty she is. I've never seen the likes of her in my entire life, on a screen, in person or printed in a glossy magazine. But... damaged, I'd say.

She says, in her Texan drawl, "Once you jump the wall, you will be exactly 1,285 feet from where I nab you at the cliff at the end of the field. At your fastest sprint, over uneven ground, barring injuries, I calculate 136 seconds."

I think she likes me. She volunteered for this mission despite its high probability of failure. Well... I'd like to think she likes me.

She continues, "Just before you start running, signal me with three flashes from your bright beam flashlight. I'll be parked in the bluffs with my engine off. Once I see the flashes, I'll set to meet you at the rendezvous, the edge of the cliff, 136 seconds later. I have to keep my engine and lights off until then. Cuz if I sit there like a dipshit waiting to be hog-tied in a rodeo, those bad guys will hit me with a grenade launcher hours before you even see me. So, I'll wait for the flashes and then be there for you, sugar."

"No worries. I'll get there. I just gotta run like a rabid dingo. She'll be awright... love." I turn up my Aussie. We both smile.

Jean Jacques glances at the both of us. Then gets back to business.

PRESENT
WATSON COMPOUND, NORTH PERIMETER

I flash three times directly to where Teska should be parked. I start my watch countdown for 136 seconds and bolt in a straight line. I gazelle my way over small bushes and stones on an undulating field.

The first ten seconds are serene. The cool air nurses my airbag-slapped face. I feel limber and energetic, thanks to adrenaline and the Cadbury lollies. Stadium lights come on, interrupt the peace and illuminate the terrain. *A fly on a white wall.*

"I stand out like dog's balls out here!" I say to Crutcher over the com.

Vehicle engines rev. Hummers. I hear two. Then, sounds like three dirt bikes. Those are going to be faster; but shots from their pistols will be less accurate than the Hummers topped with riflemen. The race is on.

"Looks like a batch of vehicles entering the arena, two Hummers and three bikers, others to follow," says Crutcher.

Bikes'll be right up on me and I still have—*let me check my watch*—100 seconds. Need to slow these pricks down. The inaccurate fire over bumpy terrain, my vest and my luck are my biggest hopes for survival. Otherwise, as Teska would say, I'm a hog in a rodeo.

I pull out a tube on my belt containing star-shaped spikes that look like metal jacks from the kid's sidewalk game with the red rubber ball. One of the dirt bikes gains.

"Biker at your six, forty-five yards and gaining fast," says Crutcher.

Biker number one unloads his semi-automatic in my direction, no bullets come close enough to worry about. I estimate his approach, pop the top off my tube of tire-piercing jacks and spray a line behind me. He doesn't notice what I did, because three seconds later I hear him tumble, off my tail.

Crutcher says, "One biker down, two to go, plus the two Hummers gaining. Riflemen on the beds."

Pop! Crack! They fire at me.

The second biker spotted the tire jacks and drove around. His aim is better. Bullets whiz by me. By the sound of it, he takes small jumps in the air, and uses the steadiness of flight to aim and fire. *This tosser must be some sort of motor-cross enthusiast. Right fucking beauty.*

This gives me an idea, which I need because in four seconds he'll be close enough to pop me off, and I still have thirty seconds left to hit my rendezvous. I pull out a grenade and drop it on the ground before going over a small hill which will block the blast from behind me.

11

Sprinting, I cover my ears and open my mouth as it goes off. The bike tumbles in a clang of parts right behind me. *Piece of piss. I'll do the same to the next biker.*

But I don't hear the third bike.

"Third biker MIA. Can't see him," says Crutcher.

The Hummers are catching up. They're too heavily armored for a grenade to do anything, unless it's right under and that's too hard to make happen. I'm still twenty seconds from rendezvous.

There's no sign of Teska yet. *Did she see my three flashes?*

As I pass over the crest of a knoll, a high-cal bullet punches me in the back and I soar through the air, once again in Superman pose. The plates in the vest blocked penetration. Still a wrecking ball in the back.

I land face down in the dirt and slide a few feet. Fifteen seconds from the bluff. The two Hummers seconds away from the hill behind me. My heart pounds in my chest and hammers in my ears. I still don't see Teska. *What the fuck am I going to do? I'm a dead man.* One asshole on foot against these fuckers? "Wade Maley, the Aussie cunt who slowed the human trafficking trade a smidge before dying." That'll be on my fucking tombstone. Although... my name is already on a tombstone.

An idea flashes: the Hummer driver saw me get hit and disappear over the hill. He expects me face down in a heap, right here, when he drives over the mound. He'll slow a bit as he comes over, to stop in front of my body.

I push myself up, roll onto my back and slide-up the hill behind me. The nose of the Hummer appears over my head like a star destroyer. I hear the orchestral Star Wars movie theme. The wheels roll past each side of me. As predicted, the driver slows, confused to see no one anywhere. He stops, looks around. I ninja onto the back of the Hummer, and come up behind the rifleman who leans on the roof, looking side to side. I snap his neck before he has a chance to scream. *The driver will hear the commotion and look out the window.* I point my .357 over the side. He pops his head out and I shoot him point-blank.

The neighboring Hummer team to my left pulls up, hears the shot, and its rifleman turns in my direction with his gun. I roll backwards off the passenger side as he sprays ordnance. He's well-exposed compared to me, so I take my time and aim, while he pumps bullets in my direction. Two shots take him out.

Teska's helicopter appears near the bluff, a hundred yards away, and a rope ladder dangles. The driver of the second Hummer is the only remaining hostile in proximity. Aside from trying to run me over, risking driving off the cliff himself, he has no way to incapacitate me. He can't reach out the window and shoot me while I'm running with any accuracy. I sprint towards the rope ladder. Counting down, 10, 9, 8, 7, 6, 5... a hundred-yard dash in ten seconds. Then, I see him. The third missing biker stands up from behind a bloody bush in front of me and shoots from fifteen feet. The bullet hits my right thigh and cracks my femur. The bulletproof material is flexible. It may not allow penetration, but a bullet is still a crowbar in full swing. The pain is blinding, and I almost pass out, but rageful adrenaline numbs it. *Thank you QuadFilium for the pain training.* I switch to hopping on my left leg. *Thank you Sergeant Crutcher for the one-legged squats.*

Bush-hider shoots me in the chest twice. The vest is well-armored so aside from slowing my hopping ass down, I keep going. I don't bother to pull out my gun, he's so well-armored and has so few vulnerabilities. I have a better chance dodging bullets than trying to do a cowboy showdown.

He takes two more shots. The first hits my left arm above the elbow, cracking my humerus. The pain is unbearable. My limb goes limp. My vision, a spinning kaleidoscope. My body goes into shock. The world goes foggy.

His third shot is a clicking sound. Music to my ears. He wasted his bullets on me when he was on his bike. I recover my senses. Even if he has another pistol, by the time he pulls it out I'll be swinging on a rope ladder. I hop and fight to stay conscious.

Bush-hider charges me. *Now I'm rooted.* I have two limbs weaker than a sunburned snowflake and a collection of broken ribs front and back. *A little kid could kick my ass.*

With my working arm, I pull out my pistol and aim for his mouth, the only unarmored spot on his whole body. I pull the trigger mid-hop ten feet away. The bullet goes through the center of his lips and clangs against the back inside of his helmet and whips his head back. His body flops forwards.

I hop to the edge of the bluff, grab the rope ladder with my one good arm and step on a rung with my one good leg.

Teska flies the chopper away as bullets glance off the armored fuselage. The ladder spins, giving me a view of two more platoons of guards, tearing across the field towards us. *We had seconds.*

Chapter 2
Teska Lando, Texan Pilot

Wade grabs my rope ladder and I spin the chopper away from the scene. *Good God almighty, I'll be dipped and rolled in cracker crumbs! Close fucking call!* He can't hold on too long with those injuries. There's a plateau 300 yards away. I bring the chopper to hover over it and descend to drop him off. I can't see him from here, so the medic opens the side door and looks down.

"He's good. He is on the ground," he shouts.

I do a little turn and land twenty feet away from Wade, keeping the engine running.

"Patch him up and load him in, fast!" I tell the medic. I run over to Wade, lying in a heap, tangled in the rope ladder. The medic works on him.

"Thanks, love," Wade says to me.

"You had me worried there for a moment, Wade. Seeing you hopping around like that..."

"I was fine. All under control. She'll be—"

"...Awright?" I cut him off to finish his signature phrase in my best Aussie accent.

"Americans never sound like real Aussies," he says.

"You Aussies would never admit it if we could," I say.

"Probably true. You know back there I was more worried about how goofy I looked, hopping around like an unco," he says.

"Unco?" I ask.

15

"Aussie slang... an uncoordinated bloke. We used to call the goofy kids that in school when they tried to play sport."

"What an asshole."

The medic notices the flirty banter. I catch both blokes glancing at me up and down as I stand there. At my body. Even now, in the grip of a life-or-death struggle, with unbearable injuries, guys still have the nerve to check me out.

The medic injects Wade with painkillers and we load into the chopper. He removes Wade's armor, bandages him and I take off from the plateau. The chopper is rigged to dampen the deafening sound of the propellers so we can hear each other speak in the cabin.

"Teska, I'm pretty sure I'm high from these painkillers," Wade says.

The medic chuckles and says, "It's true."

"How bad are the injuries?" I ask.

"I think he broke his femur and probably his humerus. Maybe ribs."

"See... not bad," says Wade.

"Jesus almighty. You got more guts than you can hang on a fence," I say.

"She'll be awright."

We both chuckle.

"Ouch! Okay, okay laughing hurts," says Wade.

"That confirms it. The ribs are broken." says the medic, who leans back on his seat and puts on headphones.

A few minutes of silence pass as we move over the hills and valleys below. Wade looks calm.

"We have about an hour to get back. Want to listen to some music?" I ask.

"Nah...Maybe we can chat. Get my mind off that whole

experience."

"Sure. Any subject in particular?"

"Yeah, how did you end up here?" asks Wade.

"...probably the same way you did. Scopulus," I say. Scopulus, Latin for "cliff." I'll never forget mine. A huge moment in life. It's when everything's fucked and you want to die. Jean Jacques coined the term to describe the moment in your life when you are ready to be recruited for QuadFilium.

"Sure, of course. What was yours?" asks Wade.

"It was brutal."

"Everyone's is. Did Jean Jacques show up at just the right moment?"

"Yeah. Minutes away from me killing myself actually."

"Bloody oath. What happened? Tell me. Every detail. I want to know," says Wade.

"You want my story right now?"

"Yeah sure. Why not?"

"You need to rest."

"I need to focus on something."

I start to think about my scopulus. A devastating experience. I fly over a small town and more hills on the way to our base in France.

"Okay, well, normal Texan country girl life until ten. Then, everything changed when I was the only survivor in a plane crash. Not a puddle jumper plane, a real big jet with hundreds of passengers. I lost my whole family... parents... sister. An orphan. I spent the next seven years in foster homes, all but one had the added benefit of perverted-ass pedophiles. At first, I said nothing because I was scared shitless and didn't know any better. But one day a schoolteacher suspected something and asked me about it. I told her. And next thing I know I'm back in the orphanage and the guy, my foster father, ended up in jail. Anyways, this happened two more times in different foster homes over the next couple years. Starting out great and then the older brother or uncle or father loses it. Didn't help none that puberty was making itself known to the world by giving me more curves than a barrel of snakes... with these fat bags big as Dallas. The last guy who tried to do this shit with me, my foster father's brother, actually blew his own head off after I called the police on him for the sick shit he was doing.

"When I was old enough to be on my own, I decided to try out real relationships with real guys. Found some good ones, but they each turned out to be douche bags. One super-nice guy videoed our bedroom activities and put it out on the web. And he was the nicest of the few guys I dated. Guess he had horns holding up his halo. By twenty years old I was pretty certain that all men were hard-wired to be fucked up perverts, and couldn't help it.

"Right about when I was 100% done with all men in the universe, I met this mild-mannered churched fella named Jeffrey Miles. He was honestly a good person. Never weird. Really cared about me. We fell in love and moved in together. He paid for my education, piloting, which was what I always wanted to do. It was real love, I'd say. Didn't know what it was 'til then.

"One night, I decided to surprise him and show up to his hotel room in a town where he was working, 200 miles away from where we lived in Austin. I knocked on his door and he opened it without checking the eyehole, maybe thinking it was room service. Some naked bitch was standing behind him. Jeffrey was in nothing but a robe.

"Now, ordinarily, a woman in a moment like this freaks out

pretty bad and starts screaming and shit. I went numb. Absolute despair soaked my soul like a bucket of acid. Everything went watery thin. I could only hear distant echoes, like on a foggy ship, rocking. I stumbled down the hall, not saying shit, while Jeffrey yelled my name begging me to listen to him, telling me it's not what I think. That shithead actually said that. He even tried to grab me, but I broke free. That was the last time I saw him."

I look over at Wade. Although his eyes are half closed, he listens.

"I turned my phone off and drove back towards Austin. I had a mind to jerk the wheel and end it. I was certain it was the only solution. But I had a cat at home named Spider and I wanted to find her a new home before I offed myself. Wouldn't be fair to her. She didn't do nothing wrong. That was the worst night of my life.

"When I opened the door to the apartment, I froze and snapped out of my funk, cuz Jean Jacques him-fucking-self was sitting there on my couch with my cat purring on his lap. He was so fancy looking in his suit and clean-cut hair an' stuff, ain't no way he was a burglar. Didn't ride into town on a mule. He looked more like a politician or a news anchor or something.

"I grabbed for the gun we kept in the drawer next to the door. It wasn't there. I turned back and he was holding it by the barrel. He'd unloaded it. He told me this is going to be the most important night of my life, and that I needed to listen to him. I told him I'm calling the cops. But, he was calm and asked me to hear him out. He handed me my cat.

"If he wasn't so fancy and chill, and if my cat didn't approve of him, I think I would have just run out of there. But, he seemed so sincere. And since my life was over anyways, no

19

family, no fiancé, nothing left, maybe this guy has something I should hear about. That's what I was thinking... and if not, fuck it, I'll kill myself. Nothin' to lose."

"He told me about QuadFilium. How it has a twenty-year contract. How they'll fake my death and replace my teeth. How they kill bad guys, sex traffickers and other criminals who get away with shit all the time. He told me the statistics and the benefits. He told me I get ten million dollars at the end of the whole thing and can live wherever I want as a real person with a new identity. That he has billions of dollars. I asked him if he's a kidnapper, and why I should believe him? Why don't I just go to the cops and tell them about this murderous secret group. He said they won't believe me and would throw me in the loony bin. He told me to trust him.

"He said QuadFilium is Latin for Four Leaf because good luck is the primary quality that he looks for in a recruit. He told me the fact that I survived the plane crash, and a few other close calls with death, like when I fell out a third-story window when I was thirteen, or when one of the foster family members, ex-army, tried to kill me before he killed himself; all confirmed it. He said this is why he has been keeping an eye on me for years, waiting for the right moment to swoop in and recruit me. Seemed like he'd been tracking my every move. But one thing he said that really clicked for me.

" 'You are done with this life. QuadFilium offers a safe environment where you are highly valued. All efforts directed at the eradication of documented human trafficking crimes. A strong, positive future where your talents are developed and nurtured. Where you are judged by merit and honor, not your... silhouette.'

"It struck a chord. And he told me any romance was

forbidden during the initial months of training. That was a relief. I loved the idea of a new start with a purpose and strong goal. Killing pedophiles sounded kinda weird but also kinda great. Sure as hell wanted to do that already. I asked him if I could keep the cat. When he said yes, I was like, 'I'm in.' "

Wade says, "And here you are. Flying me away from an army of psycho soldiers... not in Kansas anymore."

"Ha ha. Yeah, no shit."

"This drug's making me woozy. I'm gonna close my eyes now , but thanks for sharing."

"Get some rest. I'll wake you when we get there," I say.

I think about when I joined. Intensive training. What a relief that relationships were forbidden. No one tried anything. It was the first time I felt safe from predatory men. I could be myself and live without getting hit on.

After 115 miles, I land the chopper at a QuadFilium outpost, an unremarkable, dark brown building and heliport on a rural mountainside. Impossible to find without coordinates. We enter, then descend through a hidden elevator and board an automated underground train to the QuadFilium base. Every step of the way requires a triple security entry check: retinal scan, voice and fingerprint. Each member passes through one by one. On a wheelchair, it's a bit harder for Wade.

It's a fifteen-minute train ride. I still don't know where the base actually is. That's okay. It's better we don't know.

Chapter 3
Jean Jacques Girard

"Sir, Teska and Wade just arrived," says Olivia, my secretary.

"Great," I answer.

I open the door to my office. I pause and look a moment. My reflection in the glass, "Jean Jacques Girard, Founder" etched on the front. I close the door behind me. The office is clean, minimalist, glass and metal. It's been polished to a gleam in my absence. I pick up a note on my desk. I am to meet with one of my staff from the Estates Department, who handles repairs. He has been considering resignation from QuadFilium and I'd asked for the appointment with him. I pick up my phone and dial my secretary.

"Yes, Mr. Girard?" she says.

"At risk of repetition Olivia, you may call me Jean Jacques if you wish," I respond.

"Yes, sir, of course. It's easier to say 'Mr. Girard,' " says my American secretary.

"Ha! Of course. Well, can you call for Ian? I'm ready to see him."

"Of course."

Ian Braddock. I open his file and review recent entries. It says he had aspirations to become a field agent, derailed by a knee injury. Since then, he has not been as enthusiastic about his position here. He has been at QF for eight years. I hear a knock and Ian enters the room, politely nods and says, "Sir." I stand to greet him and direct him to sit across from me. He wears a repairman's jumpsuit, has dark blonde-hair and ears that jut out a trifle.

"Ian. How are you doing?" I ask.

"I'm fine. Thanks for taking the time to chat," he says.

"Of course. Anytime. So, it seems you had a loss on failing to make field agent. And now you are considering resignation?" I ask.

"Yes, sir. The excitement of direct action and the goals were really what I signed on for. I love helping out with maintenance and repairs. I have a knack for it, but honestly, Sir, I'm unhappy," he says.

"Okay. Well, your objectives are vital. You've learned a great deal and you are a valuable team member. In twelve years, you'll matriculate and receive your full ten million-dollar ending bonus," I say.

Ian nods, and says, "I've told myself that for the last five years, since my injury. But I can't help but think about the family I want to have, and the other things I want to do with my life. I don't know if it's worth ten million to me at this point."

"I can't fault a man's aspirations. Let me tell you a story. Let's see... I am fifty-four now. French and Jewish. I'm married to Madame Frances Girard, as you know. Madame is heiress to the fortune her grandfather built with his cosmetic company, *Estrelle*. When I was in my late twenties, after Frances and I married, I found myself in an executive position with *Estrelle*. I managed exports and imports for Europe. One cold day, a year into the job, at the Port of Le Havre in Northern France, one of my men received on our dock a misrouted shipping container. The port foreman called me down to see. It was full of dead bodies. Little children and some adults, piled randomly on top of each other. The sight and smell made me vomit. The most macabre thing I'd ever seen... it violently disturbed me... my family endured the Holocaust. My grandfather died in Auschwitz.

"Uniquely, and impossibly, all had died except one nine-year-old girl. She had survived without food or water for twenty-nine days. Frances and I adopted her. Her name is Carmen. We contacted the Gendarmerie Nationale. It turned out these people were being shipped to Europe to be sold as sex slaves. We hear and read about it. But firsthand, it is another thing.

"The police and the law enforcement tried, diligently I might add, but they came up short, maybe one suspect who disappeared. But I couldn't let it go. I retained ex-police detectives and PIs, whomever, to track the perpetrators. In the process, one of my investigating detectives was murdered. At a loss, I hired mercenaries, assassins, underground types, Mafioso. I couldn't rest and carry on with life as normal. Justice had to be served. My Carmen's entire family was dead. We loved her as our own daughter. She had been shipped to be abused, drugged and made into a sex slave. When used up, harvested for her organs. An evil only rivaled in history by the Nazis. I wasn't going to relent."

"The assassins at last found a number of the criminals responsible and executed them. A dozen or so. This interrupted a great deal of the traffic coming through the port. While satisfying, it wasn't enough. I became obsessed with the number of missing children and the black-market organ trade. Multi-billion enterprises. In the United States today, there are more slaves in bondage than before its Civil War. I convinced my wife to fund QuadFilium. I built this organization. We have eliminated hundreds of traffickers, and freed thousands of victims.

"But there's something you need to know, Ian. Every member of this group, from the cook, to laundry personnel, to the field operatives, is 100% vital, irreplaceable and a hero. No one is more valuable than the other. We cannot exist without a cohesive, self-sustained group. Repairing items on the base has as much to do with freeing enslaved captives of human traffickers as unlocking a cage, opening a door and letting a kidnapped child free. Just as much."

I look at him expectantly to invite his response.

He says, "I never really thought of it that way. I forgot the real reason I joined..."

"Okay. But you're brave. You aren't afraid of action."

"That's right."

"Well, just because you can't rappel down the side of a building doesn't mean you cannot be a more direct part of the action. There are operative roles you could fill. Transport, communications, logistics. There's plenty you could do on our missions."

"I'd like that." Ian smiles and his ears move back and look larger than before.

"Then it's settled. I'll have HR replace you. You'll be reinserted into special forces training. We'll design a role for you."

"Wow... Thank you, Sir. That sounds fantastic. I definitely want to stay and be part of this."

"I'm glad we had this talk," I say.

Ian gets up, shakes my hand and leaves. I make some notes in his file.

Brett Meyers, my top advisor and friend, walks into my office.

"Well, it looks like Teska aced the mission, Double J," he says. "That was a pretty dangerous one. I'm surprised you sent her. She's so new," says Brett as he sits where Ian had been sitting. He insists on wearing nice suits, even though it's not required.

I say, "Her part was relatively safe. She insisted on it. It was Wade's that was impossible. Decidedly impossible. I was worried he would not survive." I try not to betray the mixed feelings I have, but Brett was a very successful trial lawyer. If he can read the mind of a stoic-faced juror at twenty feet, I'm sure he can see right through me.

"You okay, man?" he asks.

I turn away and change the subject, "There's going to be a party to celebrate the successful mission. Taking out Alistair Watson was our most significant, single accomplishment to date. We undo their human and organ trafficking structure and take out their top managers, things will really start to dissolve."

"We're going to need to target top clients, to quell the demand. It'll kneecap the kidnappers. If word gets out that buyers are starting to die, shopping will hit the toilet, and shut off other human trafficking entrepreneurs," says Brett.

"I agree. Now... let's go see how setups for the festivities are going."

We exit the office, down the hall and into the Commons, QuadFilium's large hall that doubles as a staff lounge and venue for base events. Preparations for the party are underway with workers bringing in gear and lights and setting up a microphone on a small stage. Wade, Teska and a dozen others laugh and cajole on a circle of couches in the center. Wade, in a wheelchair, wears removable leg and arm casts which he displays like trophies.

"Tonight, we celebrate! Wade, Teska, you are guests of honor," I say. The group cheers a little and Wade flexes his working limb.

"Don't break your good arm patting yourself on the back," says Teska.

"C'mon! You're impressed!" says Wade.

Brett adds, "Wade, you're the only guy I know who struts sitting down."

The group laughs, and Brett and I return towards my office.

My phone rings. It's Carmen.

"Hello, honey."

"Hi, Dad. Mother and I had lunch today. Are you two doing okay?" The question strikes like a jab for which I was unprepared.

"Where's the 'Hello, how are you?' " I ask, parrying her attack.

"Whatever. She said we aren't spending Christmas together this year because you'll be working. You'd never let anything get in the way of family Christmas, unless you and Mom are fighting. I can just tell."

"No... I just have an important project that I cannot skip. I tried and really can't. Your mother and I are fine." I sound convincing.

"Okay. Tell me if you aren't though. I don't want you lying to me. 'Lying leads to crying and dying.' "

"I thought that was my line," I reply.

"Yeah, well, you should follow your own rules," she says. She has no idea. Her statement sticks a pin into every area of my life.

I laugh, "Okay, honey, I will. Love you. Bye," I say.

It's been a year since Frances and I were intimate... she's

27

been cold and angry. Frances's intuition isn't faulty. It's a razor knife that cuts through my pretenses like a surgeon. Her suspicion, *Teska*. She hates the girl... and she's right. I can't get over my infatuation. While I've never strayed, I've also never had this much sexual attraction for anyone before. The only thing that dulls it is to focus on my work. The next mission. The next mission.

I decide to call a meeting of the strategists.

"Hey, Brett," I say.

"Yeah?"

"Can you gather the strat team? I want to go over ideas for our next mission."

"You bet, Double J," says Brett.

"Oh, and by the way, after the meeting I'll call you. I want you to see the progress we made in research and development," I add.

"Love it," says Brett.

Brett leaves to arrange the meeting. I sit down and make some notes. I'm not halfway finished when Brett messages me that the strategists have gathered.

I walk in and take the seat at the head of the conference table. The QuadFilium War Room is all business. A high-tech cube. No windows. No cameras. Its walls, floors, and ceiling are lined with hidden grids of copper mesh, creating a Faraday cage. Nothing gets in. Nothing gets out. Screens line the entire wall on the left side. Kris Connelly sits to my left. To his left sits Heidi Flannagin, a top strategist. Heidi is Caucasian, in her fifties, a former madame for a successful prostitution ring serving top-level execs, entertainment superstars, Wall Street wolves and anyone else that had the money and inclination to pay for the services she offered.

To my right is John Crutcher. Mid-fifties, Black, a former Marine Special Operations platoon lieutenant with a powerful physique and military presence. At the far end of the table sit three apprentices, one for each of my strategists, and Brett.

I start, "We need to move forward fast on our target list for the next-level managers and several of their top clients in Alistair Watson's human trade. Kris, do you have a list of proposed targets?"

"Yes, sir, right here," Kris says. A list of twenty names appears on the screen. "These are some of Alistair's top johns. Four Europeans, four Americans and one Australian."

Heidi says, "We could send in teams to terminate them and make having sex slaves unhealthy."

"Do we have a *full* list?" I ask.

John answers, "No. Alistair's trafficking business supplies hundreds of slaves a day. It has well-hidden and guarded distribution units all over the world to house, prepare and distribute the 'merchandise'. Top clients purchase one to five slaves at a time from dealers in their region. We identified, for example, the Los Angeles location. LA has 260,000 millionaires. We estimate one thousand are clients. The LA distribution center sells 150 to 200 per week. Our intelligence unit hacked electronic ledgers but were only able to gather the names and contact info of three clients. They keep most of their records in a handwritten book to prevent leaks. We don't know the other 997 some-odd clients. Those names will be in the notebooks at the distribution centers."

"Alistair is eliminated. We can expect people are going to be looking over their shoulders. What's your take, Brett?" I ask.

Brett answers, "The numbers are daunting. Yeah, we kicked them where it hurts, but business will continue, with the next guy in line taking over and running the show."

I frown.

"But you have a point. How do we break the business at the roots? That's the question. We cannot eradicate every single member of the organization, as well as the thousands of clients. And we know what happened the last time we reported the whereabouts of one of these distribution centers to the FBI. Four dead FBI agents. They moved and set up shop in a week elsewhere. This criminal operation is well-connected. Spies, bribes, they work with impunity."

Brett stands up and puts one hand in his suit pants pocket and moves his other hand while he talks. Ever the lawyer. "I have another idea. What if we close down an entire regional center and free its slaves? Based on Kris's numbers, there'll be hundreds of captives in any one of these major facilities, or distribution centers, as you call them. We go in, take out the personnel, and free the slaves, and feel like a bunch of Abraham Lincolns."

"Hopefully we do not get assassinated in the process," says Heidi.

Brett nods. "We confiscate the ledgers and send a gift basket with a note to the names in there: Free your slaves or die."

"I love that idea. I think LA sounds good." says Kris.

Heidi says, "I like it. We make a statement. Hit several local clients, so word gets out… record the termination live."

I pause and consider.

How many people work in one of these regional distribution centers?" I ask.

"The one in LA has about forty personnel including a sales unit," answers John.

"We'll put together the tactical program and present it to you," Heidi says.

"Sounds good. Meeting adjourned," I say and walk out.

I start my daily executive inspection of the QF facility. Unlike CEOs or military generals, I prefer a daily eyes-on inspection of the entire facility and personnel. I walk to the training wing and watch new recruits practice hand-to-hand combat, fire weapons and lift weights. My eyes linger on Teska for a moment longer than necessary. She's in the mobile firing range unloading on a series of moving targets.

My calendar beeps and I check my phone. I have a meeting with Jenny. She's three days away from hitting her twenty-year mark and retirement. I retrace my steps, but steal one more glance at Teska without slowing my stride. Wade appears in a wheelchair. He rolls down the hall towards me.

"Sorry I can't give you a proper stand greet, boss man," says the always cheerful Aussie. He throws his good hand up in a military salute, even though a salute is not mandated.

I laugh. "How are you feeling, Wade? I heard you cracked seven bones but no full breaks," I say with a smile. Young men love their battle scars.

"Right now, I'm feeling tip top, but that's partially cuz they got me on happy pills. Otherwise, I'm choc-a-bloc with aches and pains, 'specially when I sneeze. Crickey, those ribs hurt! But at least I get to be a bludger for a couple weeks," he answers.

"I thought I was good at Aussie slang. 'Bludger'?" I ask.

"Lazy bastard," he explains.

"Ah, thanks. Well, heal up soon. The next mission is a doozie, and you're going to head the team," I say.

"Wish I was Wolverine sometimes, magic healing powers," says Wade.

"Well, you have some magic in you, *mon frère*," I say, countering his Aussie with French. "I'll see you around, I'm almost late for a meeting."

"Cheers, boss." Wade wheels away.

I walk to my office. When I enter, Jenny Summerville stands to greet me with a sheen of glass in her eyes. She forces a polite smile and nods her head at me. I give her a gentle side hug and walk around to my desk. She's sad but keeps it to herself well. Nice hair, nice clothes, fit, in her forties.

"Well, this is it, then?" I ask.

"I can't believe it. QuadFilium has been my home for the last twenty years. All my friends are here, so many memories, so many moments I'll never forget. I'm going to miss you, Mr. Girard."

"The departure team manager tells me you are going to live in Italy. I must say, I can't argue with that choice. I'm sorry I don't keep up with everything but are you and Eric still together?"

She looks away, "We... decided to split up. Eric wants to finish his twenty. He has five left."

"Is it because he'll receive less money if he leaves now?" I ask.

Jenny wipes her eyes. "He says it's a matter of honor and pride. He agreed to do twenty years and he wants to uphold his promise. He also said he'll try and wait for me."

Loyal members straining their relationship because of logistics? I don't like it.

"And you would prefer to remain in a relationship with him?"

"Oh of course. I love him. But I respect his choice."

I punch the intercom. "Olivia," I call my assistant, "get Eric

Meyersfield up here right away, please." I hang up the phone. Jenny looks surprised.

She says, "Please, Mr. Girard, I mean... It's fine. Please don't trouble yourself with this. You have so many important things to attend to."

"Jenny, this *is* very important. QuadFilium isn't martyrdom."

Eric is escorted into the office and I stand and shake his hand.

"Jenny, could I talk to Eric alone for a few minutes?" I ask.

"Of course, I'll wait outside the office," she leaves, dabbing her eyes and fidgeting.

"Eric."

"Yes, Mr. Girard."

"If you could stay with Jenny and still remain at QuadFilium would you?" I ask, point blank.

"I love her, Mr... Girard. Yes. But I am a man of my honor and I would never want to let the group down," says Eric. His eyes are a little red with dark bags.

"What if I set up to have you fly to her location in Italy every second weekend and spend it with her? You could maintain your relationship that way, plus you will have annual vacations you could spend together. Would you want to do that?" I ask.

"Well..."

"We'd arrange the cost of transportation."

"Oh wow... Yes, I would find that arrangement... well... incredible, really." Eric's eyebrows raise and he straightens up in his seat.

"Let's find out if Jenny wants that too, shall we?" I say.

Eric gets up and opens the door. He calls out Jenny's name

and she comes back in, her eyes darting between the two of us.

"Would you be happy with an arrangement of having Eric visit you every second weekend for the next five years while he finishes up his contract, plus annual paid vacations?"

Jenny sits down and looks at each of us again.

"Eric? Do you want to do that?" she asks.

"Yes, sunshine, I do." Eric's eyes get watery.

"Yes! Of course! I can't even believe it. This whole last six months has been torture knowing I was going to possibly lose you," exclaims Jenny. They embrace. Jenny's body shakes slightly as she begins to cry. A salty tear purges through a dry duct into my eye and I blink it away.

"Thank you so much, Jean Jacques. This means so much to us," says Jenny.

"Thank you, sir," says Eric.

I stand up and shake both of their hands.

"Eric, I have a little more to discuss with Jenny before she continues her departure process."

"No problem, Mr. Jean Jacques, I'll head back to my work now. Thanks again. You're a real gentleman, sir," says Eric as he leaves with a little bounce in his step. I take a deep breath to hide my sentiment, and allow Jenny to compose herself.

I go over with Jenny the matter of maintaining security, including a detailed cover story for how she got her money and how important it is that she never reveals the truth of her past here. She agrees. I let her know that the Departure Unit will outfit her with all needed documents for a new identity, including a passport, and will prepare her on answers to any questions she is asked, but the personal communication from me to any soon-to-be-former member adds gravity to these rules.

"Do you have any misgivings about the line of work we do here or the execution of criminals without due process? Any unhandled experiences in the group?" I ask.

"I mean... I see the courts and law enforcement fail to handle the situation. It allows the criminality to flourish and ruin so many innocent people's lives. If I'd been trained as a field operative, I would have had no hesitation pulling the trigger, even though I find violence sickening. My only problem has to do with the agents we lost in the line of duty. I know it comes with the job and blame no one for it. I know the extensive measures we take to prevent it. But, I loved them. They're part of my team," she answers.

I place in front of her the gold and emerald four-leaf clover that we gift to all retirees.

"You have worked hard these last twenty years. Your contributions have saved the lives of untold thousands. On behalf of the survivors whose lives you salvaged and the staff and officers of QuadFilium, you are deeply thanked."

She cries a little harder, smiles and nods at me through the tears, collects her new piece of jewelry and comes around to give me a hug. She leaves my office.

The mission celebration begins in an hour. I get up to complete my inspection rounds. I'd planned to bring Brett along to show him the most recent R&D, so I call him. He shows up and we head over to the Bat Cave, as Wade likes to call the Tech Wing, where innovations and tools are fabricated, medical and tactical. I open the door to the medical lab. The space brims with beakers, colored liquids, vials, test tubes, scopes and white-coated personnel.

"We're working on the next level of RhinoSkin fabric. The current version is made by splicing spider DNA into silkworms and cultivating the threads into highly durable fabric," I say to Brett as we walk towards Dimitri.

"Incredible stuff. When can I get a suit tailored in it?" asks Brett.

"We're doing that already for mission operatives. For undercover stuff. But yes, you should have one as well. We're testing ways to make it even better. We want to handle the flexibility issue so a bullet can be relatively harmless to the wearer. Rather than just being impenetrable, we need it to form-fit the body but allow less of a dent inwards when the bullet hits, distributing the blow throughout the fabric."

"Of course," says Brett.

I show him prototype samples. The Director of the R&D, Dimitri Abdromonova, comes over and greets us. "Comrades, please let know if need help." He smiles.

"Yes, can you tell us about the healing potion?" I ask.

"Yes, I explaining. Accelerated healing serum for repair damaged tissue and bone faster than natural. Stem cell already well advanced and we use. But we also get healing power of tongue and eye," says Dimitri, "they fastest healing organs in body."

"Yes, if I recall correctly, the eye will heal a scratch in twenty-four hours. A skin scratch takes four days, or a couple of weeks for deeper ones," says Brett.

"Da," says Dimitri. "We isolated healing properties of eye tissue repair cells and combine with skin steroid and natural skin components to serum. And stem cells. Apply to hemorrhages reduce healing time to half."

"Fascinating!" says Brett.

I jump in, "He also harnessed the tongue's ability to heal rapidly and replicated this directly on bone and muscle reconstruction in combination with nutrient saturation and stem cell accelerants. He's using Wade as a test subject. He's left a couple of his broken ribs to heal on their own, as a control."

"I love it."

We walk to the Weapons and Devices unit, a large room with half a dozen work tables in the center, each displays unique project components. The walls are lined with shelves of every conceivable tool, fastener, adhesive and raw material one could require. On the periphery are drill presses, welders, 3D printers and dozens of other fabricating tools.

"This is where I feel like Bruce Wayne," I say.

"Yeah, me too," says Brett. "Hey Dimitri, how did you make our ear and eye devices so they could avoid metal detectors?" asks Brett.

"Mainly use silicon parts and virtually undetectable amounts of metal. Very detailed x-ray reveal only tiniest specks, easily fool metal detectors and bug-sensing devices. Operative safely blend without detection, but give us access to everything hear and see."

"So you spy on me in the bathroom, Double J?"

"Very funny."

"It took me a minute to get used to that, by the way," says Brett.

"It takes some time for new members to adjust to their every move recorded and viewable. Only one's thoughts are private."

"Indeed."

I look over at a nearby table and see a bloody band-aid on the counter, "Dimitri, this is disgusting. Get it out of here."

"This actually spy prop, sir."

"Oh... How so?"

"Look at these." Dimitri holds three minuscule tools. A razor, a handcuff key and a tiny syringe. "Can place these under bloody band-aid. Stick to body. Even bad guy not touch."

"What's in the syringe?" Brett asks, holding the miniature syringe up close, studying it.

"Adrenaline and drug for super strong."

"How fast does it activate?" I ask.

"Five second," answers Dimitri.

"It's so tiny," says Brett.

"So, this all goes under the band-aid? It fits?" I ask.

"Yes sir. Even if strip search, no one touch bloody band-aid. No one want to get disease. Even bad guy."

"I can see that. If I had a criminal subject stripped down and under interrogation and saw that, I'd leave it alone. Well, at least until now. Brilliant move," I say.

Brett and I look around at other gadgets. The exploding cigarettes, laser watch, night vision sunglasses, a set of air pods that are also an electromagnetic pulse device.

"How's the phone gun coming along?" I ask.

"In testing. Want to see?"

We walk over and enter a soundproof room adjacent to the Weapons and Devices unit. There's a table laden with guns and bullets and a target placed at the far end of the room. We put on safety headsets. Dimitri picks a typical cell phone. It's slightly thicker, like it has an after-market battery pack. He points to the top of the phone towards the target. His pinky and index fingers hold the sides, and the heel of his palm supports the base. On the target a small red dot appears. Dimitri points the phone gun. He triggers it, and it fires and Dimitri's arm jerks in recoil. A bullet hole appears where the dot was.

"Phone is hot for minute but look normal," Dimitri says as

he hands me the warm phone. Brett and I inspect it.

"I can't even see the barrel," says Brett as he prods the top of the phone, where did the bullet eject?"

"Top opens for shot, and for moment of cooling, and close tight after," says Dimitri.

"What kind of bullets?" asks Brett.

"We make all gun components with plastic, so can take on plane if want. Bullet is little smaller than .22 caliber."

"Great work Dimitri. Brilliant," I say. We remove our headsets.

We look at a few more gadgets. Then, make our way back towards my office.

As we walk along the hall, Brett asks, "Hey by the way, does Dimitri have a girlfriend?"

"Actually, he's gay. Even though there are other gay men in QuadFilium I guess there's no mutual attraction there. He's more or less celibate. And finding a relationship outside QuadFilium means you have to lie about your life or it opens the door to external influences interfering with the group. Off base relationships have other obstacles... limited time off... no place to go. It doesn't stop people from dipping their toes in speed dating, bar-room hookups and playing the game," I say.

"Have you been looking at my AV feeds or something?"

"Haha! Yeah right. Trying to stop it is simply unrealistic, even if I object to it on moral grounds."

"Is that your stance?" asks Brett.

"I'm not a fan of promiscuity."

"Fair enough. You know, I can't help wondering what's the deal with Teska."

"She and Wade have been flirting... who knows where that will go?"

"Yeah…."

"We have fifteen minutes until the celebration. I have some work to catch up on," I say.

"Yeah. I need to get out of this suit and into some party clothes." Brett leaves.

I have a nagging thought. The AV feeds from QF members. The time I saw Teska changing after a shower. The only time in twenty-four years I broke the rule: AV feed is never to be used to invade a person's privacy. I'm the only one who doesn't have AV devices installed. No one can ever know what I see or hear.

Focus, Jean Jacques. Get back to work. I check my prospect tags, the fifty-seven people I've marked for future recruitment. I scan through the batch of daily reports and find one of particular interest: the young Chinese girl who was tagged at age fifteen, and who we've followed since. Li Yun Fei. She was one of two survivors in a factory fire. The report says she is now eighteen years old, her mother just died, and her father is ill. We have learned the death of a parent markedly destabilizes younger people. It is also one of the best times to recruit. Becoming his or her new point of stability. Otherwise, they could turn to vice, drugs, promiscuity. Yun Fei's scopulus is imminent.

I pick up my phone and call my wife. She doesn't answer and I leave a message that I'll be home around 11:00. I leave my office for the party.

Chapter 4
Teska

I take a quick shower and put on some casual clothes for the celebration. Spider purrs against my leg and jumps onto the bed, hoping for a petting. I briefly oblige, but I'm almost late so I hurry. I dab on some makeup and check myself in the mirror. No matter what I do I look slutty with these tits. And when I hide them, I look fat as a town dog.

I suppose this blouse is as tasteful as possible, I need to go. I pour a little bit of cat food into Spider's bowl, refill her water and leave, walking fast. I join a few others in the hall to the Commons.

I walk in. Tables of finger foods, drinks, fruit, desserts and beverages line the right wall. At the end table are various wines, beers and a bar, complete with a bartender for cocktails and fancy drinks. A raised platform with a microphone sits against the back wall. The whole left side of the room has couches, a makeshift dance floor and small tables to hold drinks and plates of hors d'oeuvres. The room is dim except for the stage platform. Pleasant music fills the room.

I walk over to the food and get a small plate of hors d'oeuvres and a wine cooler. I move to an elbow-high table and start munching.

"I guess you chose that table to rule out any possibility of me joining you," says Wade from his wheelchair.

I laugh, "Oh no! I didn't even think about it," I say.

"That's flattering," says Wade.

"Shut up, asshole," I say as follow him to a circle of couches.

He chuckles and says, "You call me that a lot."

"For obvious reasons."

"Fond of assholes, makes me think you're weird." We laugh.

Wade glances me up and down. There's something organic about it. Not creepy. I notice the ink on his arm. It looks swirly and tribal. "What's that?"

"It's a fern bud."

"Does it have any special meaning?"

"It's the Maori symbol for life and growth. I got it after a very traumatic incident."

He stated that with finality. Doesn't seem to want me to pry.

"Seems like everyone is here for this," I say. There are almost 100 people gathered in the room.

"Yeah, its choc-a-bloc. Aside from the few security patrols and the field personnel, I think everyone came."

"Ladies and Gentlemen, thank you all for coming." Jean Jacques mounts the platform and begins into the microphone.

"Tonight, we celebrate some heroes: the Mission 271 team and Jenny Somerville," The whole room looks around, identifying the guests of honor mentioned. Wade and I smile as they clap. Jean Jacques lists Jenny's achievements over the years, in the accounting division. She successfully set up front companies to help QF hide their expensive transactions, and these survived several government audits over the years.

"She has saved thousands of lives from her contributions. Ladies and gentlemen let's raise our glasses and give a toast to Jenny Somerville for her work, and let's use tonight to thank her and say our goodbyes." Clapping fills the room.

"Now, let's talk about the latest operation we completed, Mission 271.

"With intel gathered by the hacker team led by Ashkay Kapoor, Agent Wade Maley broke into the most secure compound ever to be breached in the history of QuadFilium, and per our intel, a base that has never been trespassed or escaped from since its creation. With the help of his teammate, Teska Lando, they barely made it out alive, and I'm sure that all of you want to see some of the footage." The crowd cheers in agreement as Jean Jacques lowers a screen.

Edited with music and sound effects, video of the action fills the screen. The editor cut out Wade's blinks and any gore, featuring mostly Wade's acrobatic and skillful exploits. Throughout the presentation, people look over at us, smiling and admiring. Wade is a real three-jump cowboy. More guts than you can hang on a fence. And it doesn't hurt that he is hot as a billy goat in a pepper patch.

The video sequence plays through and includes my POV from the helicopter. Wade runs across the field, deals with the Hummers and the final hostile hiding behind the bush, and his final leap onto the rope ladder. The editor did a fine job making it like an action film. Loud and long cheers cap the video and nearby guests give us pats and high fives.

"All made possible by technological innovations from our very own director of Research and Discovery, Dimitri Abdromonova!" Dimitri receives the same loud admiring cheers. He smiles.

Dimitri's general unkempt and unattractive appearance contrasts with his row of perfect white teeth. Everyone at QuadFilium has them, thanks to dental implants on arrival.

"Last but not least," Jean Jacques continues, "Our strategists and techies for this mission are its unsung heroes," Wade cheers and whoops in agreement, "Ashkay Kapoor, Heidi Flannigin, Kris Connelly and John Crutcher!" Additional toasts and revelry follow.

"Enjoy the night and don't hold back. Everyone sleeps in tomorrow!" Jean Jacques finishes up his toasts and presentations and walks off the platform to a final applause.

By now I've had two wine coolers and the third is half-gone. I feel the de-nerving effects. After a half hour of congratulatory conversations with other members, Wade and I, with too much to drink, start to talk. It's deep. Means something. Not just social BS. He never told me about what inspired him to come to QF, what the final incident was that pushed him over the edge. His scopulus. I don't know that he wants to. He dodges my questions with more questions about my life.

"This Jeffrey bloke, seemed like a good one. How do you suppose he ended with a less attractive girl to step outside with?" asks Wade.

"How do you know she was less attractive?" I ask.

"It's impossible that she wasn't. This is not the least bit of a come-on, but you are hands-down, bar-none, bottom-line, the most attractive human being I have ever seen, in print, in life, or on a screen," he says. I feel a blush and look away.

"Whatever," I say.

"I'm not even going to try to prove it to you with evidence or arguments. And you're no ditz either, fun to talk to and all that good stuff. So, I don't understand why this guy felt compelled to cheat on you, when he'd put so much effort to make a great relationship."

"I guess some guys just have an obsession and aren't monogamous. That's the only thing I could figure," I say.

"Do you suppose it's possible that he *didn't* cheat on you?"

"You mean he was in his undies with a sexy, nearly naked girl in his room because they were just friends hanging out? I would have to be dumb as a wagon wheel to believe that," I say.

"Okay, okay, fair enough. But just suppose, and maybe I shouldn't say this, but suppose the scopulus was a setup...to accelerate your arrival to QF? I'm just playing devil's advocate here. I know a good many blokes, and this guy really doesn't sound like the cheating type," says Wade.

"Even if it was a setup, he went for it and took the bait, so fuck him. When I was with Jeffery, I had plenty of opportunities to step out of bounds, with god-like male specimens, and the thought never crossed my mind. I loved him." My eyes start to moisten and I look away.

"Good point. Just a thought. Where'd it happen...the town...the hotel?" asks Wade.

"It was the Hampton Inn in Stephenville, Texas. Why?" I ask.

"I've been to Texas so I was just wondering...but I've never heard of either," he says. *Oddly specific question for him to ask.*

Chapter 5
Wade

I roll over and give Jenny a congrats and goodbye hug, which requires her to lean down. She sits and we chat for bit and I decide to ask my random question.

"Hey, Jenny I have a question for you. I know you keep precise accounts of every transaction that goes in and out of this place, right? So, what if I wanted to see a list of transactions from about a year ago? Would that be possible?"

"Well, we don't allow access to the general crew. Is there a specific one?" asks Jenny.

"Yes, I want to know if there was ever a payment made to a hotel called the Hampton Inn in Stephenville, Texas around that time," I ask.

"That rings a bell. Why are you asking about that?" she asks.

"I might have mission business in that area and wanted to see if it's a place we've already been to," I say, flashing my most charming smile. American sheilas are often enamored by the Aussie accent, thanks mostly to Hugh Jackman. Hopefully that oils up the machinery in Jenny's mind.

"I usually don't get asked about these things from field operatives, but I don't see any harm in checking for you."

"Thanks, love." We part.

I wheel over to Jean Jacques who looks like a stiff, conservative officer trying not to be too buddy-buddy with the privates. I respect that. If we saw him on the piss giving the place the liquid laugh, we'd probably feel less a need to comply to his serious orders, and that could jeopardize operations. I mean, I personally couldn't be fucked if he took his shirt off and started twerking, but that's me. Others might judge a person's skill in battle by it. I don't. I look at the competence in the line of fire, and Jean Jacques scores an A-fucking-plus on that in my book.

"G'day, mate, howzitgoing awright?" I ask.

Jean Jacques chuckles, "Sometimes I think you exaggerate the Aussie slang, but to answer your question, I'm doing fine. Yourself?"

"Yeah, good. Healing up. Well, I reckon I need to defend your accusation, good sir. I feel like I've toned the Aussie vernacular down so cunts can understand me better," I say.

"Saying the 'c' word is toning it down?" he asks.

"Well… saying it less than usual is. In Sydney or anywhere in Australia, that word has no slightest offense to anyone. But I said it to you just to fuck around. Even little girls will say things like, 'you're a funny cunt,' without even thinking twice. But around you guys, even the hard-core Hell's Angel yanks and ex-mob guys are offended by it. Bunch of up-yourself, sanctimonious cunts if you ask me."

Jean Jacques laughs out loud.

"Otherwise, yeah pretty much everyone in Sydney says it all in one breath, 'G'day-mate-howz-it-going-awright?' I'm not putting on a show, it's how we really talk."

Jean Jacques recovers from his laugh and nods.

"Just came over to say thanks for the good wishes and for letting me do that crazy-ass mission. Feels good to be counted upon and to make a difference," I say.

"You earned it, Wade. I don't know anyone who could've

pulled that off," says Jean Jacques.

"Cheers," I say and roll away.

I chat it up with Kris and get a few stories out of him from his bad old days as a criminal. I notice Teska steal glances my way every now and then. I'm not sure if I should get close with her. Seems a slippery slope. Lots of baggage and if we break up, I gotta live with that shit for a long time afterwards in close quarters. But she is real nice looking, so much it takes heaps of willpower to resist. And she's quite fun to joke around with. I'll have to weigh the pros and cons. Meanwhile, I've got some things to check out.

Teska is a bit legless from all those wine coolers, hopefully not about to purge 'em onto the floor. I roll on over, a bit typsie myself.

"Looking a bit pissed up, love," I say.

"I can handle it," she slurs. "I'm heading back to my room. Can I use your wheelchair as a walker?" she asks.

"Have at it," I answer.

She gets behind me and pushes me out of the room and down the hall. She takes me to my room door instead of hers. I unlock it and she pushes me through the door and lets it shut behind her. My heart jumps its beat rate.

"I know you're afraid of having a relationship with me, Wade. So, this doesn't mean anything," she says as she bends down, leans her face towards mine. As she gets closer and her eyes go from half closed to fully closed, I can't help but notice a direct view down her blouse. She kisses me. I don't pull back. Lust's heroin rushes my veins as our lips connect. The sweetness of her wine cooler tickling my taste buds. She pulls back and smiles, eyelids mostly closed. Time stops. A voice in my head screams.

"That was real nice, Wade," and she walks out. I sit still for a good two minutes while my heart rate drops from 200 to something more tame. I try to make heads or tails out of what just happened.

I lift myself off the wheelchair and wobble onto the bed still playing it back in my head. After an hour of blinkless staring at the ceiling, I fall asleep, in a state of confused ecstasy.

The next morning, I wake up to the sound of a ping on my phone.

"Looks like you were right. Two rooms were rented at the Hampton Inn in Stephenville Texas, about twelve months ago. Hope that helps! Love, Jenny."

Holy... fucking... screaming... dingo shit. Fuck me. There is no way that can mean anything else than the fact that our organization was somehow involved in that crazy thing with Jeffrey at the hotel. Could they have set that up to expedite her arrival? I can't tell Teska anything. Who can I talk to? And what the fuck was done? Who did this? Jean Jacques had to be involved. Did someone conspire with him? I'm already fucked since my AV feeds have me asking Jenny about this, and her response text. If some monitor sees these, they'll alert Jean Jacques and he'll start running it down to find out what's what with me. *Fuck me...*

This starts to make me wonder about the incident that got me over the edge, that led me to QuadFilium. *Peyton.*

The PA system chirps. "Urgent meeting at 0900 hours, conference room, all members of the team of Mission 271." I look at my clock. It's 0845. That's fifteen minutes from now. *What could be the problem? I thought we were sleeping in today. Is it about this stuff I just started to look into? Or about Teska kissing me last night?*

49

I get ready and roll down the hall. I get to the conference room a few minutes early. Kris Connelly is there, Teska runs in after me. The rest of the strategists and Jean Jacques enter. Although the analytical portion of my brain tells me that this could not possibly have anything to do with kissing Teska or asking Jenny about the hotel, I feel nervous. I hide it best I can.

Chapter 6
Jean Jacques

I wait until everyone is settled in the conference room. All personnel from Mission 271 sit or stand around the table. A couple of them look a little haggard. They drank last night and expected to sleep in. This couldn't wait.

I deliver the message point blank.

"Thanks for coming, everyone. We have some bad news. Brand new intel reveals that we did not, in fact, kill Alistair Watson."

Let it sink in for a moment.

"We killed a decoy."

Wade betrays no reaction.

I continue, "He is alive and well, and operations of his energy company and human trafficking business have not halted. The man was even better prepared than we ever expected. Our inside contact also reveals that Wade's image was captured on cameras. There's contracts out on him for ten million."

Teska looks at Wade, worried. Wade retains his stoicism.

"We have no idea how many bounty hunters have Wade in their crosshairs, but obviously this puts us on high alert. Wade, you aren't leaving the base anytime soon unless under strict cover, is that clear?"

"Yes, sir," replies Wade.

He probably feels foolish, "Wade, do not blame yourself. Decoys are near exact replicas. Even his own staff, aside from top aides, didn't know it wasn't him," I say.

"We should have done our homework better," says Kris, standing up.

Wade says, "I dig what you're all saying, and thanks for caring about my tender feelings, but the real problem is that fucking murderous knob is not only still out there fucking over the world, but he's on triple alert now. Much harder to kill. I had a feeling there was something wrong with the tosser I hit. He looked like Alistair but he was goofy and awkward, didn't match with pre-mission footage we had of the real bloke. I should have predicted a decoy, and hit the right bloke. Fucking pity, that. So now what?" says Wade.

Brett chimes in, "Double J, I think we should still take out the regional center in Los Angeles. Just as planned."

John says, "Meanwhile, we re-strat Alistair's termination. We have a lot of homework to do. We need to identify decoys, how many, where the real fucker is, and when is our opportunity."

"How much longer until Wade is fit for combat?" I ask Dimitri and the medic standing next to him.

"Wade respond well to accelerated treatment with test serum. It has working. Heal fast. One week 80%. Two week 95%. Three week 100%," says Dimitri. The medic nods in agreement.

"Then mission strike time is two and half weeks," I decide. "Full preparations move forward. Create the tactical plan, pick the team players and begin mission simulations in the next five days. Ashkay, get the blueprints for the distribution center. Do full virtual simulations of all possible scenarios. John, oversee it."

Ashkay and John nod.

John interrupts, "Jean Jacques. Permission to make a request."

"Go ahead," I answer.

"This fuck-up is on the strategy team, not Wade or the techies. I feel a tribunal is in order for myself, Mr. Connelly and Miss Flannagin for this costly mistake. A mistake that threatened a valuable operative's life and wasted time and resources, and makes the next missions more difficult." John sits.

Kris and Heidi, already feeling guilty, nod in agreement.

"Granted. It will convene tomorrow morning at 0900. Pick five jurors amongst the crew. I will choose three of them to pass judgment and sentencing... and I'll preside as the tribunal director."

They nod, and everyone gets up to leave the room.

"Wade, wait back," I say. He nods and the others file out.

"You okay?" I ask.

"What, are you my psychologist now?" asks Wade.

"I need to have your, how do you say, 'mojo' on for this next mission, and can't have you stuck in your head."

Wade says, "I have no slightest attention on my feelings. I know what I signed up for, boss. I know my life is on the line, and that I have to take the lives of others, and that there will be gore, setbacks, and other bull shit. Fuck my feelings. Let's be effective and get this shit done. That's all I care about."

I look at him. He is calm and determined.

"Fine, soldier. But come to me anytime if you need to discuss anything. " Wade's eyes give the slightest flick. *He's got something he's not talking about. That eye flick.*

"Thanks boss," Wade says. He turns and leaves.

I call Brett, "You nearby? Can you come back to the

conference room?"

Brett enters moments later.

"Double J," he says as he comes in.

"How did we fail to allow for the possibility of decoys?" I ask.

"We've never seen before except for heads of state. None of our missions had that issue."

"Let's ask Kris about this," I call in Kris. He comes right away.

"Boss?" says Kris.

"Have you ever seen use of decoys?"

"You know, boss, I have. Cartel leaders do it all the time when they make dangerous public appearances. But I've never seen them so paranoid that they take it to their private lives. That's why I didn't include it in tactical," says Kris.

"Unreal," Brett says.

"Okay, Kris, thank you. Let's fast forward Mission 272, Regional Distribution Center, LA," I say. Kris nods and leaves.

"Have you thought about how we are going to penetrate this LA slave factory?" I ask Brett.

"In fact, I have…"

Chapter 7

Wade

I leave the War Room feeling about ten different things at the same time. But mostly I am pissed off at the wasted energies of the whole group. To sneak me in there, we had to tap the lines, which was nearly impossible. We found out Alistair's compound ordered a large new fridge for the kitchen. We bought the same one and built a false back in. They stuck me inside and switched the fridges for delivery. I made it through the compound's extensive delivery screenings. Doing all that, breaking in, almost dying in the escape... all for nothing. How did we not know about the decoy? It's probably a new thing, otherwise Kris, Heidi and John would have prepared for it.

I wheel over to the med bay to get my next session of serums and physical therapy. I'm a little hung over from last night being on the piss, but today's news shook me out of the stupor. I enter a white, well-lit room, with white-coated personnel attending patients and stocking supplies. There are medical table beds, baths, shelves full of supplies and cupboards neatly arranged around the open space.

The medic greets me as I come in and directs me over to the x-ray machine. He plops me down and takes shots of my leg and my arm. We look over the developed images.

"Remarkable recovery rate, Wade. Look at this. It's 60% better than normal healing time." He has other film of healing bones that show the same number of days but more obvious fissures. Mine are smeared lines. He sits me on a chair and prepares the serum injection. The needle is long. Although I am actually kind of afraid of needles, I don't show it. What's the point? You're getting the shot no matter what, so pretend like you can't be fucked and you feel like a tough guy, and look like one too. These support personnel aren't going to feel too inspired if their top operatives are a bunch of pansies. Keep it tough-looking for them... and for personal pride.

He injects me on the top of my thigh right into where the break is. Dimitri enters.

He looks at the x-rays. "Impressive," says Dimitri. I get the arm injection for the humerus fracture.

"How your breathing is now?" referring to my broken ribs.

"Still hurts to cough, sneeze or laugh."

"Where?" he asks. I point at the two spots that were left to heal on their own, both in the front where I got two bullets in my chest armor.

"It looks like experiment conclusive. Serum work. We should now use on these bones too, accelerate healing," he says. The medic injects these spots as well. Six total. The medic then applies a vibration tool to my ribs. It shakes out the debris in the break and lets the edges of the bone find their way together like puzzle pieces.

I think about Teska. The kiss. The Jeffrey thing. I don't know what to do with this information. Maybe I am just being paranoid. To top it off I have a bounty on my head. How long does something like that last? I guess until the bounty comes off the market. When either I or Alistair die.

Chapter 8
Jean Jacques

The team of strategists chose five crew as their jurors to ask questions and issue findings and any sentencing. I picked three out of the five. At 0900 I walk into the War Room, where we hold such hearings. Tribunal members are seated, reviewing the documents that were used to prepare mission 271.

"Have you studied the files?" I ask the group.

"Yes, sir. We are all familiar with them now," answers Cody, one of the mechanics who works in the vehicle bay.

I say, "Good. Are we ready to see the interested parties?"

"Yes, sir."

"Bring them in."

The jurors and I sit on one side of the conference table, and the three accused, John, Kris and Heidi sit opposite. The tribunal is kept polite. No accusatory flavor or disparaging looks from the jurors. I start a recording device and read off the particulars, "Tribunal Order number 102, on the matter of negligence on the part of the tactical team for mission 271. Names are John Crutcher, Kris Connelly and Heidi Flannagin. Juror number one may proceed with questioning."

"Thank you, director. When you created the strategy, did you discuss the possibility of a decoy?" asks Cody.

John answers, "We did. I asked both the other strategists if it was a factor we needed to consider. They both responded that in their experience in the underground world of criminal enterprise, prostitution, hired guns, etc., they had never been aware of decoys used in the private life, only in public appearances."

"Okay. Kris, how do you suppose this error could have happened?" asks the juror.

Kris responds, "I think that Heidi and I may have never seen the use of decoys in private settings because we were simply unaware of them. We probably did deal with decoys and never knew it. They don't introduce themselves as decoys. I suppose a very select few know they are actually decoys."

"Okay thank you, no further questions at this time," says juror number one.

"Juror number two, do you have any questions?" I ask Joyce, from Household staff.

"Yes, Heidi, do you have any further to say on this?" asks Joyce.

"I only want to say that we should have gone the extra mile to check into this, but we chose not to. It was sloppy. I take responsibility for it," she says.

"I have no further questions," says Joyce.

"Thank you. Juror number three, do you have any inquiries?" I ask Dr. Vizcarra, our dentist.

"I do. Which of you feels most responsible for the miss?" he asks. All three raise their hands.

"I have nothing further," the doctor says.

"Meeting adjourned. The tribunal has three hours to formalize its findings and adjudicate any further actions necessary. Meet back here at 1300 after lunch," I say as I get up and leave.

I go back to my desk and find a note from one of the monitors. "Important internal security matter. Discuss in person." It's signed by Paula G., an AV monitor for five members. Wade is one of them.

His flinch yesterday. I head down to the monitoring bay and to Paula's station. She grabs a flash drive, and we head to my office. We sit down and she inserts it in my computer monitor and types in the security code to access its content.

The first thing I see is Teska, at the party a couple nights ago. We hear Wade ask her if she thinks it's possible that the incident with Jeffrey was a setup. Her answer, "No, but if it was, Jeffrey took the bait so he is still a piece of shit." Then Wade asks her for the name of the town and hotel where she found Jeffrey. She answers and asks why. Wade gives a paltry excuse. The video cuts to Wade convincing Jenny to look if QuadFilium rented rooms that time in Stephenville. It cuts to a confirmation text Wade received from Jenny.

"He is conducting an investigation of his own. He suspects Jeffrey was set up," says Paula while looking at me. I need to explain the matter to allay any suspicions.

"I can see that you could have your own questions. We rented two rooms that night because I predicted what would happen. We had to be there for timing purposes. There was no setup. The extra room was for my assistant," I explain to her.

"Makes sense. Just so you know, I've never had reason to doubt you," says Paula.

"Thank you for bringing this to my attention. I'll take care of this. Keep Wade's monitoring more frequent and report anything else," I say.

On her way out, Paula turns and says, "Oh, Teska kissed Wade in a drunken daze after the party. Nothing else." She leaves.

Even more adventure to deal with now. *Wade does not lead a boring life, does he?* A tinge of mammalian jealousy pokes at my stomach. I better nip this suspicion of his in the bud. Having my top field operative not trust me is dangerous in the extreme. His suggesting to Teska the same could fray and loosen the fabric of the group. I hadn't expected a romance yet.

I punch my intercom, "Olivia, can you call Wade to my office?"

While I wait for him to arrive, I review his profile. Wade's field tests show results several percentages higher than the best operatives to date. Reaction time, pulse recovery rate, situational assessment speed, autonomic nervous system control, marksmanship, and simulated intuition are all at record levels.

Wade rolls in on a wheelchair.

"It's been an interesting and eventful last few days, Wade," I say.

"Fair dinkum," he says.

He's been shot five times, broken or fractured seven bones, made an impossible escape, celebrated a triumph, kissed a beautiful girl, had his triumph deflated, got placed on a Class A hit list and lost trust in a group he dedicated his life to by coming across seemingly incriminating evidence.

I cut to the chase, "The monitor sent me an alert."

"Not surprisingly," Wade says, straight faced.

"You think the Jeffrey thing was a setup?" I ask.

Wade answers, "Not based on a judgment of your character. It's just the only explanation I could come up with given the facts."

"Okay, tell you what. Ask me anything you'd like," I say, knowing that a blunt demand to accept and never question authority would never work on Wade. He's intuitive, self-determined and most of all, Aussie.

"Why did you rent two rooms that night?" asks Wade.

"I predicted the infidelity would be going down that night. I knew Teska might find out. I had to be there to catch the moment of scopulus," I answer. "The other room was for my assistant."

"I guess that explains it then," he says.

"You seem unsure," I observe. "Why?"

"I'm almost never surprised by what people do. I see patterns and they hold pretty true. Even unpredictable folks are predictable. If there's a glitch in the pattern, I find an explanation. Jeffrey is not the cheating type, not at the stage of the game this went down. He invested so much into Teska. He enhanced her life. He cared about her. That had to be the case for her to blossom, knowing how touchy and fragile she was. It couldn't have been fake or sporadic. For him to just betray her like that is a major glitch, even if tempted and set up. I just don't see it," he says.

"Happens all the time. Some wife never suspects her perfect, conservative husband is stepping out with a mistress. The families of serial killers talk about how normal their father or husband seemed," I say.

"That's not how I see it. I see it's marketed that way by the media so everyone can be afraid that their next-door neighbor is a cannibal, so people will be in fear and watch more news and buy more papers or click more websites. Pure marketing. But the real serial killers are pretty off. Ted Bundy is the most famous for seeming normal but being a killer. But if you watch him and look into his life, he was actually an outcast growing up. He wasn't all that normal. He didn't have close friends or relationships like Jeffrey. Just happened to be good looking... goes a long way... a lot of natural affinity towards good looking

61

people. I understand, comparing cheating to killing people isn't a fair comparison," says Wade.

"I can see your point. I understand your questions," I say.

"I've never had any reason to question you or your purpose and ideals. In fact, you are probably the one person in my whole life I respect the most. So even thinking this feels disloyal. But for me, logic always trumps feelings and hunches. This Jeffrey guy's infidelity was a glitch in the pattern."

"Well, we didn't set it up. I saw it coming and seized the moment. Since you don't have firsthand knowledge of Jeffrey, do you think, perhaps, Teska's perceptions were colored? Trauma can warp and exaggerate a person's recall. Make good people great and bad people horrible. He was her knight in shining armor," I say.

"I suppose that's the only possible alternative," says Wade. "Mr. Girard, I appreciate you taking this head on with me. I feel I can put it behind me for now and move forward onto the next mission."

"That's what I needed to hear. If you *ever* have a question or issue, I want you free to speak up," I say. He leaves.

I can't tell if he's convinced.

Chapter 9
Wade

I make my way over to the physical therapy office and get into the hot tub. I need to spend half an hour soaking in very warm water mixed with some healing elixirs. First step is the hot part. Quite nice really. Then, I switch to cold for ten minutes and allow the cold to penetrate to my bones. I start to thinking.

Jean Jacques's reassurances made matters worse. I have even more questions about Teska's recruitment.

While it's all fine and good to say the end justifies the means, and that sacrificing things for a better cause is justifiable, where's the limit? At what point do we say it is immoral, unethical?

Was ruining Jeffrey's and Teska's happiness to expand the ranks of QuadFilium a worthy sacrifice? It's like asking someone, "Would you agree to kill a baby if you knew it would save a hundred people's lives?" I'm sure Jean Jacques faced that. It begs the question: Was my own scopulus incident a setup?

The warm bath puts me into a calm reverie. I close my eyes.

I suppose that Jean Jacques is monitoring a fair number of tagged prospects, hoping for a life changing incident to take place, so he can swoop in and snag the recruit. These life changing incidents don't always come, and he has to drop it and move onto others. I'm sure some are intensely more valuable than others. In the case of Teska, I have to wonder if the value he placed on her had to do with something more than her value as a team member. Don't get me wrong, she is highly skilled, and contributive, there's no question about that. But the type of behavior Jean Jacques may have been involved in, setting up the sundering of a happy couple, instigating suicidal urges, to go to that level, one's own judgment would have to be clouded. The main things I have seen that make that happen are: money, justification of crimes, past unresolved trauma and lust, quite the overpowering mental fogger. Lust is the impetus that seems most likely.

Digging away like a wombat burrowing, Jean Jacques's inner beast could have taken over his sense of judgment. As he spent more time stalking her, he could have become infatuated, then obsessed, telling himself all along that he wasn't, that he was strong enough to resist.

One day, he realizes that her future is secure with this guy Jeffrey, and that the likelihood of a traumatic incident, strong enough to create a decision to change or end her life, is low. Jacques panics and comes up with a solution. Maybe even contemplated taking Jeffrey out. But was too good a person. He probably convinced himself that setting Jeffrey up and baiting him was actually better for Teska. If Jeffrey gave into it, it is safe to assume that he would have anyway in the future, thus ruining her life at some point down the line. He probably had it all "explained" that he was, by testing Jeffrey, preventing a future tragedy for her.

The only problem is, I don't see how this angelic bloke would have even taken the bait. It's logical. I don't know if it's true. So how the fuck did he end up in his damn skivvies with a naked sheila when Teska came to the door? Fuck if I know, but I can't stop wondering.

I start to feel a bit dopey from the steam. This is without

question my favorite part of physical therapy. The attendant informs me that we're ready for the next phase. Cold water. Not my fave.

"Alternating cold and hot accelerates healing by getting the fluids in and out of the affected areas. Sports doctors heal sprains and injuries much faster this way," says the medic.

"Right-ee-o."

I need to recall the details of my own scopolus. I need to look for glitches. I close my eyes and return to the time...

Late one night. Probably almost 4:00 a.m. I am alone, just left a club in Sydney and hear some noise around the corner. People talking in an alleyway.

"What are you doing out so late, little girl?"

"Where's your dadda?"

I look around the corner. There's a very young girl getting harassed by a couple of junkies. A recent former athlete and a construction worker, my body is more prime than average. I sprint, jump in the air, and kick one guy in the head and land on and tackle the other. The little girl rolls away from the brawl and crouches several feet away. The head-kick guy was out. The other, still conscious, wields a knife, swings at my leg from his position on the ground. I move fast but the edge nicks my shin. He's put all his might into the thrust and falls forward exposing his ribs. I drop and punch his side, leaning my weight into it. I feel several cracks beneath my knuckles. For all I knew, one of his lungs collapsed. I hit him hard. The wind's knocked out of him. I kick him in the head and he's out.

I help the girl get out of the alleyway into a well-lit sidewalk. She is darker skinned, perhaps aboriginal.

"Are you hurt?" I ask.

"No... but you're bleeding," she replies, out of breath and

panicked. She points at my leg.

"She'll be awright. We need to call the police."

I call them on my cell phone. While we wait, she starts to calm down from hysterical shaking and crying to a more controlled breathing. I give her my coat and ask, "What's your name? What are you doing out here at 4:00 a.m.? How old are you?"

"Um… I'm Peyton. I'm thirteen and my dad runs a bakery. I get here early every day to start up the ovens thirty minutes before he arrives… at 4:30. His health isn't good, diabetes and arthritis and stuff. He comes into the shop from 4:30 a.m. to 8:30 a.m. every day but then I run the store from then 'til the evening.

"Where's your mum?"

"I have a two-year old brother and she looks after him."

The cops arrive and arrest the two scumbags passed out in the alley; and take our reports.

"Good on ya, mate. Helping out like that. Not too many folks do that anymore," says one of the cops.

"Let's go ahead and git you back to your mum," says another cop, reaching for Peyton's hand.

"No, no, officer, I really have to go to the bakery and open the shop and start the ovens. I have to," said Peyton.

"Miss, it's highly unusual… a victim, especially a young girl like you to just carry on. The trauma, and all that. Let's get you home. Take the day off."

Peyton starts to cry.

"What's wrong?" I ask.

"We can't close the shop, even for a day. We're too poor. We can't even miss a single day."

"Okay, okay. Stop crying," says the cop. He looks up at me,

"Sir, can you escort her to her dad's shop?"

"Of course," I said.

We thank the officers for their help and head down the dark sidewalk. The street cleaners are out, and drive along the road, sucking up the trash from a night of partying. Arms come out of the bottom of the vehicles and spray the sidewalks down and suck up the waste.

"You don't go to school?" I asked.

"I do homeschool after I turn on the ovens. I work at the bakery until 8:00 p.m. when it closes."

"Every day?" I ask.

"Seven days a week," she says

I couldn't rightfully stand there and not feel a strong desire help Peyton and her family. She is of aboriginal descent, and sadly, too many have ended up poor and without much.

"You know what I'm going to do? I'll walk you to work every day. I'll meet you at 3:30 a.m. and get you to the bakery at 4:00. You can start the ovens."

"Wow… thank you. Why?"

"Cuz I feel like it, that's why."

Over the next four months, I did this, every day. I became her older brother. I tried to teach her what I knew. Our lives were completely different. I grew up in a lower middle-class white suburb, playing footy, going to school, parties, taking vacations, field trips, school plays, travelling to cities to play other teams. When I told her about these things, she loved the stories. It was a wider world. I brought her on hikes, to sporting events, and beach trips. I took her to the Blue Mountains and saw the continent from the top down. She'd never been but a few blocks from her tiny house. The fresh air, the space, and a connection with nature flowed life back into her. I watched her grow into a brighter person, bigger dreams, a taller posture, a feeling of hope.

One night, I'd been to a party and was on the piss. I fell asleep at maybe 2:00 a.m. and woke at 4:00 to the sound of an alarm that had been ringing for forty-five minutes. This was the first and only time I'd missed picking her up and walking to the bakery. I ran to the bakery, only to find the place dark and empty. I looked around everywhere. There was no sign of her. I ran back to her house as fast as I could through dark and quiet streets, panting and sweating, smelling of booze. I went inside. Her mother was there, already awake, looking confused. Her father was just about to leave for the bakery.

"She left over an hour ago. She was not with you?" said the mother, dread forming on her face.

The next two weeks were pure trauma for me and Peyton's family. The cops had no leads on where she could have gone. She either ran away—impossible—or was kidnapped. The kidnapping of young teenage girls was the sex trade. The grief and rage were unbearable. I felt like I was tied down, being forced to watch my own sister be slowly killed and raped in front of me while I could do nothing but watch and scream. It was my fault.

That's exactly when Jean Jacques showed up.

Chapter 10
Jean Jacques

The tribunal on the three strategists has issued its findings and endorsement. I read it aloud: "Twenty-five hours of general crew community service on personal time, and a retrain of two classes: boot camp and Strategy 303. Both classes emphasize the requirement of double checking and assist to overcome the disease known as 'assumption.' "

Ironic. Kris wrote Strategy 303.

Each of the strategists agree. They leave the tribunal and I package up the proceedings and content, put them in an envelope, and set them aside to be placed in archives.

Mission 272 rolls forward. I sent a unit to LA to gather detailed intel on the human trafficking distribution center's labor, delivery schedules, patterns, systems and security protocols. While we knew a great deal through Ashkay's electronic recon, nothing's better than direct observation.

Wade has recovered, and is running around again, rebuilding his strength. Once a team goes into mission mode, there is a contagious buzz in the whole base. Everyone's wired up and excited. I extend work hours to triple-check all requirements, plans, and intel.

It's one week to mission launch. Brett sits in my office waiting for me. I sit down across from him. This is has become a mission ritual: I detail every aspect of the mission to Brett, and he looks for holes.

He asks, "Okay, Double J, we've covered the operational

details. Now give me the full low down on mission command."

"On 'go' day, the field team departs the base to a satellite hangar and takes a private jet to Los Angeles. I'll remain here as will the strategists. But, the audio-visual feeds from all operatives will be on display in the war room 24/7 from the point of landing until mission completion. The strategists and I will watch the feeds full time. The mission is set for thirty hours. No one will sleep throughout. The Mind Team consists of myself and the three strategists, others as needed. We will not leave our station unless we need to use the bathroom. The mission support crew brings us what we need.

"While the field team is in the air, the Mind Team will rest a full eight hours, minimal. We wake, we exercise and eat a breakfast consisting of a vegetable smoothie with vitamins, two omega-3 eggs, three pieces of bacon from pasture-raised pork and coffee brewed in high PH water. Every two hours we eat a small healthy meal, usually fish or lean meat and vegetables, followed by additional vitamins. Fresh organic fruit is available at all times. Caffeine is kept to no more than 150mg every four hours. We drink a sizeable amount of non-sweet fluids with electrolytes,." I say.

"Is this an infomercial for the latest diet?" challenges Brett.

"The precision of these points is based on the previous missions and the exact formulae for success. Mental clarity is 100% vital. Sugar and caffeine burn you out fast. Few simple carbohydrates are provided to the Mind Team during an active mission. Success requires the team leader and strategists have constant alertness to all details of the mission and maximal attention on same. It is against QuadFilium protocol to enter the Mind Booth when the 'mission active' sign is on outside the door, unless there is a crisis that threatens lives, or a support crew member brings in scheduled sustenance. The red-circled light outside the door will, during violent action, prevent even the support crew from entering until it's turned off.

"It is forbidden for the team leader or the strategists to have cell phones during active engagement. The team leader has the majority of the direct contact with field agents, unless delegated to others. During violent confrontations, high-intensity moments, each strategist is assigned to one or two field agents for direct monitoring and communication, as the team leader will not be able to speak with and monitor all of them at the same time.

"These combined regimens keep one clear and focused for thirty hours straight despite no sleep."

"I don't see any holes in any of that. Sounds good. But I have another question for you, Double J."

"Shoot."

"You got something going on? You don't seem as... undisturbed as usual."

He's picking up on the Wade issue, the Teska issue, the family issues. He's good. I can't have him around to Sherlock these clues right now. We have an involved mission to execute. He will pull strings and sniff things out, like a good plaintiff's attorney. I need this to wait.

"I'm good. Just perturbed about the fact that we got the wrong Alistair."

"...makes sense."

I get an idea.

"But on another note. I have a scopulus that coincides with this mission. In China. You're the only one I trust to do it. Her name is Li Yun Fei. It looks like she's ready."

"China? Never been."

"She is an incredible prospect. And since I can't go, you're the guy."

"Okay...but you've never had anyone beside yourself be there for a scopulus."

"I'll be full time in the Mind Booth and we can't miss this one. Her father is expected to die any day. Her mother is already dead. She's young. She'll be desperately grieving.

"We know, desperation breeds degeneration," says Brett as he looks me right in the eye. *Is he reading my mind?*

"You'll be briefed as soon as possible. Can't miss the scopulus window."

"Okay. Will do."

"I'll have Logistics inform you."

"Alright then. I'll go to Records and pull up her file." Brett leaves. I breathe a sigh of relief.

I leave my office and head to the tactical training center, field simulation training room. Each operative is equipped with a virtual reality mask. From my vantage point, they look silly as they weave around and jump over invisible obstacles. John Crutcher prepares them for the assault. Most of our field agents will be deployed for this mission. A risk, but worth it. This mission will not succeed unless properly manned.

Chapter 11

Teska

Mission 272, Alistair Watson's Los Angeles Distribution Center. The field team is on a private jet from France to LA.

For the past two weeks we drilled and devised tactics for every scenario. The overall mission objective: Eliminate all personnel and save all captives. A logistics team went ahead. Been there ten days, gathering intel and doing preps.

Wade is our action group leader. He runs the assault teams.

Nine hours 'til touch down. We take melatonin tablets so we can sleep until just before we land. Once we touch down, no sleep for thirty hours at least.

We wake up eight hours later at 0400 and get our grub and coffee. We suit up in our gear. Which in my case is lingerie, tighter than a wet boot, covered by a trench coat and bright, naughty-girl make-up. Lookin' like Jessica Rabbit was a stripper.

Wade comes over, "Finally, they took my recommendations on the new uniforms."

"Ha ha. Very funny."

"You gonna be okay?"

"I'll be fine."

"Never doubted it. Just be careful, okay?"

"She'll be awright," I say.

"That's my line!"

I wink and walk the plane's exit stairs. My foot hits the

tarmac and a car pulls up and stops.

It's 4:05 a.m. They drive me to a shady part of East LA near the LA River, a dry concrete drainage channel, except when it rains. They drop me off on a corner, under a bridge where women strut their wares, and look for a pickup. All I can think of is Chili Peppers, *Under the Bridge Downtown*...

I walk down the dark side street and stand twenty feet from the group of prostitutes. Two of them see me and head over, wearing dark makeup and choker necklaces.

"Who the fuck are you and what makes you think you can be here?" one asks. She has a deep voice. Used to be a man.

"Just working like you," I respond. The other one behind her, eyes me up and down.

Deep-voice lady says, "Get... the fuck... outta here... you dumb bitch! We been working here for a year. Go somewhere else!" They hold their stances, arms akimbo and glare. They look to be early thirties trying to look seventeen with pigtails and colorful girlie stuff, which are worn and unclean. Both of them have matted and greasy hair. They pull out pepper spray canisters from their clutches and aim. Like quick-draw McGraw, I pull a snubnosed .22 from my own clutch and point.

"I can shoot you even if you pepper spray my eyes," I say calmly staring them down. They freeze.

"Back the fuck off," I instruct them without blinking. Wolves to sheep. They tuck their pepper spray away, and walk backwards.

A car pulls up. It's not the guy I want. I pull my trench coat tighter. He drives past me shopping the others who wear next to nothing. He picks one up and drives off.

After an hour, and a few more johns that don't fit the bill, a van drives up and looks at me carefully. He's my guy. Sgt.

Crutcher sees him through my visio feed and confirms it to me through my internal radio. This man looks for younger girls to pick up. I smile and he slows. I open my trench coat, and the streetlamp illuminates my body. His van stops. His head jerks forward. He doesn't take his eyes off me and reaches over and opens the passenger side door. I start to walk over —

"Hey, new girl! Anyone who gets in that van, we never seen again," calls out another prostitute, not one of the first two.

"Thanks, sugar, I can take care of myself," I say.

"Don't say I didn't warn you," she trails off and walks in the other direction.

These women recognize this guy. That's a good sign. Our intel found freelance collectors bring in quality merch daily. They're paid for each one that meets standards. Some valued higher than others.

Heidi Flannagin estimated that I would be Category 1A: very young, pretty, girls, boys or women with "exceptional physical qualities" between fifteen and twenty-five years old. This guy reckons he struck gold. His eyes don't waver as I approach.

I get in the van and shut the door. He drives. He's Hispanic with very short hair, buzzed, uneven, to a quarter inch. Cuts his own hair. Edges ratty. He wears a loose pullover and jeans. The van is unclean, with food wrappers and discarded pop cups. The floor mat has dirt pressed into it and the window has the smears of dust mud and bug body parts pushed to the sides by windshield wipers.

He keeps looking over at me. I can sense his body wants to sample mine. He is fighting between pulling over and getting some action of his own or going straight to the distribution center. I sit motionless. It confuses him. Most prostitutes get in the car, start feeling the guy up, and negotiate price. I don't. Which may be worse. It makes him more eager.

"I charge fifty dollars for thirty minutes," I say and I put my hand on his leg. He keeps looking at my lacy chest.

In a thick Hispanic accent he says, "Das fine. Ay dios mío, you are a mamacità like I never seen."

His eyes shift about. He glances at the time and then at the side of the road. I assume he contemplates pulling over and getting it on. My bet, if they find out back at the warehouse, he'll get his ass kicked. Of course, I know this type of man. His mind clouds over... tells him it's worth it... that everything will be okay... that this is a once-in-a-lifetime opp. The same drugged-up face I saw in men who molested me. Nothing is more important to them at that moment. He starts to slow down, and I wonder if I'm going to have to suck this guy's dick. Not something on my list of goals and objectives.

He pulls over and abruptly grabs my left breast, then the right. He's strong and squeezes hard. He squeezes harder and I breathe in sharply. He reaches over to undo his seatbelt and his phone rings.

"Ay! Puta!"

He answers. "Hello?... si... okay... si... probly like fifteen minutes... oh, ten minutes?... si, okay boss. Si, okay, okay, adiós." He is angry now and he replaces his seat belt and drives on. He mumbles something in Spanish to himself. Then it sounds like he mock-mimics his boss's voice in English. Then strings of angry Spanish, arms moving around here and there. I remain motionless for the most part. He's got a beef with his boss. What a surprise.

We pull into the back of a warehouse. This is the place.

He says, "I'm sorry, mamacità," and he pulls out some

handcuffs and smiles at me. I feign surprise and weakly scream, and wiggle and try to fumble for the door handle. He grabs my body and sinewy-strong arms cuff me. I struggle and act freaked out. He slaps me and says, "You better shut the fuck up, puta, or else we hurt you!"

I look at him with tears in my eyes, convincingly terrified. I whimper and tuck my head down.

"Good girl. Stay quiet and you won't get hurt."

He comes around to the passenger side and pulls me out, fondling me in the process.

"You have the best tits I have ever fucking seen. And they don't feel fake. You're going to be worth a lot, señorita. I wish I could try you out. I could have if my stupid boss didn't call." He laughs. I keep my head down and act sad and terrified.

I hear Crutcher alert the other team members, "Phoenix going in."

I blush embarrassment as I remember that Crutcher, Kris and Jean Jacques are able to see anything I look at, including my body in this lingerie. I don't much care, but I hate the change in men when a woman's body turns their reason into something else. They act different.

I'm brought into an office in the back of the warehouse. Three guys smoking. One looks at me. The other two glance up indifferent, then do a double take. One stands up, stares at my body and exclaims in Española. The other one, white guy, stays seated but transfixed, the cigarette falls out of his mouth. The first guy throws his cigarette on the ground and comes over.

He takes out a pair of medical shears and methodically snips off my clothing. The other guys in the room look me up and down. I'm not a living person to these guys, more like a hot rod that just rolled into the garage. They quietly exclaim to themselves. Most of which sounds religious.

I look down and see my naked body. I hear in my audio feed one of my strategists cough uncomfortably and realize that my visio feed is on the Mind Booth screens. I look up.

He inspects me closely. Looks at my face, my eyes, touches and squeezes my lips, then examines my teeth and gums. He cups and lifts my breasts, feels their weight and squeezes them. He sees the bloody band-aid on my lower back and leaves it alone.

"Small injury on lower back, still bleeding. Blue eyes. Perfect teeth, lips round and plump. She looks nineteen years old, maybe twenty. We can say seventeen. Breasts are fucking massive, real, still firm, maybe double G. Take off your heels," he says to me. The guy in the back notes details.

I take off my shoes and he measures my height and weight. "160 centimeters. Five three. 126 pounds."

He continues to feel up my breasts. It takes everything in me not to head butt this fuckface's nose into his brain. But I keep my face lookin' like a cat in a dog pound.

"Be strong, Phoenix," says John.

The guys take turns feeling me up. They are rough and it hurts. One brushes the band-aid by accident. The adhesive is stronger than duct tape, thanks to Dimitri's foresight. It holds.

Four more girls are brought in. The men go back to business mode and wrap up my assessment. I am placed in a nightgown-like garment and my kidnapper brings me into the next room. In there is an old woman with reading glasses and brilliant, dyed red hair, with grey roots about an inch long. She's the cashier or something and looks at the ticket my kidnapper hands her.

"Category 1A? It's been a while...." She pulls down her

glasses and looks me over.

"No shit," she says. "Sorry honey, the rest of your life is going to be a little different than you dreamed." She sighs and puts her glasses back on, counts off some cash and hands it to my kidnapper. He looks happy as cream gravy and pockets the money. Old cashier lady gets back to business and kidnapper-dude marches me to a set of stairs. We go down. At the bottom is a door with a bouncer. We get buzzed through. Then two more bouncers and doors.

I enter a large underground warehouse with a couple hundred cages in long rows, housing all manner of human merchandise, but most are young girls kidnapped in an open market or on their way home from school. All wear the gown thing I have on. Most lie aimlessly on the ground or look jumpy as spit on a skillet. Some look out of their cages, and observe the hell they were forced into. The strong stench of piss, feces and unbathed bodies hits me. There are two closed doors on the left. The back wall to the right has a closed door. The room has a high ceiling with exposed pipes, ducts, beams and wiring. Fluorescent fixtures keep the den of hell well lit. The air feels thick. More humid than the dry LA outside.

I count a dozen attendants. Some administrative, some serve food and water, and others deposit or withdraw people from cages. It has the feel of a slaughterhouse where nonchalant workers mutilate bodies and chuck parts on conveyor belts while they listen to playlists on headphones.

I see attendants bring a group of ten nude captives up a ramp and through a door. Per pre-mission intel, they bring them to a tiled cleaning bay and hose them down. Make-up artists go to work, finishing the pre-sale ritual.

The ground floor above us is a fully operational textile

factory, complete with modern looms and machines that make wholesale bolts of fabric. Happy Fibers Textiles Incorporated.

Trucks pull up and load slave merch. Then workers install a fake wall in the trailer, and load bolts of fabric to the top. It's worked for years. The fabric dampens any sounds from inside and makes the compartment soundproof. Most of this intel was gathered in the last two weeks. The advance prep crew planted hidden cameras and audio bugs. From these the strategists composed their plan.

Another attendant leads a batch of folks in another direction, straight to the shipping area. They're the chaff. The unsellables. Many slave buyers want workers and aren't particular about age or gender. But insubordinate slaves, especially if they aren't sexy, are worth more as organ donors and raw material for a gallon of fuel in Alistair's processing machines than they are as anything else.

Every drop of profit leached from every human body.

It's hard for me to watch the slavers herd the unsellables away. I know they'll pulp and process them like yard mulch. It's still possible to save them, if they don't leave the shipping yard before we complete our mission. It's possible.

They place me in a cell with another girl, uncuff me and give me some water. My cellmate doesn't move from her prostrate position. She looks about mid teens. Maybe African or Hispanic. I can't see her features, only her dirty black hair and a body that's thin as a gnat's whisker.

"Do you speak English?" I ask. She doesn't move. I touch her arm and she pulls away. I tug on her shoulder a little more and she half-heartedly pulls away again.

"Do you speak English? I ask again. Still no answer. I pull on her harder and try to turn her over on her back. She resists and I increase the pressure. She rolls over. She tries to hide her face from my view as if I am a blinding light.

"It's okay. I'm not going to hurt you. I might be able to get you home to your family," I say. She finally steals a glance at me, confused. At least I know she understands English. I see her face and it appears she's Pacific Islander, maybe from Fiji or something.

I whisper, "I'm also a prisoner here, but I might have a way out. I need to ask you some questions. How is your English?"

"It's fine," she says in good Aussie English.

"How long have you been here?"

"Much longer than the others. Two weeks."

"Why?"

"I was kidnapped in Australia at a market when I was shopping for my family and shoved into an SUV. They brought me somewhere dark and scary and then put me on a boat."

Tears form in her eyes and she looks away.

"On the way here, I... I... was raped several times, it's... I lost my virginity. When we arrived, I threw up a lot. They keep the sick ones away from everyone until they are healthy before they bring them upstairs. I kept puking but I had no runny nose or sore throat, so they checked. I was pregnant. They gave me an abortion this morning.

"How old are you?"

"14."

Sexual abuse at such a young age is dehumanizing. If you thought you had value for your intellect and creativity, or thought you deserved respect and honor, you learn that you do not. You are meat. Not a soul or a source of imagination and contribution. You are moist friction for a man's satisfaction. Your thoughts and dreams are nothing. You are a pleasure device, with no opinions or feelings. I know. It happened to me.

The girl sits up and says, "You are the prettiest woman I've ever seen. Have you been raped, too?"

"Yes, I have. When even younger than you," I answer. "My name is Teska. What's yours?"

She answers, "Dolly."

I hear some commotion over to the side, a young girl screams, and a male attendant yells at her. He drags her in handcuffs down the aisle between cages. She twists and yells curse words at the top of her lungs. She has crystal blue eyes and golden hair, angelic, like one of those cherubs on church paintings. She looks about 13 and going through puberty with knobby knees. He brings her through the door at the back wall and closes it. It mutes the screams. But I can hear. She doesn't relent. A few moments later, the screams stop.

"Do you know what they do to people in there?" I ask Dolly, who shakes her head and shrugs. The recon mission attempted to discover what each job and each room was for but was not able to discover what that one was.

Twenty minutes later the same man carries the blonde girl back through the same aisle, past our cage. She is limp and her eyes are bruised with a trickle of blood on the inside corner of one eye.

Bile rises in my stomach and a lightning bolt of terror courses through my body which turns into a seething, violent, screaming, murderous rage. They lobotomized her. To make her docile. They purged her rebelliousness to make her marketable, brain dead, and cooperative.

"Be strong, Phoenix. Follow the plan." John reminds me. He must have detected that my heart rate doubled. Dolly sees my wild eyes, draws her head back in fear and stares at me.

"You hate them," she says.

I nod. I control it. I breathe and hold myself still.

I think to myself, *follow the mission regimen precisely*.

I have no chronometer but my internal clock tells me it is near 0730. I try to study our cage's lock mechanism and cannot see it. I study the others across the aisle. They require no keys. Metal latches hold the cages shut and steel plate surrounds them preventing captives from being able to reach. Attendants open them without keys. I scan the warehouse and survey the personnel scene. It also provides QuadFilium command in the war room the view through my ocular feed.

My own cage has a few dirty blankets, a bucket for waste and flimsy tin trays and cups. An attendant can access these through narrow horizontal slits in the bars. The buckets cannot fit, so they must empty them less frequently, perhaps when removing or depositing captives. These buckets are primarily responsible for the penetrating odor.

"How long do most people stay in here until brought out?" I ask.

"Not long, usually only a few days." This syncs with our intel.

Crutcher talks in my ear, "We want to go live at 1030. Be ready." He expects no reply.

The rest of the team has assembled near the factory. My job is to prevent the captors from killing the captives when the team busts in. I have three hours to figure that out, while I watch these scum-sucking bottom-dwellers degrade people by the minute. Some personnel come and go. A shift change.

"Do these guys change up at this time?" I ask Dolly.

"Yeah, the night shift goes home and some day shift guys come in. There's a lot more day guys than night ones."

More people come in and fill into the jobs. They laugh, drink coffee and kid around with each other. I hear the night guys talk to the day guys about sports, or whatever seems to be on their mind, all nonchalant like. The guy that groped me walks into the room with a new guy I don't recognize. He describes something to the new guy. He points at me and mimes breasts with his hands and laughs. The new guy laughs with him but looks at me. The gown thing I wear hides my figure. But the look on new guy scares me. Predatory. Carnal. Same look as guys who molested me in the past, under the grip of something more powerful than they can control when they decided to strike, that it was worth it to take sexual advantage of me no matter the cost.

I'm worried he'll try before 1030, because there's no way I'm going to simply submit to that without a fight. That could throw off my go-live mission targets. It was hard enough to keep myself from breaking heads on the first guys I met here.

We went over this in tactical planning. The first solution: Do everything possible to deter the man from trying. The second: Feign illness to repel, and third: Submit. I have a problem with that last one ... but I won't jeopardize the mission. Me in here is a major advantage for us. In past busts, the captors destroyed the evidence by killing the captives. Often, by torching the entire place with the prisoners in their cages. This destroys the evidence, except for burnt dead bodies. But worse, it kills the very folks we are trying to save. I came in to prevent that.

If this new pervert tries something, it could be a problem. There's not likely to be a lot of willingness happening on my part, even if I analytically know I should.

Dolly sits up. I sit down next to her.

"Where did you live in Australia?" I ask.

"Sydney." She answered.

"Are you of Aboriginal descent?" I ask.

"Yes," says Dolly.

"A friend of mine is from Sydney. His name is Wade."

"That's weird. I never met anyone named Wade, but my cousin always talked about a guy she knew with that name. She used to keep a photo of him with her all the time. She said he was her guardian angel and wished he would come back. But he died in a car accident or something."

"Huh...And he lived in Sydney? What did he look like? Did you see the photo?"

"Yeah, I did. Real hunky cute guy. Athletic, dark hair, a small amount of hair on his face and some good muscles. My cousin said he used to help her all the time and she loved and missed him."

"Interesting."

"Why?"

"Nothing. My Wade's from Sydney too."

"This place fucking stinks!" A guy yells from the other end of the room. Chats stop. Slumpy shoulders go upright. This must be some head honcho. Older, clean-cut, slicked back hair. Hispanic. Scars on his face.

"Get these buckets fucking cleaned out and hose this shithole down!"

Warehouse personnel freeze and look like daddy just came home in the middle of an unapproved party.

"Now!"

Everyone springs and hustles, busy as stump-tailed bulls in fly season. A mid-level manager type stands as new boss man approaches. He's nervous but tries to stand tall and brave. Hold his position.

Boss man says, "Do you like working in filth, Carlos?"

"No sir."

"You like to sit around and breathe shit? What the fuck, man? Have some pride!"

Boss man's face is less than an inch from Carlos's.

"Yes, sir."

"I'm coming back down in an hour."

He walks out. He holds his arms out to the side when he walks, like a moseying cowboy.

A cleaner walks over to our stall and aims a weapon at us through the bars while pointing to the corner of the cell.

"He wants us away from the door to take out the waste bucket," says Dolly.

We scoot over and he opens the cell door. He keeps the weapon more or less trained in our direction, grabs the bucket, the blankets and the food tins and leaves. He latches the door.

I ask Dolly, "Have you seen this boss guy before?"

She shakes her head, no.

I tell her, "There might be a chance to break everyone out of here. I'm going to need you to help me open all the cell doors, okay?"

Dolly nods, nervous. We both watch the attendants open and close the cage doors, to see how it is done.

"I'm also going to look for a book that I need to take from here. It's a ledger with a bunch of handwriting in it, names and numbers in columns. We'll only have about sixty seconds to do all that so I need you to open cages and get others to help free everyone, okay?"

A guard enters the cage across the aisle. I point out the mechanism to Dolly and we watch how he enters the cell and re-latches when he leaves. I estimate 200 captives, two to three per cell and eighty cells. At three seconds per cage, if the captives help, it can be done. The assault team will create a diversion which will bring most of the personnel up to the main factory floor. I'll need to secure control of the basement and dispose of all hostiles. Any captives not freed will not make it.

The whole place is in a cleaning frenzy. Attendants remove shit buckets and blankets. A guy with a hose makes his way from cell to cell. He fires through the bars and washes down the floors, walls and the captives. Shrieks come from the cells as the powerful hose douses them in cold water. The hoser yells at them to shut up. Behind him, a guy with a squeegee pushes the water towards drains.

Hoser and squeeger get to us and start hitting the walls and floor. Dolly and I are in a corner to avoid the spray.

"Move over, cunts! I need to hit the wall behind you. We jump through the stream and cold powerful jet slaps hard. He hits the wall and then tells us to step forward and slowly spin. He jets us down in our night gowns as he makes lewd comments about our wet clothes plastered to our bodies. I check the band-aid on my back. Still on.

It's about 8:45 a.m. by the time the hoses stop. They let us soak and shiver for twenty minutes and then come back with clean gowns and throw them at us. While I change, the pervy guy stands right outside my cell and stares. He swallows. He turns and walks back to the guy that felt me up when I arrived.

I read his lips. He says, "I'm going to hit that after inspection. Wanna go in on that? Might need to hold that one down."

"Yeah man. You got it." They fist-pump and separate.

The place is cleaner, damp and cold.

Head-honcho re-enters, "Okay! The place smells better already! How many weeks of piss and shit did you guys hose off?" People laugh but no one answers the rhetorical question.

Carlos, the supervisor, has laughed along with everyone which catches big boss man's attention, who clearly doesn't appreciate this. His sharp look cuts the laughs off. He cowboy-moseys towards Carlos, who's not laughing or smiling no more. Two inches from his face. Silence pervades the room. Only the sound of dripping water accompanies this episode.

"I'm glad you can find humor in this, Carlos. So... so glad."

"Yes, s-sir."

"It makes me think though, that if you didn't enforce a clean space before, that a) you probably are unclean yourself, and b) you might not keep it clean in the future, because you aren't accustomed to cleanliness as habit."

"I assure you Mr. Salazar—"

"*Do not fucking say my name!*" Salazar punches Carlos in the stomach hard. Carlos keels over and pukes.

"Get me some rope." Compliance is instant.

Salazar grabs a towel and throws it on the ground.

"See, you're already making this place dirty again. Clean up your puke."

Carlos uses the towel to mop up his own vomit.

"Strip this fuck and hang him from that beam upside down!" Three guys jump in and carry out the order. They roughly pull off his shirt, shoes, pants and underwear. Then tie a loop around his ankles, chuck the other end over a beam, and pull him up.

"Someone get me the hose!"

Salazar proceeds to hose Carlos at full power. Carlos shrieks and jiggles like a fish on a line. Salazar cruelly goes out of his way to point blank the genital area. Carlos screams in pain while Salazar laughs and looks around to make sure everyone laughs as well... which they all do... all nervous as flies in a glue pot.

Carlos passes out, probably from the combo of pain and hanging upside down too long.

"He seems quite clean now. Cut him down," says Salazar.

They lower him to the ground. His inanimate body flops sideways.

After thirty seconds, a dazed Carlos comes to. Salazar squats down to keep his two-inch-from-the-face thing consistent.

"Carlos, think you understand cleanliness now?"

"Yes-s, s-sir."

"Good boy. Your momma must have been too busy sucking dick for crack to teach you this shit. You are still the fucking manager of this shithole, but the rest of the day, I'm sorry to say, you are going to stay up there in your fucking birthday suit." Salazar points at an elevated spot above the cells on the wall opposite the entry door.

Salazar directs a couple of boys to tie him up on the ledge and display Carlos to the whole group in his birthday suit.

"Run the place from up there today."

"Yes, sir."

"You!" Salazar points at another bystander, "Cut him down at 4:00 p.m!"

"Yes, sir" says the bystander.

"You guys still need to listen to him. He's your boss. Have fun, Carlos. And do you think we can keep this place a little cleaner in the future?"

"Yes, sir, for sure, sir."

"Great." Salazar flashes a brilliant smile and leaves.

What an awkward pose for Carlos, with his junk out on display. Arms outstretched, like a crucifixion. He's no Chippendale's dancer either. Pot belly, balding and pretty hairy overall. He starts crying after the boss leaves and I would probably have felt sorry for him except that he has been running an enslavement operation and deserves several lifetimes of pain and humiliation.

Perv guy seems to be wasting little or no time. Only minutes after the boss leaves, he walks over to my cell and unlatches it. He roughly grabs my arm and walks me over to a side room, opens the door and shoves me inside, a small room with a table and two chairs, an interrogation room perhaps. His buddy follows us inside.

"I have several STDs I should warn you," I say to him.

"Shut the fuck up, cunt. So do I, and I don't give a shit." By now he is already starting to undo his pants. He is in a hurry. I estimate that it is 9:45 a.m. Still forty-five minutes until the cavalry arrive.

"Take your gown off." he says.

I hesitate, and he open-palm slaps me on the side of the head. My left ear is ringing.

"Take it off!" he whisper-yells, to avoid discovery, but his face is contorted into rage. Hot as a stolen tamale. *How am I going to navigate this?* In pre-mission preps I agreed to take one for the team if this should happen. But now that I am here, right now, confronting these rapists, who have STDs, I'm not too keen on submission.

I feel a small trickle of blood on my left ear. I reach and lift off my gown as rapist number one readies himself, pants down. Boner out.

"Dude you were not fucking kidding about this bitch! I've never seen such fucking huge tits on a skinny bitch like this. And they're real! Damn!" says boner guy.

"That's what I was saying, bro. Hurry up I can't wait to get some of that shit, too."

Boner reaches forward and I reflexively grab his thumb and twist his arm around nearly breaking his hand. He yipes in pain and pulls back.

"This cunt needs some fucking restraints!" says the other guy, and he pulls out some handcuffs and comes behind me. The two of them wrestle my arms into position and lock them together with the cuffs behind and attached to the chair. Rapist number two holds me from behind while Boner massages his painful hand.

"That was a pretty fast and strong move there. Where did you learn that? Jerking guys off?" They laugh.

Looks like he's over it now and ready to get his groove on. He comes over and starts with the fondling. This buys me a little bit of time and might be the first time I was happy to have some creep feel me up, postponing the next thing.

I reach the band-aid and slowly peel off one side of it so it flops open. I can feel the handcuff key and grab it. Rapist number two, behind me, leans over to watch and can't see what I'm doing. The fondling continues and is getting more intense. I undo the cuffs but don't quite take them off yet, leaving them loosely in place. I grab the mini syringe with the hormones and steroids in it and I plunge it right into my back. Within a couple of seconds I feel an acute boost of strength. The rage inside of me is a tempest. *Did Dimitri put PCP in this shit?*

I grab the last tool, the razor, and I grip it in my fingers. The blade is only three quarters of an inch, but that can still do some damage.

Boner man pulls my legs forward and spreads them out, feverishly excited. As he gets real close, I let the handcuffs drop off my wrists and fling my elbow back into rapist number two's mid-section, knowing he'll bend forward, and follow that with flinging my head backwards. The top back of my head connects with his the center of his face. I feel his nose collapse, like stomping on a scorpion. Crunch!

Like a bullwhip, I lash my body forward and headbutt rapist one in the nose and teeth. The juice I took doubled my strength, pain tolerance and aggression. The top of my forehead craters into the center of his face.

I swing my blade around and slice at the base of his manhood, severing it halfway through. It hangs open and pissing out blood.

I flip around and swing wildly at the stunned guy behind the chair. He yells while his nose gushes. I reach up with the blade and slice at his neck. Two tries does it, and a sprinkler of blood sprays my body in crimson. He topples to the ground.

Both hostiles are motionless, and I stand fully nude, covered in blood, and watch my first two kills bleed out. As the puddles form, I can only think of the abusive molesters, rapists and evil fucks that damage and kill the helpless, just for their few minutes of sexual satisfaction. Savages.

I assume the yells from inside this room have alerted the folks outside. I can hear naked Carlos yelling from his perch to check out what's happening.

John Jacques, with his subtle French accent, talks into my earpiece, "I can't blame you, Teska. Just be ready for the mission plans to change a little bit from here."

I snap back to reality. *I'm on a mission.* The Mind Booth just saw that whole thing unfold. I may have just ruined the entire operation by not letting the rapists fuck me.

The doors fly open and armed men take in the scene. I'm quickly subdued to the floor face down. The men drag the victims and me out of the room and Carlos sees us all. The two rapists are still bleeding out and blood continues to pool around their bodies.

"What the fuck happened?!" Carlos yells.

"Looks like these two assholes tried to get some action and got a little more than they wanted," answers one of the armed men.

"Get her into surgery! She's too out-of-control! And cut me down from here!"

One of the guys starts walking over to do so, and another guy points his weapon at him and says, "Don't do it. The big boss told me to shoot anyone that tries to cut Carlos down. He said even if the fucking building is on fire, leave him up there."

"Are you kidding me?" Carlos asks.

"That's what he said, boss."

"Get her into surgery!"

Two guys lift me up and start heading towards the lobotomy room. I struggle violently, knowing they plan to kill my brain, my drive and my life force and in only a few minutes.

All of a sudden, an alarm goes off.

"Mission is a go." says Jean Jacques to me. He must have just triggered the upstairs team to go for it.

A loud speaker announces, "A group of inspectors have appeared to look at the factory upstairs and everyone needs to get to their stations in the textile factory *now*!"

Chapter 12
Wade

// Wade, Teska's position is compromised and they are about to take her into a lobotomy. Mission is go," says Crutcher into my ear piece.

Oh, my fucking God, I can't let that happen.

I answer him, "Boss man, I need to know the status as we move forward on this. Tell me when they are about to do it, because come hell or high water, I'm going to stop them."

Jean Jacques answers, "Definitely."

I and six suited men and one woman approach the entry to the factory and knock on the door. A voice says through the intercom on a small metal box, "Hello, may I help you?"

One of our American operatives answers, "We are with the Labor department and are doing a random inspection of your facility. Please let us in."

"Yes sir, of course. May I see the papers legitimizing this?" he asks.

"Of course," says the operative, and he displays the papers to the camera.

Sounding as pleasant as Mr. Fucking Rogers, the knob on the intercom says, "Please give us a couple of minutes. We need to shut off a few of the machines for your safety before we invite you in."

Jesus fucking Christ, we don't have that kind of time. Teska could have an ice pick halfway through her eyeballs by then.

I'm heavily considering breaking all protocols and busting

my way in.

Jean Jacques gives an update to the team, "From what I can see through Teska's feed, all the workers downstairs are scrambling up to man the factory right now. Teska just entered the surgery and is being strapped down to a bed."

I tell the American he needs to be urgent on this so he hits the intercom and says, "You are going to have to let us in right away."

The intercom guy answers, "Yes, sir, we will be 100% compliant with your requests. We are following state and federal guidelines of safety right now by powering down the machines, otherwise we could just as well be fined and penalized for unsafe operations."

"We can have you shut down for just delaying this order. Let us in."

"Our labor union has informed us that bullying threats from government agencies, especially in California, are subject to lawsuits against the agency threatening us, and you could lose your position, sir. In fact, we are already recording this conversation."

I'm getting more than impatient now. I whisper to Jean Jacques, "What's her status now?"

"They are trying to sedate her. She's twisting around wildly."

I tell the American, "Tell him he has twenty seconds to open the door or else we will be forced to call in units to engage."

He is halfway through his sentence when the doors open and a friendly host greets them.

"Welcome to Happy Fabrics Incorporated. Come on in." Big cheesy smile.

Jean Jacques briefs the team, "I cannot tell how many hostiles are still downstairs, but we all know that once engagement starts, the bad guys are instructed to torch the place and fuck off. We saw how the back entrance works. Wade, you hang back and let the others go inside the factory. I want you entering the back way. Waste no time!"

I don't go inside with the rest of the crew but briskly walk to the back loading-dock area. On the ledge where trucks do their loading and unloading are two blokes happily filling a truck with bolts of fabric, here at Happy Fabrics.

"Just inside to the left is the entrance," says Jean Jacques.

"Can we help you?" asks one of the loaders.

"Yes. I'm part of an inspection team that just arrived here to see the factory. Can I look around a little bit?"

"Yeah Sure. Be our guest." Such accommodating wankers.

Jean Jacques sounds more urgent, "Wade, she has just been sedated and her eyes are closing, we won't be able to see anything only hear what they are doing. There is very little time."

I can't help but notice his concern for her in his voice. It's parental and frantic... or even passionate. Normally Jean Jacques wouldn't be rash to save an operative when the whole mission could be compromised, but in this case he sounds pretty fucking urgent.

I act swiftly and engage the two truck-loading tossers. The first one is facing away from me and I just swing an elbow to the base of his head. Instant unconsciousness. The other guy screams "Hey!" but I cut him off with a chop to the throat, and I sprint towards the door just inside to the left of the loading dock, as he falls to his knees.

The door is metal and locked. It won't budge.

Jean Jacques, "Try knocking. Politely." I do. I use a little silly ditty of a playful knock. A smiling old-ish woman with freakishly bright red hair opens up the door. I swing it open the rest of the way and punch her square in the face, and she falls back. I run past her towards a stairway.

Jean Jacques describes what I'll be seeing, "There are two well-armed bouncers in front of the next two doors. You will have to take out the first one quietly or else the other one is going to spray his Uzi all over you as you turn the corner."

I leap down the stairs landing to landing and see the first bouncer. He is a good 300 pounds and half a foot taller than I am. He sees me sprinting towards him and reaches for his gun. I already have a knife out, winding up like a pitcher.

In training, we were taught to angle the blade flat when throwing into a standing target so it will fit between the ribs. I loose the knife at his chest and with a deep hollow thump it embeds itself to the hilt right into his heart. By the time I get to him he is falling over, dead. I don't break my stride.

Jean Jacques sounds frantic now, "Wade! I can hear Teska's feed, they are about to insert the spike into her eye!"

"Fuck! Where is the operating room?!" I ask as I run down the next set of stairs, this time I have my semi-automatic out and I don't give a fuck if people hear me shoot it.

"Right as you enter the main floor in the basement, it's the closed door in the wall to your right! Hurry!"

I turn the corner and the next bouncer is there, more wily and agile and quickly reaches for his gun. I put two bullets in his head and jump over his falling body, then kick open the door behind him. There are two guys in there, one armed and the other running towards a gun on the table. Right as I come through, I get a shower of bullets, but my gun is already out and I shoot the shooter in the head. Two of his bullets hit my stomach, but it's plated under my suit. The other guy grabs his gun and swings it up to shoot me but I beat him to it and unload two shots into him and don't even look back. I veer right for the door.

Some little girl in cage yells, "She's in there, Wade!" pointing at a door against the back right wall. Even though I care about one thing and one thing only right now, saving Teska, I can't help notice both the familiarity of this girl, how she knew I was Wade, Aussie accent, and the fact that there is a naked Hispanic dude propped up above the room, high on the wall with his arms spread out like Jesus.

I sprint towards the door and leap at it with a flying kick. Time slows down for me. As the door flies open inwards, I see Teska's profile on the bed and a guy with a pointy instrument halfway down into her eye socket. He jumps back in shock and lets go of the tool as I pump bullets into his body.

The tool remains upright, stuck inside her skull. I delicately grab the tool handle and pull it out from the inside of her left eyelid and a small pool of blood forms around the inside of her eye.

"Goddammit!" yells Jean Jacques, just as I think the same thing.

I hear the rat-a-tat-tat of machine gun fire going off upstairs. The team has engaged the enemy. I leave Teska on the bed for a moment so I can suss out the scene. I need the coast to be clear before I bring her out of there, or else I risk getting her unarmored body hit in the line of fire.

The naked bloke is screaming frantically from his perch, "Somebody cut me down! Hey! Someone get me down from here!"

The little cage girl yells, "Wade! Let me out! I'll open all the cages!"

"Yeah okay!" I say, and I run over and I open the lock to her door. Crickey, this girl reminds me of Peyton.

She runs out of the cage and starts unlatching the cell doors.

Into my ear comm Crutcher says, "Your backup will be entering the basement, Wade. We need to get everyone out of there."

Just as he says that the far wall of the basement erupts in flames and one of the bad guys runs off to the side throwing an empty jug away. Torching the place. Naked Jesus still screams to cut him down. I would if I thought he was a captive, but he looks like he belongs up there.

The little islander girl runs around frantically opening all the doors and getting the other captives to help her open the others.

Two of my guys bust in and start helping direct the captives out the back way up to a transport waiting for them.

I run back for Teska and lift her off the table. The pain in my stomach where the two bullets hit my armor plates shoots into my body. Too much to withstand. My body resists. I reach under my coat to my back and rip off the bandaid. I pull out the thumbtack-sized syringe and plunge it into a vein on my hand. I feel instant invincibility. I throw Teska over my shoulder and run out into the main room. It's half consumed in flames and the little girl and the two operatives are shoving people out the door to the back way.

The flames have almost reached naked Jesus and he's still screaming and wiggling like a some sort of TikTok dance challenge.

I ask the girl, "He's a bad guy, right?" She nods. I nod back at her as the flames reach him and his shriek is piercing. I get the fuck out of there, carrying Teska on my shoulders.

I run up the stairs three at a time and get to the metal door. Trampled to death by the two hundred captives is the bright-haired older woman I punched earlier. Her hair is pressed into the floor like a red greeting mat and her eyes are wide open staring up at the ceiling. Her mouth looks like it's smiling.

I get Teska over to the medic van a quarter block down the way and place her inside. I join her in there. She's still out cold.

John Crutcher talks to me through my auditory feed, "Wade, you should head back and lead the mission to its close. There's nothing you can do for her by staying there. Your team is right mid engagement and needs you." I know he's right and it takes everything I have to leave her there and run back to the scene on the factory floor.

I hear police sirens faintly in the distance. The gunshots got them called in. We have maybe one minute to get done and get out of there.

"Status Alpha One?" I shout on my team leader channel.

"All hostiles eliminated on the factory floor. Sweeping the premises for survivors."

"Good! Transport leaves in fifty seconds. All must be on it!"

"Alpha Two! Status!"

"Two captives didn't make it out of the flames, but all others did. The place is fully ablaze now!"

"Did you get the ledger?

"I'm sorry boss I didn't. It's probably burning up right now,"

"Shit! Shit! Shit! Transport leaves in thirty-five seconds. Get your team on it now!"

I get to the large lot at the back of the factory and see the two hundred gowned captives in a large group standing away from the building. Smoke pours out of the back door, and my two guys emerge. The operative's transport backs into the lot and I yell to the Alpha Two team to jump inside.

I announce to the group of captives, "The police are on their way. They will help you to safety!"

"Thank you!" yell several from the crowd, along with various other-language exclamations from non-English-speaking freed captives. Most are in total shock and say nothing.

I run back to the transport and jump inside and as I reach for the door to close it, I hear someone calling my name.

"Wade!" coughing loudly and emerging from the billowing smoke is the little girl running towards the transport. The sirens of the police cars are getting louder and they are now only seconds away. She is carrying a book and waving it. "You need this!"

For fuck's sakes, she has the ledger!

"Stop!" I tell to the driver.

"We can't, the cops are here!" says the driver.

"Stop for three seconds right now!" I yell.

The truck stops and the girl reaches up and grabs my arm. I have no time to try to get the ledger from her and let her go so I pull her aboard and shut the doors. The driver peels out through the alley just in time to miss the arrival of the local authorities.

Chapter 13

Jean Jacques

"We need to get Teska to the nearest MRI!" I yell, to the medics.

Dimitri interrupts, "Sir, MRI will kill her. The small amount of metal imbedded in eye and ear implants will get pulled out and rip through head like bullet. Powerful magnets used on MRI machine."

"*Merde!*" I yell.

Dimitri says, "Sir, right now we not know extent of damage and cannot know unless remove devices and this not possible. Taking out device will blinding her."

I think for a moment. "*Merde!* We need to think of a solution while she is on her way back here."

I turn my attention back to the mission screens in front of me. All operatives are now in the transport headed out of LA.

Wade brought with him this little girl, but I was too focused on the Teska matter to understand why he'd have her board the transport with the rest of the operatives. I ask the tactical leader, "John, why is the little girl on the transport?"

He answers, "She found the ledger and brought it to Wade as the vehicle was leaving the scene. LAPD was seconds away from arriving and this was a spur of the moment call by Wade. She grabbed his arm. Didn't seem like he had a choice."

"Wait, he's talking to her. Let's listen."

We turn down the other volumes on the screens and focus on Wade's. Filling the ocular display is an image of the same girl that was in the cell with Teska. The one who helped free the captives.

"What's your name?" asks Wade.

"Dolly," the girl answers.

"Dolly. That was very brave. You're a hero, you know? You saved a bunch of lives back there," says Wade.

Dolly blushes and nods.

The transport driver says, "Ten minutes to local operations base. Be ready."

"Dolly, I'm going to have to let you off. You can't come with us."

"But where will I go?"

"We'll alert the local authorities and they'll help you get back home. Where's home?"

"Sydney."

The screen shows Wade blink twice.

"I know that town pretty well...How'd you know my name when I ran in?"

The girl says, "I've seen your picture before, Wade."

The heart rate monitors show a ten percent increase on Wade's heart meter. I lean in closer. *What is this all about? This little girl knows Wade from Sydney? This could be a problem.*

The girl says, "I saw your picture. My cousin Peyton had it."

Wade's heart rate monitor jumps from 80 to 120. This is bad.

Peyton's kidnapping was Wade's scopulus. It's what drove him to join Quadfilium.

A very, very touchy matter.

Wade asks the girl, "I thought she was kidnapped...?"

"Yeah, she was, but she made it back home. It was a

103

miracle."

Wade's visio feed shakes slightly. Heart rate 130.

"Do you know anything else about it?" asks Wade.

"No. She said she was blindfolded and didn't see any of her kidnappers, ever. She was treated nice. Then one day they got rid of her... dropped her off near home. The police never found out who did it."

"Wow... and she is... okay?" asks Wade.

"She was kind of troppo for a bit but she came out of it. She talked about you a lot and she said you died somehow. She was really, really sad about that."

I talk into Wade's earpiece, "Wade, listen to me. We're going to give this girl over to the authorities and walk away, do you understand?"

Wade says to Dolly, "Excuse me a moment." Wade gets up and walks away from the girl.

He says to me, "Boss... as you can imagine I'm pretty troppo right now, too."

I answer, "Yes, this is remarkable. I can only imagine what you're going through at this moment. But look, this girl will get taken home to her family in Sydney, and she'll tell Peyton that she saw you, and no one will believe her. We need to count on that. You are a verified corpse, registered and recorded. The only thing you can do now is tell her that you don't know anyone named Peyton and that it must be a coincidence that you have the same name as this other guy named Wade."

Wade replies, "Okay boss. I'll tell her that."

Wade walks back to the girl.

Chapter 14
Wade

Dumbstruck and numb. So much to process. I just killed a dozen men, got shot twice, saved two hundred slaves just in time to witness Teska mid lobotomy who might be brain dead, discovered that Peyton is alive and not in the slave market, and to top it all off, I have a contract out on me for ten million dollars. Each of these facts are individually unconfrontable. To deal with them all in the same instant is a mind-fuck.

The information I've just gotten about Peyton's kidnapping tells me that it was fake. Jean Jacques must have set it up to manipulate me into joining QuadFilium, and then he released her when I was a full member of the team. This also tells me that it's likely that the Teska-fiancé-Jeff-thing was a setup as well. Our lives are lies.

Vertigo.

But I'm also filling in some holes. Some puzzle pieces appear, some gaps fill. The vertigo calms.

I walk over to Dolly and kneel, "Dolly, I don't know your cousin Peyton. You must have me mistaken for someone else," and I wink at her as I say this, so she knows I'm lying. I used the eye that doesn't have the camera installed. I can see it registers, and she knows it isn't true. She nods back.

I say, "So, we are going to let you out here and within a few minutes a police officer will pick you up and will get you home to Sydney. You've been very brave. You saved many lives. You were the most important part of this mission. You are special, Dolly. Don't forget it."

She nods again. Probably in numb shock from the last several week. Kidnapped... probably raped... rescued, and now this. Complete overwhelm. But she looks proud and she should.

Dolly asks, "What was the name of that pretty woman who came in and shared a cell with me? Is she going to be okay?"

I say, "She survived. Let's let you out here."

The transport stops and we let her out in front of a police station. We tell Dolly to go in there and tell her story. We wave goodbye and I sit down. My mind buzzes like a blue-ass fly. I close my eyes.

John Crutcher talks: "Wade. Well done. Duty's top priority. Focus. Once you hit the base, all operatives have thirty minutes to take a break and gear up for Phase II."

"Yes, Sarge," I say. "What's Teska's status?"

John Crutcher answers, "Still unconscious. We don't know the extent of damage. They pumped a lot of narcotics and anesthetics into her, add to that the thumbtack syringe, we're looking through a drug haze at a traumatized woman. We can't get an MRI because she has the devices in her eye and ear, and they have small metal parts. All we can do is wait until she wakes up and take it from there."

I say, "Keep me posted?"

"Of course. Now, focus on Phase II."

"Ten-four," I say.

Chapter 15
Madame Girard

I sit in my bedroom, in a chair once owned and sat in by Napoleon himself. A server brings me tea. The same tea the Queen of England drinks. I bathe in opulence and yet I'm completely and utterly depressed. My eyes are red and puffy. I've been crying for the last hour and resisting the urge to drink. Okay, one little sip won't hurt. I gulp down a shot of Macallan 25 and wipe my mouth.

Carmen comes in an hour and I don't want her to see me like this, flying in for a vacation. She suspects something and I keep telling her everything is fine.

I shower and run alternate hot and cold water on my face to decrease the puffiness. I come out and use creams and makeup to rescue my face. It's organic, my brand, *Estrelle*. The largest cosmetic and beauty care company in the world.

I step back and look. The whites of my eyes are still red. I drip Visine and they whiten up nicely. But I still look old and haggard, still have wrinkles no matter how much "penetrating moisturizer" and anti-wrinkle cream I use. I look at my figure and it leaves much to be desired. No wonder Jean Jacques isn't attracted anymore...I'm not attractive!

Oh no! Don't do this to yourself. You're going to start crying again! Just get your clothes on and start about your day. You'll get into something productive and forget about it.

I get dressed, put on my shoes and check my phone. Carmen will be here in minutes. I make some tea and eat a snack.

"Mother!" Carmen runs into the house and up the stairs. She is thirty-four and looks great. She's a Latin beauty with glossy black hair and golden-brown skin, and her eyes are nearly black.

We exchange anecdotes about each other's lives for the first hour. I catch up on her dating scene, and all the gossip we can think of to tell each other. Then, she looks at me point blank and says, "Momma, I know there's something going on between you and dad. You can't hide it from me."

I reply, "Why do you keep saying that?"

"Because it's obvious. The two of you were so happily in love and cute together. You used to tell and retell me all the stories of how you met in California, how surprised he was to find out that you were a billionaire, how you hid that from him for the entire year you dated. And that time in college when he tried to climb into your window but you were on the fifth floor, so he got arrested..."

I look away as my eyes begin to mist Carmen sees it.

"Mom, what's up?"

"Ummm... well... it's true... the sparks in our marriage are now more like an ember glow, but that doesn't mean we are failing—"

"Mom! You look depressed. Like, actual depression."

"Okay, Carmie, I've been very unhappy for the last year. It's true."

"Why what happened? Did Dad cheat on you?"

"No, no. But it seems like he isn't in love with me anymore. He may even be in love with someone else. I have no reason to believe that he's acted on it. But I sense it and have evidence that it's true. It kills and crushes me..." I start to cry again.

Carmen puts her arm around me.

"Mom, I'm so sorry," Carmen says and comforts me as best she can. "I have to admit, it makes me want to punch him in the face. Tell me what you know."

"I already feel it's very unfair that I am telling you any of this. I should just talk to my therapist. I don't want to give you the wrong impression of your father… that's just not fair."

"Mom… I've learned a lot about great people, amazing, great people that do amazing things, and… they're not perfect. Dad has always been 100% true, loving and my hero. I won't let anything change that. But I'm sick of being told everything is fine, when I know it's not.

"I also don't think it's fair for me to hold you two up on some pedestal. It's almost weird how perfect you two are. A bump in a very smooth road is normal."

I answer her, "You're right, dear. I'll tell you what, I'll make an appointment with my therapist for tomorrow. I'd rather not get you sucked into the details… okay?"

"Okay Mom, but you can always talk to me."

The next day, I call my therapist and ask for an appointment. He clears his schedule and invites me over right away.

I walk into Doctor Garnier's office. He smiles and indicates the couch. I lie back and look at the ceiling. It has colorful images of clouds, birds, and rainbows painted by a muralist, which makes me feel both serene and a little psycho, like I require mild gentle images so I don't trigger.

"Madame Girard. Please, tell me what's happening," says the doctor.

"Yes, Pierre. I have been very unhappy for the past year. Does it show?"

"You, madame, always look healthy and vibrant, to me but I see a dark cloud swirling. Tell me what's been going on?"

"Well… I have secrets. For two and half decades, I've told no anyone. But you're my psychiatrist, bound by patient-doctor privilege, a sacred trust, and, you're an honorable man. I feel I can talk to you about it. Am I right?" I ask.

"Of course, Madame. I've never violated that trust in the forty years of practice. It is against the law. And, it's against my word."

"Thank you, Pierre. And if what a patient tells you is illegal? Do you have a duty to report it to the police?" I ask.

"Only if they express intent. But I will say that no matter what you tell me, I will not betray this information to the police." says my doctor.

"Well my secrets do not express intent."

"Then we're fine. But even if you did, I assure you I would not report you. I will simply never betray a patient's trust."

"Thank you doctor. If you don't mind, I'd like to put our phones in another room… what I am about to tell you can never be recorded or repeated."

I scan the room for any other electronics that could act as recording devices and see nothing obvious.

"Of course," he says.

He takes both our phones to the closet twenty-feet away and places them under a blanket.

"I think we're fine, unless you yell," he laughs. I find comfort in his humor. I start to relax.

"Proceed," he says.

"Twenty-four years ago, I funded my husband's creation of a secret paramilitary group called QuadFilium. It is located in a secret base near Grenoble. It has over 100 staff, some of whom are assassins. We kill human traffickers, murderers, organ harvesters. We have saved thousands of victims and have killed hundreds of terrible people," I tell him point blank. I listen. No slightest change in his breathing. No clearing of his throat. I look at him and he does not blink.

I continue, "We recruit people to fake their deaths and join QuadFilium. The business we conduct is under shell corporations and LLCs. In twenty-five years there has never been a breach of security."

I continue. "Do you recall the Belgium Port Massacre last year?"

"Of course. Fifty men were found dead in the port of Brussels. Authorities determined the operation was carried out by elite professionals who left no clues. Reports recognized the murder victims were all members of a human trafficking organization," says Dr. Garnier.

"That was us," I say.

He nods.

"And last week we attempted to execute Alistair Watson."

"The owner of Bio-Gen?"

"Yes, the fuel company."

"That's right. I saw him receive an ad honorem degree from Oxford on the BBC for his alternative energy accomplishments."

"Yes. Those accomplishments were actually his father's. He runs the largest human and organ trafficking operation we've discovered to date."

"Alarming."

"Indeed."

"You said you tried to kill him?"

"Yes, but we killed a decoy. A look alike."

"I understand."

"I hope you're not checking off 'insane' or 'delusional' on your note pad there," I say.

"The thought, of course, crossed my mind... but I have never found you to indulge in fantasy or delusion. And any such operation as the Belgian port massacre would have to be executed by a private mercenary group with substantial resources. I also know, your husband's family found Carmen in a human trafficking shipment. You told me several years ago. So frankly, it rings true. I believe you," he says.

"Thank you, doctor. That means a lot." At this point I tremble. If this secret gets out on the loose, it would cause the death of not only my husband and likely me and Carmen, but also the 106 members of QuadFilium. But I have to tell someone and I trust this man.

"Continue," he says.

"Jean Jacques and I have not been intimate in over a year, ever since I found out that he was obsessed with a Texan tramp named Teska. This started fourteen months ago. I hired a P.I. to follow him on one of his recruit missions. He'd been spending more and more time on these and less and less time being affectionate with me. He was even temperamental. In our twenty-six years of marriage this had never happened. I had to look into it. I broached the subject a number of times with him. But got nothing. He even stormed out on me a few times, complaining I was being accusative and suspicious for no reason.

"The P.I. monitored Jean Jacques. Not an easy task as Jean Jacques is well acquainted with undercover trade craft. While not trained himself, he knows a lot."

"Intriguing, Madame."

"The P.I. remained hidden, changed his car every day...

altered his appearance and attire... varied his patterns. He was able to place hidden cameras in Jean Jacques's car."

"Sounds like a Hollywood film, madame."

"My life... yes. Jean Jacques spent considerable time watching Teska, setting up video cameras of her and her lover, Jeffrey, and tracking their every move. He's... um... very careful about whom he hires. He studies them for months or years before he recruits them. But, while he does this for any of his recruits in the final stages, there was one particular incident that set me off."

"Interesting recruit system."

"I know. He's obsessed with getting only the most perfect personnel. He feels it is his key to success. But that's a whole other story. The P.I. came to my house. We went into my office. He said he had something to show me. He put his recent footage on a monitor for me to see. One of the cameras set up was located in Jean Jacques' car behind him, able to view the monitors Jean Jacques watched. One night, a video of Teska wearing nothing but her underwear appears on the screen.

"Jean Jacques says out loud, 'Oh my God, I love you.'"

"Oh, madame..." says Dr. Garnier.

"My heart sank into my stomach. I ran out and to my bedroom. I looked in the mirror and saw the wrinkles around my eyes, the lines flanking my mouth, the bags, the looser skin on my neck, my size B breasts, and I cried. I screamed at the mirror, 'You fucking ugly old hag! You're ugly! He hates you!' and I broke the mirror. My aide came in and found me sobbing in tears, broken glass all over."

"Did you ever confront Jean Jacques with the evidence?"

"Not exactly. A few nights later when Jean Jacques returned, he tried to make a sexual advance, and told me he loved me. I couldn't go along with the charade and I pulled away. He put on a show of concern and tried to find out what my problem was. I kept refusing to tell him. Finally, I said I could tell that he'd lost interest in me. I said I felt it was related to his pursuit and surveillance of Teska."

"And what was his response?"

"He denied it with a deadpan face. At that point, I felt I'd lost my husband forever. He lied to me, admitted only that as a man, he couldn't help pay attention to Teska's uncommon physical eccentricities, but that it meant nothing to him and that his family, Carmen and I were the most important things in his life. Yet I knew he wasn't admitting a powerful infatuation, despite my heavy prying. I've rejected any advance he's has made since. You know... excuses... busy... tired."

"I have six non-profit foundations of which I am either the chairman or on the board. I fund them all. Including one that works with police to help reintegrate former slaves into society. And I am writing a book on raising a child who's lost their family, based on my experience with Carmen."

"I understand. Please continue..."

"I toured all my foundations... Brazil, Indonesia, India, and the US. Jean Jacques and I had brief business-like talks here and there. They became less and less frequent. He knows I am slipping away from him."

"Did you continue the surveillance?"

"I stopped the P.I. work when Teska became a QuadFilium member. No P.I. could ever gain access to its operations base. Also, I decided to leave it alone. The information I received disturbed me to no end, left me crying in hotel rooms at night. I tried to become numb to it and focus on my social betterment foundations and book. But I am not over it. 'Hell hath no fury like a woman scorned' is a fact."

"I have seen this phenomenon countless times, my dear," says Dr. Garnier.

My doctor, truly the most soothing voice, and I feel so safe talking to him.

"I have not decided what to do about it. The budget for QuadFilium is incredibly high. But, I have not stopped funding it. I believe in the cause deep in my heart. I know it saves the lives of thousands of helpless victims. I sign the checks whenever asked, and always will."

"I see. And you mentioned your daughter has been catching on...?"

"Carmen talks about it all the time... asking why her father and I are never together... if we still love each other... what's happening to our family? I tell her that we are so passionate about our work that it consumes our time and attention. She sees the sadness in my face and doesn't believe me. Like I said, she's an extraordinary young woman."

"Of course, she is. Let's talk about the early days. Has your husband always had a wandering eye?"

"Jean Jacques and I first met as freshmen at UC Berkeley when we were seventeen years old. We lived on the same floor in a dorm building called Putnam Hall."

"Do you suppose he was attracted to your wealth?"

"He had no idea I was a billionaire's daughter. He loved me for who I was. We were both from France living in America so this made us instant companions. We helped each other adapt to our new and exciting surroundings.

"I was pursuing a degree in Literature with a minor in Women's Studies. Jean Jacques was at Cal's business school. Within a few weeks, we couldn't stay away from each other. He carried my books for me to the library. We studied late every night. We'd walk the campus to our dorms under the stars, past the campanile and the sprawling lawns lit by moonlight. During the day, we'd picnic and feed the squirrels, who became our pets after a while. We named them after our favorite French cartoon characters."

"Sounds quite enchanting."

"During spring break our first year, when we both returned to France. I invited him to my home outside Paris to meet my family. By this point, we were so in love and for all he knew I was a peasant. He didn't care. He loved me. He thought I was beautiful and unmatched. He always joked that he had to travel ten thousand miles from home to find the love of his life, who lived only a few dozen miles from his own home in France."

"When he visited my family's estate for the first time, he was taken aback with the wealth and extravagance. He asked me why I'd never told him. I said that I'd never been able to tell who my real friends were when I was the daughter of the richest family in France. It was one of the reasons I'd gone to America—no one knew my family. It was the '80s and the internet of today did not exist. American tabloids didn't care about me or my family so I was safe from paparazzi."

"Yes, of course. So touching a story."

Although my eyes are open, I am no longer looking at the ceiling. The mind's eye consumes all of my attention and I can smell the fresh-cut grass and feel the breeze on Berkeley's campus. I feel like a teenage girl again as I talk.

"The liberal views of Berkeley had an effect on us. We cared about changing the world and making it a better place. Sure, there were other elements that went along with being a Berkeley liberal, like free love and excessive substance abuse,

116

but we didn't go along with those ideas. We knew they were a mockery riding on the tails of the real goals of the liberal views."

"Sounds blissful."

"That was such a happy time. We married when we were juniors. When we graduated, my family hired Jean Jacques as an executive trainee to oversee inventory in French ports. It was during this job that we found Carmen. Jean Jacques quit his job and dedicated himself to combat human trafficking. As both my parents had recently passed away, I was heir to a fortune, and able to fund Jacques and my passion to free slaves."

"Very generous of you, madame."

"But, despite being the richest woman in the world, as a *woman* I'm broken. The love of my life looks outside to quench his lust. Nothing burns more. A lump in my throat forms every time I'm reminded."

A tear rolls down my right cheek.

"My cosmetic business hires the most beautiful women in the world to advertise our products. I see the men around me fixate on them. It always reminds me of Jean Jacques, and the love we've lost. I will never again be able to give him what he wants as a man. All he can ever do is pretend for the rest of our lives."

I cry. The doctor hands me a tissue.

I feel relieved. I have finally talked about the secret to someone other than Jean Jacques. I have finally revealed my true feelings about the marriage. I need strong guidance to navigate through this.

"What do I do, doctor?"

"Get him to bare his soul to you, so that he may experience the same relief that you feel now."

Chapter 16
Jean Jacques

Wade handled that better than I would have expected. I can't tell if that's a good thing or a bad thing. I'm worried about him. It normally takes me a lot longer to handle him and his Aussie stubbornness. Perhaps, the issue with Teska… her unconsciousness… undiagnosed condition has him focused.

I say to John Crutcher, "I'll be gone for the next thirty to sixty minutes but close by. Message me when Phase II begins or if the slightest thing happens concerning the mission."

"Ten-four, boss."

I leave the Mind Booth as the troops replenish and prepare for Phase II.

I find Brett in his office. He stands, worried. He expects me in the Mind Booth rather than walking about.

"What's the matter, Double J?" he asks.

"Brett, I'm worried about something. It could be one of the biggest problems in QuadFilium history. I need to talk fast because the troops are deploying within the hour on Phase II. I need to be ready for them," I say.

"I'm all ears. Say it," says Brett.

"It is about Wade. I think he's dipped his toe into the pool of disaffection."

"You think he's turning on us?"

"I do."

Brett says, "Well, we best not show Wade your suspicions."

"I agree," I say.

"But, you're going to tell me, when the mission is over."

I nod. "He stays as team leader for now. Taking him off would set him off and we'd have no idea what he'd do next," I say. "Meanwhile, when do you leave for China?" I ask.

"Tomorrow morning," Brett answers.

"*D'accord.*"

Chapter 17
Wade

We arrive at a hangar in Oxnard, just outside LA. The doors open. Our ground transport enters and the doors close behind us. John Crutcher makes an announcement over our ear comms: "One hour, and we're a go on Phase II. The elimination of several top clients and freeing their captives."

Teams of two will hit precise locations. My assigned teammate was Teska. I'll need another partner. I look over who's available, but each operative is paired. No one else remains. John reads my thoughts and he talks into my audio feed: "Wade, we need to assign you a new partner."

I answer, "Sarge, I can definitely take care of this alone. I don't want to break up the strategy and reduce the number of targets, just because we're one man short."

Crutcher tells me to hold while he discusses the matter with the strategists. He comes back on and says, "Agent Maley, a sole operative is out of the question. You sustained two bullets to the stomach, and while plated, your performance parameters are an unknown. We need you paired, or with an existing team. Get back to me in ten minutes on how you want to proceed. If you have no solutions, we'll order one in," says Crutcher.

This is a bit odd. They sent me single-handedly into the belly of the beast at the Alistair kill. Now, they have misgivings about sending me to some asshole's eight-bedroom house in Beverly Hills who might have a couple of geezer rent-a-cops? What the fuck? Sounds suspicious. They're keen bastards, so they may have picked up that my own suspicions have taken over. They don't want me on my own. But they'll keep me as the team leader so I don't freak out.

"Ten-four, boss. I'll think it over," I say. I'm not hungry but force myself to eat a protein bar. I look over the paired operatives and don't see anyone that clicks for me. It reminds me that Teska might be brain dead. I feel a wave of dread.

There are two guys to my right. A couple of younger American blokes. I think I'll join up with them.

The support team in QF is rifling through the LA ledger to ascertain which targets to hit. It needs to get done before word gets out that the LA central office and its personnel got nixed. Clients will try to call their contacts and won't get answers. They'll spook and hide out if they suspect anything's wrong. We have little time.

"Sergeant Crutcher," I say out loud.

"Go," he says.

"Pair me up with Kevin and Lance."

"Roger that."

I walk over to the table the two blokes are eating at and slide into a seat across from them.

"You guys mind if I join you?" I ask.

"Yeah, sure. I mean no, we don't mind," says Lance, the shorter but stockier one. They are both a little bit nervous with me there.

I small talk, "This oughta be a fun one. We go into some up-yourself prick's house and ruin his afternoon tea plans. Seems like a fine thing to do under the circumstances, right?"

"Yeah, for sure," says Lance.

"What about you, Kevin?" I ask.

"Yeah. I have a little sister. Someone messes with her, I'm

homicidal," he answers.

"And, if she ended up some geezer's sex toy…"

I think of the whole Peyton saga; when she was kidnapped and all I could do was scream into the night sky begging for some answers. An impossible and insatiable rage.

Kevin looks thrown off by the question but tries to hide his emotions. He answers, "I once punched out her teacher when I found out he'd insulted her art work. I got sent to juvey."

I nod. It's good he has that rage. It serves one well when it's time to pull the trigger. But his rage is so deep, there's something else.

"Was there something else that happened?" I ask.

"I don't want to talk about it," Kevin answers. And I know, she was victimized by a sexual predator.

"Fair enough, mate. Sorry to pry."

"It's cool," says Kevin. He looks down.

I continue, "What I will say is when we go in to take out one of the scum-sucking fuck faces today, let's do it in her honor. Catharsis."

Kevin brightens up, "Okay!"

"Let's get into our civvies. Hope they got some Gap or BR stuff. I want to look real preppy today," I say. The boys laugh and I finish my protein bar and depart.

I head over to the wardrobe station. By the time I'm dressed, I look like the hipster version of a country club golfer. I practice my immersion identity. Fake smile, stiff walk, and well-enunciated proper grammar spoken with my lower jaw a smidgen out.

The rest of the operatives do the same and we gather in a small assembly.

I begin, "Okay. Try to take me seriously despite my attire."

I get a couple of chuckles. One guy blurts out that I look cute.

"Well done on pulling off Phase I with virtually no casualties. While two of the captives did not make it, over 200 did. We should be proud of that. Any loss of innocent life is a major tragedy. We need to do even better on Phase II and have a zero body count, except for the pricks who deserve it," I say.

The support staff take this as their cue to pass out the target assignments for each team. There are half a dozen, broken into twos.

I continue, "These are your assignments. Reconnoiter location, contact target. You are trained immersion specialists. Be creative and stay on your toes. You'll do great. The objective is to take out the target and direct the captives out. Do not eliminate domestic staff or guards unless it is very clear they're part of the operation, and condone it. Their silence is violence. The spectators and cooperators, we don't like 'em too much."

"Don't forget, we need photos and videos, so make sure your ocular feed views captures the hit and a steady shot of the perp. We're going to send those little jewels to other clients. They'll get the message. After they're done sweating piss, some more captives will be free. We're making examples today. Read your assignments. We deploy in thirty minutes."

I walk over to Kevin and Lance and I look at their assignment sheet. Our target is a man named Maximillian Martin, stock trader and real estate investor. He has 100 million dollars of properties and a big ass house in a Bel Air gated community. That means armed with rent-a-cops. Kevin and Lance defer to me for tactical guidance. Piece of piss.

"Okay blokes, looks like we have an onion here."

"What?" asked Lance.

"We have some layers to peel before we hit our target. First of all, we have to get inside a gated community. The only way into these places is with an invite from a resident. This includes service people or guests. We can try to sneak in through a side wall or something, but they have motion sensors and cameras everywhere. If they find three fuckwits trying to jump over a wall or fence, they will have us in cuffs in no time. The cops around these upscale houses are real eager beavers. They don't get to see much action and if they miss something they're fired and blacklisted. They gotta be on the fucking ball. Fence jumping is not an option. We need to waltz in there like we belong."

Lance asks, "And how are we going to do that? I can't really think of any way in that isn't obvious. Not without someone on the inside."

"That's what we gotta do," I say.

"How?" says Kevin.

"I have no idea. We'll figure it out as we go," I say.

"Sounds fair I guess," says Lance. He's a little more go-lucky than Kevin, who looks like he wants all the shit to line up in a neat row.

"We improvise," I say.

We head out of the hangar looking like a Ralph Lauren billboard and get into the civilian car provided. We drive into the city and head towards the Bel Air target area. I look for a parking spot. I find one a few blocks away from the entrance to the gated community. We are close to UCLA and there are plenty of young joggers running around the neighborhood, mostly college students staying in shape. Some of them look like real princesses and some just ordinary health-conscious folks.

We get out and I tell the guys, "Chill out and lean on the car, look cool." They oblige.

I walk around the block and look at the pretty houses. No one would ever imagine bondage and slavery goes on behind some of these doors. I feel a nice, dry breeze on my face. I see why people love this place. It's real bloody nice. Sydney weather isn't much different aside from the humidity is a bit worse. Not terrible, but noticeable. A smatter of pedestrians walk along the sidewalk, a woman with her baby carriage, a couple, and here we go, two nice-looking sheilas going out of their way to look as appealing as possible. They got the white yoga pants, sports bras and designer shades. I put on my best bad-boy look and smile at them as they approach.

"G'day ladies, how ya goin?" I say.

They walk right past, not even looking up from their phones. And here I thought the accent would do the trick.

Four other seemingly good prospects walk past us and I ask them about parties in the area and none of them seem to be in the in crowd of Bel Air shindigs. Nor are they very interested in strangers.

"Ashkay. This isn't going too well," I say out loud, knowing he can hear me and answer.

"Roger that. What do you suggest?"

"Use your searching powers to find out what parties are happening in Bel Air Crest, and who near me you can find that I can proposition. Right now, my next plan was to find some four-leaf clovers and shove them up my arse for instant absorption."

I hear some chuckles in my audio from the Mind Booth personnel.

"On it," says Ashkay.

A few minutes pass as a few more pedestrians pass.

Ashay says, "Okay I did. Searched and found a Facebook

FOUR LEAF / WADE

post that says there's a party in Bel Air Crest at some guy's house named Carlo Law. I got the address here."

"Well, that would be useful except they won't let me through the gates. Find some way of maybe ..."

"I got this Wade. Give me a moment."

I walk over to the other blokes and chat em up for a few.

"Team Leader," says Ashkay.

"Go," I respond.

"I hacked in and found his guest list and tapped the GPSes on the phones of the first ten women on the list. One of them is walking down a street not far from where you are. Couple blocks away, on a street called Beverly Glen. Not sure if she is with others. But her profile says she is 28 years old, loves dogs and Soul Cycle, and works as a personal assistant. Her name is..."

"Don't tell me her name. I'll botch it if I know too much. Let me take a stab at it organically."

We get in the car and drive over to Beverly Glen, find a spot and get out. My blokes assume the same James Dean pose on the car while I walk down the tree-lined street, purposely looking like a tourist.

"She's only fifty feet away from you now, heading right towards you," says Ashkay, tracking her moves.

I look down the sidewalk and see two women, both wearing yoga pants and sports bras, shades and one is walking a dog. She's slightly taller than the other. Must be the one with the dog.

"G'day ladies! Can I trouble you for a moment?"

I can see that they are mildly enamored by the Aussie accent. That throws a couple points on the one-to-ten scale for me.

"Yeah sure," the taller one says. "Are you from Australia?"

"Yeah, love. So, listen… I heard Bel Air has the best parties in LA, but I don't know anyone here, so I was hoping to try my luck by standing on a corner and asking," I say.

"Oh! We go to parties here all the time," says the shorter one, exchanging glances with the other.

"Really? I know we just met, but I'm just a fun guy trying to have a great story to tell when I get back to Oz. Any chance you can help a tourist like me get a real behind-the-scenes LA experience? I'd really like to go into one of these gated communities and rub elbows with some real LA elites."

They look at each other. Tall one says, "We might have an idea."

They step aside and chat about it. Acting a bit coy. Giggling and looking back over to me. I still got the touch it seems.

"We know a few parties happening tonight," says Taller.

"Oh yeah? Could you get me into one? I'd hate to come all the way over here from across the wide Pacific and miss out on a Bel Air party!"

They smile at me and one of them says, "I think we might be able to get you into a party in gated place." They start texting and looking at their phones.

While they are waiting for the answers the shorter of the two asks me, "Which city in Australia are you from?"

"Sydney. You been there?" I ask.

"No, but I've always wanted to go. Aussies are pretty cool." She's flirting and I notice her friend looks over at her and notices.

"Hey, you know I got a couple of mates with me as well. Think they can join in?"

"Are they cute?" one asks.

"Ha ha! I don't know that I've ever described a bloke as cute! But I reckon so, yeah. They are fresh out of the military. They're standing over there."

I point at Kevin and Lance, who lean against the car, arms folded. Looking badass.

"I need to check with the host if I can add three people to the guest list," says Taller. She walks a few steps away with the phone to her ear and her other hand holding a leash with a little fox-looking dog, with hair well-groomed and brushed to a shine.

I hear her say the name Carlo. This is looking hopeful.

She hangs up and walks over.

"Okay yeah! Looks good. They said they need me to text your names so they can tell the gate keeper who is on the list."

"Yeah, my name is Jack Warren. And my two mates are Jonathon Carter and Billy Mitchell." She types them in and sends it off. I hope I remembered the phony names right.

"Well, I'll tell ya, you ladies are real nice to help me out with this. I just showed up here today praying to God that I'd be able to get into a party in a Bel Air community. Seems he sent down some angels to grant me my wish."

Giggles and blushes.

"Just go to the gate any time after seven and tell them your names. They'll ask for ID and you should be fine," says one of them.

"Beauty." I wave goodbye and walk away towards where we parked. Kevin and Lance look at me.

"I got us into Bel Air Crest, mates. We go there any time after seven, say our names at the gate, and we're in," I say.

"How the actual fuck did you pull that off? I thought we were going to have to parachute in," says Lance.

"Charmed some sheilas and flashed these pearly whites," I smile. "They hooked us up. But hey what are your guys' aliases? I hope I didn't get that wrong."

"Jonathon Mitchel and Billy Carter," says Kevin.

"Fuck! I got the names backwards. Shit. Okay. I can't run back and tell the ladies to change the names. That'd be fuckin weird. We'll just have to sweet talk the guard and show him the mix up."

John Crutcher talks into my earpiece, "Smooth move, Wade. Well-played. Let's hope the other guys get in, too."

"Sarge, how come you didn't help me out there and throw me the right names? Or you, Mr. Jean Jacques Girard?"

"Wade, Mr. Girard isn't in the Mind Booth right now. He stepped out. I scrambled to try to check the aliases but wasn't fast enough. You were on your own."

"That's odd," I say. "I thought the Mind Booth was filled 100% of the time, except for extreme emergencies or quick bathroom breaks."

"Copy that, Wade, you are correct. That is protocol. He will return shortly," says Crutcher.

Makes me wonder if he was suspicious of me and acting on it. Or if he was checking on Teska. I feel the energy drain out of me at the thought of her. I didn't fully realize how much I cared, until she got into real trouble.

"Thanks, sarge. I look forward to it." I reply.

"Ten-four. Execute mission target and out of there," says Crutcher.

Chapter 18
Jean Jacques

I'm talking to Brett when the message comes through from John Crutcher letting me know that Wade had asked about me and where I was.

I end the conversation and head over to the Mind Booth. John fills me in. All operatives are set to hit their targets around the same time tonight.

I sit at my console which allows me to talk to specific agents or to multiple ones at once. The screens show live feeds from each. From my console I can change which ones I see in front of me.

I adjust to focus on what Wade is viewing. He talks to his two sub-agents, Lance and Kevin, aka Billy and Jonathon. I listen.

"Okay, so you two wankers are gonna follow me like a couple of go-lucky pricks looking for a good time. You can't be all stiff and proper. Although I did say you were both recent ex-military so looking a bit like you have a stick up your ass won't hurt too much. Come up with some good stories to tell, about how you saw action in Afghanistan or some shit. Make it real."

"We are going in at 1930. Can't go at 1900. Too eager. And we want a crowd. We blend in and get lost. On my cue, we meet up outside, and head to the target's house," Wade says.

I cannot tell if Wade has a hunch about my suspicions. God, I wish these devices could read minds. I speak into his earpiece, "Wade, I'm back and I have been briefed on your tactic. Sounds good. What is your backup plan if you don't make it into the gated community?"

"My backup plan is to come up with a new idea on the spot," says Wade.

"Sounds reassuring," I say.

"Well, I had absolutely no plan before I came up with this one. But the objective was clear. It led me to where we are now," says Wade.

"Fair enough. I'll be here every step of the way."

"Except hopefully when I drop the kids off at the pool," says Wade.

"Huh?" I ask.

"When I use the loo, the dunny, the bog. I wish you guys had set up a smelling device in our noses so you could smell what we do as well as see and hear," says Wade.

"Ha ha, funny," I say.

"Cheers. We'll make it happen, boss," says Wade.

"Copy that. I have all the confidence," I say.

Wade continues briefing his men.

I call the medic, "What is Teska's status?"

The medic answers: "Still unconscious. Pulse, blood pressure, breathing normal."

"Copy that. Over," I say.

I look over each of the operatives. There are six teams out in various parts of LA, preparing to take out top clients and photograph or video their demise as warnings to other clients.

We gave Wade the hardest one, in a gated community in the richest part of LA. My only concern on this leg of the mission is that Wade has a very high price on his head. Although no one knows his name, there is plenty of footage of him from the Watson compound security cameras. Probably twenty bounty hunters, paid assassins, are looking for the ten million price on his head. Some have the resources to tap into facial recognition software used by Homeland Security, Apple or Google. Walking around a neighborhood shouldn't be a huge deal. But the camera equipment used in these affluent areas poses a real risk.

If Teska doesn't come out of her coma, we are going to have to remove her devices and do a proper MRI. It's possible she has internal brain bleeding and would require surgery to save her life. She is on her way to QuadFilium. Only an MRI will tell us a proper diagnosis.

Brett seems to be with me on my Wade suspicions for no other reason than he trusts me. I need to be prepared in case Wade does something rash. And I need internal backup. John Crutcher is key. He treasures Wade and trusts him.

Chapter 19
Wade

Me and the boys head over to the Bel Air Crest gate on foot. As we approach, the guard says, "You guys going to the party?"

"Sure are!" I answered.

"No problem, gotta see some ID."

"No worries, mate."

We pull out our fake ID's and hand them over.

The guard inspects them against his list and says, "You're good to go but I don't have these other guys on there."

"Mate! There's got to be some mix up. They are for sure on the list there," I say.

"No, man. I can't let them in," says the guard.

"Well, could there be a simple misspelling or something? Maybe they switched up the names? Officer, we traveled a very long ways for this party. Do you mind checking that? See if there's a mix up?"

"Uh... sure, I guess." The guard looks through and a few moments later says, "Ah hah! Look at that! They did switch the last names. How the heck did you know that?"

"Mate! I used to be a bouncer in Sydney. Happens all the time," I say.

"Fair enough. You guys have fun. Let's not get too loud, yeah?" says the guard.

"Struth, mate." The guard pretends to know what that meant and waves us on through.

It's just before twilight, so we can still see. We walk into an immaculate neighborhood with manicured lawns and perfect tarmac I could eat a meat pie off of. The trees and bushes are sculpted into works of art. The houses are straight out of that old show *Lifestyles of the Rich and Famous*.

We wander around the neighborhood a bit to canvas our target. To not look too suspicious, we pretend to be architectural enthusiasts and admire the various facades and front yards of the mansions. We mosey on up to the target house and suss out the scene. Two casually dressed guards sit at a table on the front porch and based on their expressions and poses they look ex-military or ex-police. They don't see too much action out here in Gucci-ville, so they aren't alert. We walk up near and gaze at the place. It's a majestic, stately manor with white columns and sculptured fountains, all screaming how rich this geezer is.

These guards must have seen some of this guy's sordid shit. But, *innocent until proven guilty* is one of our mottos. If it wasn't, we could just pull out our nine mils right now and blaze into the place like cowboys, popping off obstacles in a video game. Hitting innocents is one of the worst possible offenses in QuadFilium. It results in a tribunal and significant penalty. There's only one instance in QuadFilium history where an innocent was badly injured by an operative. No innocent has ever been killed by QuadFilium. But innocents have been killed by perps in a few of our missions. A very contentious point in the organization.

The guards look over at us, annoyed. We gesture and point at the design elements we see from the front. We are actually trying to figure out our basic strategy. One of the guards seems bothered by how long we're standing there, approximately one full minute, and comes over. I was hoping for this. I want to see my opposition up close.

"Let me do the talking," I whisper.

"Good evening boys," says the approaching guard.

"Evening, officer," I say. Automatic importance feeling, elevate him to police or military.

"Can we help you?" he says.

"Yes, actually perhaps you can," I say. "My mates and I were wondering why the architect chose Corinthian columns for the façade but they don't have fluted shafts. Seems like the ionic order. Rather odd to mix orders in Classic architecture."

"All Greek to me," he says with an impatient tone.

I laugh. "Greek indeed."

When he walked, I watched his movements. He doesn't carry a visible gun. A loose shirt to hide his piece. I suspect that standing out in front of a house in California with a visible firearm is a huge no-no. The owner would have protestors picketing, and conspiracy theories going viral about his abode. Not the kind of attention a paranoid pervert likes. But having casual looking blokes out front wearing Tommy Bahama doesn't draw attention, and provides good guard detail.

He stands there observing us, looking impatient. Waves his hand in a "Well, be off then," gesture.

"Oh yeah, no worries. We happen to be real enthusiasts about that sort of stuff. Being out here in Cali we couldn't miss the opportunity to see the real gems this place has to offer, since the rest of the city mostly is, frankly, pretty ugly, buildings-wise."

"Yeah, well, there you go..." he says. He looks at his watch.

I can tell he's about to verbally ask us to move along, but I'm not done.

"Hey officer, did you happen to be a policeman before?

You seem over-qualified for this gig," I ask.

"Yeah," he says.

"Ever see real action, or have to take out a perp?" I ask.

"Actually, yes. There were two times I engaged active shooters and... well... had no choice."

"Wow, you must have some badass stories."

"I've been known to tell them from time to time..."

"I'd love to hear them, but hey, gotta run to a party! Oh my name's Jack Warren by the way. Pleased to officially meet you. And you are Officer...?"

"O'Grady."

"Please to meet you Mister O'Grady. Thank you for your service."

He flashes a fake smile and turns around to head back to his table and chair on the porch. We walk towards the party house.

Kevin asks, "Hey Wade—"

"Jack," I correct him.

"Sorry, Jack. What do you make of that guy?"

"I notice his mosey's crampy, rusty joints and jiggly parts. He's not prime, but I reckon he's competent. The only thing I was hoping to find out is if he is aware of the geezer's sordid shit. Nothing in his answers and our brief chat told me one way or the other."

Lance asks, "Yeah."

"What I can tell you, this bloke is bored and works in a gated community, has zero action in his life. He probably gets paid well and enjoys semi-retirement. The force he was on pays him a nice pension. Add this gig in, his retirement fund is growing. He's the alpha in the duo. The fact that I was friendly to him and he flashed me a fake smile does make me think that he has misgivings about stuff. Unethical shit eats away the soul and spirit. Movies make it seem glamorous. It's real life. So, if he's seen any of the bad shit that goes on in there, he's had to ignore it, he'll be a sad chap. He looks a bit like that."

Lance says, "And all I noticed was the flower pattern on his shirt."

I laugh. Lance is well-trained in observation. The sarcasm is his way of complimenting mine.

"His impatience tells me the boss is home," I say.

Kevin and Lance look at each other.

We head up another street to the address of the party. At the open front door, not surprisingly, the two sheilas hover. I wouldn't have recognized them if it wasn't for their ditzy giggles. Gone are the yoga pants and the ponytails. In are push up bras, fake eyelashes and flowing hair. Vacuum wrapped dresses, short on bottom and top. They work it.

"Oh my God! Hey Jack!" one says to me.

"Hey you!" I smile and give a small hug. I introduce my mates and we merge into the crowd, grab hors d'oeuvres, and sip drinks. The girls are a bit clingy. It could make it more difficult to strategize with my agents and head over to our target. But at some point, they'll go to the dunny together to powder their noses or whatever, and we can spring off.

I look around the joint and see a scene just like the movies. So much privilege jammed into one space. Each of these folks must have been raised with golden spoons up their asses their whole lives, polished from head to toe. Perfect tans, chiseled physiques, perfectly dyed hair and expensive clothes. Most attendees aren't too old. A few are already drunk or lit up with some substance. They've created a small dance floor in one of the several living rooms.

One of my operatives seems to be keen on a Latina lady and is talking to her somewhat intimately. The other is a bit of a wall flower and shy.

The girls mention they need to hit the bog, so the three of us group together and find a spot where we can't be heard. We go over our tactical plan and decide to part in sixty minutes when it's dark.

We spend the next hour piss-farting around in the party. Seems like the more gregarious agent got his groove on with the Latina girl, freaking on the dance floor like it's going out of style. Must be fun for those in the Mind Booth to watch.

Dark comes and I give the signal. By this point, the girls who invited seem expectant and want to take it a bit further. They are touchy-feely and from what I can tell, the two of them are specifically focused on me. Most blokes would dig on this. What I dig on is how to bugger off without them following me.

"Jack, did you want to see some of the rooms upstairs? They are real nice," one of them asks, real close to my ear, steaming it up.

"Sure, yeah," I say. Meet you there. I'm just going to hit the loo."

They hold hands and walk towards the stairs. There is no doubt what they have in mind. I do in fact hit the bog and then go straight out the front door. A good thirty-feet down the block I see my blokes and head over to them. The two naked sheilas in that upstairs room might be disappointed, but something tells me it won't be too hard to replace me.

We get to the target mansion, and in a shadow, look at it from across the road. The same two guards chat at their table on the porch. They haven't noticed us.

While we were at the party, Ashkay ran the name *O'Grady*

139

through all the police personnel databases in the US, and found a large number of them. He took but the image from my ocular feed and crosschecked. His name is Mike O'Grady. But more importantly his daughter's name is Samantha Sterne and her daughter's name is Olivia, a two-year old. They live in Otto, Cattaraugus County, New York at 117 Cherry Hill Road in a small two-bedroom.

I walk up to the property line and call out, "Hey O'Grady!" I sound a bit drunk. He walks over both amused and annoyed, accustomed to being left alone, where everything runs like clockwork. Disturbances are glitches in his Matrix.

"I wanted to hear one of your stories. I've never met anyone involved in one of those." The mild slur in my voice pins me as less dangerous. Just a drunk kid.

"What happened to the party? It's sort of early...?" he asks.

"Boring as shit, mate. Tell me a story... please,'" I say.

"I guess it wouldn't hurt," he says. He begins at the beginning and gets into the details. Meanwhile, my agents head to the side of the property behind bushes. On my cue, they rustle the braches. The other guard is closer. When O'Grady hears it, he stops talking and waves him to check it out.

When guard number two reaches the bushes, my two agents tackle him to the ground. O'Grady hears it, knows it's an attack, reaches for his gun and turns. I leap over the short hedge between us, tackle him to the ground, disarm him, and squeeze my hand over his mouth. He can't make any noise, but can hear me nice and clear.

I tell him, "Now listen to me, Mike O'Grady, and do exactly as I say. I have three assassins right outside 117 Cherry Hill Road in Cattaraugus, New York. They're set to break inside and kill Samantha and Olivia if you try to be a fucking hero for the geezer in there."

It's amazing how much eyes tell you. This man went through terror, rage and despair in three seconds. He nods eagerly.

"Just to be clear, I have audio and visual directly to these goons in your daughter's front yard. If you try anything, they will know in real time, and break through the front door and shred the place." He nods even more eager.

I look over. Guard number two is prostrate, gagged and immobilized. The agents shove him out of site and out of earshot. A moaning man, gagged, is still gonna draw attention.

I tell O'Grady, "You are going to tell me exactly where Maximillian Martin is in the house. You are going to tell me the layout, the security scene and the personnel scene, and then you are going to let me through the front door."

I de-gag him for a moment and he tells me the scene fast. Although he's terrified, he manages to keep control, the sign of a man who has seen real action.

I lift him up and drag him over to the front door. The entrance requires a card swipe and a number code to de-activate a magnetic lock. Then, a key is used to unlock a dead bolt. I free up one of his hands. He looks up to the corner of the porch and this draws my attention to a camera. I assume that Mike O'Grady knows that if footage shows him let me in, no matter the reason, he'll be terminated and killed. I pick this up as he hesitates to draw out his card.

Now, I have no idea if this tosser is aware of the human trafficking scene going on inside this exquisite domicile. But if he really doesn't know then it's not fair for me to end his life here, which, essentially, I'd be doing if I make him let me inside. But if he does know, this fucker doesn't deserve to live whatsoever and is part of the problem, part of the disease. And his silence is violence. I don't care what the reasons are, participating in it is a death sentence.

I grab his collar and lift his face right up close to mine and I ask him, "Are you aware that Maximillian is a criminal, sexual predator who owns little girls?" I look deep into his eyes when I ask him this. If he is aware, he will flinch at the end of my question and look away slightly. If he is not aware, he will not break eye contact but look at me to see if my question is for real. Sadly, this nice old ex-cop flinched. I pull out his gag and I ask him where the girls are kept.

"I don't know," he says.

"Fine. Punch in the fucking code right now or else your daughter and granddaughter will be terminated immediately," I say.

He reaches forward and swipes his card and keys in the code. I re-tie his hands to a nearby post and gag him.

The three of us enter the house, guns drawn. It's dim. Only light from the kitchen filters through and illuminates the grand entry. We hear a faint sound coming from upstairs. Everything is marble including the grand staircase to the left. I signal one operative to case the bottom floor while I head upstairs with the other. The upstairs sound increases. I send my operative down the hall at the top of the stairs past the room with the sounds. I stop in front of it. O'Grady's description matches. I get nausea in the pit of my stomach as I realize the sound is sexual.

I kick the door in, and catch him in the act which means my ocular feed does as well. The sudden noise startles him and both he and the girl shriek and dart off the bed in opposite directions. I throw a blanket at the girl and aim my attention and gun toward the criminal.

The room is dark. Faint moonlight filters through the curtains. The walls are a dark wood paneling, with chair rail and wainscot. The bed board is taller than an average man.

Maximilian jitters and reaches his hands out in a futile attempt to ward off my bullets. I look at him. Covered in greasy sweat, with pathetic terror.

"I will give you whatever you want, I will give you any amount of money that you want. Please! Don't kill me," he begs.

"I'll tell you what. I'll consider letting you go if you tell me how many slaves you bought and any other confessions you'd like to add."

"Okay, okay. I… I um, like little girls, it's a problem I have, I know…"

"How many?"

"Six… six… sixteen!" he manages to stutter out. "I'm sorry! I'm sorry! I know I'm sick. I'm *sick*! I know! I have problems!"

I'm getting all this good material. I'm keen to shoot the bastard, but shots are loud, even with a silencer, and in this neighborhood will bring on the cops in no time.

Jean Jacques pipes into my earpiece, "You need to make an example of him. We need other clients to see the pain and what they should expect to soon experience. Make it gross, painful, torturous."

I don't revel in torture or death. I hate torture, but I hate human trafficking more.

Jean Jacques yells into the comm to my downstairs partner, "Go to the kitchen, get a bunch of knives and bring them up to the room!"

The other upstairs operative comes in and brings the girl out.

"What are you going to have me do, boss?" I ask Jean

Jacques.

"You are going to painfully and slowly kill that bastard with knives. Throw them."

"I don't want to do that," I say.

Maximilian sees me talk to the air. Confused.

"It *must* be done! We need to have footage showing it! And I need your operatives to watch! We need their footage as well! Do it. Goddammit, *do it!*"

I remain silent for a moment. Then I address Maximilian, directly, "It's a shame that in your last moments, the point where you could have saved yourself, you lied to me. We know that you have purchased thirty-five slaves, yet you tell me sixteen. Well… that was pretty dumb of you."

"No, no, no! the others were not for sex… domestic staff!"

"Oh! Really? Interesting! Thanks for clarifying!" I yell.

My downstairs guy shows up with of block of kitchen knives.

Jean Jacques says, "Make him hold out his arms and throw the knives into him! Wade! Do it! You will save thousands of lives with this! *Do it!*"

"I can't," I say to Jean Jacques.

"Goddamnit! *Do it!*"

"I'm against this shit. Cruel and unusual."

"A merciful death will have *much less* impact! Show him going through *serious pain!*"

"Sarge?"

"I know how you feel, Wade. Do this for the team. Do it for the lives you will save. Do this for the captives that will be saved," says John.

Maxmillian sees the block of knives, starts to shake and cry.

I know I should do this. I don't want to. It makes me sick.

144

But it will save lives. Other clients see this footage and will quit, free their slaves, and never buy more. It's the right thing to do. I don't want to do it, but I must.

"*Do it*, Wade!" yells Jean Jacques.

"Hold your arms out to your side. *Now!*" I yell at Maximilian.

He does. His shakes jiggle the baggy flesh hanging from his arms. His wails of grief and terror increase in volume. I walk over and grab his sock off the ground, ball it up and shove it in his mouth. He'll get louder.

I walk to the block of kitchen knives on the dresser, select a heavy, sharp one. I feel the weight in my hand and mentally assess the move I intend to make. I throw it hard at one of his arms and it plunges through his forearm and fixes itself into the wood paneled wall. He screams, but the gag dulls it. He is naked, fat, bald and ugly as sin and whimpers like a baby.

I hate doing this. I can't well justify cruelty. I want to just put him out of his misery. End it. Move on.

Jean Jacques says, "Wade, I need you to make this guy's death as bad as you can and I need you to watch it as it happens. Same with your operatives. We need the video of a man dying horribly. This will save lives!"

The look in the man's eyes pleads. It feels indulgent to do anything but just separate him from mankind and end his life. I'm not against the death penalty. But cruel and unusual isn't my thing. Right now, it's my duty. I see the point. It will save lives.

I take out another knife and I fling it at Max. It plunges into his other arm, and plasters his body against the wall. He looks just like the guy in the regional center we busted yesterday. Pinned up. Naked. Arms outstretched.

The next one goes into his stomach with a meaty thud. I try not to retch or gag.

I throw every knife in the block, each one landing where I aim it. Each one results in painful groans, and more blood. He looks like a porcupine is glued to his chest. He finally goes lights out. Game over. I run to the bathroom and puke.

"Let's get out of here," I say to the operatives. We leave the girl wrapped in a blanket in another room and we run out the front door. As I walk past him, I see the shame in O'Grady's eyes. I stop and look directly at him.

"You dishonorable fuck," I say to him.

A tear forms in his eye.

"There's a little girl up there. You get her back to her family," I say.

He nods, tears stream down.

"Think of Olivia. Your silence is violence. Make it right." I leave.

By now, Ashkay and his team have captured and are editing the footage into a gruesome montage for other clients. From the ledger we sent Aksay, he's gathered the names, found the email addresses.

We walk down the street again and act intoxicated as we pass the guard station.

"Did you guys hear a scream up that way?" asks the guard.

"Yeah mate! Some dipshit from the party acting like an arse!" I say.

"Okay thanks! You boys have a good evening! And don't drink and drive," the guard says.

"Cheers, mate!" I say.

We get to our car and head back to the remote base.

Chapter 20
Jean Jacques

Phase II has been a flawless success. All operatives hit their targets. My tech team threw together the videos and forwarded them to the hundreds of clients we have records on. We already receive replies from terrified customers saying they have released their captives. No casualties.

There is one team actively wrapping up, and that will conclude Phase II. We'll get everyone back to the base.

Teska has arrived and is in the ICU. Dimitri is there. I head over to see check the status.

She lies on a bed motionless, unconscious. I hear on the heart monitor a steady beat. Nurses and doctors chat and look at instruments and charts. Dimitri looks unhappy.

I approach the lead surgeon. A middle-aged man, named Doctor Wisner.

"What's the status?" I ask.

"We cannot perform an MRI yet. Our only reference point as to how deep the instrument penetrated the brain is Wade's visio footage of the lobotomy. Based on the video analysis, it penetrated three point four inches past the plate that separates the eye from the brain. It is impossible to tell what damage was inflicted but worst-case scenario her frontal lobes were completely severed and her body shut off. If she comes to, there's no predicting what her cognitive functions will be like. We tested brain pressure and it's only mildly elevated. It suggests, there is no guarantee, that there is no active bleeding," says the surgeon.

"Okay. What are our options?"

"In my professional opinion, she needs to have the devices removed so we can perform an MRI. With and without contrast. Only then can we really see what we're dealing with. Failing to do so, there's a high chance of a permanent coma or death," says Doctor Wisner.

"I see. And what will happen to her sense organs if we remove these devices?" I ask.

"She will be blinded in her left eye. Hearing will not be affected," says the surgeon.

"Okay. How long can we wait for her to wake up before... it's *too* long?"

"Mr. Girard, it has already been too long. We should not wait if we want to preserve cognitive function at all. More importantly, if we want to prevent mortality," he says.

"Okay. Do it," I say.

"Yes, sir," says the doctor.

"Dimitri," I say.

"Yes, Mr. Girard," says Dimitri.

"You made these devices. Is there any way to prevent blindness when removing it from her eye?" I ask.

"I know nothing for this. But I can accelerate my healing research to see for cure," he says.

"Do that," I say.

"Yes, sir," he says and walks out of the room.

At the door, he stops and turns, "Actually, Mr. Girard, there is one solution which we can try."

"Yes?" I ask.

"Eye transplant. We need a donor though," says Dimitri.

"Hmmm, okay," I say and walk back over to Doctor

Wisner.

"Hold off on the device removal for just a moment," I say to him.

"Yes, sir," he responds.

I go back to the Mind Booth where the strategists organize the return of all the operatives.

I ask Crutcher, "Is the last team still in action?"

"Yes, sir. There is one team active. They're in target's house now, about to execute mission objective."

I look up at the screen and I see the team's ocular live feed on screen. I speak to the team leader, "Alpha Six leader, hold for one second."

He responds, "Copy that, what's up?"

"We plan to do a transplant on a downed operative's eye. We need... donors."

Long pause. "Okay sir. Specify the requirements," he says.

"We need as many different eyeballs as possible removed from the targets and placed in ice," I say.

"...yes... sir," he responds.

"This is the only chance the operative might see again. How many targets down in location?"

"Three."

"Okay. Harvest one from each. If there are any others, do the same," I order.

I see the team leader order his sub-operative to find a cooler in the kitchen and fill it with ice. I force myself to watch the team leader remove eyeballs and place them into the cooler. The targets are already eliminated, but I can't look away. It's not fair to have the operatives suffer through this while I remain aloof and detached.

The team leader collects a total of four eyeballs. If one

matches blood type, we're good.

I leave the Mind Booth, head to Dimitri's lab.

"Prepare for the transplant. Replacement ETA eight hours," I say.

Chapter 21
Madame Girard

I sit on my patio couch, and reel with the knowledge that I just revealed a twenty-four-year secret. I'm surprised at the relief I feel. But, I broke a solemn promise never to speak of QuadFilium. This has soaked my relief in fear.

The only excuse that numbs the burn is that my husband has been unfaithful, even if only in his heart. This too is a betrayal.

I've trusted this doctor with my life. He has always been there for me. He's never demonstrated a hint of duplicity. Besides, what he could do with this information?

I walk back into the house feeling a sense of direction and orientation restored. I have a solution, albeit a bit far-fetched. How likely is it Jacques will bare his soul? I'm not an expert in human behavior, but my doctor's advice seems simple, rather brilliant, and a bit terrifying.

Carmen greets me and she comments that I look better. I'm grateful she doesn't ask for particulars. A soft breeze comes through the open patio doors.

"What are you thinking about, honey?" I ask.

"I know that we support many charities and do a lot of philanthropic work, but I never understood why we don't turn our attention on the slavers. They killed my family," she says. She has mentioned this before.

"We do as much as we can. We aren't the military or law enforcement. It's really their domain," I say.

"I know. I just wish we could do something. For years, I've read the news reports. It looks to me like there's some secret group killing off the bad guys. They find these abandoned trafficking centers with bodies of the slavers strewn all over the place. And the slaves, when freed, what happens to them? Who do you think that is?" asks Carmen.

She is passionate about it.

"Could be a government with secret forces like the CIA or something."

"That makes me want to work for the CIA!"

"I know, I know. I'm a very peaceful person, Carmen. But if I had one shot at those who did that you and your family, I wouldn't hesitate to take it, despite the repercussions," I say.

"Me too," says Carmen.

Chapter 22
Wade

We get back to the Oxnard base. One last team still needs to arrive. We ready for the trip home. I think about Teska, and I ask John for an update.

"She's still in a coma, but we have to get an MRI. To do that, we have to remove her devices.

"She'll go blind!"

"Yes. But when your last team arrives at any moment, they have a cooler with four eyeballs on ice. The surgeon here will attempt a transplant so she can retain her eyesight."

"For the love of God, you're kidding me! There is no other choice?" I ask.

"Roger that. Meanwhile, the devices come out to do the MRI and prep her for transplant," says John.

I look up and see that final team pull into the hangar.

"Okay, I'll get all these pricks onto the plane straight away so we can bugger off and get home," I say.

Thirty minutes later we lift off the tarmac. I already made sure fresh ice was in the cooler. We go full throttle to be back in time for Teska.

We've been in the air for two hours. I look around. Most of the operatives are asleep or watching a device. Only a couple chat. I get up and sidle to the back of the plane and grab a parachute. No one notices. When I discovered that Teska was still in a coma and could die, or at least likely be brain dead, I made my decision.

I grab my bag of stuff, prepared ahead of time, and keep the parachute next to me. I wait for turbulence. The Captain issues the obligatory fasten seatbelt order. Everyone complies. Except me. I wait until everyone is belted in and secured.

I walk to the emergency door. My estimate, the plane is travelling at about 750 miles per hour. People have limbs ripped off from the pressure at these velocities. But I've trained on this. I know the right body position.

I fling open the door. The noise is deafening. The whole plane screams with sirens. It jolts in one direction. Everyone in the plane wakes up and looks at me. I wave good bye and jump ship.

I am the first fugitive in the twenty-four-year history of QuadFilium. This is what I think as I make my way towards Earth, miles below.

At first, I see only clouds and sky. I catch a view of the door I just ripped off, as it barrels down below me. In free fall, I spin and look up at the plane rapidly making its way across the sky. I have no doubt that QuadFilium will send operatives. It won't be hard to track me. I still have my implanted devices with GPS. This is the one thing I've had the most trouble figuring out. Right now, they see what I see. They hear what I hear. Which presently is nothing but howling wind.

I get a comm through my feed. It's Crutcher.

"Wade, I know you can hear me, and you're in free fall. Can we talk when you land?"

He's playing the good guy. But if that doesn't work, they have other methods and none are considered off limits. Desertion is the third worst crime in QuadFilium, behind premeditated murder and the delivery of information to the enemy that puts QF personnel at risk.

I've already thought it through. I yell to Sergeant Crutcher, "Mate. I will talk to you, but not for long. You already know that I am over Montana. Try me after I land. We'll talk."

"Thanks, Wade. Talk soon."

I pass the cloud layer and notice that I'm headed toward a city. Must be Billings, Montana. I'd wanted to land in the outskirts. But, I see the plane door below me and it's headed straight toward city center. What are the chances? That door smashes into a city, it could kill people.

I tuck my arms to my side and make an arrow out of my body to reduce wind drag. My drop speed increases. I turn my shoulders and bullet in the direction of the door. It flips around so catches more drag than me. The city sharpens. Distant objects grow fast. I'm a minute away from the door at my descent rate, and maybe fifty seconds after that from splat down. The air stings and freezes my face.

I don't have a plan. But I can't let it kill someone. That'd be on me.

After fifty seconds, I reach and grab the door. I spot an open, less populated zone. I use the door as an air boogie board to cut my way towards it. Angling the door while holding it stiff allows me to scoot sideways rather than dead drop. But I'm out of time. I need to pull the chute or I'll hit the ground at 200 mph. I'm still over the city. I calculate the last possible second.

"Pull the chute, Wade!" says John, who watches my every move.

"*Pull the chute!*" yells Jean Jacques. Perhaps the most intense I have ever heard him. Both are right. I'm directly above suburban houses.

I yell back, "The door could bust through the roof of a family's home! I'm no fucking murderer. I'd rather die."

155

An empty baseball field is not far away. There's a soccer field filled with children next to it. I have two seconds until broken legs, death or both. I aim for the baseball field, hold for three seconds, and kick the door in the field's direction. I pull my chute. It's too late. The ground rises towards me at 150 miles per hour. The chute opens and slows me. But not much. I'm above a neighborhood. The door crashes against the baseball field's outfield fence. Home run. Nobody there.

I crash. Impact.

I'm underwater. In a swimming pool. And in the deep end, too. Lucky, lucky, lucky. And I didn't even have to shove four leaf clovers up my arse.

Phew...

I'm alive. I don't have any broken bones. Bloody oath, mate. I look up to the sky and thank my imaginary guardian angel. My chute floats above me.

Fuck me.

A family runs out to see what just landed in their back yard. I hear them chatter as they pour out the door. The chute covers the whole pool.

I get out from underneath the canvas and look at the gathering.

"Cool!" yells a little chubby redhead with freckles.

"By golly, son! Are you okay? How in the heck did you end up in there?" says the dad.

"Cool!" says the kid again. I notice a shy little girl hiding behind her mother, who is looks at me in disbelief.

I look up in the sky. I see two small black dots. Two operatives followed me out of the plane. No surprise. But, they're miles away, maybe thirty miles east. It'll take them an hour to get to me at the fastest. I climb the pool steps, dripping.

"Well, mate, thank you. In fact, I am part of an elite military unit—"

"Cool!" yells the kid again.

"Patrick! Let the man talk! Don't be a ding dang idiot!" says the dad.

"It's fine, mate. I don't mind."

"Thank you for your service," says the dad. "Can we help you somehow? Need a change of clothes?"

"Well… Yeah that would be really great. Thank you."

The mom pipes in, "Thank you for your service! Do you want to stay for supper?"

"Thanks for the offer, but I'll need to leave in the next five minutes. I parachuted in and I need to get to the nearest hospital or doctor's office right away," I say.

"Oh, my Lord, are you hurt?" she asks.

"No, ma'am, I'm fine. I parachuted in so that I could get to a medical facility, one as fast as possible. It's part of my mission," I say.

The kind family gives me some clothes they don't really need. They fit okay.

The dad says, "Son, want me to give you a ride into town to the hospital?"

"I feel I have imposed way too much. I landed in your backyard, and you gave me clothing. That's more than enough," I say.

"Nonsense. We're God-fearing folk around here. Helping a traveler is a good deed. You came from the sky, for crying out loud! You sacrifice for the service of others. I reckon it's odd you sound like Crocodile Dundee. Ain't American. What branch of the military are you in?" We head towards his pickup.

"I'm in a confidential, multi-national unit," I say.

"Like Interpol or something?" he asks.

"Something."

We get into his pickup and drive off. He describes the landmarks and tells me their stories. I listen, but I'm aware that two operatives are finding a vehicle right now and will be driving down the highway honed on my GPS.

I see a podiatrist office a block into the town and I say to my good Samaritan, "Whoa, whoa, this is fine. This place is fine."

"A podiatrist? They don't even look open," he says.

"It's totally fine, this will be great. Thanks!"

"Okay! Good luck! And thank you for your service!" He salutes me and drives off.

I walk over to the office door and suss it out. Small place, perfect for what I need. Closed. Off hours. I go around to the back alley and find a door, with a dead bolt. I look around and see nothing useful. I walk down the street and see a liquor store, a diner, a cleaners and a hardware store. I enter the hardware store and buy a pry bar and duct tape.

I go back to the alley and do a quick sweep of the area. No one. I stick the pry bar between the jamb and the door and I lever it hard. Cracking sounds. The wood rips away at the dead bolt.

A shove. It pops open. I slip inside. It's dark and smells antiseptic. I'm not familiar with podiatrist offices as I've never had any foot issues. I find and enter the x-ray room. Inside is a large machine on the floor, intended for x-raying feet. X-ray-proof lead-filled blankets hang on the wall. That's what I'm looking for. It will block the bloody GPS signal that tells QF exactly where I am. I know that lead blocks it, but I don't know what else does. I'll have to find out. QF techies track also track a

GPS on my phone.

I grab as many of the lead blankets I can, five in total, and I carry them out the door.

"Wade, I'm ready to talk," says Sergeant Crutcher.

"Go for it," I say.

"What are you doing?" he asks.

"Figuring out how to block you guys tracking me. These x-ray-proof blankets should do the trick."

"Okay... why are you running?"

"I don't feel it's safe to say why I am running. All I can say is that I need to do this, and you will most definitely see me again."

"But what are you doing?"

I stop answering.

"Wade?"

He realizes that I'm done answering.

I walk to the bus station and buy a ticket from a machine with cash. While I make the purchase, I keep my left eye closed, the one with the camera in it, so no one can see which city I've chosen.

By my calculation, the two operatives are ten minutes away, know my exact location and are barreling down on it. I walk over to the bus-boarding location. As I board my bus, I look at my phone and use a search engine to find how to jam radio and GPS signals. Once the data I want is on display and downloaded, I tuck the phone back into my pocket. Soon it won't have any signal.

I find a seat in the far back and I cover myself from head to toe in the x-ray-proof blankets. At this point, my signal has gone blank. No location, no ocular feed, and no audio feed to QF.

The bus moves forward, and for the first time in seven

years, I have privacy. Stuck under blankets unable to come out. This is not comfortable. The moment I emerge, their blips will start blipping again. They'll know exactly where I am.

Chapter 23

Jean Jacques

QUADFILIUM, MIND BOOTH

"It's been three hours since Wade went rogue," I say to Kris Connelly, John Crutcher, Ashkay and Heidi in conference room.

"Where do we stand?" I ask.

"We fired two operatives from the plane when he jumped. He saw them, of course," says John.

Heidi says, "We also flew in a four-man team from here. Last known location, Billings, Montana. He got on a bus and went dark. Destination unknown."

Kris says, "With no GPS the operatives will have to employ good old fashioned detective work."

Heidi adds, "Bus station had eight departures in our window. Three for the West Coast, two South and three for the East Coast. We asked the depot manager...to have the drivers report any passenger covered in blankets. This is what they got."

Heidi plays back the bus depot clerk's response, "First, I don't know you two guys. Second, these are long trips. Half the passengers are covered in blankets. Sorry gents, can't help you."

"Police uniforms would have been better," she says.

I say to Heidi, "I want an operative to track each bus. I can't unless I turn the plane around and send the whole force back there," I say.

"Boss...Teska's eye replacements are on that plane...." argues Heidi.

"Exactly. Fuck!" I think a moment. "The plane stays on course." I check the plane's location on GPS monitor. "It's over Michigan. Three busses are headed in that direction. Drop two operatives off now. They check out the East coast busses," I say.

"Great idea," says Heidi.

I order two operatives to parachute out of the plane and track the East Coast run, meanwhile our two operatives in Billings really have as much as they could learn about the destinations of all the busses that just left.

We've all been up for 30 hours and are cross-eyed and weary, but I don't have a precise plan yet.

Kris Connelly asks, "What do we do?"

I could send the whole organization. Maybe I should. But what does that buy us? How much force do we use to subdue him? What do we do with him? We don't keep people here under force.

I should have predicted this when he began snooping around about Teska's recruitment. When the little girl from Sydney appeared at the warehouse, his suspicions confirmed, he turned.

"Now we have the most skilled field operative in QF history, on the run and in possession of all our secrets," I say.

Ashkay adds, "Also, he is under the heaviest bounty imaginable, and there are untold numbers of assassins searching him out. Luckily, he is extremely 'off the grid.' No one knows his name, and if they do find him listed under Wade Maley, they will see that he is deceased, and this will confuse them. Or impress them. This will keep him safer from the facial recognition software hacked into by the more sophisticated bounty hunters searching for Wade. Many of these guys have connections into the government and can tap into the

Homeland Security software that uses this."

"Sir, is there anything we don't know?" asks Kris.

"Good question. I'll think about it," I answer.

Chapter 24
Wade

I was so tired, I slept six straight hours. Now I gotta piss with these blankets on my head.

I'm also hungry. I stand up with forty pounds of blankets draped over me and head to the on-board bathroom. I feel my way along. Must be getting some weird looks. I get to the loo and open it. I'm greeted by a pungent fog of urine and feces vapor.

I hold my breath, do my thing and get out of there. I hope my signal remained hidden. This blanket's worked so far, otherwise I'd have been in QF custody hours ago.

Back in my seat, still under the blankets, I look at my phone. I study how to jam or block signals. I can't well spend the rest of my days walking around under lead blankets.

Chapter 25
Jean Jacques

"Sir, the plane has arrived. The crew with the transplant eyes is in the tunnel," reports the transportation engineer.

"Thank you," I say as I run in the direction of the underground train's arrival platform.

It has been almost twenty-four hours since Teska went comatose. When someone goes into a coma, if they don't come out within the first couple of days, they tend to stay in it for a long time. We'll pull out the devices and run the MRI, unless she comes out of it in the next hour.

The train arrives. The doors slide open.

"Take the cooler to ICU, now!" I say to the operative holding it. He runs into the building. I follow. We hand it to the surgeon and he thanks us. The operation will take five hours. Teska will be temporarily without her ocular and audio devices while she recovers.

I go back to the Mind Booth to follow up on Wade. Thus far, his signals have not resurfaced. I call in Ashkay.

"Talk to me. What do we have?" I ask.

"Both of Wade's devices are GPSed. These and the feeds for visio and audio are radio waves. The devices are EMP resistant but will be interrupted if an EMP is triggered close to the devices. They can be turned back on if an EMP deactivates them but only if we have Wade. It's a procedure that requires close contact with the devices. Also, there are simple things that can block the signals," says Ashkay.

"Such as?" I ask.

"The myths about tinfoil hats and concrete bunkers have some truth. You can block radio signals with foil. Wade might figure it out. Maybe he fashions some head gear. But, he has to see at times. Signals could leak. And then we can find him."

"Right now, he is covered in lead blankets," I say.

"Aside from several feet of concrete, it's the best signal blocker. We have no way to know where he is," says Ashkay.

"Can we somehow increase the sensitivity of our instruments into his frequency?" I ask.

"No. We have the most sensitive settings for all QF agents. Rarely are feeds interrupted... deep tunnels... basements... underground parking garages," says Ashkay.

"I've seen that. Okay. Keep an eye on any signal and let me know," I say.

"Okay boss... one other thing... Wade's a very close friend. Is there any reason for why he's doing this? A lot of us are wondering."

"Fair point, I need to brief the crew," I say. Brett calls on my cell. I step away.

Brett says, "Hey boss, I'm in China."

"Good."

"Things okay there?" he asks.

"Uh... yeah."

"Jean Jacques, it's time we talk," says Brett. "Talk."

"What do you want me to say?" I ask.

"The stuff you're not saying. You are hiding something. About this Wade thing." says Brett.

I lower my voice. Brett's too perceptive.

"Couple things. Wade's smitten with Teska. They kissed last week."

"Really?" says Brett.

"Yes. She initiated it." I say. "Since then he's been on a conspiracy kick about her scopulus, thinking it was a setup by me."

"Was it?" he asks.

"No," I answer and pause.

"Why would he think that?" asks Brett.

"Because Teska described her scopulus and he didn't think it could possibly have gone down that way without a setup."

"Okay... It still seems like you aren't saying something."

"Want the truth?"

"Of course."

"I've got my own thing that I've never sorted out."

"What?"

"She was naked. In front of a mirror... on her ocular feed I was watching. I didn't turn it off." Blood rushes to my face.

"Okay. I'm jealous but yeah that was bad. What else?" he probes.

Damn him. I hesitate.

"It's kind of weird. I *wanted* Teska's fiancé, Jeffrey, to cheat on her," I confess.

"So?" Brett says.

"I felt disgraceful that I was so eager to have Teska's fiancé break faith with her. I desperately wanted him to, and when he did, I was ecstatic. The feeling itself, of wanting that, was and is dishonorable. Repulsive to me and my view of my own character. I pride myself on having a purity of purpose and of thoughts. Such low-level compulsions make me dislike and not trust myself. It violates everything I stand for," I say.

"I see," says Brett. Seemingly satisfied that he has the answers he needs. "Well, we need you on your game, and not in a state of introspection. Your effectiveness diminishes like that," he says.

"True. How do I achieve that?" I ask.

"Get over it."

"Fair enough. And Wade's departure. What do I tell the crew? They idolize him." I ask.

"Of course, they do. You can't run him down... say he's a coward. No one will buy it. And, you can't say he doesn't trust Quadfilium. It plants doubt," he says.

"I'm fucked, either way," I say.

"The team doesn't want either of those to be true," he says.

"What then?" I ask.

Silence. Brett's mind whizzes...

"It's passion. Wade met the little girl at the warehouse. She's the cousin of his adopted little sister in Sydney, who he lost. They look identical. When he hears that she might be alive, he takes off to save her. He doesn't want to weigh down QF. He has to do it on his own...," Brett says.

"Chivalrous, loyal... it's brilliant, Brett," I say." And I'll tell them that we will help Wade reunite with her, and that he doesn't have to go rogue to do it."

I call for a full crew meeting. They assemble in the Commons. Aside from those on active measures, and security, everyone is here. I turn on the remote PA so all those not in the room are plugged in and can hear. I walk to the podium and look across a concerned crew.

"Friends and fellow freedom soldiers, most of us are aware that our top agent, Wade Maley, has gone rogue under the category and label of 'deserter'. He's not. Let me explain..."

Chapter 26
Teska

I wake up to a sound in my audio feed. The last thing I remember is a needle going into my arm in that Los Angeles human slave distribution center. I was tied down and about to get lobotomized. *Had I been?*

I look around. White walls. An I/V tube. A machine mimics my heart beat. No one around. I am in an ICU bay at QuadFilium. I can hear something. It's Jean Jacques talking into my audio feed. He's talking to the crew. Must be a base-wide meeting.

"Friends and fellow freedom soldiers, most of us are aware that our top agent, Wade Maley, has gone rogue under the category and label of 'deserter'. He's not. Let me explain...

"We all know Wade to be the finest operative in QuadFilium history. We've reviewed all of his visio and audio feeds and noted that he jettisoned after he spoke to a young captive at the Los Angeles distribution center. The captive happened to be related to the person most involved in Wade's own scopulus.

"Before Wade came to QuadFilium, he had a traumatic experience in which his adopted younger sister was kidnapped. No one could find her and Wade assumed, as did the police, that she was taken for human trafficking purposes. Wade discovered from the young girl he found in LA two days ago that his adopted sister is in fact alive and well.

"We all know how emotional the scopulus is. Wade was

169

affected by these events and took things into his own hands. We believe his plan is to find and reunite with her.

"Unfortunately, we pieced this together after Wade had blocked his signals. We can't tell him we support his reuniting with his adopted sister, in a way that protects Wade and QuadFilium. There are complications. Public record has Wade dead and buried. Any QuadFilium action might involve authorities and complicate matters. Plus there is a massive bounty on Wade's head. He's already in danger. If he surfaces assassins will kill him.

"For now, we all must keep our duties going while we find Wade, let him know we are on his side, bring him in and help him find his sister, not punish him."

I hear distant clapping. Their questions and concerns answered. Mine are not. I hear the doctors come in the room. I close my eyes. My heartbeat monitor beeps faster.

A doctor says, "Her pulse is up from 60 to 85."

"Check it out," says the other doctor.

One of them comes over and grabs my hand and feels my pulse. I do everything I can to control my breathing and remain limp.

The doctor shines a light into my eye.

"Pupil responds to light."

"Is she conscious?" asks the other doctor who walks over to inspect.

"Teska?" one asks. I remain inert. One of them jiggles my arm. Limp.

"Tell the boss."

One leaves and returns with Jean Jacques a minute later.

"Teska are you awake?" Jean Jacques gently shakes me. I show no sign of life. He asks the doctor, "What's this mean?"

"It means she's moved from comatose to catatonic. We should move forward the surgery and MRI. And fast," says a doctor.

"Okay. Remove the devices and do the MRI," says Jean Jacques.

Hmmm... I've been unconscious since the LA mission. They think I might have brain damage and want to do an MRI. This requires the removal of the devices, so the MRI magnets don't pull the metal parts out and kill me.

I want the devices gone. *Roll with it.* They wheel me into another room.

"Since she's no longer comatose, we need to anesthetize her with a general," says a doctor.

I feel a needle enter a vein in my arm.

Chapter 27
Wade

My bus is headed to Austin, Texas. The best I can guess, we're in Wyoming. I'm hungry, and these lead blankets feel like lead blankets.

I've read and committed to memory the download on how to block or jam the signals. It appears I can hide underground, in a basement or in a parking structure. Anywhere that has lots of dirt or concrete between me and the sky. There are aluminum foil contraptions that should block the signal. I thought these were reserved for conspiracy freaks but looks like there is some truth to it. I'll have to figure out how to do that with my eye and ear GPSes without looking like a complete weirdo.

We're coming up to a stop. I need to get out and sort this out. I have a small peek hole I can see through by folding my blankets.

Casper. That's a town we're pulling up to. Perfect. I can be a friendly ghost here. I get up to walk off, still wearing the blankets. I can hardly see where I am going. I feel my way along and exit. I hear a group of guys waiting outside the bus. They have deep voices and are jovial, like some sort of team of guys hanging out. When I leave the bottom step, I land on one of the guys' feet. It's hard. I came off a high step.

"Ouch!" he yells.

"Hey, mate, sorry about that!" I say, muffled through my blankets.

"What the fuck, man? Fuck you under blankets for? Pull

them off, fucking weirdo!" he says.

"This jackoff sounds like he's from England or something," says another.

Two guys rip off my blankets. Unbalanced, I topple over. Now I'm exposed to the open air and my GPS will register my location. QuadFilium knows where I am within twelve inches.

"Who the fuck is this guy?" says one of the group of men standing outside the bus depot.

I get up off the ground, surrounded by six blokes. These chaps wear cowboy hats and baseball caps, facial hair, jeans and the shirts and vests I've seen truckers wear. They're young. Like a football team out on the town. In fact, that's what they remind me of considering their size. Larger than average. Much larger. Mildly slurred voices and angled postures. They're intoxicated.

The guy whose foot I stepped on is pissed. He leans into me and says, "Hey fuck face, watch where you're going. Answer the fucking question! Why the blankets?"

Each has six inches and thirty pounds on me... a good supply of muscle and medium supply of fat.

"Gentlemen, and you specifically," I look directly at the guy right in front of me whose foot I stepped on. "I am sorry for the trouble. I'll watch where I am going. I'll just be on my way."

The foot guy spits in my face and says, "You ain't goin' nowhere, faggot. Ain't no sissy English homo going to show up in our town wearing blankets and stepping on feet."

Another one chimes in, "What the fuck's your story, dude?"

My lack of fear aggravates them. They're bullies, accustomed to cowed victims. Four of them tilt forward, two lean back. In these situations, body pose tells all. The two leaning back don't want to fight. The four leaning forward do.

173

The prick who pulled my blankets is the alpha. The other guys want to impress him. The guy whose foot I stepped on seems the most eager to prove how tough he is to the alpha tosser. I'd rather not get into a fight with these testosterone junkies.

The bus pulls away. It's just the seven of us on the side of the road.

"You guys really don't want to do this, trust me," I say.

"Yes, we do," foot guy says.

"Look, I'm sorry for being a weirdo wearing blankets over my head and for stepping on your foot. I'd really like to just be on my way now if that's okay," I say.

"Nope," says the guy who spit in my face.

"Fair enough. I have a question. Are any of you guys a caretaker for someone? Like a grandparent or a little child?" I ask out of thin air.

The four pugnacious boys leaning forward furrow their eyebrows, unamused by a question from the weirdo guy. But the two boys leaning back both give a tell. When I asked it, one looked to the side fast, in reaction to the question. It tells me he probably does care for someone, so getting fucked up would cause some serious problems for an innocent. He has a child or a grandparent or a disabled sibling, someone, and he's the guy that feeds and helps. His feet are pointed away from me. The other guy, tilted back slightly, also gave a tell. His foot flinched when I asked the question. I scan him. He wears a ring. He's married. Could've knocked up a girl and has a kid. It's not the kid's fault.

"You aren't the one asking questions!" alpha says as he turns to his boys and says, "I knew this faggot was a weirdo, kick his ass!"

Foot guy, on my right, was the first to reach for my neck,

while the guy on my left swings a wild right hook towards my face. I turn my head directly into the right hook and head butt his bunched hand. As the knuckles connect to the top of my forehead, metacarpals crunch like brittle sticks. As predicted, the guy to my right, thrown off balance, misses and stumbles forward and leaves his instep next to my right foot. I kick down on it at the apex of his arch. I hear the crunch of bones collapse under my heel. Like stepping on a bag of crisps. Alpha prick launched forward to join the attack, but was thrown off by my unexpected defense. He pauses, leans back and prepares to relaunch. With a tight fist, I chop down on his collarbone, the strike angle and point of contact dead-center of the floating collarbone with the tip of my pinky knuckle. All my force is concentrated on that one small surface area. It connects and the bone cracks in half. Alpha's shoulder pulls towards his neck with no collar bone to separate them. Knees buckle and he drops. The guy whose foot I crushed writhes in pain on the ground. Broken-hand-guy, to my left, cradles his injury.

The two guys in the back look baffled. Pupils fully dilated. They hesitate. Fight or flight. Their buddies were crippled one by one by a maniac guy with an accent. Is it worth it? They're asking themselves. And I'd rather not hurt these chumps.

Three guys on the ground. Three guys stand. I say to one, "I don't plan to fuck up these two jokers because, they're either caretakers or fathers," I slowly walk towards him. "But I don't really have the slightest problem fucking you up."

I size him up. I notice his right knuckles are knobby. Healed boxer's fractures on the third, fourth and fifth metacarpals of his right hand. Crooked nose. Been in fights. His stance indicates boxer, martial arts training. The other three jokers had no plan. This guy is organized in structured hand-to-hand combat. Maybe ex-military, maybe boxing, maybe a streetfighter, the deadliest. He sized me up when I incapacitated his buds. He steps back. I recognize the position. A Muy Thai attack stance. Worthy opponent. He lunges at me with a parry of blows that would easily take someone out and give the others free reign to kick me to pulp. But I predict his move and only need to see how he initiates. Once he does, I visualize the whole motion. It requires he lift one leg for a second. Instead of moving to block the strike, I step over and kick out the one foot he's standing on. His kick lands on me, but isn't supported by a planted foot, so he falls to the right as I sweep his leg out from underneath him. He reaches for the ground as he falls towards. When his fingers hit the ground, I break them with my heel. I knee him in the center of his face, breaking his nose. Two more crunches for the road.

The last two guys standing are torn between defending their mates, trying to attack me or self-preservation. They're fucked and I truly don't give two shits.

I look at them. One shakes a little. I say, "Mates, I need some things. If you get them for me, I won't kill these blokes. If you call the police, they will get even more hurt."

They agree to my terms.

I send them for tinfoil, a cap, sunglasses, an eye patch, a hoodie, a pile of grub, water, some tools, a sleeping bag, flashlight, bug net and a mess kit. I tell them they have about ten minutes to get these items.

As I wait for these two wankers, I prop up the broken chaps, moaning in pain. I arrange them like a simple and unnoticeable band of drunken youngsters leaning against a wall. I take all of their cash. 125 dollars. I tell them to shut up or I'll break more of their bones. They comply.

They give up their ATM cards and pins, after some mild threats and well-placed finger pokes. I head over to the ATM machine at the bus depot. I take out the maximum, five hundred dollars, from each account, not feeling the least bit bad.

By now, QuadFilium operatives have my location and Jean Jacques and Crutcher have agents on their way. Wasn't quite ready for that, but at least I can test out the GPS jammers I'm about to fashion.

The two wankers come back faster than I expected. They must have split up to get the supplies. One guy was smart enough to get me a bag to carry everything in. I knew these pricks were caretaker types.

I grab two of the wankers' phones and use their face ID's to unlock them. I change the passwords and place them in my pocket. I get up to leave and say, "Cheers mates! Thanks for the hospitality! By the way, I'm Australian, not English."

No one answers and I walk away, towards the edge of town. Then I hear Jean Jacques in my ear feed.

"Wade? Can you hear me?"

Chapter 28
Jean Jacques

Teska is under general anesthesia to receive her MRI and transplant. One of the harvested eyeballs was a blood type match. I leave the doctors alone to carry out the procedures. I re-enter the Mind Booth to find out what happened with Wade.

As I walk in, I see the blips light up and Wade's video and audio feed come to life. He's on the ground looking up at some young ruffians. GPS says he's in Wyoming in a town called Casper.

I tap into the audios of the active operatives who are in search of Wade. "Delta Corps, come in! We have a signal and a location! Do you copy?"

All answer in the affirmative.

I order three operatives to Wyoming to track and follow the real time GPS signal and send the other three to Texas. Wyoming lies directly between Montana and Austin. Wade's headed to find Teska's ex-fiancé, Jeffrey.

This will get complicated if Jeffrey gets involved.

The three going to Austin ask why I expect him to go there. I say I'll brief them on the way.

The Wyoming team has a three-hour-travel-time estimate. I need to talk some sense into Wade.

I say to the six operatives, "You are all on operation Hide and Seek. The target objective is Agent Wade Maley back here. Deadly force is prohibited unless he engages first with intent to kill. But stop at nothing to contain him. Use tranquilizers, sedation, or incapacitate to capture. Now, *go!*" They acknowledge.

I turn to Wade's feed and watch a street fight with six thugs. Wade dismantles them, and sends two on errands, including buying tinfoil. He's already figured out the tinfoil can diminish the radio signals in his devices.

He walks away towards the edge of the city. I say, "Wade? Can you hear me?"

He answers, "How's Teska? Is she still out cold?"

"I'm afraid so." I cannot tell Wade about the device removal. "But the doctors are optimistic that she'll be fine."

"That's a load of wank. How the fuck do they know? They can't even do an MRI to look at her brain. She's got fucking devices in her head. They're guessing?"

"They are doing what they can," I say, to skirt his questions.

"Wrong answer, mate. If you're not going to tell me what's what, but spin your PR bullshit, I'm not going to tell you what you want to know," he says.

"Wade! Wait—" The screens blip and feeds go black and silent. He put the blankets over his head. He's off the grid. His last location was 241 meters southeast of North Poplar Street. He's a needle in a haystack. But, a much smaller haystack now.

John, Ashkay, Heidi, Kris huddle in a scrum in the Mind Booth.

"Heidi, talk..." I say.

"Chip on his shoulder. What's the deal? As much of an asshole as Wade can be, I've never seen him show anything but admiration for you. That was blatant disrespect," says Heidi.

"It's a combination of factors. You heard what I said to the crew," I say.

"Sure, but what's the back story?" says Heidi.

"He's fallen in love with Teska. She initiated intimate contact with him last week," I say.

"They had sex?" says Kris.

"No, she kissed him. But they've grown very close over the past four months. The last mission cemented the bond. Things went haywire when Wade met the girl in LA. She recognized him. Wade had adopted a young aborigine girl as his sister. Her name was Peyton. Peyton had shown the little girl a picture of Wade. Peyton was kidnapped which culminated in Wade's scopulus," I say.

"The girl knew Peyton?" asks Heidi.

"Jesus Christ, what are the odds?" says Kris.

"QuadFilium personnel possess an intangible. Luck. I imagine it falls under that," I say.

Kris chimes in, "So he's freaked out. Thinks his own and maybe Teska's scopulus were staged. He's headed to find this Jeffrey guy. You want to beat him to it."

"This is fucking weird. A catastrophe," says Heidi.

"It's actually a screaming emergency. We need to *prevent* a catastrophe," I say

Kris says, "We need to deploy an ambush. Jeffrey can't know he's being tracked or used as bait. Does he have any training? Military background?"

"No," I say. "None."

"Do we have fresh intel on him?" Heidi asks.

Ashkay answers, "I've done a cursory study in the last half hour. He's not doing well. There's very little on him since he was found cheating on Teska and she supposedly committed suicide. He ceased all social media. His electronic signature has gone silent for the last twelve months. He's part of an AA group, and has two prescriptions for antidepressants. Otherwise, we don't have anything on him, besides paycheck deposits and groceries. No travel, minimal phone use. That's it."

"Do we know where he lives?" asks Kris.

"He pays rent for the same apartment," says Ashkay.

"We need to get there before Wade, and set the trap," I say.

"He'll expect that." says John.

"Of course he will. But he can't avoid it. He has to *contact* Jeffrey. Wily or not, we catch him," I say.

"We need a net around Jeffrey, track every move, cameras... audio... phone tap... stakeout. And, he can't know it," says John.

I nod. "Identify every person that comes within fifteen meters of him, and remain invisible," I say.

We go over the details. The Wyoming team will locate Wade. The Austin team will cast the net around Jeffrey.

I head back to the surgery.

Teska's devices removed, MRI done and the eye transplant complete. She's still not conscious but not comatose. The chief surgeon examines the results of the MRI. I walk over.

He says, "Good news and bad news."

"Okay, tell." I say.

"Good news is that she has no obvious brain damage or extant internal bleeding. She has a small cut where the two frontal lobes connect. The connection remains intact, which means the lobotomy was incomplete. The cut may or may not influence her cognitive function. It'll only be demonstrable when, or if, she comes out of her dormancy," he says.

"What's the bad news," I ask.

"We cannot identify the etiology of the semi-coma, or catatonia. Without a cause, there's no solution," says the doctor.

"I understand. How long until the anesthetic wears off?" I ask.

"It did. Twenty minutes ago," he says.

"Gotcha. Thank you, doctor." I go and look at her. She's lying on her back on the operating table. Her new eye bandaged. According to doctors, successful eye transplants result in good vision within a few days. We can't use Dimitri's super healing serum because it's derived from the eyeball. Her eye is the point of attention. There's more to be done. There is no hurry at this point. She is out of touch. What's curious is she's responsive to stimuli in the environment. Her good pupil adjusts to light. Her heart rate changes under duress. She reacts to pain, but otherwise unresponsive. I consider praying to God. Something I haven't done in decades.

I think to myself how much I'd like to turn back time and redo everything. I look down at Teska, the most striking beauty I've ever seen. Even now, I hold myself back. Don't touch. Don't look.

Chapter 29
Teska

I come to after my operation. At this point, I have no devices in me and I have another person's eyeball. I hear chatter. It sounds like it's coming from next door. It's the voices of the lead surgeon and Jean Jacques.

Their conversation ends and I feel the presence of one of them next to me. I keep my eyes closed and remain calm and still.

The man stands there for several minutes. I cannot tell what he's doing. I only hear shallow breathing that sounds anxious and an occasional swallow. He leaves.

So much to process.

Chapter 30
Wade

I look through the small slit in my blanket fold as I walk along a remote country road. To the side and under the road is an entrance to a large drainpipe, tall enough to walk in at full height. I enter and make my way in several yards to ensure radio signals won't make it to me then remove my lead blankets.

I go deeper. The light dims. I grab a flashlight out of my bag and turn it on. I see some signs of life down here. An old candy wrapper, a coke can, empty bottles of booze. I hear a noise down further. Scuffling. Animal or human. I'm ready for either. I walk deeper.

I see a homeless man. He sits against the curved wall and squints into my light, smiling ear to ear, flashing his few teeth.

"Do you always walk into a person's house without knocking?" he says.

He wears dirty clothes. His face is wrinkled and brown with deep grooves. Like a walnut shell. His arms are covered in grime and scabs. Hair is clumped into short scraggily ropes.

"Sorry mate, you got room for another?" I ask.

"I charge a lot for rent," he says as he bursts out laughing at his own joke in a unique, high-pitched machine gun shrill. I chuckle at his good humor.

I'd prefer a hotel room, but this place offers the protection I need from the radio waves, while I figure out how to scramble them with a head gear that I intend to fashion. The other problem is that at any point, if I use my phone for anything, I'm made. Ashkay will pinpoint my exact location. I remove its sim card and power it down.

"How much?" I ask my new landlord.

"A place like this? It even has an indoor pool!" he says. He points at a puddle of scum flowing down the center followed by his signature cackle.

"Will twenty bucks a night cover it?" I ask as I pull out a bill and hand it to him.

"Well stick a bottle rocket up my butt and call me Yankee Doodle! Ain't nobody ever walked into these sewers and handed me a double sawbuck before!" followed by the now annoying, shrill laugh.

"Today's a special day. What's your name?" I ask.

"Melvin the Great!" he answers. I realize his shrill laugh bookends most of what he says. A defense posture. Most would-be assailants probably flinch at its loudness and suddenness.

"Nice to meet you, Melvin, and thank you for the hospitality. My name is Wade."

We talk for a bit. He tells me a story I've heard too often before: loses his daughter in a car crash, becomes an alcoholic, wife leaves, mortgage foreclosed, and loses his job because he was drunk and stinky; and, my guess, partly because of that fucking laugh, not that he's aware of it. It all ends with him on the streets. He has been here for six years.

He tells me the drainage system wends its way throughout the city of Casper. You can get to most places through it, by popping manholes. While he talks, he keeps up the intermittent cackle until he dozes off and mumbles his way into dreamland.

I'd downloaded into one of the stolen phones a number of

videos on how to fashion tinfoil hats to block radio waves. I follow the directions and line my hood and jacket with a few layers of foil. I pull the hood over my head and try to cover my face as much as possible. I'm concerned the ocular device signal in my eyeball is not shielded. I guess I'll have to test it.

It is getting dark. I set up the camping gear and make a small fire. I eat a meal of hot dogs and beans like any good American cowboy. I put out the fire and roll myself up into a sleeping bag with a net on top to keep out the bugs. Melvin is still out for the count. Been snoring for a couple of hours now.

The next morning, I put away my gear and make a plan to test my hoodie shield. Melvin shows me where the center of the drainpipe network is, about a quarter mile northwest from our camp spot. There's a manhole cover above. A pinhole of light illuminates the ladder leading up. Every one or two hundred yards there are other similar shafts leading up to street level.

I tie a rope to the manhole cover, so I can tie it off after re-entering and make lifting it impossible from the top. I seal off any other manhole covers within a 100-yard radius using the same rope method.

I pop up through the center manhole and stand next to it. Now I'm fully exposed to the world. If there's a signal coming off me, the operatives will be on me in minutes. Little doubt they're in Casper waiting for the "Wade signal."

I scan the horizon and look for any signs of QuadFilium agents. They'll use their immersion tactics and be almost unrecognizable.

Several minutes go by. Several cars and pedestrians pass. Still no sign. I will give it an hour, and if they don't show, I can assume the tin-foil-hoodie-cloak works. I see something.

On the roof of a building, the slightest movement above

one of the low walls. That was enough to tell me that they made me. My cloak is not sufficient. I walk towards the open manhole next to me and start to climb back in. Two operatives emerge from the crowd near the outdoor shopping zone, sprinting towards me.

I'm halfway down into the hole when I feel the powerful plunge of a tranquilizer dart penetrate my chest below the collarbone. I look up and see a smiling sniper pulling back his gun over the small wall on the roof. Fucking bastards! I recognize all three operatives. Two men, one woman. Good mates of mine and great agents. Now I'm in direct conflict with them. A choice I had to make.

I'm woozy and lose control of my muscles and consciousness. I have three seconds until the sedatives take effect and knock me out. I scurry down the hole, reach up and pull the manhole cover over the opening and blank out.

I wake up dazed and disoriented, near my stuff at the camp spot. There's a gentle fire. I'm in my sleeping bag. *Was that all a dream? How the fuck did I end up here?*

Melvin and his five teeth greet me with a smile and his broken-record laugh. He holds a dart and looks at me. "Youz gots a lot more to you than could be reckoned at first glance! You must be the fugitive!" he says, in his best Tommy Lee Jones impression. It's awful, and his few ivories make him lisp.

It seems that Melvin followed me to the central manhole. When he saw me fall in a clump below with a dart sticking out of my chest, he jumped in. He tied off the rope that was connected to the manhole cover and sealed the entrance. Then he removed the dart and dragged me back to our home base and tucked me in. The operatives likely tried the other manholes, but they were sealed.

"How long have I been out?" I ask.

"Three hours," he says.

"Well, that means they couldn't get into the manholes and we successfully evaded them." I say.

"Oh no, they finally made their way into a manhole. Even came down in these parts looking for ya. Heard 'em coming a couple minutes 'fore they arrived here, on account of the echoes. And I managed to hide you in my secret spot," he says and points to a small metal door in the side of the drainpipe.

"The door is sealed shut. But if you lift out the hinge pin here, it opens up backwards," he says.

He pops the pin with a little metal rod he keeps handy and opens the door from the hinge side. There's a small closet space inside.

"I threw you and your stuff in there and stayed in my spot," he says.

"You saw them?"

"Oh yeah! I talked to them. Real nice folk. They wore civilian clothes but seemed like military. Must be undercover FBI or something. Man! You are full of surprises! Why's the FBI after you?" he asks.

"I'll explain later. So, they spoke to you?" I ask.

"They sure did. I told them I ain't never seen or heard of you. They offered me all sorts of good stuff including money and booze and other great things to spill the beans. I held strong. Showed no sign that I had ever had any inkling about you," he says.

"You're kidding. Why didn't you turn me in and get the reward?" I ask.

"Because you are the first person in ten years that has been nice to me," he says.

This is the first sentence Melvin has said that wasn't followed by the laugh. Looks like I have a new and loyal comrade. *Lucky you, Wade, or else the operatives would have had your arse.* Chances are they'll come looking this way again. They know I was down here. They'll search, find a goose egg and they'll be back.

The manhole I used was the center axis point of the culvert system. There are dozens of miles branching out from that midpoint. It'll take days to canvas the whole web of tunnels.

It seems in my cockiness, using myself as bait, I underestimated the other QuadFilium agents. I learned my lesson. I got away with it by sheer luck....

I add more tin layers to my hoodie, but maybe more important, I fashion an eye patch to block its signal. Looks weird. I place a few layers of foil over the inside left eye of the sunglasses, to hide the ugly patch. Now, I have to test it, but I need to be safe about it. This time, I recruit Melvin to help.

We go to the opposite side of the city and Melvin pops up through a manhole and stands near it. I wear the hoodie and glasses. I climb up and expose only my head through the manhole. There is no doubt that radio waves can reach me.

After forty-five minutes, there's no sign of them, Melvin claims he looked at every passerby and driver that came anywhere and says that none were the folks he met the day before.

I assume my shield works. Time to plan.

Undoubtedly, Jean Jacques figured I'm headed to Texas. He'll send another detail to monitor Jeffrey.

Chapter 31
Jean Jacques

// Delta Team leader come in, do you copy?" says John Crutcher. We are in the Mind Booth we've barely left in days.

"Delta leader, go," says our operative in Austin.

He touched down an hour ago and found Jeffrey's apartment building. It is currently 1800 hours local and likely Jeffrey will be home soon. We watch the ocular feeds of the three operatives on this leg of the mission. They're huddled in a car across the street. Cars pass, a lady with her dog. A jogger with blue hair. We can't keep them there too long as they look suspicious. A black Ford Fusion pulls up. It matches the lease description Ashkay hacked on line.

"We have an ID on the target. That's him," says Delta leader.

It's Jeffrey. He pulls into the apartment building and the gate to the garage closes behind him.

"Good. Commence Operation JT," says Crutcher. Jeffrey Tracker. Wade would have come up with a better title but we're too exhausted to be creative.

The operatives spend the next twenty-four hours placing bugs and cameras inside his apartment and car. GPS trackers in all his shoes. Ashkay manages to tap his phone. This gives us another GPS, and we can hear his audio and see with it when it's out of his pocket. Thanks to Ashkay and some black-market software he stole from NSA.

All angles of the building are covered: Outside looking at the building, and from the building to its surroundings.

There are dozens of cameras to monitor for any sign of Wade. We set up an all-hands-on-deck, and recruited other QuadFilium staff to keep 24/7 eyes on the screens. Ashkay installed a facial recognition function on each camera to identify Wade. But we expect him to be clad in face and head-hiding apparel to block our signal from his devices.

We observe Jeffrey. He's a miserable fellow with a slow and slouched gate, a downcast look, a grayish complexion, and a lackluster personality. This poor sap has given up on life. It's not been long enough to ruin his handsome features. He has rings under his eyes and put on a few pounds from a year and a half ago when I saw him during Teska's scopulus. He was more full-of-life then.

We watch. He approaches his apartment door at the same time his neighbor, an attractive woman in her late twenties, comes out of hers. Ashkay has identified all neighbors. This is Molly.

"Oh, hello Jeff!" she says, glancing down at herself. Girl checks herself out. Sign of possible affection, wanting to be attractive.

"Hello, Molly," returns Jeff.

"I'm sorry I was loud last night. I had some friends over for game night."

"I didn't hear anything."

"Okay… well, the invitation still stands, join us anytime," says Molly.

"I'll think about it," says Jeff.

"You always say that. Don't you think it would be good for you?" she asks.

"Probably. My therapist sure thinks so," says Jeff.

"He or she is right," says Molly.

"I'll think about it."

"The classic line of Jeffrey."

"Okay, Molly, well, I *will* think about it."

"Please?"

This girl has a crush on Jeffrey and tries to get him out of his doldrums and into living life again. Would be good for him.

"Okay, I promise. I'll go to one of your game nights in the next couple weeks."

"Yay! Great! I'll make you stick to your word on that!"

"Okay, okay," says Jeffrey. Half a smile comes out and he walks into his apartment. He groans and sighs.

I say, "Delta leader, we expect Wade to show in the next forty-eight hours. My take, he'll have eyewear and a hat or hoodie. Be ready, vigilant at all times."

"Ten-four, boss."

Ashkay busts into the Mind Booth and says, "I just got Wade's location!"

Kris exclaims, "How the fuck?"

"I checked the hospital ward in Casper. I found the names of the guys Wade beat up. I hacked their phones," says Ashkay.

"Unfortunately, there are three phones and they're all going in different directions. One appears at random spots throughout the city and then goes dark. I suspect Wade, but it could be someone else who travels through the culverts under the city and pops up here and there. Another is on a steady path through Colorado straight towards Texas. The last one's been sitting in the same spot for the last few hours."

"Colorado's the most likely, but we can't take chances. Team Beta is still in Casper. Have them check it out," I say.

John Crutcher says, "Hide and Seek team leader do you read me?"

"Hide and Seek leader, go," says a voice.

"Tech leader is sending you a cell phone GPS map. Trace it down, fast. It could be Wade. Don't approach. Just find the signal and report. There's good chance this is a red herring, but it's the closest one we have right now," says Crutcher.

"Ten-four, Sarge, on it." he says.

"Ashkay, you are a genius. I didn't think it possible," I say, impressed. The others chirp in their attaboy's. Ashkay is unaffected. He doesn't give a shit about admiration.

"We are close to the signal. Wait. It disappeared," says Hide and Seek leader.

"Move to the spot where it was. You'll find a manhole," says Heidi.

A tense pause in the Mind Booth.

"Ten-four on manhole. Entering," he says.

We see the team go down the hole and lose their signals.

"Wait!" I say to another agent, who is not underground. "We'll lose your signal. Turn on all body cams. We'll review when you are back out."

"Ten-four, sir."

Five minutes later they come back up, their signals back on.

"Hide and Seek leader here, Wade is not down there. We just uploaded the body cam footage."

We review the cams's footage.

The team watches the whole thing.

They enter the culvert and run fast. Wade could outrun them. He's the speediest in the corps. But they gain on someone. The footsteps pound louder. They turn a corner and see the homeless man they interrogated yesterday. He stands and laughs.

"Where's Wade? We ain't buying your story this time, old man," says Hide and Seek leader. The old man is wearing new clothes, has a decent haircut and looks cleaner.

"And, I have no idea where he is," he says with a loud laugh. It's not funny.

"Okay," says Hide and Seek leader, "you look mighty different from yesterday."

"Wade gave me a pile of cash and checked me into a hotel last night, and gave me these clothes. I took my first shower in months!" Shrill laugh.

"Do you have the slightest clue where he is?" asks the team leader.

"Absolutely not and I certainly would not tell you under any circumstances if I did. Even if you offered me a million bucks or threatened to kill me. Wade is my friend and I'd die for him."

I talk into the team leader's audio, "It's okay, you verified it wasn't Wade. Target two is next. Let's get out of there."

Hide and Seek leader to Melvin: "Your loyalty's noted. See you around." They depart the tunnels with echo of laughter fading off into the darkness.

We brief them on the travelling GPS we believe is Wade on a direct line to Texas. Ashkay was unable to tap the microphone and cameras on the phone only the GPS. South on Interstate 25 at sixty-five miles per hour.

If the team takes roads, they'll never catch up. If they wait until he reaches Texas, it gives Wade more opportunity to lose the signal if he ditches the phone.

Logistics locates a nearby hangar and contracts a now handsomely paid pilot to fly his puddle jumper and land near the interstate ahead of the signal's trajectory. They should be there in the next hour.

Chapter 32
Wade

Just past Denver. I'd love to sightsee and hike. The place is nice and fresh. Don't much like bus rides, although I can sleep in them pretty easy. I can't lower my hoodie or take off my glasses or else they'll pinpoint me. I'm sure I look bit emo to other passengers, who dart suspicious glances.

I hear the moan of an overhead prop plane. I look out and see it's quite low. Landing nearby I suppose.

QuadFilium guys aren't going to give up. I reckon they'll have Jeffrey and all his possessions, movements and thoughts wired. If he jerks it, they'll know how many strokes.

How's Teska doing?

Ten minutes later, the bus slows down in the middle of the highway. I look out the front window and I see three small figures growing larger. One of them has a silhouette and posture I recognize. QF. Fuck me! They made me again! How the fuck?

I look down at my stolen phone. They must have traced it. *Must've been Ashkay! That brilliant bastard*

I jump out of my seat and look for the emergency exit. It's a window with a fancy lever on it to pull and release the pane. I pull it. Alarms blare, the panel requires some elbow grease—which I provide—and comes loose. The driver yells something, a couple people scream and I leap out of the bus as I glance to see how far I am from the three QF operatives. The ground blurs beneath, a good thirty-five miles per hour. The agents are a fifth of a mile away and this time I don't have an airbag on my chest.

I leap, tumble and land hard on a moist field. Thank you, Denver, for your precipitation, otherwise I'd have road rash up the ass.

I look back. They got the bus to slow down by standing in the middle of the highway. Now they are 400 yards away and running towards me.

I assess body damage. Any twisted ankle or broken bone in the lower body and I'm fucked. Aside from some cuts and contusions, I'm good. I run in the opposite direction. The question now is where the hell am I going to go? Will this be an endurance test to see who drops first? It's not likely someone will pick up a panting, sweaty hitchhiker in a hoodie and sunglasses, which technically, I can remove for now as they got me spotted anyways. Gotta think fast, run fast.

I'm on a long stretch of road surrounded on each side by forest. Worst case scenario, I leap into the woods to hide behind trees and rocks, but it won't get me where I need to go. I still have the phone I stole off the alpha jock prick.

I dial 911.

"911 what's your emergency?"

"I have three psychos chasing me down Interstate 25 south of Denver... I'm running as fast as I can!" They hear my frantic breathing.

"Okay sir, where exactly are you?" says the operator.

"Interstate 25 at East Greenland Road running north but on the southbound side, trying to outrun these freaks! They have guns! Please hurry!" I say.

"Okay sir, we have a highway patrol officer near you. Avoid all confrontations with suspects. Can you describe them?" she asks.

"One woman, white. Athletic. Two blokes. Also athletic. One darker skin, one white. They have guns! I'm losing my breath, can't talk much more. I'm in a hoodie, alone, please don't let them catch me!" I yell.

"Okay, sir, thank you. The patrolman is almost there. Can I have your name?" she says.

I hang up and run like dingo on the hunt. I glance back, they are still 400 yards away. They saw me make a phone call.

I see the police car heading towards me. I stop and wave and point at the three figures sprinting up the shoulder.

He skids hard in front of them and bleeps his siren.

"Freeze! Hands up!" he says through a bullhorn on top of his car.

I can't say I'm not getting a kick out of this, but I will say that I can't be brought into a police station to give a statement. I'm technically dead, have no ID, and this will keep me in their custody for too long. I bolt into the woods. The police officer pulls his firearm and trains it on the three operatives. I hide behind a tree and watch the ordeal go down.

This cop has clearly never seen any real action. The gun shakes in his hand. He yells something at them while they all stand there with their hands up.

I hear another couple of police cars approach from the distance. I slip into the woods, zig zag around and drop a few items including the tracked phone. Any sniffing dogs they may send won't have a clear path of travel.

I make my way to East Greenland Road, leave the forest and walk towards the highway. Out here in woop woop. I take off my hoodie and glasses, put on my friendliest face and stick out my thumb. There's a decent flow of traffic and I catch a ride.

A big smile did the trick.

"Where you headed?" the driver asks.

"South!"

"Hop in!"

I climb into the passenger seat of a Ford F-150, with a real man's-man-looking bloke, complete with a handlebar mustache and a red plaid flanno. Could be a true blue lumberjack, considering his hands are one big fat callous.

I put on the hoodie and glasses.

"Whatchu wearin'?" he asks.

"I'm real sensitive to light."

"Fair enough."

We shoot the shit. He drives three hours south down Interstate 25 into New Mexico. He's headed to Santa Fe, so we part at the 84 and I walk alone down the highway. By now it's dark, and I keep my thumb out and hoodie and glasses off. Well after twilight, I finally get picked up, by a nice woman. Probably has ten stray cats at home. Bit of a hippy, based on the strong smell of incense and cat dander in her car, deep raspy voice, leathery skin and colorful clothes. Not complaining, love the ride, the company, the forward progress. I put my hood and glasses back on.

She asks lots of questions. I decide to tell her the truth, for no other reason than it's too unbelievable, I can get away with it.

I tell her about the secret group I am part of, how I escaped and have GPS trackers in my head, hence the sunglasses at night, and how my death was faked so I could be a fully committed member. She soaks it all up and goes right into her theories about Area 51 and the Loch Ness monster. Great stuff. She swears she saw Big Foot one day when camping. She admits that she was high on mushrooms at the time but is positive the poor creature exists and is victimized by the cruelty of men.

She gets me all the way to Lampasas, Texas around midnight. She offers to give me a place to hole up for the night. I except.

Sure enough, she has a pride of cats. Not sure if its ten or twelve, but a good lot for sure.

"I have a small spare bedroom. You can sleep there, honey," she says.

"I'll rest as best I can with the hoodie and sunglasses. It's been a few days since I took a shower. I can't do that wearing these."

"Oh no. That's a shame. What can we do about that?"

"I apologize about my smell but the ideal safe spot would be a deep basement or a shower surrounded by a faraday cage."

"I know just the thing! My good friend Harold has an underground bomb shelter he built during the Cold War. It has a shower and food supplies. He'd let you use it! He's in Johnson City just outside of Austin. You get some sleep and I'll take you!"

Austin is music to my ears. *Luck.* I accept the invite, considering I'd be at even further disadvantage if I stink to high hell.

The next morning we head over to Harold's place. This bloke is sixty-five going on ninety. Must have fried up his whole nervous system with a copious consumption of drugs. He yells instead of talking and has wild eyes that never seem to blink, but gaze off at a distant spot, making everything he says seem meaningful and profound.

I'm an appreciative guest. My new tie-dyed lady friend,

who I finally learn is named Maude, briefs Harold on the whole thing. He gives me a conspiratorial nod despite the unlikely nature of my story. The secret military group, bugs in my head, faked death, all believable to him. He welcomes me into his safehouse.

"Son, you can use my bunker any time. It blocks all signals coming in or going out, even from outer space."

"I am so thankful mister Harold. This is great!" I say.

After I shower and clean up, and put my hoodie and glasses back on, I get upstairs for some good tucker.

They share stories about protests and concerts and hikes they have been on. I thought the movies I watched about American hippies were exaggerated. Not in this case.

I rest well and sleep the night in the bomb shelter. Zero noise or light coming in makes for restful sleep. The next morning, after breakfast, I let them know that I need to depart.

"Come back anytime. *Mi casa es su casa*," says Harold.

"Afraid I don't speak that language," I say.

"My house is your house. I mean it."

"There is a very high likelihood that I will take you up on that offer, my friend."

I leave and head for the road leaving a pile of bills in his mailbox. Doubt he'd accept them if I tried in person.

I head south toward Austin but I need to be prepared.

Chapter 33
Teska

My internal chronometer tells me it's about 0200. My eye's covered in a bandage. There are people up and working but only a handful, mostly the staff in the Mind Booth. Support staff do shifts to keep the Mind Booth occupants fed and alert as they track what they call the "Wade crisis."

They think I'm still comatose or catatonic. They don't know I know what I know. I sneak out of my bed and look into the hallway. Empty. I sneak down the corridor, aware cameras are watching me. I hope no one happens to be look at the monitors. I've seen the inside of Security Control Central. There are hundreds of screens. It's not likely they'll notice me.

I get to the door marked, *QuadFilium Lab, office of Dr. Dimitri Abdramanova,* and walk inside.

I grab a bag and fill it with spy items of every sort, including a small breathing apparatus with compressed oxygen and a pile of astronaut food that comes in neat packages and are labelled things like, "Roasted Crispy Duck," and, "Filet Mignon, Medium Well." I get the watch with a laser, the exploding gum, the pen gun featured in every spy flick, an electromagnetic pulse device disguised as a small pair of airpods, a can of spray paint. I run to my berthing and grab the purse I had on the mission, which contains a passport and a .22 handgun. I change out of the gown into regular clothes and put a few spares into a bag.

I sneak out with my bag of gadgets and spray paint the

camera lenses in the hall near the trash chute, so they cannot see what I am doing. I sneak into the back of the kitchen and find an airtight trunk used for transporting food long distances. I bring it over to the trash chute and balance it on the edge. I place my bag of supplies inside and climb in and fasten the top on as best I can from the inside. I rock my weight to tip it over the edge and slide down at a sharp angle and pray there is some cushion at the bottom.

After about ten seconds of sliding I slam into the dumpster, cushioned as hoped by other loosely placed trash, and wait inside the box rather uncomfortably, for three hours, using the oxygen supply to keep me alive, and enduring the building temperature making it hotter than a honeymoon hotel. I'm glad this thing is airtight, otherwise I'd be breathing acrid, decaying food gases for hours and therefore sick as a dog passing peach pits.

The nurse checked on me moments before my escape and only checks every three or four hours, so I should be fine. Also, the likelihood of them guessing my current location fast enough, even if they find me missing, is very low; there is no footage of my escape, and I have no GPS to track me anymore. The platform beneath me starts moving.

Fifteen minutes later it stops and I feel myself being slid onto another platform. I can hear the faint sound of garbage men doing their thing. Then I suddenly realize that the truck compacts trash. The arms will throw the bin's contents in and a loud hydraulic press will crush everything down, me included.

I feel the lift as the arms of the truck carry the dumpster into the air. I pop open the top and lift myself out, gadget bag in hand. The bin I am in starts to tip over towards the hole in the roof of the truck. I leap out towards the edge.

Having been completely motionless for several days, both in an actual coma, and then in a fake coma, then stuck in a box for three hours, my muscles do not perform with the same reliability I normally enjoy.

I end up missing the edge and falling into the truck's dump hole. I scream as loudly as I can, hoping my voice rises above the noise of the machine. The bin is emptied, bits raining down on me, and the walls of the truck start pressing towards me.

I scream in French, "Stop this now! I am inside the compactor!"

At least I am pretty sure I said that. Well, it worked and the guy in the driver's seat heard me and halted. Two men climb up and look down at me in bewilderment. They help me out of the pit of trash.

One of them speaks English.

"I went to pull something out of the dumpster and fell in and hit my head and went unconscious until this moment"

"Incredible," he says. I tell him a whole story about how it all happened. He and his colleague nod along as I tell it, asking me questions along the way.

They believe me. The men kindly take me in to their cabin, despite my horrid smell, place me in the middle of the cab between them and drive towards the city.

"What happened to your eye?" says the one on the right, who speaks English, pointing at the bandage I have over my left eye.

"I poked myself with a kitchen tool while making dinner," I say.

"Ouch. Sounds painful," he says.

"Yes, it was," I say.

"This dumpster is so far away from the city, I wonder how

you got out here?" he asks.

"I walked for hours to find this dumpster. I really thought my wedding ring would be in there. I lost it last week and I was told that this is the dumpster that belongs to the house I was staying at when I misplaced it," I say.

"Interesting. We have never been able to figure out how this trash gets here," says guy on left. "The bin just appears here full every week, and there are no buildings around anywhere, just this track that carries the bin. We've never seen this before. Do you know where it leads?"

"I supposed it came from the rich family house up in the mountains, and they have some sort of underground railroad to carry their garbage out from the house. I was a guest at that house when I lost my ring, and I was told this is the dumpster where they would have thrown out their trash," I say.

"How fricking rich would you have to be to have a railroad for your rubbish?" and he laughs hysterically for a few moments. I smile, hoping they are buying it, but not caring that much if they don't.

We get into town and they let me out on a bank of the River L'isere in Grenoble. I thank them for the help.

Part A was a success. QF has no way of knowing where I am and no idea how to track me down. Poor Jean Jacques has two rogue agents now. The question is, how in the hell will I figure out how to connect up with Wade?

Chapter 34

Jean Jacques

*"*Mr. Girard! Please come to ICU right away!" yells one of the nurses into the Mind Booth, ignoring the confinement protocols. *This must be very bad.*

I break into a near sprint towards ICU. The nurse fills me in: "Teska has vanished!"

I get to the ICU. The doctors, Dimitri, hospital staff all stand there aggrieved.

"Have you checked her room?" I yell.

"Yes, sir," one answers.

"The Exercise Rooms? Bathrooms? Lounges? Closets?" I ask, frantic.

"All of them, sir. We swept every inch of the base. She's not here," says a hospital worker.

"Check the hallway cam footage!" I say.

We run to a monitor in the closest office. I punch in my access. Hallway cameras are black. I move into the hallway and check a camera. Black spray paint covers the lens.

She spray painted it. That does it. Seals it. Teska's escaped, intentionally. She wasn't in a coma. She faked it, so we'd remove her devices for the MRI. She knew it and went through with it, posing as a catatonic victim. Dear Lord. Now we have two rogue agents and three operatives in police custody in a small town in Wyoming. I get dizzy. The overwhelm of it. I've been in the Mind Booth for a week, sleeping almost not at all. I don't know if I can withstand another major setback.

I steel myself and say, "Gather the strategists and meet me in the conference room in five minutes."

"Yes, sir," says Dimitri.

I run to the Mind Booth and tell John Crutcher to stay on Wade. We have a problem as Wade times two.

I head to my office and sit down at my desk and try calm myself. I take a few deep breaths and gather my wits. I walk into the conference room two minutes early. Everyone is there.

"Teska has taken an unauthorized leave from QuadFilium. She has no GPS trackers, ocular or audio feed. She is on her own," I say.

"Sir, may I venture...?" asks Dimitri.

"Of course," I interrupt. "Say it."

"I noticed missing items in my stores of spy gadgets and custom weapons. It appears she took dozen things," says Dimitri.

Kris Connelly pipes in, "Okay, so she has a survival kit with her, big deal."

"There are two things she took that have GPS chips installed," Dimitri smiles.

"How long have you known?" I ask, getting angry that he didn't say anything sooner.

"I noticed it on the way over here, a minute ago," says Dimitri

I activate a new team of operatives to deploy and find Teska by tracking the GPS signals in the pen gun and so-called James Bond watch she took from Dimitri's supplies.

Ashkay pulls up the map with a small glowing blip. Her location. She's moving through the city of Grenoble. Both signals come from the same spot.

A team of three, assigned the name Delta Two, fires via the

underground rail. They land in the vehicle bay on the outskirts of the city. They drive into town and park outside a hotel from where the signals emit. They are dressed in plain clothes and armed with tranquilizer guns.

"Go straight for the target. Walk in the hotel like you're guests and kick down the door to the room she's in," I say, not wanting to lose opportunity. We watch their feeds as they enter the hotel lobby. They head for the elevator. Since the GPS only shows a top-down view, we cannot tell which floor she's on. It's a five-story building. We only know that she is in the northeast corner of one of the floors.

"Floor one is the lobby and restaurant. No rooms. Each of you take a different floor from two through four and hit the room that corresponds to the signal, at the same time. If no joy, head to the fifth floor and break in all together. Hurry!" I say.

Chapter 35
Teska

I sit in a hotel room on the fifth floor. I hear a loud bang on the floor just below me. It only takes me a moment: QuadFilium operatives. They must have a GPS signal from something I took. GPS doesn't show altitude, only a top-down, two-dimensional view. They don't know which floor I am on. Right room. Wrong floor. My luck gives me a small head start. I have thirty seconds to get out of here before they bust into my room. I'll need to ditch this stuff and figure a way out of this building. Stairs? Elevator? Nope. I look out the window and see a fire escape. I move to my bag. I grab the EMP and stick it in a metal kettle from the kitchen stove in case it also has an embedded GPS. I put the lid on and put it in my bag, leaving the other spy gadgets in the room. I climb out the window and head down the fire escape, trying to be light-footed despite the clangy vibrations when I jump onto each landing. I'm down to the second floor when I hear the *thump*. They just kicked in the door to the room I was in.

I make it to ground floor. I run and look back and see two operatives looking at me from the fifth floor fire escape window.

"Teska! Wait!" says Helena, a Danish operative who I trained with. I ignore her and run faster. I glance back again and see her and two other agents leap landing to landing down the fire escape. Two of them are much faster than me.

I turn corners and wend my way through the roads and

alleys between shops in Grenoble. This part of the city is not tight, small, crowded streets like other European towns. More open and wide, fewer holes to hide in. I am at best thirty seconds ahead of them. I turn a corner and see a man. He carries some food out the back of a restaurant. He throws it in the garbage can and goes back inside. I catch the closing door and jump inside. The man notices and yelps in French, "You can't come in here!"

The door closes behind me. I face him and say, "I'm being chased by some men, please help me hide in here."

Chivalry... please.

We are in a foyer between the restaurant kitchen and the exit. Mops and brooms, a shelf with cleaning supplies. The mingled smell of wet mops and delicious food.

"What?" he asks.

"Those men are chasing me." I say, frantic, helpless.

"Oh my God... we need to call the police."

"One of the men is a cop. It won't help," I say out of breath.

"Why are they chasing you?" he asks.

"They're drunk and horny," I say.

His eyes furrow. He looks to the side. Then looks at me. He nods, "I'll help you hide, come with me."

He takes me upstairs to a small room above the restaurant. It looks like a teenager's bedroom. An unmade bed with a faded red comforter, a small desk with a laptop, a pile of books on a shelf, and some mugs with tea bag tags hanging out. Clothes on the floor and a lounge chair. A couple posters on the wall. The bathroom is open, and the light is on.

"I apologize for the state of my room. I'm so sorry, I never have guests, and," he sighs, "I have been lazy..."

"It's fine, monsieur, thank you so much. I'm so scared.

Thank you," I say.

"No problem, mademoiselle, please rest and catch your breath," he says as he takes the dirty clothes off the lounge chair.

"You are so kind," I say.

"I need to check on the restaurant. I'll come back in a little while. You'll be safe here."

I sit on the lounge chair, catch my breath, start to brainstorm how to deal with this. They haven't broken down the front doors of the restaurant, so I assume dumping the tracking devices and EMP air pods into my tin pot worked on any GPS. I have no idea if the air pods EMP will work to disable Wade's devices, but it's worth a try.

The kind man returns with tea and snacks.

He asks, "Where are you headed?"

"I was staying in the hotel up the street. These men broke into my room. They knew exactly where I was staying. I don't feel safe there. I'm just an American girl on vacation."

He nods. I nod with the puppy dog eyes of a damsel in distress.

He thinks for a moment and says, "You can stay here if you like while you decide what you want to do."

"Oh, I couldn't impose on you like that. You have been so kind already—"

"Nonsense. I don't even sleep here every night. Only when I have to open the restaurant early. I live at home with my family. Please, feel free. I'm sure you would do the same for me," he says.

"Oh, thank you so much!" I say, and I get up and kiss him on the cheek. He blushes a nervous nod.

He shows me around, provides me with a towel and fresh

linens, and says he'll bring up more snacks and things to drink in case I need them.

"What happened to your eye?" he asks.

"I poked it with something. It's almost better though."

"Okay, call me if you need anything," he says.

"I left my phone in the room. I have no way to call anyone. I feel pretty unsafe without one, actually. I should probably go out to a store and get a disposable one," I say.

"Well. Safety's most important right now. I'll go and get one for you, okay?" he offers.

"You have been so nice. I will figure out a way to repay you as soon as I can," I say. I pull out some francs and fan them. "I don't have much but it should be enough for a phone." I hand them to him.

He leaves to get a burner phone. I look outside the window down at the street. A homeless man looks through the garbage can where that my savior dumped food. He pulls out a chunk of something and starts nibbling. I'm a bit grossed out and look further down the street. A couple walks together. A man smokes a cigarette, a couple of teenagers are gossiping.

I realize I have been deprived of simple life moments, sheltered away for the last year in a military compound. It's not a bad thing. It's just something that is, something I've been part of. An intense military mode, non-stop, so all of this, this "ordinary" life has become unfamiliar to me. I'd forgotten what it was like.

My life has been so regimented and every little thing so meaningful. The meaningless, unimportant nothings have been absent. I see them now and I feel outside. Like this world is a fishbowl and I am looking at through refracting glass and water.

I inventory remaining assets. A few items of clothing, the EMP in the kettle, the .22, five throwing knives, fifty-six dollars and a toiletries bag. I get up and walk over to the bathroom mirror. I have not really seen myself in almost a week. I have a bandage over my eye and seepage has made its way to the surface.

I peel slow and gentle and rinse my eye. I open it and look. This is someone else's. The white part is completely red, but the center is light brown. My natural eye color is blue. I now have one brown eye and one blue eye. I don't know that I've ever seen that before. I've seen people with green and blue, but not brown and blue. Vision in the new eye is blurry. The pupil is dilated. Things look twice as bright in that eye. My new friend returns with a phone.

"Do you need anything else?" With my bad eye closed, I decline. I thank him too many times. My luck has held.

I sleep through the night, a sound sleep. I wake to noises of people walking outside and the gentle chatter and footsteps of town life. I smell fresh baked goods and croissants in the morning air. I'm starving.

I'm sure the QuadFilium team searched every possible place. They came up empty.

Now... how to get to Wade...

Chapter 36
Jean Jacques

Delta Two team returns, no Teska. Delta One team stands at the ready, close to Jeffrey's apartment house, and waits for Wade to surface.

I need some rest. I'm burning the candle at both ends. More, I'm terrified about what's happening to my group, my family, my team. Things are falling apart, like my limbs are being ripped off my body. Things could not be any worse.

I haven't even spoken to my wife in a month, and my daughter in a week. I have five missed calls from Frances this week.

I walk to my office, sit back at my desk, and sigh. I look at the ceiling and relax my body and close my eyes. After a minute, I grab a glass and pour myself a Scotch. It feels good going down my throat. Stings just enough.

I should call my wife. Might as well give it a try.

"Hello," she says.

"Hello dear, I'm so sorry. I've been 24/7 on a mission. It's ongoing but I didn't want to ignore your calls. Is everything okay?"

"Yes and no. I know you are busy, but I talked to my therapist. I had a bit of a breakthrough, but we need to talk in person. When can we do that?" she asks.

"How urgent is it? To be honest, right now we have the most pressing and life-threatening issues I've ever faced in QuadFilium's twenty-four year history," I say.

"What's happening?" she asks, knowing that we are on an encrypted line.

"Two rogue agents left QF unauthorized and are on the run," I say.

"What?" That's never happened before." she asks.

"Never," I say.

"I can't believe it. Who?" she asks as she knows many of the members.

"Wade and Teska," I say. Knowing the second name slaps. She'll appreciate the truth, though, rather than me dancing. She's going to know soon enough anyways. There's an awkward pause on the other end of the line.

"Oh my. Together?" she asks.

"No. Separate. First Wade blew mid mission, two days ago. Teska left the compound yesterday."

"She did? How's that even possible?" she asks.

"She spray-painted the cameras and went through the trash chute," I say.

"Unbelievable... but you have devices to track her? And Wade?" says Frances.

"Long story, but no. We aren't getting their signals," I say.

"Why would they do that? she says.

"I have my suspicions but I don't have the time to explain them all right now," I say.

"Of course," she says. She sounds caring, less standoffish. I think, this is the only real conversation we have had in months. It's not about us, our family, our relationship. And, it's something we both care about.

"We still need to talk soon. Please, make that happen," she says.

"Of course, honey," I say. We hang up.

I'm back in the Mind Booth. I'm starting to think it should be called the Mind Fuck.

"Did we get the goddamn operatives out of jail yet?" I bark.

"Yes sir," says John Crutcher.

"Good. How?" I ask

"They escaped," he responds.

I hold my breath.

"It was actually pretty easy. They all had bandaids on their backs, the ones that Dimitri made to help on these scenarios. The cops cuffed them for transport, they grabbed their handcuff keys, undid the locks and bolted when they moved them from the holding cell to the main block," says John.

"They ran out of there! Just like that?" I ask.

"Yes, sir. Just like that," he says.

"Are they clear? Where are they now?" I ask.

"Clear. On their way to meet up with Delta One team in Austin. ETA fifty minutes," he says.

Chapter 37
Wade

Time to get hold of Jeffrey. And somehow avoid a well-trained and effective team of at least three QuadFilium operatives. They'll have every single aspect of Jeffrey's dwelling cased and staked. More like six operatives now. I doubt the Wyoming Andy Griffith was able to hold onto them at the local police department.

Not to mention I'm still bugged and wearing eye and head gear to prevent detection. I'd be spotted if I attempt to waltz into Jeffrey's apartment and knock on his door.

Took a cab to Austin. I have to find where Jeffrey lives. I walk into a café and steal an unlocked phone off a table and run out. Too fast for the owner to notice and chase. Two blocks down, I hide in another café. I search the web to find where he lives. It's easier than I expected. I type in Austin White Pages and with a few clicks I find eight entries for Jeffrey Miles in Austin. Only one age range fits. His address is listed. I type his name into Google. Jeffrey Miles... Austin. I tap on images and see a whole bunch of Jeffreys. There's one with him and Teska.

They look happy. She, child-like happy. Contented. Jeffrey is a decent looking bloke. Aside from big ears that stick out a little, he's a handsome guy, wholesome. Neat brown hair, button down shirt. The stance of a software engineer or something. A bit vanilla, but a well-kept boke.

I run back to the café where I took the phone. Out front on the street is my victim. He calls on someone else's phone. He paces, agitated. A girl stands nearby with her arms crossed. The phone lender. He looks up and sees me and yells, "That's him!" and runs towards me.

"Sorry mate!" I say, as I set his phone down where I stand and bolt in the other direction.

"What the fuck?!" he says. He stops, confused, and bends down for his phone.

"Fuck you very much!" he yells. I reflect that was a clever way to say both ideas in one phrase.

I hail a cab and direct the driver a block away from the apartment address. I look around trying to figure out how I am supposed to suss out his place with QF crawling all over it. I see a rooftop restaurant on a building and head over.

I come out the elevator to a wide-open restaurant, five-star by the looks of it. Fancy half-tuxed waiters carry bottles wrapped in white cloth. Well-dressed patrons sit at tables spaced along its edges with nice views of the Austin skyline. A reception desk with an over-groomed older gentleman in a full tux next to an even more impressive woman with glossy healthy hair. Brushed at least 200 times, no doubt.

"Can I help you, sir?" asks the nice concierge man, taken aback by my hoodie and glasses. I stand out like dog's balls here.

"I'm cool. I'm supposed to meet up with a group."

I look over to my left and see a large party at a long table with one seat empty. They sit on the side of the building I need.

"Name?"

"Actually, that's them over there," I pretend to wave at them with a big smile and start to head over, "I can make my way, no worries."

"Umft…"

I walk past him towards the table. He doesn't stop me but follows.

I stand near them but peer over the edge and look at the Jeffrey's apartment building and case the scene. The entrance. The garage. The parked cars on the street. Passersby.

"Sir?" asks the kind concierge gentleman.

"That's not the gender title I prefer," I say.

He blushes annoyance.

"I'm sorry. And may I ask which you prefer?"

"Actually, that you assume my gender makes me not want to eat here. I'm leaving."

"I'm so sorry, Si—, I mean. I'm sorry for assuming..."

I walk towards the exit. He follows behind.

"We're very inclusive here... ah... come back any time," he says as I push the elevator door. It opens. I enter without a word.

I walk out onto the street and hail another cab to head back to Harold's place.

"I knew you'd be back!" says Harold.

"Thanks, mate! Cool if I crash here again?"

"Absolutely!"

Harold and Maude have been amazing hosts. Feeding me well, letting me use the bunker. We sit down at the dining table.

"What's your plan, Wade?" asks Harold.

"Well, I gotta talk to this bloke but there are six trained operatives waiting for me. Several dozen cameras, watching, day in and day out, 24/7. All waiting to identify me, incapacitate me, and bring me back to the base where we work. Makes it a bit hard to have a chat with him, which is what I need to do."

"Hm," says Harold, as he looks pensive, considers the issue, and tries to hide his excitement to be part of this. "Do you have any ideas?" he asks.

"I was thinking of attaching a bungie cord to my ass, run up to him, give him a big hug and shoot backwards to wherever I came from. That's as far as I got," I say.

They laugh. Harold slaps his knee.

He presents an idea, "Why don't I just go and talk to him? Catch him after work?"

He pauses, a mischievous smile.

"I want in on this mission," he says.

"Crikey! That's brilliant! They'll have him bugged so it might be best to hand him a note rather than talk. The note will need to convince him. You could hand it to him and then he and I could meet up."

"Sounds good to me, I love it!" says Maude.

"Yeah! I'm in!" says Harold.

They push me sheets paper and pens. I head down to my bunker and start writing.

The letter reads:

Dear Jeffrey,

My name is Wade and this is a very important note regarding Teska Lando that will change your life. You must read this in private with no one around. Do not point your phone camera, either front or back, towards this note. Please go to a safe place and read it.

Do not read it aloud or to anyone else.

Teska is alive and I can prove it. Her death was faked after the hotel room incident two years ago. Keep reading this note and I will prove to you that it's not fake.

The last time you ever saw Teska was in a hotel called the

Hampton Inn in a town two hours north of Austin called Stephenville. She saw you in a room with an underdressed woman, you in your jocks and a robe. She left, staggered out of the hotel and refused to listen to your pleas.

You returned home to find her gone. You were then informed she died driving her car off the road. It caught fire and blew up. You were told it was a suicide. You never saw her body because it was not her in the car. Her teeth were extracted and used to help 'identify' the body with dental records. Her death was fake, a setup, and I can prove it. This is no scam. I'm risking my life to tell you this stuff.

I will tell you a few things about your relationship that she told me that there would be no way of me knowing about unless she was alive today.

She said her arm always fell asleep while cuddling with you. You have a tattoo of a fish at the bottom of your stomach, cuz you're a Pisces. Whenever you told her you loved her in the first few months, she would cry a little. You guys made each other 'pinky dinky' swear, which was your sacred oath to each other that you weren't lying. And the night she left the apartment, for the last time, the gun and the cat were missing because she took them with her. Her cat's name is Spider. I've spent some time with the little rascal. The most notable thing about Spider is that she likes to bite men's hands but she never bites females' hands.

You might think that I could have somehow learned all this stuff some other way, and this is a ruse to play on your loss and take advantage of you. I can assure you, it is not. To prove that, I want you to check your shoes and see if you can find a foreign object, a small electronic device placed in the heel or in the lining. This was put there because I defected from a clandestine group who setup this whole charade. They know I might try to contact *you and placed it there. They have bugged you, are tracking you, and have planted cameras and other surveillance items all over your apartment, your stuff and your car. This is so they can catch me when I attempt to contact you.*

I believe you to be innocent in that hotel room that night. It was a setup and a frame job. I intend to hear your story.

If you want to ever see Teska again, which I have not yet worked out how to do, follow my instructions.

They can hear everything around you. They can see anything your phone camera points towards, front or back. They can see every text you send or receive, every email you have and every social media private message you share. There are concealed cameras in your house, watching you.

Do exactly as I say. Make sure the bug you removed from your shoe goes back in the shoe. Leave work at 5:30 pm today. Look and act normal, business as usual. Get in your car. There is a car wash two blocks from your place of business called Jim's Super Shine. Pull in and have your car go through the wash. Order a full wax job so it takes a while.

Go inside the building and into the restroom. Lift out the rubbish bag and find another bag underneath it. In it you will find shoes, a wig, glasses, a jacket and a pillow to stuff in your shirt, to add weight. Put these all on as a disguise. Place your shoes, phone and jacket in the rubbish bin under the existing bag.

Outside in the lot, close to cars being dried by carwashers, will be a white SUV with a key inside. The SUV will have a white chalk mark on the driver side front tire. Walk over to it, get inside and drive away. The agency will not recognize you. They will believe you're still in the building per their GPSes and will not be alerted to your escape.

If the stake-out team gets worried and goes in to check on you, we will already be talking and discussing this matter and trying to help each other solve this mystery that's ruined your life.

In the car will be directions to a safe location where we can meet and talk.

I'll be waiting for you there, expecting you around 6:00 p.m.
Wade

I read the note aloud to both Maude and Harold and I tweak it up based on their suggestions. I hand the note to Harold and say, "Okay, mate, we are going to head into the city tomorrow morning, rent an SUV and a hotel room, buy some supplies and set up the whole operation to go down when he gets off work."

Harold, mission-eager, agrees. I strategize in detail how Harold will wait for Jeffrey when he leaves his apartment and follow him to work. Then will run into him at work and slip him the note while holding up his *shhh* finger and walk away.

We'll head back to a hotel room rented in Harold's name and wait for Jeffrey to knock on our door. We expect he might carry a weapon in case of a con. It's Texas, after all.

"One condition that I ask, in order to be part of this," says Harold.

"Yes?" I reply.

"I want to be there for the conversation," he says.

"Mate. I cannot allow that. I am incapable of having a sensitive and important meeting with someone in the room listening." I say.

"Why?" asks Maude.

"I want to witness history! And be part of it," says Harold.

"I know, I know. And I doggone wish I didn't get all weird

and tongue-tied when someone else is in the room. But the truth is, mate, when I am having an important conversation with someone, life-changing and meaningful, where the slightest wrongly timed answer or slight eye shift could spell total failure, I can only do it alone or else I stutter and botch it up. I get self-conscious. Please, guys. It's my biggest weakness. I swear. Maybe a mental illness, I dunno. I'd love to include you guys. You both are my new best friends. I pinky dinky swear."

This closes them. They concede. I'll be alone with Jeffrey on the first conversation.

We wake early the next day and head into town. Harold drops me off a couple blocks from Jeffrey's apartment. Harold parks nearby but not too close. He has a photo of Jeffrey handy to spot him and follow him to work. I'm carrying Maude's phone so he can call me once he's on the way to Jeffrey's place of employment.

I assume QF operatives are engaged in immersion tech and blending in, perhaps at the workplace and in the apartment complex. This poses a problem if they see the old man slip a note to Jeffrey. Triple red alert.

A call from Harold, "I'm on him. Two cars back. So, he can't spot me following him."

"Great work, Harold! Not too worried about him spotting you, but better safe than sorry."

"Hey! I know my spy moves, Wade! I've been training for this my whole life!"

"Right-ee-oh, matey!"

"He's pulling over. Looks like he's going into a parking lot. We're at some office building. I'm pulling in. The address is 147 North Lamar Blvd," says Harold.

"Copy, call me when you are done."

I coached Harold how to run into Jeffrey in the company bathroom and ensure no one else is in there. Hold up his *shhh* finger, hand him the note, and walk away. On the outside of the note I wrote, "Read this right away. Show no one. Jeffrey's eyes only."

Twenty minutes later I get a call from Harold: "Done, Captain!"

"Great work! Pick me up."

He does. Harold describes the note delivery, "You'd be so proud of me if you could have seen how slick I was. I walked around the office. People kept asking if I needed help. I said 'no.' Then, Jeff asked. I faked a gimpy leg and asked if he could help me find the men's room. When he got me in there, I did the *shhh* finger, handed him the note and left. He stood looking at the note bewildered. I'm sure he read it right away!"

I smile and compliment Harold's immersion tactics and smooth improv. What an asset. "Well done you old hound!" Harold giggles with happiness. We arrive at the hotel room, rent an SUV and gather needed supplies. At 1645 we head over to the car wash and leave the SUV where I want it, key in the car, chalk-marked tire. In the car wash bathroom, I take out the trash liner, place the bag of stuff described in the letter, and replace the rubbish liner with its contents back over the bag.

We head over to the hotel where we expect to meet Jeffrey and settle in. I station Harold in the lobby so that Jeffrey recognizes him and adds a sense of familiarity.

It's now 1745, and if everything goes according to plan, Jeffrey is in the car wash bathroom changing while staked out operatives wait outside in a car.

1805 rolls around and I hear a timid but hopeful knock at the door.

"Come in," I say, having left it unlocked. I'm across the room.

Jeffrey opens the door, pokes his head in, and checks the scene. His eyes rivet on me.

"I apologize for my odd look," indicating my hoodie and glasses. "I'll explain why I have these on and you'll understand. I'm Wade," I say.

Jeffrey, nervous, nods. I knew he'd come. He's depressed and willing to die to find a shred of hope about Teska. I banked on it. He enters with his ridiculous disguise, the fake fat belly, a wig, a hat, glasses and brand-new, too big, shoes.

"Jeffrey, you don't need to wear the disguise right now if you don't want to," I say. He sheds most of it. Still a good-looking bloke, actually. I should have expected, considering where Teska lands on the one to ten scale. I hand him a warm burger, "Go ahead. It's your dinner time. We want you distraction-free for this conversation," I say.

"Thank you," he finally says something.

"No worries," I say.

He looks around, less terrified. "This seems really weird... like a *Black Mirror* episode," says Jeffrey. "But you knew things Teska would never tell anyone she didn't trust. If you're this elaborate to steal money, you'd deserve it for all the homework you put in," he says and smiles a little. I return it.

"What's all that...?" he indicates the hoodie and glasses.

I answer, "This may sound like *Black Mirror*, but imbedded in my eye and my ear are live-feed audio-visual devices that stream data to the agency I've been working for. They also have a GPS on me. I suspect you found one in your shoe, yeah?"

He nods.

"I wear metal-lined clothing and glasses to block the

signal," I say.

His eyebrows pop up for moment, and he looks to the side.

"This is the weirdest thing that's ever happened to me."

"I know. Bear with me, we'll sort it out. First things first. Can you please tell me what happened that night?" I ask, as he wraps up his burger.

Jeffrey says, "I was on a business trip in Stephenville and I get this call from the front desk of the hotel. A lovely lady on the other end of the line says that I've earned a complimentary one-hour massage as the 10,000th guest of Hampton Hotels that year. Then she apologizes and says the only available time over the next week would be in the next hour.

"I was happy to get a free massage, so I agree. A very good-looking woman shows up with a massage table and sets it up in the corner of the hotel room. She tells me to keep on my underwear on and lie face down. Nothing unusual. Standard for any massage. She works the massage for about half an hour when I hear a knock on the door. Without thinking much of it, I roll off the table, throw on a robe and walk over, and open the door. Tesk's there. I'm shocked, surprised, and happy. Teska goes rigid. She looks at me in my robe and underwear. She looks past me. Then it happened. A look of shock, horror and despair on her face like I'd never seen. I look back, and the woman masseuse has nothing on but a sexy bra and panties. Full-on lingerie. I'm stunned. I turn and Teska walks away down the hall. I chase her, beg her to listen to me. Just like you said in your note. She gets away from me and runs down the stairs. I run back to my room to put some clothes on. Something I've regretted every second for the past twelve months. I should have followed Teska even if I was only in underwear.

"In my room, the woman has on her clothes and is packing

up.

"I yell at her while I throw my pants and shirt on asking her why the fuck she was undressed? She gives me some bullshit about freedom of movement. I don't argue. I run outside, jump in my car, and hit the ignition. I put it in drive, but it's dragging. I check and all four tires are flat. I know then it was a setup. The whole thing. I call Teska over 250 times the next two hours. I manage to get an Uber but they don't come for thirty-five minutes, being out in Stephenville. The cab company says an hour. I call the cops and report my slashed tires. They say it'll be over in two hours before they can inspect. But I'm already in the Uber by that point trying to get to our apartment."

I hand Jeffrey a glass of water. He drains it.

"I get there and she's gone. So's the cat and some of her stuff. I notice the gun is also. I call the Austin cops. Austin PD arrives and I tell them everything... the massage lady, the whole thing. We call the concierge of the Hampton Inn and they don't have a massage service, and don't give complimentary massages to anyone. Outside massage companies can come at customer request.

"The cops think I'm cheating on my fiancée who they think slashed my tires before she left. I argue the massage lady was a scam and a setup. They don't believe me. Men on business trips hire personal masseuses all the time or just hit the strip mall massage parlors and often conclude in pricey happy endings. They make more money."

Jeffrey stands and paces. I listen...

"A few days later news of her death comes. She wrote a suicide note, citing my infidelity as the final straw. It was definitely her handwriting.

"I'm not suicidal, but I was close. Teska was the best thing that ever happened to me. I couldn't have been happier or more loyal to anyone. I never cheated on her. Why would I?"

I nod agreement.

"The suicide note, my alleged infidelity... the cops dropped it. They were unwilling to help. I tried to explain the whole thing was some sort of a weird-ass con job. People, including some in my family, began to think I was crazy. I was the only one who believed me. I stopped talking about it kinda knowing I'd never resolve it.

"Then I got your note. The tone was genuine. The information accurate. Someone else in the world didn't think I was a fucking wack job."

I answer, "I got all that, mate. You ain't no wack job. You just confirmed what I've suspected all along."

"Is it true? Teska is actually alive?" he asks.

"Yes. But she's in a coma."

Chapter 38
Jean Jacques

"What the fuck do you mean you lost him?!" I yell.

"He entered into the car wash and never came out. After an hour, we went in. His car was done and waiting. He shed all of his trackable material, his shoes, phone and jacket," says Delta Two team leader.

"How did you guys miss that?" I ask.

"Wade must have gotten him a message that we never saw or heard. There's no chance that Wade has come within 100 feet of this guy. We had agents directly on him 24/7... phone, shoes, jacket bugged. His apartment is covered in cameras—"

"I know!" I say. "Goddammit! He's made contact with Jeffrey. I tracked Jeffrey for months after Teska's scopulus. His family tried to have him committed to a psych ward because he was ranting on and on about never cheating on Teska, and how he was framed. That guy went nuts after Teska killed herself. Now he and Wade... together?! Who knows where it will go?"

"Copy, sir," says the team leader.

My phone rings. It's Frances. I send it to voice mail. She calls again ten seconds later. Again, voice mail. I'm worried. She knows I get back to her as soon as possible if I'm in the middle of something urgent. She calls again.

"I'm sorry everyone. I need to take this call. Come up with a solution by the time I get back!" I say.

I go to my office and take her call. By now, I'm nervous something bad has happened, maybe Carmen.

"Frances, what's happening?" I say.

"This is not Frances," says a deep, raspy, dignified, and 100% familiar English voice on the other end of the line. "This is Alistair Watson."

I freeze in shock, then hit the record button.

"Where is Frances? Why do you have her phone?" I ask.

"I'm entertaining her. And your daughter, Carmen... so pretty they are."

My heart stops.

"I know about your clandestine shenanigans. Grown men playing toy soldiers, so boring. You are responsible for violating my compound and dispatching my favorite decoy. You made an abattoir of my entire Los Angeles distribution center and a number of my premier clients in LA. You've been... *very*... *disruptive!* You will do exactly as I say, or I dare say, my men will ravage them with pleasure before they enter Elysium Fields. Not to worry. We *recycle* everything."

I fall to my knees and vomit on the floor. My body shakes out of control.

"P... P... Proof of life..." I stutter.

A moment later I hear mumbles and whimpers. Both voices. It's them.

"What do you want? *Anything*," I blurt.

"Well! It's Christmas time for me then isn't it? Oh that's right, you celebrate Hanukkah. Nevertheless, I'll make a list and check it twice. Let me see,... to start: stand down all active measures against my organization. Add two-billion dollars as recompense. Lay bare the location of your base. And most important, I want the man who broke into my compound, dead or breathing. That should co-opt you sufficiently..."

"Done. Please don't hurt them," I say. Sobbing.

231

"I'm a gentleman, aren't I? As a show of good faith, you will give me the coordinates to your base. Now. Don't tinker…" demands Alistair.

"45.187 latitude and 5.003 longitude," I rattle off.

"I'll call you in an hour. Oh. Would you be so accommodating as to place a flare outside your base? So less cumbersome…" he says.

"I will," I say. He hangs up. I stand frozen. *How did he discover us? How the fuck?*

I activate the emergency alarm and pick up the PA, "All crew, I repeat, *ALL* crew. *Code Red.* Drop what you are doing and go to the Commons for an emergency briefing in two minutes at 1410. Be there!"

All muster up in the lounge. People note my puffy red face, bloodshot eyes, and vomit-stained coat. I don't give a shit.

"Officers and crew be advised. This is a Code Red. The secrecy of our location has been compromised and is known by Alistair Watson. It's expected he will attack in twenty minutes or less. We are evacuating to secondary base immediately.

"The following actions, without delay. All crew pack one duffle of belongings, write your name on it, and be on transport bay below in ten minutes. Security will initiate data destruction protocol and bring backups. We will travel to secondary base where you will set up and man your posts. Dismissed! Go!"

Everyone snaps in unison toward the door. Like an hourglass of sand, they pour through the doorway and down the hallways. I run to my office and grab my phone and wallet. I open my safe and grab The Kit, a small, locked box of items required for a Code Red.

I run to my dwelling, grab a duffle bag and fill it with personal effects, toiletries, a few other odds and ends that fit. I pause and press my face into my pillow and scream as loud as humanly possible, until I feel my vocal chords tear, and my lungs empty. I pull away. There are two wet spots where my eyes were. I grab my duffle and run.

At the transport bay dozens have already assembled.

I go to the train car, where the throng waits, and open the door allowing them in one at a time. I count as people enter. No one can be left behind. Alistair could bomb or invade the base.

There are nine operatives off base, plus two runaways and two human resource people in China on the recruitment of Yun Fei, including Brett. A total of 106 QuadFilium crew, thirteen off base. There should be ninety-three on this train.

I keep count. The last person enters as I count 92. One person is still on the base.

"You," I say, pointing at a group of crew in the train car, "I need fourteen able-bodied to step forward. In an instant, fourteen muster on the transport bay.

"I need a fast errand."

I send one person for each of the thirteen off-base crew members to go to their respective berthings and retrieve obvious necessities and return. They have six minutes. The remaining crew member I send to find the one who's missing.

I gather the council of strategists to the front car, Kris, Hiedi, John, Ashkay and Dimitri.

"You guys stay here. We need to plan. I'll be right back," I say.

I run off the platform, upstairs, to the vehicle bay. I grab a flare and run to the training paddock, which is outside. I see the landscape filled with training equipment, obstacle courses, swimming pools, tracks, and several wide-open fields. I break open the flare and throw it on the tarmac and look up. I hear the faint hum of a distant helicopter, its thumps growing louder. I run back to the train, wondering if I'll ever see this place again.

When I get back to the transport bay, thirteen of the errand team store duffle bags labelled for the off-site crew.

But the member I sent to find the missing person is still gone. I decide to wait one more minute. We do not leave people behind, but I can't risk the lives of the entire crew.

Sick Bay. I sprint up into the compound and break into the infirmary. In bed the remaining crew member watches a movie with headphones. He's ill and in quarantine. I yank him out of bed and tell him that we are Code Red, invasion imminent, and we need to leave now. I grab a blanket and we run. I send him to the transport bay and go to the PA system box on wall. I snatch it and click on.

"Max, I found him. Run to transport bay, right now!"

I drop the PA and sprint. As I enter the transport bay, I can hear the chopper overhead. I run inside the tunnel.

In the lead car, I catch my breath and I look at the strategists. Stares wait for guidance, an explanation, a chance to help.

These are battle-hardened experts. They've seen life from the top down and the bottom down. The worst of man and his best. Trials of life and death, betrayal and loyalty, love and hate. A test of faith that bonds camaraderie and welds a force power that, together, forge through storms of fire.

Now they look at me. Search my face for answers. Hope for understanding.

I begin, "Wade traded info to Alistair to get the bounty off his head. He revealed mine and my family's identity. Wade's the only person who has had the time to make contact with Alistair. He has jeopardized the lives of every member of

QuadFilium, and my family. The order now is: 'Shoot to kill.' "

Chapter 39
Teska

I set up the phone the friendly restauranteur host gave me and test it out. It has some internet functions and otherwise is a basic cell phone. I need to get out of the country and to Texas, urgently. Wade will most likely go there to connect up with Jeffrey. I look through what flights exist out of France and it appears that I can get to Paris where there is a direct flight to Austin.

I have little money but I have the fake passport from the previous mission, naming me Jessica Adams. I need to find a way to get some money, get to Paris and get on the plane to Austin. Right now, the QuadFilium operatives have no possible workable plan. They do not have the manpower to canvas the entire city. Unfortunately, with my blue and brown eye, and my noticeable physique, I stand out, as Wade would say, like dog's balls. The operatives could have spread the word to keep an eye out for me, offering a hefty reward and a contact number, and thus flush me out with many searching. And of course they will be at the airport and train station, looking for me.

I'll need a disguise. Also, if Ashkay is on the ball enough to make me a fake passport that will actually work as a real one, he can probably set up an alert to tell him if the passport ever gets used. I'll need to figure out how to solve that as well. He'll know to look for Jessica Adams.

For now, sunglasses and baggy clothes will have to get me around. I get cleaned up and pack up my things. My friendly

French host gently knocks before conning up the stairs to check on me.

"Thank you again for your incredible generosity and know that I will most definitely repay you in the near future," I say.

"My pleasure. It is a tradition for a classical man to help a damsel in distress. Thank you for choosing me to be your knight in shining armor, and I am sure the karma will figure out a way to repay me if you are not able to. Please, you have no debt to me. I must tell you though. I was offered a substantial reward to provide information as to the whereabouts of a woman of your description. Someone came to my door," he says.

I get nervous, and ask, "And?"

"I played dumb. Claiming to have never seen you," he says.

"You most definitely are my knight in shining armor," I say and I give him another kiss on the cheek. He blushes and ushers me out the back door and waves goodbye, smiling.

I walk down the street keeping my eyes on every human body in as wide a radius as I can see, ensuring with each identity I verify it is not a QuadFilium operative.

Money. How to get some. Hmmm. I think over the various supplies I have and find the small snubnosed .22 revolver in my bag. I check that it's loaded and walk through town, over to the seedier part of the city, hoping to run into some drug dealers, who tend to have extra cash. I see a couple kids running around on a street corner, playing around but also talking to random adults, and watch.

One of the adults walks away from the kids and into a side door of a building. Must be the dealer's operation center. Perfect. I have no qualms stealing money from those fuckers, but smart dealers keep a hefty protection detail handy, especially so close to the street. I'm sure any time that door opens, they pat the guy, or girl, down at gunpoint to make sure there is no threat. Waltzing in there with my .22 is going to simply get the firearm taken away from me. If I try to use it to incapacitate the bodyguard detail, I'll only slow them down. A .22 is weak and unless you hit the exact right spot, doesn't neutralize a strong man. I've even seen a .22 bullet glance off a man's head from a shot thirty feet away. Four or five body guards, themselves armed with 9 millimeters and .38s or even .45s, unless I am Wyatt Earp, they'll jump on me like a duck on a June bug.

I'll need to get past the body guards, assess the scene and improvise how to escape with the loot.

I watch for another hour, gaunt twitchy guys and gals going in, coming out with a small brown paper bag, looking around all shifty-eyed and then heading out into the street like a regular everyday normal motherfucker.

I decide to play my assets. I unbutton my blouse down to the second to last button at my stomach, and place the .22, luckily a snubnose, in the fold under my left breast. Being a size H there's enough of an overhang to hold the gun in place. It's pressing my left one up a bit and throws the balance off. I find a couple of maxi pads and stick them under my right breast to hold that side up as well. Now it feels even. I'm otherwise wearing tight clothing, showing no bulges in the pockets, no weapons, no threat. I hide my stuff and head over to the door.

I walk in. The door guy's eyebrows raise as he swallows, looking me up and down but eyes landing in the middle upper area of my torso. He must be accustomed to seeing ragged, haggard zombies, not healthy fit women. One guy drops something. Door man looks back at the others pointing at me, as if to say, "Do you guys see this chick?"

I say, "I need some meth."

Door guy pats me down but fails to lift my breasts and check under them, however he does not fail to squeeze them and stroke them, same with my ass. I'm again faced with a strong desire to mangle a man's face, and I suppress it.

The dealer looks up at me through an open door, a bald guy who looks like his head has been squashed in a press, wider then it is tall. And he looks so crooked he could swallow a nail and shit out a corkscrew. He welcomes me in with a real million-dollar smile.

Straightening up his posture, he asks, "What can I do for you, madame?"

"I need some meth," I say.

He looks me up and down, up and down, and finally just stares.

"Can I get a discount?" I ask, licking my lips slowly and lifting one leg to the side, like I'm posing at a burlesque show.

"Perhaps...I actually have a coupon that's quite easy to earn." he says.

"How do I earn this coupon?"

He lowers his voice, "Well... you know... if you... play around with me a little bit."

"Sure, but not in front of these goons. Send 'em out?" I wink at him, give him a half smile. The familiar glazed look appears on his face. The one that precedes the careless actions of a dumb man with a boner. He gets up out of his chair and sends the four guards out of the room into the foyer, closing the door behind them.

He looks giddy as he turns back from the door towards me.

I immediately thrust both hands forward, one into his throat and one into his solar plexus. He can't breathe, he can't talk, he's on his knees, hands to his neck, trying to catch his breath or make some noise. With his mouth wide open his head proportions look a little more correct. I pull out my .22 and aim it against his forehead and whisper, "I have no slightest problem spraying your brains all over this floor. I fucking hate drug dealers. So, don't make any noise or I will kill you and then kill your four fat, lazy guards."

Gasping for breath with a red face and eyes tearing in pain, he mouths the words, "What do you want?"

"A huge pile of cash right now in my bag." Talking low so the meatheads out there don't hear me.

"Open your box and hand it over right... the fuck... now," I say in a loud whisper. His eyes show me fear. It must be a lot, and he knows he'll have to either explain this to his boss, or somehow replace the money before he turns it in to him, or else he'll lose some digits or limbs, or his squashed head.

His hesitation tells me he is debating whether to try to disarm me or to go with the flow. I interject his train of thought, "I have killed before and I will happily kill again," He suddenly looks at my eyes and furrows his brows, no doubt noting the brown and blue combo. I guess he's savvy enough about chromosomes to know that I have someone else's eye installed in my head because the brown, blue combo is genetically almost impossible.

This convinces him. He deduces that I must have ripped someone's eye out of their head and got mine replaced, which is itself is some next-level expensive and unavailable medicine. He's not dealing with a fake. He opens the box and empties the cash into a bag.

By now he'll believe anything I say. I pull out a lighter and throw it on top of a shelf too high to access without standing on a chair.

"That lighter is C4 and I can detonate with this small button that I have in my hand," I show him a keychain. "As I walk out of here, say nothing, pretend to be satisfied and happy and let me get all the way out of sight before you say a word. If one of those fuckers comes chasing after me, I'll blow the place up. Let me walk." He nods. I mess up his hair to feign a sexual encounter and walk out. The guards see me with a bag, thinking it's meth. They smile at me. One tips a hat. I leave and power-walk down the street, unharmed, rebuttoning. I get to a safe spot and count my winnings. About 45,000 dollars. Much better than I expected.

I google the nearest travel agency and walk a few blocks to get there. I pay cash for a ticket to Austin via Paris, leaving later that day. I decide on first class as it is an eleven-hour flight, plus I have all this money, why not spoil myself a little?

I walk out with my ticket in hand and flag a cab for the theater district of Grenoble. My flight leaves in five hours.

On the cab ride over I decide to call Jeffrey's phone. I remember his number. I begin to dial it and then realize that Ashkay has Jeffrey's phone bugged and will see this call from France and keep track of it, knowing it's me. He will probably even figure out how to triangulate the coordinates and find my exact location. I decide I can do it and then throw the burner away after.

Chapter 40
Jean Jacques

The whole crew heads to the alternate base. It's a near identical replica to the existing one, a bit smaller. There are four crew members there at all times. They keep it clean and test the equipment. I call ahead and brief them on our arrival. The alternate base in-charge sounds stunned. This has never happened in QuadFilium history. She'd been wondering if her job was even useful.

I call the external teams in the US.

"Team leaders come in," I say.

"Here," they both say.

"All operatives, briefing in three minutes."

"Ten-four," they both say.

"Sir, are you certain Wade gave us up?" asks John Crutcher.

"Yes. I can't fathom any other possibility. He's AWOL. In military units that's treason, the brig, and…"

"But, the death penalty was eliminated," Crutcher interrupts.

I look at him.

"Wade has risked the lives of over 106 dedicated, well-intentioned people, as well as the lives of the future captives and the slaves we will free. The moment he did that, he relinquishes his rights to fair treatment and due process," I say.

Kris pipes in, "Sir, we shouldn't be rash—"

"*My daughter and wife are kidnapped and in the hands of*

Alistair Watson!"

Silence.

"What!" says Heidi, breaking the silence.

"He'll have his men rape and kill my family, if I don't get him everything he wants!"

Longer silence.

"Sir, the teams are assembled," says the Delta One team leader.

"Good. Pay attention. *Everyone,"* I say, sternly, unusual for me. "Wade Maley is officially in high treason to QuadFlium. He has revealed the existence of QF to Alistair Watson. It's resulted in the kidnapping of my wife and daughter. He's likely instigated the unauthorized departure of Teska Lando, another high-value asset, now AWOL. They had a recent romantic encounter and share disaffected communication. He is dangerous and responsible for putting all of your lives in danger. And now, my daughter and wife.

"No mercy in Wade's apprehension. Lethal force is authorized. The agent who takes him down will be highly decorated."

"This may all be a shock to you. You may think this is unfair. *I don't give a shit! Find that motherfucker and neutralize him!"* I scream.

Long silence again.

"Answer me!"

"Yes, sir, say the two team leaders.

"Everyone! Answer me!" I scream.

"Yes, sir," say all operatives at once. Except one. I see the sole silent dissenter on Ashkay's laptop AV feeds. A stoic silent face. Vladimir, from Kazakstan.

"Vladimir, step forward," I say. He does. "You did not

answer in the affirmative?"

"Sir..." he says in this Russian accent, "I cannot bring myself to be okay with killing Wade, after all he has done for me."

"Get on the next plane here. You're a traitor."

"But sir..." he says.

"That's an order!" I say

"Yes, sir," he says.

"Leave for the airport, now" I say. "Any objections or *feelings* from anyone else? Last chance. When I disengage this call, it's on you. Whoever shows any sign of complaint or disaffection is considered someone that is okay with my wife and child being raped and killed by homicidal maniacs. For what? So Wade can get a bounty off his head and save his own hide. Anyone else?"

Silence.

"Go!" I yell.

And disconnect.

I look at Ashkay and say, "Monitor Jeffrey's phone and listen to any calls. We should be at the alternate base in five minutes. Set up the new Mind Booth before you even take a piss," I say.

He nods.

I look every one of my strategists in the eye.

They all nod, except John and Dimitri.

The QF contract that all new arrivals sign covers this scenario. If an agent goes enemy, he's terminated. Everyone knows this. They're thinking about this clause right now. We all signed it, knowing it would never happen. It has.

Then my phone rings. It's my wife's phone again. Alistair.

"Hello?" I say.

Alistair says, "Mr. Girard. My pilot's confirmed the base location. Thank you for the flare. You're a true gentleman. Next, I require a certain agent's head in a box."

I walk through the train car and into an empty car.

"He is out alone right now. In fact, he is AWOL. I have six top operatives tracking him down with orders to shoot to kill on sight, and bring back the body," I say.

"I'm aghast, such disloyalty. Don't you agree? I have a dozen contracts out on him, you're prescient enough to conclude. Between your expertise and mine, we should find him lickety-split. Where was he last seen?" asks Alistair.

"We know he's in the Austin area, right now. My operatives are on the ground," I say.

"Excellent. Describe him," asks Alistair.

"He's likely wearing head gear to prevent us tracking his implanted GPS devices. He's Australian," I say.

"Fascinating. You chip your personnel like stray cats and puppies. I must try that. It sounds fun," says Alistair, in his whispery confident English accent.

"If you catch him before I do, your two-billion-dollar recompense adjusts to 1.99 billion," he says, "The ten million is the current offer on his head."

"Got it," I say.

"One item more... comment, advice , take it as you wish. You and your kind consider yourselves moral and admirable, your work humanitarian. But you have no idea what lives these people live before they end up in my grasp. They are from slums. I give them an opulent domicile in comparison. They are besieged by disease and death. I give them health and hygiene. If they are dying, their organs are used to save lives. It's so easy to sit on your self-congratulatory, ivory pedestal. My research shows you went to some top-league school in the US, and think you know about everything. You don't know piddle-shit. We're the same, Jean Jacques. We are the same," says Alistair, and hangs up.

I ponder a moment, and then walk back to the adjoining car and strategists.

"Wade provided the QF information Alistair wanted. He still wants him dead. Top priority is Wade's acquisition and conveyance of his body, dead or alive, to this fucking psycho," I say.

Heidi asks, "Why's he want Wade dead??"

"Wade broke into his compound, killed his men, including his decoy, led the slaughter of his men in the Los Angeles distribution center. The video of Wade's kill on his Bel Air client went viral on the dark web. Does that answer your question?" I say.

Heidi gives a sheepish nod.

"He appreciates he has our balls in a vice, but still wants Wade on a platter or he hurts my family," I say.

Kris Connelly reads the group, stands, and says, "It's definitely odd. We go from loving and working with Wade, to killing him. In my years of dealing with the mafia, the mob, the darkest elements, betrayal by people close to you is common. It's hard to imagine Wade doing such a thing. But, since he did, we deal with it. We can't wish it away or pretend it didn't happen. We need to back up Jean Jacques and find this fucker."

Ashkay and Heidi express reluctant agreement. John and Dimitri look at the floor.

We arrive at the secondary base. All report to their stations.

"Strategists, straight to Mind Booth, activate operative cameras and audio feeds, track Jeffrey's phone real-time, run the Teska sit and reset operation status on both. I'll check on each crew member, make sure they're operational. Meet you in Mind Booth in one hour."

I check the crew. The setup, in most cases, is identical to the earlier base. Little familiarization is required. Even the berthing area has the same blueprint and room numbers. Each crew member enters their own berth, places their stuff, and heads to respective positions.

After an hour and fifteen minutes, the place is up and running. I head back to the Mind Booth.

I say to the Mind Team, "You need to know that Wade was pushing the idea on Teska that her scopulus was a setup. That QuadFilium somehow made it look like her fiancée was cheating on her, when he wasn't. She found him in a hotel room with a naked woman. Wade will try to convince Jeffrey the same. Pay attention."

"On it, sir," says Ashkay. The rest of the group nods.

Chapter 41
Wade

Jeffrey breaks down on the news that Teska is still alive. Falls to his knees and just bawls. My hand on his shoulder, I lend support. He sobs. After a few minutes, he settles down and drinks some water. We sit up talk about plans.

I tell him, "I want you to take this burner phone, return to your apartment and go back to your routine. Yeah, they know you ditched your stuff and escaped. They may try to contact you. But go ahead and pick up your car from the car wash and just carry on, like nothing has changed.

"Every day, find a way to get away from the shoes and the jacket, and call me on the burner. I need to know anything you notice or any contact from these guys."

"I have so many questions, I can't think with all this," says Jeff.

I say, "I understand. Now that I know the true story, I'm going to make this right. I promise you, to the best of my ability, provided the Lord lets her out of the coma, I'm gonna see to it you see her again. Then the two of you decide where your life paths go."

"Thank you, Wade. Question: Am I safe?" says Jeffrey.

"The unit always takes every precaution to not hurt an innocent You're an innocent. No one has ever taken out an innocent. We don't do it, mate, so no worries on that. But I'd be remiss if I fail to warn you. We're armed, guns go off, and shit happens. People get killed. So, you being connected puts you at risk. I will do my best to protect you," I say.

Jeffrey nods, takes the phone and leaves.

I call in Harold, who waits in the next room. I know he feels left out. I sit down on a couch and brief him. He strikes me as the kind of guy who feels vindicated by any conspiracy theory he proves. I further wonder about my own scopulus, Peyton's kidnapping, her return to her family weeks later unharmed. Reeks of setup. I can't fathom another possibility. Who ever heard of a little girl getting kidnapped and returned home safe, with no ransom? Doesn't happen.

"What's our next move, agent Wade?" says Harold.

"Next move is, we see what the deal is with Teska. If she's out of her coma, she needs to know that her scopulus was a setup. She needs the right to decide."

At risk of betraying my location, I could contact Jean Jacques and try to get him to admit the scopuluses were staged. Maybe in exchange for me turning myself in.

It'd need to be a careful plan. Right now, the operatives are too close. They'd be on me in minutes. If Jeffrey plays it cool, maybe they think he's been sitting in the bathroom for an hour. More likely, they've already found his stuff jammed into the rubbish bin and deduced we made contact. The next few hours will tell.

I wonder how many QuadFilium staff had a similar thing to get them to join.

Harold and I drive back to his place. We go down into the bunker. I take off my hoodie and glasses. A relief; they're bloody uncomfortable.

After a short rest, I throw on my getup, and go upstairs. I sit down for a dinner Maude's thrown together. The tinfoil in the hoodie makes bothersome crinkly sounds whenever I move.

We chat and Harold tells me his whole theory on how the world pandemics, like SARS and COVID-19, are political tools and ways to make powerful people more rich. Fascinating how much he knows, or believes he knows. Lots of it seems implausible to me, but hey, if someone told me ten years ago that there was a secret modern military monkhood that killed bad guys and had chips installed in their heads, I'd have laughed at them.

I tell him mission stories. He and Maude lean towards me, fascinated, soaking it all up.

My phone rings. It's Jeffrey.

"Wade, you're not going to believe this. I just got a call from Teska."

Chapter 42

Teska

TEN MINUTES EARLIER

I get out of the taxi in the theater district, go to a local park, and sit on a bench to call Jeffrey. I'm more terrified of this than when I rescued Wade in my helicopter under a hail of bullets.

I call Jeffrey's number. At first it goes to voice mail, ignoring the random international number. I call again. Voice mail. I call again, and he answers annoyed, "Hello?"

"Jeffrey, it's me," I say.

"T-Teska?" he says.

"Yes," I say.

"You... you... you *are* actually alive," he says. I hear heavy breathing and the vibrato of a mounting sob. The way he said *actually* tells me he is in touch with Wade.

"Yes. I am. And I'm sorry for not listening to you. To this day, I still don't know the truth. But Wade, whom I think you met, didn't believe you cheated on me..." I say.

"It's true. I didn't," he says.

"But... the girl... she wasn't wearing much, neither were you. How'd that happen?

"She was sent to my room, a free massage. My eyes were closed. You knocked. I go to the door. She undresses. She was placed there, so you'd freak out. It worked. I didn't even know she was undressed until I saw your reaction and turned around."

251

My mental wheels turn, grind, and squeal. My body curls forward on the park bench. Tears fight their way out of my eyes.

Wade was right.

All the suppressed emotions I've had over the last year and a half rush in and flow out as tears gush from my eyes. Uncontrolled sobbing on each end of the phone line.

I have no doubt that QuadFilium strategists are listening to every decibel of this conversation. Jean Jacques exposed for his dishonest recruitment tactics. But do the others listening believe us? Or him?

I know time is running out. They already have my position and are heading my way.

"Jeffrey, we're bugged. This conversation is being listened to by a group in a room. There are operatives surrounding you right now," I say.

"Yes, Wade told me," he says.

"They're triangulating my position and will come for me any minute. I need to get off the phone. Tell Wade I'll meet him where you and I had our first date. Don't say it aloud. Only you and I know that location. The agents won't. Get Wade there in three days at 6:00 p.m. Don't say it out loud or let the location be discovered in any way. Do you understand, Jeffrey?"

"Yes, of course," he says.

"They can hear you at all times, but they can't always see what you are seeing. Figure out how to get him the message."

"I will. Teska, I love you," he says.

"I loved you more than can be described. I spent the last year hating you. Now I'm confused," I say.

"I understand and don't blame you," he says. "We'll sort it out."

"Yes. Goodbye," I say.

"Goodbye," says Jeff.

I hang up the phone and sit on a park bench shaking. Deep breaths. I walk around and regroup. I focus on a chestnut tree, two pigeons on cobblestone, a streetlamp. A couple more deep breaths and I calm down. I walk two blocks to the banks of the L'isere river. Tour boats dot a pedestrian boardwalk. I walk and watch the boats come and go. I drop the phone into a departing boat. The operatives will track it and find a group of South Korean tourists.

I go into a convenience store and buy another burner. On my way out, I drop my .22 into a trash can. I make my way to a shopping street lined with tourist trinkets, small eateries, small theaters, costume shops and cafés.

My flight is in four hours. I have some time to prepare. If I make it to the Austin airport, I'll need to be a completely different person. QF operatives will be there, waiting for me.

I see a costume shop named *La Penderie.*

Wigs, uniforms, superhero outfits, goblin masks and other props line the shelves and racks in the center of the store. A young college-age girl with dark-rimmed glasses smiles and says something in French, probably asking if I need some help.

"I only speak English," I say.

"No problem," she says.

"Okay, great. I need a realistic mask, ya know, doesn't look like a mask."

"I have some great ones. Come..."

We walk past Easter Bunny, Santa Claus, Iron Man and Big Bird costumes on display. At the end of the aisle, she selects a life-like latex rubber head mask of a bald, old, overweight man. I put it on and adjust it so the mouth and eyes match up. I look in the mirror.

I love it.

I remove it and select fake glasses to hide the gap between the mask and the eye skin, and to try to cover the brown versus blue eye thing I got going on. If I'm not talking and no one is looking at me closely, this will work.

I find a large man's jacket, a couple of small pillows to add weight to my physique and some puffy gloves to hide my feminine hands.

I jam these in my soon-to-be carry-on luggage, a shopping bag.

Flight in three hours. I'm concerned that there will QF operatives at the Grenoble airport, when I try to board the plane. They know I intend to go to the US and will be waiting.

I get in a cab and head to the airport.

When I arrive outside the terminal, I scan the departure lanes for any sign of surveillance. So far nothing. I pay the driver in cash, grab my bag, and walk into the terminal. I notice two hundred yards down, to the left, two agents spot me and head in my direction, walking fast. The airport's crowded. Think fast.

I walk up to a French-version TSA agent and say, "Sir, those two guys over there tried to give me some luggage to take on the plane. I told them 'no.' Now they're following me and look aggressive. I'm scared. And I'm late for my flight. Can you get me through security?"

"Okay, mademoiselle, go ahead," he points, "In front, that line over there. I'll deal with these characters," he says.

I walk to the zig zag security line and look back as my guy hails two more agents and approaches the operatives, who look *too* suspicious, no plane tickets, no luggage, and hyped-up. It's not helping their cause. My security guy is all up in their grill being my knight in shining armor. Damsel in distress seems to be a good working system for me. Note to self.

I make it up to the metal detector thing. My bag clears and no alarms clang when I raise my arms for body-scan. I glance back. Four airport agents gesticulate, stand tough and gesture for the two QuadFilium operatives to leave the terminal. They see me pass security, faces bitter as gall. I get through the US customs and Homeland Security portion of the security clearance procedures and head to the gate and wait for my flight. This was easier than it'll be in Austin. Once I clear Customs, I'll be in the open. No TSA agents. No crowds. I'll be a sitting duck.

I get on the plane. It's a fourteen-hour trip, with a connection in Paris to change planes. Then a direct flight to Austin. First class is a new world to me. No one bumps me, lots of yummie grub, my legs can stretch. Never done this before. Never had 45,000 dollars in cash before.

Travel's a respite from the hammer and pound I've called my life. It gives me time to reflect without panting like a lizard on a rock. I'd started to finally get over Jeffrey and fall for Wade. Then I find out Jeffrey didn't really cheat on me. That it was a setup from Jean Jacques to push me over the edge into QuadFilium.

Who do I really love though? Do I go back to Jeffrey? Do I run with Wade–fugitives for the rest of our lives? Do I return to QuadFilium and make things better?

I have done more good for the world, learned more and grown more in the twelve months at QuadFilium than I did in the previous two decades. But the QF recruitment was dishonest, even treacherous, but also kinda helpful. My life was going fine with Jeffrey up until that night, but I was so weak that one incident was enough to make me suicidal, so how was I really? I thought my life was sweeter than stolen honey but yet on account of only one incident, contrived or not, I was suicidal. How dandy was I?

QuadFilium has been the most incredible experience. It's got its crazy times, but it's living with a purpose, saving lives for real, eradicating oppression and evil, every day. Jean Jacques was wrong, the way he manipulated me. *But would any other way have worked? And if he didn't, was there any chance I would have joined?*

I doubt it. *How many fewer lives would have been saved without my shoulder to the wheel? What would have happened with Wade's escape from the Alistair compound? Would he have made it?*

It's easy to point the finger at Jean Jacques and say he is a scoundrel, a rotten and dishonest man. *But is that true?* I don't know. So many angles.

I have a lot to think about. I close my eyes and fall into a deep sleep. These first-class seats are so worth it.

Chapter 43
Wade

"Wade, you're not going to believe this. I just got a call from Teska," says Jeffrey.

Long pause as I assimilate this.

"She's out of her coma! How did she reach you?" I ask.

"An international call to my phone. I can't even believe it… my whole world's flipped upside down. She remembered my phone number. She said she is alive and well, wants to see me and… you," he says.

"What else?" I ask. My heart pounds.

"She's on her way to Austin. She knew that we were being listened to on my phone by operatives. She told me to tell you to meet her where we had our first date."

"Okay. She's AWOL. Nuts. But she doesn't have the devices in her head so they can't track her. Cheeky woman. So clever. Don't tell me the location. You might be bugged even though you probably are not wearing shoes or a jacket, not in your house and using the burner phone, right?" I ask.

"Yeah. But I won't say. She said she'll arrive in Austin in the next day or two. Three days from now, at 6:00 p.m., you two are to meet. How do I get you the location?" says Jeffrey.

"More important, what if she's been sent to bait us into a trap?" I ask.

"What do you mean?" asks Jeff.

"Maybe she's playing their game and using herself as bait. Maybe she isn't really AWOL but trying look like it, lure me in.

We meet and they snag me. Some elaborate scheme," I say.

"Guess it's possible. All this shit's not in my world, but frankly I don't care if it's a setup. There's nothing more important to me, including my safety or life, or sorry to say, yours, than the chance to see Teska again. Her body was unidentifiably mangled and burned in a fiery explosion she supposedly did to herself. They said it was a suicide. How could I ever just go back to clicking my heels and living life? Been dead since then."

"I dig, mate. I dig. Well, let's be a team and let's get this sorted, cool?" I say.

"Yeah, man. So how do I get the information to you?" asks Jeff.

"Hmmm. I've an idea. Kind of weird but it will work. Go to the bank at lunch and ask for fifty single dollar bills. Write the name of this place on one. Today, after work, go to the city park where there are more than fifty homeless people in encampments lined up along the park's West fence. Give a dollar to each one of them. When you see the man who handed you the note the other day, give him the correct dollar. Agents won't possibly be able to get each homeless person to give up their dollar. Never going to happen. You got it?"

"Yes," he says.

"Okay. Don't be obvious. Pull all the dollars from one pocket. No separate one for my guy. They'd look for that. It's all got to look the same. Then call me," I say.

I turn to Harold, who overheard my conversation with Jeff, "Looks like you'll be playing make-believe today. Can you be a convincing homeless bloke?"

"Of course! Sounds like fun!"

At go time, we get Harold all ragged up and dirty and

drive into the city. I stop at a store and buy a nanny cam and fix it onto his collar, so I can track what's going on when the transaction happens. I set it up on my phone.

If I were a QuadFilium agent on this op, I'd surround the park and look for me. We decide to find a travelling homeless person with a shopping cart near the park and have Harold caravan in to the encampment. This way they don't see some sedan dropping him off near the park. Dead giveaway.

We find just the guy. He is struggling with two carts. I drop Harold off and he heads over to the bloke and strikes it up with him and starts pushing one of the carts.

I hightail it out of there. Undoubtedly there are half a dozen perceptive motherfuckers looking for me in every car near the park. I'd get easily made.

I park in a safe spot and watch the nanny cam. Harold moves slow, looks a bit drunk and blends in like a fart in the wind. He sets up in the center flanked by encampments stacked in a row. For the most part, the tents are identical with American flags on them. It seems like the city or some patriotic philanthropic donor provided the dwellings in bulk. Outside these tents sit residents of this small-park-town. Some chat, eat, drink. Others talk to the air around them. Interesting bunch.

Jeffrey shows up and walks along the front of the encampments He approaches each person at each tent, and hands them a dollar. He's polite and gets a lot of thank-you nods, looks out of place. Clean and tidy, with his white shirt tucked into his trousers. Looks like a nerd walking into a biker bar. He arrives at Harold and betrays no sign of recognition. Jeffrey completes his round and leaves. Harold looks at the dollar bill and holds it up to the nanny cam on his chest: "Clark's Oyster Bar."

I assume the operatives watch Jeffrey leave and look for anyone that follows him. Harold doesn't budge. When night comes, Harold moseys out of the park, after many have left. They'll interrogate everyone. Harold will have dozens in front of him.

Harold's questioned by an operative. He has no dollar on him and acts like a ranting psycho. They back off like he might be contagious. He rambles, mutters, a few blocks. He chucks his dirty coat and shirt, a cleaner one underneath, and Ubers home.

I'm at his place. He makes it back at 0100, tired but pounding his chest like the badass he is. He tells me stories shared by people at the encampment. Lost jobs, eviction, bad marriage, substance abuse. We catch some sleep. In two days, I see Teska. I need to be ready. Time for some risky recon.

Chapter 44

Jean Jacques

I gather the strategists in the new conference room: Kris Connelly, Heidi Flannagin, Dimitri, John Crutcher and Ashkay.

I brief them: "We had two operatives at the Grenoble airport to spot and exfiltrate Teska. Spot they did, exfiltrate they did not. She did a move like Wade in Wyoming, getting the authorities to intervene. They think alike. We had one operative covering the train station.

"Wade outsmarted us at the homeless encampment. We can only assume he has a rendezvous set with Teska. We have a lot to deal with right now. Wade is enemy number one. Alistair actually wants Wade dead. He saw footage of Wade throwing knives into a prime client's body and it pissed him off. We need to escalate our strategy to terminate Wade and retrieve my wife and daughter. No matter what it takes."

"Sir, you holding up okay?" asks John.

"Yes and no. Not sleeping, very stressed. I'm ready to kill anyone who had any part in this," I say.

Kris says, "We are with you, boss. Let's figure this out."

It's evident that the team is more tentative to label Wade an enemy and plot to kill him. I need to dissolve equivocation. All operatives and strategists need to be on the same page. Otherwise, we'll never put an end to Wade, and my wife and daughter will be raped and killed.

"Put all of the operatives on so they can hear. Now!" I

order. Ashkay notifies the six operatives in Austin to stop everything and listen.

Ashkay nods. I begin, "Before Wade went AWOL, he was in Teska's ear, making noise about QF. We have solid evidence. I confronted Wade directly on this two weeks ago. He denied it and stated any doubts or suspicions were put to rest.

"On the day he discovered his adopted sister, Peyton, was still alive, he flipped and went rogue. He became convinced QuadFilium had organized Peyton's kidnapping and framed Teska's fiancée, Jeffrey. Total absurdities. He then contacted Alistair and passed information about me, my wife and the location of QF. We do not know how much he was paid.

"When Alistair saw the video of Wade executing his client that we sent to his other clients, he did a 180 and demanded Wade's death. If we don't get a dead-or-alive Wade to Alistair in the next few days, my wife and daughter will be tortured and executed. If any of you are not 100% on mission, you are duped, disloyal, disaffected or all three. You'll need to step down. So, speak up right now."

John Crutcher raises his hand. I call on him, "I feel there remains a possibility that Wade is innocent of these charges, and that Alistair found out about us some other way. I can't in good conscience sanction killing him without incontrovertible evidence."

"You believe QF setup two scopuluses, and someone else betrayed the secrets of QF to Alistair?" I ask. Looking him right in the eyes.

"I don't *believe* shit. But I can't condone hunting Wade down on partial facts and assumptions. He's the most accomplished agent in QuadFilium history," says John.

I nod and say, "You are dismissed. Report to tactical

training instruction full time. You're on probation until tribunal. If you spread disaffection your sentence will reflect that. Does anyone else have anything to add?"

Kris says, "I support your plans. You are the most experienced, our trusted leader, and I back you up." Ashkay and Heidi pipe in that they agree with Kris and will go with any decision or plans I make including, if required, terminating Wade.

Dimitri stands. He agrees with Crutcher. I direct him to continue his research but isolated from strategists and operatives and all mission comms. If he violates my directive, it will impact his tribunal. I label him *disloyal* and dismiss him.

It's now me and the remaining strategists. I say, "Thank you for your loyalty and support. Let's move forward with a plan. Strategy dictates our first target is to make contact with Jeffrey. We need the location of their first date. Thoughts on this?" I ask.

Heidi jumps in, "There's no other way. We grab Jeffrey and use every possible means to get him to talk. He has to tell us. My opinion, he still loves Teska, so we tell him it's the only way to guarantee her safety. We show him Wade is a real threat."

I answer, "Good point. If he feels that Teska's well-being is in danger, he'll cooperate."

Ashkay says, "Wade has his ear. We need to counter. I know just the thing. I'll compile footage of Wade killing the client in Bel Air. When the Delta team has Jeffrey, they show him Wade summarily torturing and executing the man. It'll show Wade's brutality. He'll talk. And Wade's discredited."

Kris says, "Brilliant. I agree."

I nod. We contact the Delta leader in Austin and do a detailed brief.

The strategists and I watch our operatives' cams and those planted in Jeffrey's apartment.

Jeffrey is home eating dinner, salmon and vegetables. We wait for him to finish. Three operatives are outside his apartment door, waiting for our signal. The team leader, Alex Gonzales, is a skilled soldier and negotiator who spent time in Texas. He knocks on the door. Jeffrey flinches.

He looks through the peephole and says, "Who is it?"

"You know we've been tracking you. We are operatives from QuadFilium. We have some vital information on the safety of Teska. May we come in?" says Alex.

"Actually, I think I'll call the police. You guys have bugged my house, set up cameras, tapped my phone. It's against the law," says Jeff.

"If you call the police, we disappear without a trace. Our fingerprints aren't in any database. But, you have a history with the police... wild allegations... ya know the drill. Most important, you love Teska and you want her safe. So do we. You talked to her on the phone and know she sounded safe, healthy and strong. We helped her. Teska's now doing well. Let us in so we can talk."

"You're telling me Wade's a liar?"

"We have something to show you. If it doesn't change your mind, we'll walk. We're both interested in helping her."

"Okay," Jeffrey says and opens the door.

The three operatives enter the apartment. They're dressed casual with no weapons and they stand in the entry like guests. Alex smiles, "Hi Jeffery." A moment, then Jeffrey invites them to sit at the table.

Jeffrey says, "What do you want to show me?"

Alex answers, "Wade is AWOL from our unit. In military

terms, that means he's committed treason and is disloyal to the unit. He's lured Teska into his scheme."

"From what I hear, you guys set up the whole massage thing to make Teska think I cheated on her. I checked with the hotel. They have no masseuse service. Why'd the woman take her clothes off?" asks Jeffrey.

Alex shakes his head. "There's a predatory con racket going on throughout Texas, New Mexico and Arizona. The hotel patron is told he's been awarded a free massage. They send an attractive woman who undresses during the experience and makes sexual advances on the unsuspecting guest. He's lured and videoed in sexual acts. Then blackmailed. It's what went down with you," says Alex.

"I'd never hire a prostitute!" says Jeffrey.

"No shit. It looks like it was just the worst possible timing. Turned out to be good timing for us. When we found Teska, she was about to kill herself, we stopped her. We saved her life," says Alex.

"Oh my God. You guys didn't set up the massage?"

"We did not. Pure coincidence. The scam group was very active in that area at the time. It's tough for police, victims are not anxious to call or talk to the police," says Alex.

"Holy shit. So Wade and Teska think that you guys set it up and then they blew your *unit or whatever*," says Jeffrey.

Alex nods. "And we have no way of contacting them except through you," says Alex.

"Okay. But Wade strikes me as a competent, decent man. Ingenious how he helped me evade you guys twice with all your resources," says Jeffrey.

"Let me show you a video from last week," Alex says as he clicks an iPad. He says, "All of our operatives have a recording lens in their eye. All footage from their view is recorded. Another operative was in the room watching. You need to see this."

Jeffrey watches the video of Wade throwing a knife into a man with great force. It plunges through his arm and into the wood wall behind him. He does this with the next arm. The man is screaming in pain. Wade proceeds to throw an additional dozen knives into this man's body and watches as he bleeds out.

Jeffrey vomits salmon and vegetables onto the floor. Tears in his eyes, hands shake. He says, "What the fuck?"

Alex answers, "Can you think of any possible scenario where this would be warranted?"

"Not at all. Who was that guy?!"

"He was a suspect. Likely guilty of crimes. But that doesn't justify the cruel and unusual execution-style torture, and the pleasure that Wade clearly got out of it. It's quite sickening actually," says Alex.

"It is," agrees Jeffrey. Then, the penny drops. Jeffrey looks up, drool on his mouth, "My God. What kind of danger is Teska in?" he asks.

"Hard to say. We don't think he'd intentionally hurt her. We are certain he'll lead her into dangerous situations which could get her injured or killed. Wade has enemies. This is classified data, but he has ten contracts out on him. Assassins are looking for him. He has an eight-figure bounty on his head. If Teska is with him, she's just collateral damage. A thing assassins don't give a shit about. We've seen them blow up an entire train car full of passengers just to kill one guy," says Alex.

"Geezus," exclaims Jeffrey.

"The news stories you hear about bombings, and about

people running their cars into crowds? Many of them are actually assassinations. Not all, but many. Al Queda and Isis take false credit for them sometimes, which plays well into the assassins' cover ups," says Alex.

"Weird. But don't most of the assassins die in the process of their killing?"

"This is where it gets super weird. Those suicidal mass murderers are in fact carrying out a religious event in their minds. The priestly commanders that set it all up are sometimes just being paid by clients for hit jobs hidden as homicidal religious expressions," says Alex.

"Unbelievable," says Jeff.

"Teska is in grave danger with Wade," says Alex.

"What can I do?"

"Tell us where they are meeting tomorrow night at 6:00 p.m. We apprehend Wade and reunite you and Teska. You spend some time together, decide what you want to do. If you both want to restart your lives, we're good on that and could help. If she wants to return to our unit, that can be arranged. It's her choice. It's your choice. Most importantly, the two of you need to talk and sort it all out," says Alex.

"Okay, It makes sense." A long, silence, tense moment. "It's *Clark's Oyster Bar*," Jeffrey blurts.

"Thank you, Jeffrey. You've probably saved Teska's life."

"I hope so. How do I reach you guys?" asks Jeffrey.

"At any time, just say, 'Delta Leader, call me' and we'll call your phone," Alex says.

"Okay," says Jeffrey.

The team leaves.

"Well done, Alex. You are a master," I say.

"Thank you, sir," he responds.

Now, the ambush.

Chapter 45
Wade

"Harold, I need you to case the restaurant," I say.

"You got it, boss. What am I looking for?" he asks.

"There's a decent possibility this is an ambush. They will wait until both Teska and I are present and then probably rush in, posing as police officers, DEA, FBI and tackle us right in the middle of the joint. And take us into custody," I say.

"How do we avoid that?" asks Harold.

"Back in Wyoming, I was able to use the local police to stop them from catching me. Maybe we can do a similar thing again. Seems to be working," I say.

"So, we tell the local police force that a group of vigilante impostors, armed, fake badges are attempting to kidnap you guys. They snag the bad guys and you and the little lady walk," says Harold.

"That's the only thing that will work. I don't see us running and dodging tranquilizer darts like Neo in *The Matrix*," I say.

"Okay, so what do I do?" asks Harold.

"First thing, we have Maude call the police station and report fake police officers arrested her and stole money from her purse. She files a full report on the matter, describes the suspects, what they look like, sound like, based on details I give her.

"I call an hour later and make the same claim, using my alias, Jack Warren.

"Then you go to the Austin police station. The same one

269

Maude and I have called. The station in the district closest to the restaurant. Say you have evidence of a fake police unit, going around arresting, cuffing people, sometimes abusing them, but always taking their money and using their ATM cards to withdraw cash. You say that you've been informed they plan to attack Clark's Oyster Bar tomorrow, because they know one wealthy Aussie and one smoking hot babe plan to dine there at 6:00 p.m. There's going to be two to six fake police officers that rush in and 'arrest' them. You describe them the same way Maude and I did. Mention they have real guns. This adds credible threat to the calculation.

"Three reports in row from three random people, giving the same description."

Maude picks up the phone and does her part. They call her down to the police station and take a report. I do the same a few hours later.

The next morning, Harold heads in there with his intel. He comes back and reports, "The police are in. The captain himself spoke with me and thanked me for the intel. I told him I can't give up my source but that it is credible. He accepted it and is making arrangements to be there when the strike goes down. Looks like we are all set."

"Excellent work, mate!"

"Thanks, partner! Oh Wade, here... you might need this." Harold opens up a drawer in a console he has near the front door, and pulls out a revolver. I check it. Six bullets.

I send Harold to case the restaurant and video the layout, so I can plan with how this can go down.

I go to the store to buy some attire that might lend credibility to my new wealthy persona. But I must remain cloaked from the GPS signals in my head, so I choose a high-end designer hoodie, which I didn't think existed but it does, and sunnies, and line these with tinfoil. Ready.

I check Harold's video. Clark's Oyster Bar has one entrance facing the street and one back exit just past the bathrooms, leading to the alley behind. The front has large glass windows. The interior is your usual setup with tables in a line, two rows spread throughout the floor plan. High ceilings with two ceiling fans. On the side opposite the entrance is a display of a variety of oysters, clams and assorted seafood delights. The video shows three couples, one in their thirties wearing shorts and jeans, an older couple in slacks and button-downs, and a young gay couple in exercise clothing. I get the idea this is a hip hangout, pretty popular and serves good tucker.

I call in and make a reservation for two at 6:00 p.m. I make it clear exactly which table I want.

I put on my bulletproof skin guard under my new threads. Harold has a nice collection of junk in his front and back yards. I rifle through and find some metal plates. Kind of rusty iron bits. I duct tape these over my vital organs, heart, liver, spine and lungs. I put the fashionable white hoodie over it all, throw on the shades and reckon I look like Eminem.

Harold stations himself across the street on a bus bench, to watch the ordeal go down. The local police are staked out in vans parked on the road.

Chapter 46
Jean Jacques

"How do we apprehend them in the middle of the restaurant?" I ask.

Kris answers first, "Well, boss, the way I see it, is we get them on their way in, no commotion, no local authorities, no heroes trying to save the day."

I say, "Is that a problem? Heroes?"

Heidi answers, "In Texas many civilians carry, and look forward to being able to protect, especially damsels in distress. It's still a little Wild West-over there."

I say, "Interesting. I don't see how we can catch them on the way in. They won't be together. If we catch one, the other will be alerted and will blow the scene. So how do we nab them in the restaurant?"

Kris says, "Well, the boys in blue are respected there. Suppose we go in dressed like cops, and simply arrest the two. The whole place will back us up, pat us on the back and say 'thank you for your service.' "

I say, "I like that idea. Let's get four operatives into uniforms, complete with the badge and the equipment. Leave two outside to watch for funny business. One sniper rifle on a nearby rooftop. If Wade breaks, he takes the shot. The other in the back alley."

The strategists nod in agreement. I leave the room while they brief the Austin team on the plan.

My phone rings again. It's Alistair.

"Mr. Girard, update me on my requests, if you please. Mr. Wade appears to be off the grid. Official records have pronounced him dead and multiple database intrusions reveal his countenance absent on all facial recognition software. He is a ghost in Austin. My people are dumbfounded. You trained him well."

"He is the best we've ever had. He is also clad in head and face coverings to block the signals from the devices we installed. He won't appear on cameras in any recognizable way," I say.

"No wonder you have remained hidden for so long. And, the two billion dollars?"

"It's my wife's money. I can pay you 200 million, but Frances would have to arrange the rest," I say.

"Understood," says Alistair. "Sounds dicey though. With your resources I could see you attempting a sabotage," says Alistair.

"I don't gamble with the life of my daughter and wife," I say.

"Wise man, Mr. Girard," says Alistair.

"I will also promise, if something happens to my wife or child, I will kamikaze a wrecking ball of death on you, everyone you love, if love is even part of your sick equation, and all that is important to you. I have the ability, knowledge and resources and *that* I promise. If this concludes well, we both walk away to fight another day," I say.

"While I can appreciate your pugnacious machismo, I am not frightened by your threats. If I decide to rape and kill your family, there is nothing you could do about it, or to me personally. But, it behooves me financially and otherwise to honor this bargain, provided my terms are met. I believe we have an understanding," says Alistair.

"We do." I hang up the phone and return to the Mind Booth.

"Assemble the full mission team, both internal and field, for a briefing," I say.

Heidi gets all the field agents to stop and listen on their earpieces. The Mind Booth staff is already assembled.

I begin, "All involved on this mission, listen up. The importance of this operation cannot be overstressed. The apprehension of Wade and Teska, especially Wade, is the most important target since the beginning of QuadFilium. *Dead or alive!*

"First and foremost, we catch Teska as she comes off the plane in Austin. We know what flight she's on, departure gate and time. You can't miss her. Get her at the airport. Then put her on the phone with me.

"If she evades you, which will be the subject of your tribunal, fallback is Clark's Oyster Club tomorrow at 1800. If you have to execute Wade in broad daylight and drag his body to a nearby van, *you do that!* If he escapes, it's an irreversible failure. Your four-man police team enters the restaurant, reads him the Miranda rights, cuff him and drag him away. If Teska is with him, do the same. If any attempt is made by Wade to escape you are to shoot with live rounds, not tranquilizers. Do not recon the place before 1800. Wade or Teska will see you and abort. Do not allow any contact to Jeffrey, It'll spook him. Jam all his lines. Prepare everything now. Once they enter the restaurant, get into position and not a minute before.

"Each member of the team is to have tranquilizers and live rounds in two separate guns. Use the tranqs on Teska and live rounds on Wade. A rooftop sniper waits out front in case Wade makes a break. Another waits out back for the same reason.

Sniper, *you* are insurance. You see him exit the restaurant and not in our control, shoot to kill.

"Do you all understand me?"

All strategists and Delta team agents say in unison, "Yes, sir!"

"Good! Now get it done. I want good news!"

I exit and walk to my chambers, take a sleeping pill, and doze into the fitful nightmares I'm now accustomed to, awake or asleep.

Chapter 47
Teska

*//*Please ensure your tray tables are up and your seats are in their upright position for landing."

I run to the front with my bag and enter a lavatory. I put on the full costume: the rubber face, the glasses, the jacket stuffed with pillows, the fedora. I check the mirror. Damn good, but will it do?

I come out of the stall a new and different person. I sit in a random empty aisle seat in Economy Class. The sleeping passenger next to me rests against the window. As we descend, he wakes and double-takes me. I pretend not to notice. Let him assume whatever he wants. I don't look approachable, or friendly. He says nothing.

We land and go through the song and dance of forming a line in the aisle, take our stuff out of the overhead compartments and wait awkwardly as the door opens. I finally waddle out the door, welcomed to Austin with a smiling salutary "Buh Bye, thank you," from the flight attendants, who just spent ten hours serving us and are undoubtedly uncomfortable, in pain, tired and ready to kill someone. I give no response but a nod on account of my voice would sound weird coming from a man's body. The attendants certainly looked at me funny, obviously not recalling having seen me on the plane. But tired and disinterested, they wave me goodbye.

I walk up the accordion platform thing, enter the terminal and see two operatives inspecting every passenger as they exit, mentally ticking them off. They likely have orders to suspect every single body that walks by, omitting no one, and eliminating only the most obvious ones. Like fat, old bald men. They tick me off with almost no notice. I shuffle right between them. I head straight for a men's room stall and remove the mask, but keep the stuffed jacket and put a hat on, walking right out of a stall, hiding my face under the rim best I can.

I get through the passport check as Jessica Adams, go back into a stall and put the mask back on.

I pop out to curbside where I spot a third operative, the one who almost caught me in Grenoble. He scans, frantic, at every person. He looks past me with the same disinterest as he might give a light post, a trash can, a pile of cow shit.

I get in a cab, scot free.

I head into Austin and ask to get dropped at a four-star. One near the Clark's Oyster Club. A nice Best Western. At my request, he lets me out a half a block away, near a park.

I take my bag out. The cab drives away. I mosey over to the public bathrooms, walk into the men's, flinching at the pungent smell of urine. I enter a stall and change out of my costume. I walk out of the stall as myself, and a man at a sink looks up at me funny.

"*Je suis désolé Monsieur, je pense se bain est pour les femmes.*" I say. He thinks I'm a foreign woman who misread the sign. I head to the hotel, check in and get a room.

I shower, relax and play through the next day in my mind, conceiving all possible scenarios. So far, I have been successful at evasion.

The next morning, I put on an oversized sweater and a few scarves over my head and neck and head to town to grab some attire. So far, I have no reason to believe QuadFilium has figured out our rendezvous at Clark's Oyster Bar. But I need to prepare in case they have.

I'm spinning like a tumbleweed, trying to make heads or tails of the Jeffrey and Wade puzzle. *Do I figure out how to go back to Jeffrey? Do I restart my life with him, or join Wade and be on the run for the rest of my life?*

We'll see what tomorrow brings.

I grab a few things and go back to my hotel. Then I get in a cab and direct the driver to Clark's Oyster Bar. I ask the driver to circle the block five times. Each time I check every angle of the place for any sign of agents and I get acquainted with the layout of the restaurant through the big front windows.

I see no agents. I'm going to assume QuadFilium doesn't know our location, and plan to enter the restaurant tomorrow at 1800.

The cab driver brings me back to the hotel. I tell him to be here tomorrow at 5:50 p.m. and pay him a nice tip. He agrees.

I enter my hotel room and go straight to sleep. In the morning, I laze in bed, order room service and mentally prepare. I spend the rest of the day watching TV, a couple movies, and look up a few things on the internet. Been over a year since I vegged. Kinda nice. At 1700 I get up and shower, get dressed, get my game face on.

1750. The cab driver appears right on time in front of the Best Western where I stand with my field bag. He takes me close to Clark's and lets me out on the corner. I pay him in cash and walk down the street, scanning for agents. None. It's now 1758.

I get to the front door and peer inside. Sitting against the back wall, in his familiar posture, but wearing a ridiculous hoodie and glasses, is Wade, smiling. I cross the restaurant to him.

We hug. A long meaningful hug, the kind you see in airports outside baggage claim. His body is a solid machine of sinews and muscle. I feel metal plates he has on his torso. His embrace is a bit more savage than I'd consider normal. I can feel his emotion. Worry. About me. He was terrified I was not going to be okay. That I wasn't going to make it. He soaks in the reality that I'm alive and well. I return the clamping hug and hold.

We release and look at each other. He fixes on my new eye through his tinted glasses. The brown one.

"Crikey, you have a brown eye?" he asks.

"Yeah! Only one that matched my blood type. Both of my devices are gone. I'm untracked," I say.

"Beauty. I get the idea you planned this. Were you faking the coma?" asks Wade.

"Kind of, I woke from my coma and overheard that you had gone AWOL. Freaked me out, but I knew you wouldn't do that without really, really good reason. Decided to join you, but knew I had to get the devices removed, so I faked that I still had the coma so they'd still want to get the MRI done. They put me through the surgery, salvaged my eyesight with a replacement, and I took off in the middle of the night, through the trash run," I say.

"Un-fucking-real, Teska. Un-fucking-real. So... are... you... okay? You were lobotomized," says Wade.

"I don't think I have any dain brammage."

"What?!"

"*Haha!* Just messin'. Fully fine in terms of brain health and cognitive function. At least I think so. I've been able to think the same, coordinate my motor controls the same, and I haven't stuttered or been forgetful. Turns out they failed to complete the process, and only got the instrument inserted but didn't disconnect the lobes, which is normally what they do when they lobotomize someone. It makes the patient dopey, forgetful, and unconcerned about everything. I'm the opposite. I'm on fire. Awake. Sharp. And very concerned… about everything," I say.

A small tear jumps out underneath Wade's shades and makes a run down his cheek, losing steam an inch or two down. Only the shiny wet trail remains. He says, "I really thought I lost you," and hugs me again. As we dis-embrace I notice other customers watching our intense discussion.

I whisper to Wade, "I brought a mini EMP. I think this would work to disable your devices."

"No shit. It's definitely worth a try."

"Yes, but we need to be far away from any other electronics.

"Okay," he says.

"Well, it looks like our rendezvous went undetected."

"Seems so."

We sit down and scan the room out of habit. Wade's back is to the wall. We're at the table farthest from the door. I sit across. Twenty other guests dining, a couple waiters, a bus boy, a guy up front in charge of seating.

Wade's attention locks on something. I glance over my left shoulder, out the front window. A group of four uniformed policemen approach the restaurant. Familiar gait. QuadFilium agents. How did they know?

Chapter 48

Wade

I see their shapes through the glass. Four operatives. In police gear. Walking with a purpose, straight for the front door. That means there are more, probably one with a sniper rifle. One out back for sure.

These guys plan to come in posing as cops and arrest us. Just as I predicted. The local police and Harold expect this.

They draw their weapons and push open the door.

Kevin, the assault team leader, one of the guys I worked with in Bel Air, yells, "Ladies and gentlemen drop to the floor! Wade and Teska, you are under arrest and have the right to remain silent! Anything you—"

The front door bursts open. Another batch of cops. Real cops. The whole restaurant is full of crawling, screaming patrons, hiding under tables. Teska and I remain seated.

A real cop aims his weapon at the fake cops and says, "Drop your weapons. Now!"

Kevin's startled and thrown off. But doesn't hesitate to point his weapon at me and pull the trigger before anything else. Two shots to the chest.

As the bullets land, in what seems like slo-mo, I realize they're real, not tranquilizers. In the span of a hundredth of a second my brain analyzes the implications of this operative's use of deadly force, despite guns pointed at him by the local authorities. He has orders to terminate me at any cost.

The force of the bullets throws my body back into the wall

behind me. Teska's face contorts into a rageful terror. The Austin cops open fire on the operative who shot me and hold the other three operatives at gun point. They initiate sharp and fast hand combat, and the three real cops are easily disarmed and on the ground.

Hit by three bullets, Kevin has fallen. Teska ignores the whole scene, focuses only on me. The three standing agents see a flurry of activity outside the restaurant. More real cops coming. Backup. Likely blocking the back as well. But the agents have orders to kill me. I guess not Teska. Team leader is down. Undoubtedly, the Mind Booth is issuing orders in their ears. Something like, "Do not fail to kill Wade, no matter what!" It would have to be that. Otherwise, the team leader wouldn't have shot me, with three guns pointed at him, knowing he'd be shot.

I feel betrayed. I think of Ashkay, John Crutcher, Dimitri, Heidi, Kris. *They're ordering this?*

I can't breathe. The plates saved me. I know I'm not dead and my ribs aren't even broken. I'm winded. Teska, frantic, inspects my chest, burning her finger on a hot plate, but I see recognition in her eyes, that no bullet made it in.

She covers my body with hers, to protect me. She's figured out that there are orders to kill me and is now my shield. They won't kill her to kill me. But they will stop at nothing else to kill me.

The local police underestimated the scene, brought no SWAT. Only a half a dozen decent servicemen, it seems, who are now calling in SWAT and more backup. Likely in swarms. Are these agents going to try and escape? Or assume I am dead, and run?

I whisper to Teska, "Pretend I am dead. Scream."

"He's dead! You killed him! He's dead!" she screams while shaking my limp body. The agents have no choice but to bail. They had planned to come in and arrest us, shoot me if they failed, and bail with Teska in tow. They hadn't predicted that Austin's finest would be there to chuck a wrench into their gears.

Chapter 49
Jean Jacques

"Confirm Wade is dead and get out of there. Sniper two, how does the back door look?" I ask.

"Three cops waiting outside, guns drawn," he answers. His ocular feed shows the three police officers standing at the ready.

"Shoot around them, scare them off. Then, inside team, grab the team leader and proceed out the back!"

Sniper two unloads a shower of bullets around the waiting cops. They jump for cover behind a nearby dumpster.

Three QuadFilium agents bust out with the downed operative. Vitals readings show Kevin's heart is still pumping. But he's not conscious.

I give orders: "Sniper two, stay in position. Cover fire. Keep the cops backed off. Inside team, get in the car and get out of there."

We'd set up four getaway cars, including one in the back alley. They throw the body in and hightail it out of there. The real cops manage a few wild shots at the car as it peels away.

I ask, "Do we have confirmation on Wade?"

"We got two shots to his chest, and Teska screamed he was dead. But no direct contact with body to confirm," says one of the operatives.

"Okay. Status on the downed agent?"

"Three body shots. Not conscious. Was wearing shield skin. He's got a pile of broken bones and deep bruises, possible injured organs, possible internal bleeding. We don't have the medical facilities to care for him. He'll have to go to hospital, or he could bleed out internally," says the operative.

I say, "The cops will be looking at hospitals for gunshot victims. Peel his skin shield and change into civilian clothes. He'll look like a mugging victim who got crow-barred and knocked out. No bullets. Bring him to an ER and drop him off out front. No ID. Leave a note that says he was mugged.

"Dammit," I continue, "Wade predicted we'd pose as law enforcement and called in the local PD. Smart fuck. We don't know if he's dead or not. Keep snipers in position."

I look at the feeds from each of the snipers. One is a view of the front of the restaurant from a building top and one from the back. SWAT has arrived and begun a search for other hostiles. They'll find my two snipers. They need to withdraw.

"Snipers one and two, withdraw. SWAT will find you. Get out of there," I say.

They confirm and bail.

We have no confirmation that Wade is dead. It's a likelihood. Two shots to the chest, Teska screaming he is dead. Limp body. High likelihood. I'll report this to Alistair.

I say, "Ashkay, put together a video clip showing Wade shot and Teska screaming he's dead. I'll send it to Alistair to satisfy one of his main demands."

"Yes, sir."

Chapter 50
Wade

I continue to lie here. Limp, with Teska over me, a protective embrace. Teska says, "This place is surrounded by SWAT. What are we going to do?"

"Let the ambulance grab me. Jump on board. We'll escape," I say.

"Okay."

Police swarm the place, ensuring no hostiles remain. SWAT busts in, guns blazing, and clear each nook and cranny. Leading the innocents out in a congo line through the front door.

Paramedics come in and place me on a gurney. Teska screams, puts on a show, freaks out, and they let her on the ambulance.

My glasses are removed and my hoodie pulled back. I chucked the protective plates in the restaurant. QuadFilium agents will pick up my signal. It will take them a few minutes to catch up to us.

The medic performs a number of standard diagnostics on me, notes that I have no penetrative injuries, just burns on my chest. Offers me some painkillers. I decline. Teska acts relieved, continues feigned panting.

The ambulance pulls up to the hospital ER entrance and the back door flies open. The medics wheel me out of the back. Teska and I exchange glances and I roll off the side of the gurney and run from the ambulance. Teska follows.

And then, I realize I left my glasses in the ambulance. My

tracker is lit up.

I'm a sitting duck. I figure three minutes until QuadFilium agents are on us.

"I left the glasses. We need to get underground. Let's go here," I say, pointing at a manhole.

I lift the cover. We climb down, close the cover and descend the ladder. We are in a series of culverts similar to the ones I journeyed through in Wyoming. This one has a lot more rubbish strewn about.

"They'll know where I entered the manhole but will lose the signal from there. We need to get as far away as we can," I say.

We run through the large drainage pipes in ducked positions on account of the low ceiling. We take a series of turns at a number of forks, so they won't be able to guess our location. We run for a good ten minutes until we are at least half a mile from the original manhole. The chances they will guess our location are slim to none. Not worried; we'd hear them coming from hundreds of feet away anyways.

"What do you think happened to the agent who was shot?" asks Teska.

"It looked like he took a nice beating. Probably some organ damage, broken bones. I doubt the unit has the medical to help him. They'll have to use a local hospital or something. There's now a good batch of half a dozen or so operatives looking for us."

"Yeah. They shot you with real bullets. What the fuck?!" says Teska.

"Pretty wild. Good thing I wore the plates and the shield skin. I'd be a goner. Can't think now with *why*. There's a lot more going on than we know. Did you pick up anything when you were at QF?" I ask.

"No. Just that you had taken off. I just never imagined they'd try to kill you," says Teska.

"Must be some other serious shit going down. I thought we were all mates. Can't think of Sergeant Crutcher commanding a squad to take me out. That's some Twilight Zone shit. I need to get myself un-signaled. I need tinfoil and glasses," I say.

"Maybe not," says Teska. She reaches into her field bag and pulls out a kettle and opens the top. A set of air pods.

"Look at that beauty! An EMP. I wasn't sure if Dimitri had finished it. I asked him if it would have the power to deactivate the devices inside us. He said it would, but they could be turned on again, with the right signal at close range. This oughta work on me. Bloody nice," I say.

I fiddle around with it for a minute, and tell Teska to stand back, and make sure any electronic devices she has are well far way. I recall Dimitri saying it has a ten-foot radius on all electronics. I hope I don't lose my eyesight or hearing.

I flick the switch on near the left side of my head. An audible electrical sound emits from the device. I have no idea if it worked or not. I can still hear and see just fine.

"We need to test it," I say. "We need a rope. See if you can find one. I'll wait here." I help her remove the manhole cover above us. It brings her out in the middle of a road with little traffic. She darts off in search of a rope.

I stand in the culvert, the manhole cover above me, and consider what went down. How did they know our location? Jeffrey. They got to him. Tricked him or tortured him. I don't reckon Jeffrey to be the tough-guy type, but I also see a powerful sense of protection towards Teska. Strong enough to not say anything about her whereabouts, even if in incredible pain.

That's it. His protective impulse towards her. He could've been convinced that I was a threat to her. That QuadFilium's assistance was the only chance to save her. But how'd they convince him? Jeffrey bonded with me. On a deep-bro level. Can't imagine what they could say. It would have to be really convincing to get Jeffrey to talk, no question about it, like evidence that implicated me.

If I were in their shoes, I'd combine videos of things I'd done, edit to make it as bad as possible. Ashkay could've throw something together and make me look like a murderous psycho. The right video, me killing some bloke. Doctor it up to look all fucking weird. Show Jeffrey. He freaks out. Teska's in danger. And there you go.

It still doesn't explain why I'm a kill hit for QF. Why would they be trying to kill me? Must be something else, too. I try to imagine being Jean Jacques. What level of threat would have to go down for him to order my hit? Maybe it's related to the fact there are contracts out on me? Paid assassins searching me out. Not sure how that relates, but I imagine someone tells Jeffrey that, to scare him into spilling the beans. Fear for Teska's life, he'd do anything. But what has Jean Jacques so freaked out he'd order my death?

I need to prepare for the test to see if my signals are detectable. If I do the same trick I did in the Wyoming drainage system, where I jump down a manhole and lock them out with a length of rope, they'll anticipate it, and go down another manhole and approach from that end. This is where Teska comes in. She'll stand guard listening for it at the bottom of the ladder.

Since there are several possible tunnels, they could

approach from, I set a noise trap in two of the three nearby converging tunnels with debris. It will require them to knock it down or step on it. The noise will alert us.

Teska returns down the manhole with a length of rope.

"I got this outside the back of a workshop. Sorry, it's kind of greasy."

"It'll do," I say. I grab a piece of bent rod from amongst the debris, climb up the ladder and fit it through the hole in the heavy metal cover. I fasten the rope to the end of it.

I move the cover and pop my head out. I'm right in the middle of a street lane. No cars except one slow drifter heading my way. I lower my head and pull the cover back. The car drives over and I pop out again. Waiting. Teska hears nothing. We wait for fifteen minutes with no sound or sign of QF operatives.

Looks like the EMP worked. I'll have to assume so. Unless they are baiting me for a trap. I suppose I'll find out. I can't continue living in sewers forever. I'm not a teenage mutant ninja turtle.

Teska and I climb out onto the street and I take in the fresh air.

"We need a place to stay," I say, not sure how to broach the subject of how many rooms we should get. Best if I lay it out with no question marks. Won't budge on this until she sorts out her feelings for Jeffrey.

We walk down the street.

"Here we go. Travel Lodge," I say. It's a block away.

I walk up to the counter and say, without glancing back at Teska, "Two rooms please."

The desk clerk asks for a credit card which neither of us have. Teska places a pile of cash on the counter which the clerk reluctantly accepts.

We head up to our rooms and agree to meet up in half hour after some freshening up and relaxing. Our dinner was interrupted and the sewers offered little in the way of dining. After a long and relaxing shower, I put on the same clothes and head over to get Teska.

Teska also has the same clothes but luckily she has a massive wad of cash. We'll need it to buy a few things, and upgrade to a better hotel soon.

"You ready?" I ask.

"Sure thing, partner." Her Texas drawl seems to be more pronounced in her hometown.

"Let's get some food and make some plans," I say.

There's a small dark cloud over our heads. Our usual childish flirty banter is replaced with a pensive seriousness.

Teska knows the town like the back of her hand. We find a Mexican place and take an empty booth at the far back. I keep my view pointed out, to scan the scene. See people entering. No one behind me.

We order some stuff off the menu.

"Jeffrey…" begins Teska.

"Let's get some tucker inside of us, then talk for real," I say.

She pauses and we nibble on tortilla chips and salsa which doubles as a perfect silence filler.

Our enchiladas and tacos arrive. Australia is shit when it comes to Mexican food. When I first saw a tortilla, I thought it was flat pita bread. But I've had enough exposure to it to now to know my way around a menu.

We dig in. The cloud starts to fizzle a little. Food does that. As does sleep. As does good news. Hopefully we can handle two out of three of those by tomorrow morning.

"Talk," I say.

"Jeffrey. I'm so neck deep with emotion I can't see straight. The truth is, Wade, I've really been falling for you," she says. I knew this, but hearing her say it still makes me blush.

"Okay... but... it's based on a false premise, that Jeffrey was a two-timing tosser," I say.

"Right. And that was the foundation on which I planned a new life. Hating him for what he did. Now that's gone. My new life, its trajectory, was built on a lie. A pile of dog shit I that I bought into. QuadFilium became my home, my stable rock, and place to build from. Now they're trying to kill you. They lied about Jeffrey. I have the two strongest pillars of my life shattered. My mind is jumping around like a toad on a hot rock," she says.

"As one could expect," I say. "I faked a death so I could have a whole new life, make a difference, and follow something I believe in. Gave my life to it. And now my brothers and sisters are taking shots at me. I even thought they mighta turned you, as bait for me," I say.

"Then why'd you show up at the restaurant?" she asks.

"Because if you were bait, I would have turned myself in. You are the last person I could trust. If that's gone, I wouldn't care anymore," I say.

She looks down as she realizes she means more to me than flirting and a smooch. I'm realizing that myself. But, I don't want to take away from her and Jeffrey. I want her to consider that scene unbiased, uninfluenced by the Wade factor.

"Look," I say, "we just went through some very traumatic shit and it's going to get worse. All we've got is each other. Let's not confuse it with something else. I want you to have a clean view of the scene with Jeff, unclouded by our stuff."

She looks slightly rebuffed by this statement. Right now, she is vulnerable, craving company, someone to hold her, protect her, reassure her. I shouldn't abuse this weakened state with romance. It needs to be done right. If we end up together later, taking advantage of her now, even if she seems to want to, will make her always wonder if she should have gone with Jeffrey. Every time I do something sus, she'll wonder. I can't let the craving of the moment damage the smoothness of the roads tomorrow.

I add in, "Teska, as a point. You are by far the most smoking-hot sheila I have ever seen, known, heard of, thought of, envisioned, or dreamed of. As a bloke, I would like nothing more than... you know. It would be a dream come true. But I also know that forever, from this point forward, you'll always wonder if you should've gone back with Jeffrey. He was your rock. He provided you with a life you always wanted and never thought possible. If we get incautious and mess around, you can't view the issues with Jeffrey in a clean frame of mind. You'll blame me for it. You'll feel regret.

"If it were up to me, I'd selfishly want you all to myself, and I'd tell you to ditch Jeffrey like he's going out of style. But I know if I did that, the next few days weeks or months would be exciting and fun, but after that, you'd forever compare me to Jeffrey, and I'm sure he'll top me in many categories. Seems like a real good bloke. On point. Top notch. Next level. I don't have all the boxes checked for the perfect guy by any stretch. So yeah, do I want to stay in the same room as you tonight? Fuckin oath, I do. But wouldn't be right."

"Wow, Wade. Thanks...?" she says.

"Meet up with Jeffrey. Talk it over in detail, for hours, or days. Decide what you want to do with regards to him, without me in the equation. I'll back you up 100%," I say.

"Do you think he gave us up at the restaurant, tonight? How else would they know?" she asks.

"I thought over each scenario. The most likely is that they painted a picture of your safety being an issue and rubbed it in his face. They could've made it seem your life was on the line by our interaction, and made him the savior by telling."

"Kind of noble. But he made a deal with you, right?" she says.

"Yes. They had to discredit me. Show him footage of me killing someone or something. Talk about how dangerous it is around me. People die. Stuff rings true, cuz it is. He'd feel I was the one who hoodwinked him. He'd have no problem breaking his word with me in that scenario. And, I don't blame him. If I made a deal with some bloke, and later found out he was a thirsty, active murderer, with fairdinkum evidence, I wouldn't feel compelled to keep it. I'd feel compelled to shove his head up his own ass. They have ample footage to make me look like a first-rate psycho. They have evidence of contracts out on me. I should've predicted they would try to turn him. I should have prepared for it. Need to sharpen my game," I say and take a couple more bites of my enchilada.

"But if he was the one that gave up our position, I can't help but lose respect for him," asks Teska.

"I don't agree. He's known me for five minutes. He's known you for years. Any idea something'll hurt you, he'd be aggressive. Shows his feelings for you. Can't blame the guy for that. I reckon he'd have resisted torture, not sayin' a word, if he knew it would protect you," I say.

"Fair enough," she says.

"Right now, all we need to do is get a good night's rest.

We're both knackered," I say, as we finish off our meal, pay the bill and depart.

Chapter 51
Jean Jacques

"Alistair, Wade is dead," I say.

"Proof is in the pudding," he quips.

"I uploaded a video on the dark web. I texted you the encrypted link. Watch it," I say.

I wait a few minutes while Alistair watches the video of Wade getting shot and Teska screaming he is dead. His body flies off the chair backwards and he remains motionless, while she screams.

"Spare me the melodrama. Where's a live shot of his dead body?" he asks.

"We don't have it." I say

"That gives me pause, Mr. Girard. I witnessed this testosterone-twerp get repeatedly shot the day he broached my compound. Then he leapt, quite gracefully, onto a fucking rope ladder and flew away like Chuck Norris. Why don't you have the body?" asks Alistair.

"There was shooting in a public restaurant. SWAT arrived. I lost a man. But before he was shot, he hit Wade in the chest with two .45s," I say.

"My condolences on your loss. However, I need proof. I'm increasing contract value on Wade to twenty million. Your incompetence leads to my cost. Oh, on the two billion, let's make that euros, instead of dollars. American money is so dirty, isn't it? Your wife and daughter agree." And he hangs up.

He's right. Even I suspect he's alive. Close monitoring of

the local hospitals and mortuaries show nothing.

I also need to make an example of John Crutcher and Dimitri. Otherwise, they'll inspire defeatism and disaffection within QF. Has to be fast. I need to put their heads on a pike, in public.

I go onto the PA system, that broadcasts to all crew members.

"Attention all, we are having a full crew staff meeting in twenty minutes in the Commons. Please attend. All Mind Booth personnel can step out of the booth for the briefing. Ensure operatives in the field are patched in."

I go back to my desk, and I look at my messages. I see that Yun Fei in China is mourning the loss of her mother, the perfect chance to catch her scopulus. I call Brett in China.

"Yes, boss," he says.

"It looks like it's time to engage the prospect."

"On it. I'm going to connect up with her today."

"Great," and I hang up.

I jot down some notes for my staff briefing, then head to the Commons. The whole crew is assembled. As I enter, chattering subsides. I walk between the two bodies of chairs occupied by the crew of Quadfilium, up to the podium.

"You'd like answers, and direction. You'll have them. But before that, let me remind you that QuadFilium was founded upon a sacred pact of protection. We take into our own hands what nobody is willing or capable of doing. We make things right.

"Before QuadFilium, the number of enslaved people was on a sharp upcurve. Estimated at more than twenty million worldwide. Slavers worked with impunity, for lust and profit. Since we started, 15,000 slaves have been freed by our hands and five major slave distribution operations have been eliminated. Our actions have cut world-wide slave production by one-point-eight million."

The room applauds.

"As a humanitarian group, we fly straight into the teeth of vested interests, most of whom seek financial profit at great cost to others. Organizations like Quadfilium are targeted for infiltration and counter-surveillance using blackmail and bribes.

"We have strong evidence that QuadFilium agent Wade Maley, deserted the unit mid mission and provided information on the whereabouts of QuadFilium and my family to Alistair Watson. This resulted the kidnapping of my daughter and wife, who are both now captives of one of the most dangerous men on Earth."

A gasp or two. Then, you could hear a pin drop.

"Wade has put all of our lives in danger.

"I have ordered his termination to cut off the destruction. We all know Wade as an extraordinary competent operative. A good person. But good people can do bad things, and in his case, his actions have put your, my, and my wife and daughter's lives at risk." A tear wells up in my eye and I pause.

"Be advised, I've had to relieve John Crutcher and Dimitri Abdramanova from command structure. They refused orders to exert deadly force on Wade.

"I've never taken such action. But there is just too much at stake.

"It weighs heavily on me to be in this position. But my love for Wade, John and Dimitri cannot outweigh my duty to you, QuadFilium, my family and Mankind.

"John will be writing lessons on tactics and weaponry. Dimitri will continue his research and development. They will be on 'no-command' posts due to insubordination and polite mutiny. They will be given a tribunal.

"I expect the group to rise up, braze up, and be strong so that we remain forceful as a unit, and we push forward the purpose underlying everything we do.

"On dissent: think of the kids enslaved, the women raped and made into prostitutes, and the unwilling organ donors that have all their happiness, rights and futures ripped away for the selfish benefit of evil men. Dissent is the acid that burns through the bonds that hold us together and make us capable. Stomp on the gossipers, the complainers, the rabble rousers and the decriers. They are working for the enemy even if they don't realize it.

"If you have a concern, a question or a problem, let me know. I will listen, I will answer. I will fix it. But before you question my decision about Wade, think of the person you love most in your life... a child, a sister or a brother and imagine that person was kidnapped, captured and abused by a known murderer and rapist. Then know, Wade facilitates this by his actions. And you will see why I must act.

"In a war, command decisions may be brilliant, misinformed, or even flat wrong. Leadership isn't infallible. *Leadership* takes responsibility and acts. If it is right more than wrong, it wins. But mistakes or not, it never deviates from the purpose of the group. Never. For this group that purpose is to free slaves and eliminate enslavers. I will never break faith with that purpose. We are at war. War is messy. It's not a parliamentary debate. It's not an academic exercise. Second guessing and introspection are not part of winning. Are you with me?"

I pause and let the emotion carry my message into their

souls. I make it uncomfortable. I look each and every one of them in the eyes. They are frozen. Deers in headlights.

"Let's get it done. Your loyalty will free people and damn those who try to stop us."

I walk off at that point to applause. I feel the varied emotions connected with those claps. Some fear, others agree, some don't want to seem shocked. But everyone is afraid to be heard questioning my orders. Most will simply not talk about their disagreements with each other, and that's fine. Knowing we hear and listen to their every word adds to it. Being a dissenter is dangerous. That's at least the common thread each attendee takes away.

Chapter 52
Wade

I wake up in my hotel bed and orient myself. It's 0800. I slept well and feel fresh and energized.

I knock on Teska's door.

"I need thirty minutes," she says.

"Want some food?"

"Sure. Whatever you find is fine."

"Right-ee-oh," I say.

I head out to the street and look for a convenience store. A block away, I find one. I buy the two most expensive burner phones they have. These newest ones are full of apps and other fancy stuff which is what I need. As I walk, I program them, and I sync them up with an app about finding your friends which is basically a GPS so we know each other's location at all times.

I walk down the street and find a Wendy's. I heard a commercial not long ago that they have some good breakfast burritos these days. Sounds great. I scan the environment for any sus characters, folks that seem out of place.

Two homeless blokes fast asleep, looking like barnacles on the sidewalk. A girl walks a baby stroller and dog. A kid on a skateboard. The only guy who seems a bit odd is a pale white bloke with shades walking down the street. Out here in Texas most folks are at least just a little bit tan. He's holding a briefcase. A bit odd for this time of day and this part of town. No businesses around to speak of. If he walks outside a lot, he wouldn't be so pale. This guy doesn't walk around outside much.

At no point does his head point towards me and I cannot see his eyes through his glasses. I go into Wendy's and get my burritos and coffees. I look through the glass windows, scanning for pale man. No sign. I walk back to the hotel and go up to Teska's room and knock. She lets me in.

"Today we figure out how to get you and Jeffrey in touch," I say as I unload the food onto a brown Formica table.

"I can just call him and we can meet up in a location only he and I know," says Teska.

"I'm sure they are tracking him within an inch of his life. There's no chance they won't follow him to us. After we got him to sneak away from them earlier, they'll have tracking bugs all over everything he owns. He'd have to show up naked and bald in order to evade surveillance."

She laughs. "What do we do?" she asks.

"Meet him in a nudist colony? I may have to join you for protection," I say.

Teska laughs again. I turn my attention to the door. I heard a soft footstep in the hallway stop just outside our room. I hear a click. Not the door. Metal on metal. Could be room service. This place doesn't have room service. My smile disappears and I look at Teska.

"What?" She asks.

"Someone's just stopped outside our door," I whisper.

The click sounds like an automatic weapon. The table won't be strong enough to stop a bullet. It's cheap laminated particle board, a sponge of shredded wood fibers soaked and dried together, like a wafer, then covered in a tenth of a millimeter of plastic and called board.

"Get behind the bed!" I say in a yell whisper.

We both jump on the side of the bed farthest from the entry, just as automatic machine gun fire rips through the door and perforates the table, the wall, our breakfast, the chairs and everything else in the room. By the sounds of it, two automatic weapons. Either one guy with both arms holding a gun, unlikely, or two fuckers shooting at the same time. There's likely a third and fourth outside waiting to greet us with additional active weapons if we bail through our windows.

These guys aren't with QuadFilium. I think back to pale guy. A mercenary. A professional hitman. *Did Jean Jacques hire him? How did these guys find us?*

I assess my options: one door in and out, or the window. Ground floor.

Teska's crouched but poised to leap.

The bullet bursts last five seconds then the guns need to cool. The shredded door is no longer an obstacle. They might assume we are both dead although I doubt these guys assume. They enter and spray the room and we're done.

I pull out the revolver Harold lent me and I carefully aim it at the door jamb, twenty-five inches above the door knob, where the man's head should appear for half a second while he checks out the scene. I hold my breath and remain steady.

Two inches of head creeps into my crosshairs and without the slightest wiggle I pull the trigger. The bullet goes through his eye and anything directly behind his eye. I glimpse his partner as he jumps back into the hallway. I know right away his partner is the alpha. He would not expose his own face, only his underling's.

I imagine I'm him. *What would I do?* If he's a mercenary, he needs proof that I'm dead. I would expect the targets to be armed. I can't expose myself or I'll get killed like my partner just did. I'd roll a grenade into the room, blow me the fuck up, then come back and collect body parts to take back to my client.

I jump over Teska and roll across the bed towards the door. A hand pitches a grenade into the room.

If he was smart, he would've held the grenade for two seconds before he threw it into the room. It's a four second lag from ring pull to detonation.

In the small room's foyer, I catch the grenade before it even hits the ground. I throw it into the hall at him. He darts. I dive back into the room over the bed.

I plug my ears to prevent my tympanic membranes from rupturing and open my mouth to regularize the pressure and prevent the lungs from bursting. Teska sees me, training kicks in, and she mimics. The deafening blast shakes the wood-framed building. Dust debris and a wave of heat billow into the room. The hallway is thick with smoke and particles rain down. I hope no one got hurt besides pale prick.

There's likely at least two thugs outside the building, near our windows, probably assuming the blast killed us.

"Teska, give me your phone," I say. "Gather what we need and come outside when the coast is clear, in two minutes," I say to her.

I step over the dead underling and pale prick on the ground, his back shredded with shrapnel. I grab a cloth to put over my face, mostly to hide it but also to filter out dust, and run down the hall, with phone and gun tucked and hidden. I peer through the front door and see a van parked across the street. Darkened interior and a man in the driver's seat. It is dirty but the windows are clean. Telltale signs of a surveillance vehicle. No doubt the back is a well-rigged sniper nest with a gun trained on the window I'm supposed to be jumping out of. The hotel fire alarm blares and sprinklers spray. People start to file out in a state of pandemonium, shrieking at the sight of the dead guys in the hall. I wait to blend into the crowd and follow a batch of folks that cross the street and head in the direction of the van. As I pass it, I pop open the gas tank cover and slip my phone inside on top of the gas cap, and close it.

I keep walking. The van guys hear sirens as the various emergency response departments head towards the disaster. The driver starts it up and leaves.

Teska appears with our stuff in amongst the mob.

She says, "I checked for collateral damage. The thugs look like the only casualties. No innocents dead that I could see."

"Thank God. We need a vehicle."

"I got this," she says.

We walk down the block, along several rows of cars and she stops at a '90s Nissan Pathfinder parked on the curb.

"These '90s cars can be hotwired," she says and smashes the back seat window, reaches around and opens the door. She gets inside and does some wiring thing while I load in. The car fires up and we're off.

"Who the fuck were those guys?"

"Pro mercenaries."

"…damn… Good thing we're lucky at heart."

"No shit. I saw the rest of their team in a van drive off. We need to follow them and try to get to the bottom of this."

"How do find this van?" she says.

I hold up the phone and show the Find Your Friends app, "Let's find our friends. Better yet, let's see where in fuck's name they head to so we can pull back the line to its source," I say.

"Yee hah," says the Texan.

We follow the app and see the van is only a few blocks away, driving slowly. We step on the gas and catch up, staying three car-lengths behind. They pull into the driveway of a Hilton and park. We do too. They get out. Two of them. They head towards the entrance with a jagged pace, looking at the ground.

I say, "I'll follow them to their rooms. You get a housekeeping uniform and find me. Fast."

I grab the phone out of the van's gas tank gap and trail the guys up to the elevator. They get in. I walk past to the stairs. It's only a four-story so I go up to two and peer down the hall and listen. Nothing. I run up to floor three and see them walking down the hall off the elevator. They both enter a room in the middle of the hallway. Number 313.

Teska shows up a few minutes later in a get-up from the housekeeping lockers. There's a cart outside one of the rooms in the hall, with the worker inside vacuuming. Teska grabs the cart.

I have the two burner phones in my hand. I call one with the other and answer it. I put mine on mute and the other on speaker.

"Somehow get this in the room," I say and hand her a phone.

"Okay,"

She knocks on the door. I hide around the corner.

"Housekeeping," she says.

"No, thank you!" says a voice from the inside.

"I'm very sorry to disturb you, but, I left something in the room and I need to grab it real quick. I'm so sorry," she says, and opens her blouse a little in case they check the peephole.

Sure enough, the door opens, "Be quick," one gruffs.

She leaves in under a minute.

The guys stare down the hall as she walks away, "Come back in a few hours and make a bunch of extra money, Tutz," in New York accent. "Tutz" is a Gen X or older phrase. Noted.

She walks towards me and winks as she buttons up her blouse.

"Valuable currency in a man's game," she says.

"Can't argue," I say.

"Phone is placed," she says.

"Beauty. Want to go and change and then hit the store and buy some more burner phones?" I say.

"Copy that."

We wheel the cart back to its spot. She heads off to change and I go outside to the parking lot. There's a lonely bench on the other end with a smoker's pole next to it in the middle of a patch of grass. No walkways or cars nearby. I sit there and listen.

Thug one says, "They're the ones who knew what to do. We don't really know shit."

Thug two says, "We should call someone."

Both have New York accents. Reminds me of Kris. Probably knew each other.

Thug one says, "I don't know. I feel like disappearing. Alistair is a no-tolerance-for-fuck-ups kinda guy."

Like a two by four that name hits me.

Thug two says, "He'll shit a brick when we tell him. But it'll be a much smaller brick than if we run. We should call."

"Fuck! Alright... what do we say?"

"We just tell him exactly what the fuck happened."

"Okay, okay. Let's do it. I'll call him."

Silence as he dials.

Thug one makes the call, "Mr. Watson, hello. No sir, he's not answering because he and Carter are both dead.... Yes sir. Jason and I escaped and the target is at-large.

"Yes sir, face recognition software is activated...

"You want us back in LA?

"Okay sir, we'll drive straight there."

Thug one says to thug two, "He's pissed."

"Shit."

"He said he wants us back there to help with the next phase."

"Awww Jesus. Carter is way better at this shit. Too bad he's dead."

I hear them mumble about getting their stuff together and getting on the road.

Teska and I need to follow. We can't in this stolen vehicle.

Teska finds me on the bench.

She says, "I set up the Find Your Friends GPS app and fixed a phone to the undercarriage of their van."

"Okay, great."

She sits next to me on the bench. I fill her in on the thugs, Alistair and their plan.

I say, "I don't see you meeting Jeffrey as the healthiest idea right now."

"Yeah... not with every posse in town hunting us," she says.

"We'll make it happen. But we need to follow this down back to the real Alistair. Otherwise, I'll be dead in no time. I imagine it's not every day that a bounty hunter gets a ten-mil contract, probably payable on evidence, and with competition. People are working very very hard to kill me. Not to mention my own group. The bounty hunter assassins used face

FOUR LEAF / WADE

recognition software, hacked cameras on the web... the hospital... street cams and then the hotel. That's how they found me."

"Seriously?" she says.

"Yeah. We were a bee's dick away from getting minced."

"No shit."

"We follow the thugs to LA and get to the source. The thugs said something about having a wife and daughter of someone. I wonder if this is related to Jean Jacques recent homicidal tendencies, why he has a kill order on me. There is no scenario besides extreme deadly threat that would make him do that."

"Like what?"

"I don't know. Like if someone held a bomb over the QF and base and said, 'kill Wade or I'll drop this.' " I say.

"Or if one of his family members was kidnapped...?" she says.

"That's a good point. Seems far-fetched, but I suppose. He wouldn't do it for money. Only to hide something really, really serious, or to prevent the death of people he cares more about than he does about me."

"Which is basically his wife or Carmen."

"Yeah, or the whole team at QF. Who knows? Let's track these knobs back to Cali."

"Realize that Ashkay has face recognition as well and superior resources to Alistair's mercenaries. We took out half of one team of assassins. Who knows how many others there are?" she says.

"You're right," I say. "Let's move, and let's try to evade cameras."

We look on-line for a rental car place that doesn't require a credit card but will accept cash instead. We find one called the Ugly Duckling Rental Car Company. We get a total junker, buy some baseball caps and glasses and hit the road to LA.

The battery life on the phone under the van is max ten hours. By the time we have the rental and the disguises, the thugs are already forty minutes ahead of us.

Over the span of two hours, we catch up and have them in sight. We follow the rules of mobile surveillance and let the rabbit car stay a good distance away on the long highway, always several cars between us. Although a vigilant driver will make us after an hour or two.

We decide to rely on the Find Your Friends GPS and fall way back, disappearing from sight for long stretches. If the phone battery dies, we'll need to have eyes on them.

I think about Jean Jacques. The bloke has so many factors to consider. If his family is in danger he'd have to choose between his honor and his family's lives.

Someone has Jean Jacques's balls in a vice.

I can certainly find fault with his recruitment methods though. Dishonest. His actions traumatized the shit out of Peyton and Jeffrey. Lifelong scars on innocent souls, in order to get me and Teska onto the force.

One can argue there could have been no other way to get us. Not having us, meant fewer lives saved. At what point do we say we've gone too far or the end justifies the means? *What would I do in his shoes?*

Chapter 53
Jean Jacques

No signal on Wade for twenty-four hours. He's covered in GPS jamming clothes, underground, or found a way to deactivate his feeds.

I call Dimitri to my office. He arrives and looks irascible. I can't fault him. I've put him in a public yoke despite his loyalty, love for the group and consistent high performance.

"Dimitri, I need to know if there is any way Wade could deactivate his devices."

"Sir, yes. There is one way. Electromagnetic pulse turns off device until rebooted."

"How does one get hold of one of those?" I ask.

"I've made some for small radius electronics shutdowns. They also deactivate audio and visio device."

"Did Wade or Teska take one?"

"I can check," Dimitri says.

"Okay, do that," I say.

"Yes, sir," he says, as he gets up to leave. Lethargic, slow, he lacks his usual eagerness.

"Hold on, Dimitri. We need to talk..."

"Yes, sir," he says.

"Talk to me...?"

"I came here volunteer. I love Wade. I am loyal. You, this group, are my family. I indignant. You have shunned me to my family. Not fair."

"I don't expect you to agree, Dimitri, but I had to. The

311

group's survival depends on it. If I don't eliminate Wade, my family is tortured and killed. Your and John's dissent weakens my command. Under attack, a lack of single-minded purpose is a cancer. It destroys the group. My family will die, and my soul with them."

"You say Wade told Alistair about QuadFilium. Why would Alistair kill Wade in such case?" he asks.

"Wade cost him over a billion dollars. His video, killing Alistair's client, went to thousands of his customers who cancelled business. Wade killed Alistair's decoy and massacred his LA operation. No one has devastated Alistair more. Wade's revealing QF base elicits no loyalty in a man like Alistair."

"You confirm Wade do what you say?"

"No. The only thing I know is that Alistair wants Wade's head on a platter or else my family is dead."

Dimitri looks right at me, "I see. So, you now Alistair's mercenary."

That stings.

"That's... he's also demanding two billion euros."

"I sympathize predicament you face, sir. I wish you I could a solution. I check on EMPs, see if any missing." He leaves.

Dimitri calls three minutes later, "Sir, one EMP missing. Must be Teska has taken," says Dimitri.

"Thank you," I say.

I call Ashkay, "Where do we stand?" I ask.

"Facial recognition up in every Austin intersection and every gas station I could access leading out of Austin. Over seven thousand cameras active. So far, no hits."

"Hmm. Look through all your photos of Wade. See if there's another way to track him other than face. What about the tattoo on his wrist? Can you set up the software to detect it?

He's probably wearing a hat and glasses. Same with Teska."

"I'll check."

I hear Ashkay click his keyboard.

He says, "Hmmm, zooming in on tattoo on his right wrist, I can see it's a swirlie shape."

"See if you can program to recognize it. Follow up with me on any hit. I don't think they'll expose their faces. They're aware of our facial recognition capability."

"Yes, sir."

The six-man team, led by Alex Gonzales in Austin, has regrouped, now down to five. The agent shot is in ICU in a downtown county hospital, listed as John Doe. Not critical, but not stable. Surgery for internal bleeding, broken ribs. Ruptured spleen.

Once we locate Wade, the team is poised to strike on command.

One operative is full time on Jeffrey, in case they try to connect with him.

The Mind Booth team is now led by Heidi and consists only of Kris, Heidi and Ashkay.

Brett calls me from China, "Boss, I've made it to Ghangzhou and spotted Yun Fei. She is mid a drunken binge right now. I've studied the file three times through."

"What's your take on the approach?"

"Her father died last year. Her mother died yesterday. She has nothing left in the way of family. She watched her mother wither away to sixty pounds over six months. The cancer ate away her whole body, spine, stomach, and brain. She started having seizures. The brain cancer made her insane and cruel. Yun Fei was there for every step. It's gotta be the most depressing experience imaginable for a girl that age. She has no husband or family. Few friends to talk to. She moved in to care for her mother. No boyfriend. I'd say she's lost all pride and hope. Alcohol's become her form of slow suicide. Or, she may just jump. I'll surveille hands-on for the next twenty-four and engage at the right moment."

"That's a sound plan. Keep me apprised."

"Yes, sir."

Ashkay gets back to me, "Sir, I got 'em. The tattoo. A gas station in Lordsburg, New Mexico. It's Teska and Wade getting fuel, in hats and glasses like you said. I got the make and model of their car, and LP number."

"Okay! Put Heidi and Kris on the line," I say.

"Done," he says.

I check a map of the US. I can only assume they are heading to the west coast through Phoenix.

I say to Heidi and Kris, who heard my exchange with Ashkay, "Order the team to leave Austin, drop Jeffrey. Helicopter to Phoenix and intercept. Anticipate they'll stay in the area for the night. We'll find them when they get in front of a camera."

"Ten-four," Heidi and Kris say.

Wade is alive. Alistair will find out. I call him.

"Jean Jacques, what?" Alistair says as he answers my wife's phone.

"Wade is alive, and headed west on Interstate 10," I say

"I already know, you fucking incompetent piece of shit. He dispatched two more of my assassins after we tracked him to a hotel. Impress me. I have ten bounty hunters eager to hear," taunts Alistair.

"We assumed that he was covering his face and head to avoid facial recognition. We tweaked the software to find a tattoo he has on his wrist. We found him in Lordsburg, New Mexico, three minutes ago. Heading west in a mid-'80s model brown Lincoln Continental, license plate 1FRK7UX. I'll send you a pic," I say.

"Interesting. I have half a team at right about the same location as we speak. Seems odd that your two fugitives and my two assassins are hours away from Austin, and only minutes away from each other."

"They must be following your guys..."

"Seems so. But that does give me the upper hand. I'll need to go take care of this."

I think of Teska. His goons don't care about collateral damage.

"Mr. Watson, my daughter, my wife ...?"

"Of course. How inconsiderate of me... ladies?"

"Jean Jacques! Dad!" They're cut off. They're alive. I feel relief but terror.

Alistair says, "I expect every detail relayed to me. Between the two of us, Mr. Girard, I believe we can step on this little cockroach."

"Of course," I say. Alistair hangs up.

315

Chapter 54
Teska

We leave a gas station in New Mexico after filling up the tank. I grabbed a few external batteries for our burners. I recharge mine to full capacity and attach another battery, giving it fifteen hours of power.

We watch the rabbit car in our app for fifteen minutes. The GPS shows it's stopped on the side of the road. I show Wade, who's driving. He pulls over, a half a mile back.

"Maybe the pickle ticklers needed to take a leak," says Wade.

The other car doesn't move. Five minutes, ten minutes.

"What's taking them so long?" I ask.

"Maybe number two in the bushes. Using brambles to wipe their arseholes," says Wade.

We watch the GPS. The car backs down the shoulder in our direction. The gap is closing, a third of a mile, a quarter mile. The small speck in the distance grows in size.

Maybe they're searching. Maybe for us. Wade pops it into reverse and backs up. He matches their speed and keeps the rabbit car at several hundred feet. After five minutes, the car stops and takes off on the highway. We resume mobile surveillance and watch the GPS tracker, following them for a few miles, staying a quarter to a half mile back. But their car is going 50 mph on a highway with a speed limit of 70.

"What are they doing? Why are they going so slow?"

"Guess they're looking for something. Could have a tip

someone's following them. Looking for us on the highway, slowing down, hoping we'll pass," says Wade.

"How... did they find the burner?" I ask.

Wade says, "If they found the burner, they probably would have tagged it to another vehicle to make us think —"

"Wade! Watch out!" I scream as the rabbit car screeches at us from the right. Wade hits the gas but this piece of shit has no pick-me-up. From the back seat, a shooter starts to unload. Wade shoves me down below door level before the bullets rip through my seat and snowflake the windshield. Their car hits our back right fender and turns us perpendicular to the road. Going 50 mph, we're poised to flip down the highway. But Wade's trained in vehicular tactics. The natural inclination is to turn left and veer away from the car. Wade turns hard right. We don't flip, we spin. The rabbit car overcompensates their ram force, and goes perpendicular on the road.

They're not as skilled and lose control, flip and tumble down the highway like a hot wheels car bowled by a kid across a floor.

After 720-degrees of spin, Wade rights the car and we mosey down the highway like nothing happened, save a decent dent on the back right fender.

I look in my mirror and see a smoking wreckage, the car upside down, still spinning on its roof. Screeching traffic stops behind them.

Wade has a slight pant. My heart is pounding. We reorient, come back down to Earth and look at each other.

"Good we survived, but bad we don't know where we're going. These goons ain't dropping breadcrumbs anymore," I say.

"You okay?" Wade asks concerned.

"Fine. A bit rattled." I answer. "The bad guys knew our car. How?"

"They had some way of seeing us. Can't think of any other way."

"So, we ditch this ugly duckling piece of shit?"

"No. We keep it. We get another tail on us and follow them back to wherever the fuck in LA they're going."

"We're *bait*?!"

"Seems like the best idea. We need to cut off the head of the snake. Alistair has a pile of assassins with huge contracts on my head. One of them will lead us back to him. Somehow," he says.

"That's our plan?" I ask.

Wade says, "It's the *only* plan right now. Those car-flipping cunts were our best bet to undo this mess."

"…okay…"

"Human patterns have predictable elements. Jean Jacques is under some crazy ass influence, more powerful than his own judgment and ethics can fight. Whoever has this grip on him has made him into a mercenary trying to terminate me. Even after seven years of unbroken loyalty and performance. Jean Jacques loved me. When I ask myself who he cares more about, I think of only a few people."

"Who?" I ask.

"You for one."

That sinks in like a splinter in a fingernail.

"And…?"

"His daughter. Nothing is more important to him than his daughter. She's the whole reason he started QuadFilium. Why he dedicated his life to it. That's why it makes me think that some fucking way, Alistair got hold of Jean Jacques's wife and daughter and is playing puppet master. Jean Jacques had to do some major reorganization in the last twenty-four to forty-eight hours to get my fellow agents to hunt me down and kill me. These are guys I have been in the line of fire with. Who I have trained and mentored. And who have taught me to be a better agent, a better man. For them to switch, Jean Jacques would have to have convinced them that I am pure evil and need to be eliminated."

"What a fucking asshole!" I say.

"That's one way to look at it. Another is look at it from his viewpoint. His own daughter and wife, kidnapped. Alistair managed to find the QF location. His family's necks ready to be slit, if he doesn't dance to Alistair's playlist. Which clearly includes kill Wade or I kill yours. If I'm right, it's QuadFilium, and the assassins, however many there are, against our skill, vigilance, and our... luck."

Four Leaf.

We sit silent. Cruise, pan the environment for the next attack. It doesn't come. We reach Phoenix city limits and look for a safe place to stay for the night.

We settle on a three-star hotel, park the car a couple blocks down the road and walk back to the hotel. Wade does his two-room thing. He's right about that. It would forever complicate things. Relationships. I'm queen of that bucking bronco, the one on the ground. It'd be nice to have a man's arm on my shoulder, a hug. I'm such a wuss. Wade's the only man I truly trust right now.

We take a cab to a Walmart and buy five nanny cams and bring them back to our hotel. The whole time we wear hats and glasses. I don't know if it's enough. We disassemble them and take out the small cameras, about the size of an AA battery.

We secretly set them up outside the hotel, the lobby, and

the hallway outside our rooms and sync them to our phones. We agree to two-watch shifts so one can sleep while the other has eyes on the cams. Wade can fall asleep anytime. He'll take the first shift from 2100 to 0230. It's 1900 now.

I watch guests come and go, cars pull in and pull out, hotel staff do their jobs. Nothing out of the ordinary.

At 1931pm something catches my eye. One guy's movements look familiar. He's talking to the desk clerk. I can't see his face. He has no bags. He has a jacket and it's ninety-two degrees outside. He turns. Fuck. It's a QuadFilium agent. Alex Gonzales. How did they find us here?

I run across the hall and bang on Wade's door. He opens it a moment later. I show him the cam. Gonzales is still talking to the clerk.

Wade says, "Alex fucking Gonzales, Mister smooth talker. He'll know which rooms we are in no time. He's got mad persuasion skills."

"There's got to be others with him. We need to figure out how they found us," I say.

"True, but right now, we need to figure out how to survive. They'll have every exit covered... rooftop," he says.

 Come to my room, quick!" I say.

Wade grabs his bag and follows me to my room. I pull out my fat man mask. "Put this on and stuff your jacket with a pillow," I say.

"Brilliant!" says Wade.

He quickly dons the getup. Mask, hat, glasses, jacket and pillows. Perfect. Looks nothing like Wade. I look at my camera feed. Alex is still talking to the clerk. They both laugh at something. We used aliases at check-in. So Alex will need to use descriptions of us to attempt identification.

I say, "What about me? There's no disguise good enough without that mask."

"They won't try to kill you. They'll hit you with tranquilizers and bind you captive. At least you'll be safe," says Wade.

"I can hide. They won't find me. Oh look! Alex left. He's coming!"

"Okay. You hide. I'll walk out of here. If your Houdini works, I'll take off the disguise and get it to the clerk somehow. I'll send it in a package in the next hour for your alias, Sylvia. You keep an eye on the cams. When the coast is clear, grab it from the desk area, and walk out of here wearing it," says Wade.

"Okay! He's coming! Go!" Wade, in full fat-man garb, trots off towards the elevator and pushes the down button. I grab my bag and run down the hall opposite from where Alex will come up. I look inside a broom closet. On its ceiling is a panel to the space between the false ceiling and the roof where they stuff all the ducts and pipes. I jump on a sink and push it open. I pull myself up and through and lie across joists and watch the camera feed in my phone. Alex walks down the hall with another agent, right past Wade without even noticing him. Wade gets into the elevator. They both pull out .45s and identify our two rooms, across the hall from each other. They stand back-to-back and count to three and kick. They leap into the rooms in expert formation. No shots fired. After two minutes, they come out, and look at one another, then dart their attention around the hall.

They talk for a minute. Then they get antsy and start looking around. They check inside closets, the two trash chutes, an ice machine compartment, behind a vending machine.

They'll check the panel in the broom closet. They'll ask themselves where they'd go, if they were me. I sit on top of the panel to seal with my weight. I see Alex enter my broom closet. I hear shuffling below. After thirty seconds, I feel him push on the panel. He's a strong man. I'm 125. He could easily lift me up. But his stance on a closet sink doesn't give him the purchase to get his full strength. He decides it's sealed and leaves. Checks off "broom closet empty."

Phew.

Chapter 55
Wade

I make my way outside, shuffling like an old fat guy, which is good because I am supposed to be an old fat guy, right past another QF agent standing outside watching the front door for Wade or Teska. He even smiles a cordial and respectful greeting as I pass. I give a tired wave in return. No eye contact.

I walk across the street and go into the gas station and buy a cap and glasses and ask for a bag. Then to the loo.

How did they find us? No electronic trace. The feeds and GPS are deactivated otherwise they wouldn't need to know which rooms—they'd storm in guns a-blazing like Desperado. El Mariachi.

Programmed video camera facial recognition to look for another signature identifier? *What would I do if I was Ashkay?*

I look over my body for any signature. My wrist tattoo! That's the only way. They programmed software to look on all available cameras. They found one at our hotel and spotted us. All they needed then was to smooth-talk the clerk. Note to self, cover the ink.

In the restroom, I change out of my fat-guy outfit and put it in the bag. I put the cap and glasses on. I hold my hand over the tattoo and leave the dunny. There's a small open mechanic shop full of grease and tools. I walk near the front. There's a man under a car, and another bloke looking at his phone in the back. I find some duct tape sitting on a blackened wooden table close to the entrance. They don't notice me take it. I rip off a strip a few inches long and cover the wrist ink with it and head back into the gas station market. I buy a small pack of pens and a pad of paper.

I tape a note to the bag which says, "Happy Birthday to Sylvia." I look around the gas station for a customer I can schmooze.

A turquoise Kia pulls up to a pump. A cute college-age sheila gets out and plays around with the machine for a minute, grabs the pump and places it in her tank. I approach her and say, "Excuse me, miss. So sorry to bother you. Can I ask you a random favor?" She's only slightly taken aback. This ain't New York. Judging by her attire, her age and her good looks, she isn't unaccustomed to strangers striking up a convo with her, especially the young male variety.

I see her defensive stance, feet pointing to the side, thinking I'm about to bust out a one-liner. Maybe ask her for her number. I see the wheels turn, cookie-cutter answer loads, she isn't interested. I also see small intrigue in her sideways glance. Maybe the Aussie accent. She notices the patch of tape on my wrist.

"Just got a little cut and didn't have any plasters," I say.

"Plasters?"

"Oh sorry! You guys call them *bandaids*," I say, feigning an American accent when I say that word. She giggles.

"Look, I have this birthday gift for my sister, Sylvia, but I want it to be a surprise. She's staying in that hotel across the street there. She is supposed to come out any minute and I don't want to run into her. Any chance you'd be willing to drop it off at the front desk for me? I'll pay for your gas while you do it. Just for being so nice," I pull out a wad of bills and start peeling off a few of them.

"It's fine, I'll do it. You don't have to pay me," she says, flashing a little sideways smile. "Let me just finish up and I'll drive into the lot and hand it the front desk," she says.

"Oh cheers! You're so awesome! Thank you so much! Are you sure you don't want me to pay for your gas?"

"No thanks," she says.

I see a small gap in her passenger window and slip the money through it and say, "Too late."

"Haha, thanks," she smiles. Then a slight uncomfortable moment. She expects me to ask her for her number.

I don't want to diss the girl. I say, "It's great to meet someone so nice, helpful and cute. Any chance I can get your number? Maybe give you a call?"

"Sure," she says and gives it over. "My name is Trista."

"Neat! Never heard that name before. Great sound to it," I say as I hand over the bag.

She takes it and gets into her car. She pulls away from the pump and drives to the hotel across the street. I see her carry out the task. The agents don't pay any attention to her, aside from natural glances at a nice-looking woman.

I feel a little bit like a sitting duck. Luckily, the agents are spread out and keep tight watch on all exits. They think I'm still in there. They look a little preoccupied. Like, "How do we get in every room?"

I look around for a place to watch for the fat-guy version of Teska, scoop her up and be on our way. I need a proper stake out spot, like a building opposite the hotel, a well-concealed vehicle, or a natural barrier to hide behind. There isn't anything but a wide street and a library across from the hotel. Not a great stake out spot. I need to park in something, and not the car we've been driving. QuadFilium and the mercenaries know it.

I head over to the nearest Target. I load up on some key items, including four burner phones, three toy magnets, two cans of hairspray, a can of spray paint, two spare knives, more tape, five lighters, string, some black sheets, one set of binoculars, eight more nanny cams and a backpack to carry all the shit.

I walk out to the enclosed parking area and look around. I need a van, and, unfortunately, I'm going to have to steal one. Aside from the Ugly Duckling Rental Car company, every other rental place requires a credit card. My alias, Jeremy Nemeth, doesn't have one. They'll tell me to fuck off.

I scan the place and look for an older model. Easier to steal. I'm not really practiced at hotwiring like Teska. I see a green Ford van with a couple of tinted side windows. Looks like the Scooby-Doo van. It'll do.

I go to the side away from the store to remain hidden from cameras or security guards. I pull out the string and create a slipknot a few feet down from one end. I lever one of the knives into the top corner of the door, prize it open about a quarter inch and slide part of the string through the top far end of the door and pull it along with both ends outside the door, with the slipknot inside. I lower it and snare the thumb pull to unlock the door, then tighten the slip knot. I pull up and it unlocks. I open the door and climb into the driver's seat.

I check obvious spots for a spare key: the visor, console, glove box. Nothing. I check the owner's manual and find a valet key in the back. I light her up and take off, leave the parking lot and turn onto the road.

The back of the van has excessive junk inside I need to jettison. I look for a good spot. I see a driveway off the side of the road that looks long and deep. I pull in and go up a few hundred feet. I stop halfway up and turn the van around. I open the back doors and back up as fast as I can, slam on the brakes and the load in the back flies out. I credit Jeff Foxworthy with this move. He once made a joke that if you unload your truck by backing up real fast and slamming on your brakes, you might be a redneck. I suppose I qualify now. I drive forward and slam on my brakes again. The back doors slam closed.

Stolen vehicle and rubbish on someone's driveway. Not being a good boy scout at the moment. I look for the nearest parking garage that isn't Target. There's a grocery store lot. I pull in and go to a lonely spot, away from other cars and not well lit. I climb in the back and rapidly assemble a dark room: tape the black sheets up along the windows, make small slits to look through. From the outside, it's impossible to see in, even from up close. The windows only reflect.

I disable the interior lights and set up a couple nanny cams in blind spots, so I see every angle around the vehicle. I find the nearest car and swap license plates.

I've been gone forty-three minutes. Hopefully, fat old man Teska hasn't wobbled out. I drive back to hotel and park across the four-lane street with a view of the hotel, and perch in my surveillance nest. From my vantage point, I see two operatives. One scopes the front. The other covers the side of the hotel, the fire escape and exit door. I create three more Find-Your-Friends apps between one phone and three others, so I can track the three with the one. Best way to be safe from the agents is to track them myself and know where they are.

The main vehicle I need to track is their helicopter, their only versatile mode of transport.

I watch. Normal traffic in and out of the hotel. The outside agent studies everyone who exits. He even talks to a few. It's past 2100. Come on Teska, get out of there. After twenty minutes, I see two agents come out the front door, Alex and his deputy, Brian. They haven't found Teska. And, they haven't found me. It explains the pained look of frustration on their faces, especially Alex's. He's accustomed to things going his way.

Alex talks to the first agent posted outside the front door for a few seconds, arms akimbo. Judging by body language, length of conversation and some minor lip reading through my binoculars, I'd say they're discussing options. Looks like Alex makes suggestions and the guy discusses it. All three look shagged. It's been days of awful sleep. Now, it looks like Alex is talking to the air. Must be Jean Jacques, giving his directions from the Mind Booth back in QuadFilium through audio feed. Standard procedure would be to have them replenish rest and sustenance, while they keep the minimum operatives on watch shifts. Brian, the deputy, takes over front door duty and Alex and the other guy walk off toward the operative on side of hotel.

They're going to be a bit thin. I hope Teska sees this and seizes the opportunity. She will.

Eleven minutes and thirty seconds later I see the fat old guy exit the hotel. Luckily, it's a different watch than the guy who saw me leave, who would have noticed that fat guy left twice and never re-entered. Could've made us. Would have. This fat old guy character is memorable. Another touch of luck from the angel. Jean Jacques's own recruitment requirements backfiring on him.

Teska, as fat man, walks down the street a couple blocks and I pull up in my van. She gets in.

"Stay in the fat-guy uniform," I say.

"Why?"

"Because we need to tag their car and helicopter with burner phones so we can track them. Or, we sit around and pray all night and day that Ashkay, the genius, doesn't outsmart us again. That's like praying for Michael Jordan to be worse than me at basketball. It just ain't going to fucking happen. Ashkay's the maestro of figuring this type of shit out."

"How did he find us at the hotel?"

I lift my arm up and show her the duct taped portion. "I figure they plugged my Mauri tattoo into a supercomputer and searched every camera feed they could tap. Which apparently includes the hotel we stayed at. I can't think of any other way," I say.

"I think you're right. There's no other way, unless they have my measurements," she says.

This is the first time I have ever heard Teska mention her body without some negative emotion connected with it. It was even a borderline joke. I roll with it.

"Haha. That's a possibility."

"How do we find the helicopter and car?" she asks.

"Let's drive around the block a few times and see where the agents go," I say.

We circle back and see Alex walk down the street a couple of blocks from the hotel. He enters a small parking lot, walks towards a black Suburban, and unlocks it. That was easy. Getting the helicopter will be harder. We can follow the Suburban for that.

Alex gets what he needs out of the car and walks away with a backpack. We park near the lot. Teska gets out in her ugly ass fat-guy costume and ninja-waddles over to the vehicle. She carries a burner phone with an external battery attached to double its life. She fixes it to the bottom with magnets and returns to the van. We drive off, but not too far. She changes out of her costume and puts on her cap and sunnies, which is odd on account of the fact it is nighttime, 2200 hours.

"Let's park with a view of our ugly duckling rental car. I want to see if QuadFilium agents, or more mercenaries, identify it," I say.

"We need to do the two-watch thing... track the GPS app and wait for the Suburban to move... with eyes on the rental for any nibbles. I'll rest first. You go next," I say.

We park on the side of the road with the rental in view, mixed in with other parked vehicles. It's a medium-traffic road with scattered buildings and patches of trees in their natural habitat.

I lie down in the back of the van on one side. Teska holds watch on the other.

Chapter 56
Jean Jacques

In the Mind Booth with Heidi, Kris and Ashkay. I sip green tea and sit at the head of the conference table, now a war table. Papers, coffee mugs, and schematics are strewn about.

I get the report from the field team. They've searched as many places they could throughout the hotel.

Alex reports confirmation that both fugitives have in fact been in the building and that there are conclusive signs in Teska and Wade's rooms that they've been there.

Separate rooms. Interesting. Squelches any romantic aspect. Surprising. They kissed two weeks ago.

Alex did painstaking searches in all rooms he could access. Other guest rooms only received cursory looks for obvious reasons. Wade and Teska must have made it out undetected.

A signal comes into the Mind Booth comm box from one of the field operatives, "Sir, something just clicked. May I say something?" asks Brian, the junior deputy.

"Shoot," I say.

"When I went in with agent Alex Gonzales to find Teska and Wade, I noticed an elderly, overweight man waiting for the elevator."

"And...?" asks Heidi.

"If Teska was able to walk right past us off a plane, she had to be in disguise, right? There's no way she got off that plane, or out of the hotel, without walking past us, in plain sight," says Brian.

Kris says, "True. What does this have to do with the fat man?"

"He got off that plane in Austin."

Jesus Christ! When did he leave the hotel!?

"About fifteen minutes ago. I was on front-door watch. He hobbled out past me."

"When did you take over the watch?" I ask.

"Ten or fifteen minutes before. Ray Williams was the watch before me, sir."

I push the button on the comm box to direct my words to field operative Ray Williams.

"Ray, come in," I say.

"Yes, sir," says Ray.

Ashkay sends Ray a digital image of the old fat guy.

"Did you see this old guy leave or come in?"

"Yes, I saw him leave two hours ago."

"Did you see him return?" I ask,

"Definitely not," says Ray.

I say, "Ashkay, rewind the feed. Let's see both times this guy leaves and comes back."

Ashkay taps into Ray's audio/visual footage and rewinds it to the point where the guy left. Then he fast forwards it through to the end of the Ray's watch, when the Brian took over. At no point does the fat guy re-enter the building.

Then we watch Brian's footage and see the same old fat guy leave while Brian watches front door. Fat guy leaves twice.

"This guy never comes back in but leaves twice. How's that possible?" I ask.

Ashkay says, "The fat guy is both Teska and Wade. This woman brings a bag inside and then walks out empty handed. About an hour later the fat guy leaves. He never came back the first time!"

"Zoom in on the eyes." I say

Ashkay zooms in on the fat guy's eyes. The second fat guy. Blue and brown.

"That's Teska."

"Zoom in in the first fat guy's eyes."

Ashkay rewinds and finds the earlier footage. "No eye contact. Can't see his eyes this time.

"Wade." I say.

"Let's check out this woman that brings the bag in."

Ashkay zooms in on the woman with the bag and freezes it. A "Happy Birthday to Sylvia" label is taped on it. Wade's handwriting. I recognize it.

I say, "Merde!" I slam my fist on the table. "They walked out in plain sight!" I add.

Kris says, "Yes, sir. Looks like they're on the run. Again."

I stand up and lean on my hands. The strategists all slump a bit and rub their hands through their hair or against their tired faces.

"Ashkay, any hits on Wade's tattoo from local cams?" I ask.

"Negative, boss."

"Do you think Wade could have figured out we jerry-rigged facial recognition onto his tattoo?" I ask.

Heidi answers, "Nothing surprises me with this dude. Or, he's wearing a long-sleeve shirt."

"In Phoenix? It's ninety-five degrees!" says Kris.

Heidi says, "Wade's the Aussie version of Sherlock Holmes. His mind is a pattern-watching filter. It calculates possibilities and narrows probabilities. Then, he selects the right one, almost always. He'd know the only way was some identifiable item like his face. He covered his face. Ergo, the tattoo."

Kris says, "He thinks like us, but a step ahead. We need to ask ourselves what he thinks we think, and be a step ahead of that."

I say, "Okay."

I punch into team leader Alex Gonzales. I tell him to rest the team tonight and be ready to hit the ground running in the morning.

"All field agents need to be on their top game. You got it?" I ask.

"Yes, sir."

Heidi says, "We need to ask ourselves: 'Why are Wade and Teska headed West?' Jeff is in Austin. Meeting him seems a top priority."

Kris answers, "To follow the assassins."

As Kris says that, I see my phone ring. It's Alistair.

"This is a life-or-death chess match, people. Know every move and be three steps ahead. I need to take this call," I say as I walk out, harried. I take a deep breath.

"Alistair," I say.

"Alas, the other two members of my mercenary team were the less competent of the batch," says Alistair.

"What happened?" I ask.

"They added a red tint to the highway tarmac, compliments of your fugitives."

Silence for a moment, bracing for Alistair's reaction. All I care about is whether he harms my family. This erudite fuck is impulsive.

He breaks the silence, "Please update me at your end."

"We found Wade and his partner in a hotel. We sealed all exits."

"Brilliant. And then...?"

"They got out, using impressive disguises," I say.

"I don't know whether to be impressed with them or disgusted with you," he says.

"Despite the incredible skill of our operatives, Wade is hands-down the best agent we've ever had. He breaks the mold on field training and mission success."

"A most worthy opponent. No one has ever penetrated my compound and survived. The last mercenary team was one of the finest. You're going to have to up your game. However, if he is not eliminated within twenty-four hours, I dare say a group of ruffians are going to take liberties with your wife and daughter. I'll perform introductions personally. I promise."

Fucker. How do I answer that? Say "Okay, sounds good" and flush my pride down the toilet. Or, tell him he's a piece of shit and he shortens the timeline.

I remain silent. I look at my watch. It is Monday at 4:03 p.m. France time. I have until tomorrow same time to handle the Wade factor.

"Exactly twenty-four hours from this moment." The phone clicks off. Alistair's 'promise' impinged. I put the phone in my pocket and look around my office. The world spins. I now hunt my best man, shun some of my best strategists and loyal soldiers. My family is in deep peril. I'm a fucking liar. I need to get a grip.

A message comes in from Brett to update on Yun Fei.

"Go," I say.

"Very, very bad news, Mr. Girard. I got to her too late."

"What happened?"

"I was walking towards her building and heard sirens, lights everywhere. A crowd on the street. I wiggled my way in to get a look. A stretcher came out covered head to toe and was put into an ambulance. A dead body."

"Do we know it was her?"

"I followed the ambulance to the hospital and pried and bribed. It was her. She jumped off a tenth-floor balcony."

I drop to the floor on my knees and slam my fists against the carpet, "*Fuck!* Goddammit! I sent you too late."

"Boss, it sucks. But, you got enough going on right now. It's definitely not your fault."

I say, as a tear forms in my eye, "It feels like it. It was my only stab at some good news. This has been the worst week of my life."

Brett says, "I got it. I'm on my way back. I'll help you piece everything back together."

"If I'm here."

Chapter 57

Wade

I wake up on the van floor mid-morning to Teska's gentle rocking.

"Your turn, sleepyhead," she says, chuckling at my smushed face and scraggly hair. She looks pretty tired herself. I check my watch. Its 0330 hours. I sneak outside in the still darkness to find a place to relieve myself. I find an area hidden in shrubs. I piss and drink a half a liter of water at the same time.

I glance over at the ugly duckling rental car, unmolested, about 100 feet away. I come back. Teska's already snuggled into my makeshift bed.

"It's nice and warm in here," she says, with a smile. I return a smile and take over the watch.

The Suburban has not moved. The rental remains.

An hour goes by with no activity 'cept a mischievous raccoon that finds a rubbish bin to tip over and explore.

I see a car drive by and slow as it passes the rental. It circles again, slowing again in the same spot. Must be another mercenary squad. If they were total professionals, they'd have an auxiliary vehicle watching for watchers. They would have predicted this as bait. Most mercenaries don't deal with folks like me. Their targets are often easy access. They've likely been warned that their current rabbits are wily.

I look through the slits in the black sheets and scan the surroundings for another watcher. The new car parks forty feet from the rental. If I were them, I'd look in nearby cars, like this one. My blackout sheets should hide us. I tap into the nanny cams I've set up around the van. So far, no sign of anyone.

Then, I see movement. A man approaches the van from the shrubbery area, near where I took a piss. I can only see him in silhouette through the cam. He crouches and moves slowly. Then I see the unmistakable shape of a gun with a silencer in his right hand. He approaches the van from the back where there are no windows. He thinks he's invisible. If he has experience, he'll look for the telltale signs of a stakeout. Blacked-out windows, dirty car but clean windows. Couple windows cracked for ventilation. He should be able to figure me out, in which case all he needs to do is blow the van up and collect his check from Alistair.

The other car that scoped out our rental, for which he no doubt has make, model and license plate, waits at a distance for the coast to be clear before approach. He'd assume there's a nice surprise waiting.

I have several options with this curious bloke circling my van. I could kill him, and risk losing the tail on the other vehicle. I could incapacitate him, sneak up on the other guy and put a tracking device on his car. Or, I could wait and see if this guy doesn't figure out that I'm in here, and walks away to search for me in some other parked car.

I decide on option two, but I need Teska for it.

I wake up Teska and point outside. I mouth the words, "There's a man outside with a gun." I show her the video footage on my phone. The man moves, no noise , no twig snaps or leaf crunch. He remains hidden from the view of the van's windows and mirrors. He is all stealth and wise, but we can see him. The van has a sunroof and it's already open. I set it up for ventilation and an alternate escape hatch in case of emergency.

I instruct Teska to go through the sunroof and neutralize the guy with minimal noise. I take three lighters out of the bag from Target and pop off their metal caps. I take the first one and remove the small lever that turns the flame up and down, and hand wind the gear until it hisses. I turn it back down to stop the hiss. I do this with the other two lighters, grab some tape, two burner phones with attached external batteries, and put these all in a small field bag. Teska, without noise, shimmies her way up through the sunroof and stomach-crawls towards the back, tire iron in hand. The man leans against the back of the van, listens, looks, thinks.

Teska knows the exact points of impact to knock someone out. Luckily, one of them is the top of the head. She bops him on the correct pressure point and he crumbles to the ground. His gun rattles across the tarmac, but otherwise noiseless. She crawls back into the van.

I tell Teska my plan and scurry off into the woodsy area off the side of the road, towards the other vehicle that is scoping our rental, parked and poised for action, waiting on the other guy to give the thumbs up, hence we have little time. The other guy's unconscious. When he doesn't answer in a minute or two, they'll get suspicious and bolt.

I call a burner phone from another burner. I put one on mute and one on speaker. I place the speaker one in a dark small cloth bag. I pull out my binoculars and study the parked car. Two men inside, alert, wait for a message from the now unconscious scout, for any sign of us. I grab two of the lighters and start the gas hiss on each. A steady stream of butane comes out. I tape both lighters to a tree, pointed at a downward angle, and light them. The flames envelope the plastic cases containing the butane. In the next thirty seconds or so, the plastic will melt and provide a nice explosion, just like a gunshot.

I leave the area and hide on the side of the road. I see that both the passenger and driver's side windows are open. Both men have their elbows hanging slightly out. The back windows are not open. Damn it. I ninja my way as close to the car as possible.

The first lighter bomb gunshot sounds off. Both men's heads turn to where they heard the shot flash. They focus on a spot to their right. The rearview mirror on the left of the car is not visible to the guy in the driver's seat. The "gunshot" happens again. This is my only chance. I sneak up and drop the small bag with the speaker phone burner behind the driver seat. Neither notice.

I can hear and track them now. I sneak back through the forested area and give Teska the thumbs up. She shakes the guy awake and pushes him stumbling out into the road, in plain sight of the two men in the car. They stiffen, try to size up the scene. Their headlights come on, spotlighting their stumbling scout. Teska fires a hollow point round into the man's head, which obediently explodes out the exit side.

"What the fuck!" yells one of the guys in the parked car.

The car guys fire up the engine and peel out. Teska and I jump into our van and listen to their conversation on the speaker phone and watch their movements on the Friends app.

"Jesus fucking Christ! Where were they?" says one.

"I don't know. I heard this guy was good. Let's hit it. He's probably following us," says the other.

"Keep an eye out! See anything?"

"Not a damn thing. The roads are empty. I'd be more worried about something jumping out from the side or the front."

"I'll watch for that."

"Mike's still back there, watching from a distance."

Teska and I glance at each other. There's another guy. Probably a little ways away, maybe with night vision and a sniper rifle. He was watching the car, not the van. Lucky us. If he'd been watching the van he would have popped Teska when she shimmied across the top. Or both of us when we came back and got back in. The diversions of the exploding lighters must've drawn his attention.

Now we need to find him. Listen.

"M-dog, come in M-dog," says one of the drivers.

A crackly voice comes through the CB radio, "M-dog go."

"R-fox down. Head blown across the street right in front of us. What's your twenty? We need to get you."

"Top of the office building 200 feet southeast of target car. I'll scale down the side, wait for your flashing headlights. How long?"

"Three minutes. We're going to go around the block and will approach from the north."

"Ten-four."

Teska and I grab our guns and look at each other. We both have ideas. She goes first, "I'll take out the shooter. You cover me in case they do something unusual."

"Good plan. Let's go."

We get out of the van and head towards the building. We dart between trees, shrubs, garbage cans and parked cars to hide as we hunt. The night air is still. No sounds of cars, only a background hum of nocturnal desert insects, reminding us there's some nature in this is city. A distant howl.

We get into an adjacent parking lot, a cinderblock wall

between us and the sniper's building that flanks the street. We can see the progress of the car in our GPS tracker. Turns west on the street perpendicular to the pickup spot. Taking out the sniper and leaving the other two would disassemble their team enough to send them packing home. Keeping the two in the car alive allows us to hear the conversation.

If we don't take out the sniper guy, he'll get in the back seat and find the little bag I dropped with the phone and battery pack. He needs to go.

The building is sixty-five feet away and the only firearms we have are handguns. Hitting a moving target at night from that distance is unreliable. Jumping this wall and exposing one or both of us increases the chances of getting killed.

The sniper has, by now, packed up his gear to rappel down the back side of the building.

Teska says, "I'm not a good enough shot to hit him at this range, while he runs in the dark. I can run at him and shoot while he approaches the car."

I answer, "You could. Too risky. That sniper is trained enough to rappel down a building and man a sniper rifle. He'll assume, since his friend's head just got ceremoniously pulped, that there are other threats. He'll be vigilant. He'll wield a semi-automatic, scanning the environment. The back of his brain, his hunter mind, will look for movements. You pop out over the wall, he'll be in the crouched position, steadying his arm on his knee, one eye closed, and he'll aim at you as you run towards him. Two seconds after you hit the ground from the wall, you'll have five or six bullets in you. Best not underestimate these guys. Alistair is paying millions for the best."

"Good point. But we need to take this guy out, no fail," she says.

"Right. I have an idea," I say.

I pull out another of the lighters I bought and disassemble the top, remove the bar of flint and the spring. I coil part of the spring around the flint and hold it between my fingers. Using another lighter, I heat the flint until it is red hot.

"Get ready to run at this guy. When this flint hits the ground, it makes a blinding flash that if used at night, can impair human vision for up to ten minutes. It's a homemade flash-bang. We only need ten seconds," I say.

Teska is poised to leap the wall. I see our guy rappel down the back of the building. I heat the flint. He comes around the corner towards the street, just as the pickup car pulls up.

I chuck the homemade flash device to land in front of him and look away. This technique takes all the incandescence this lighter has to last weeks or months and brings it all out in one flash. I hear the pop and the subsequent yell.

"Shit! I can't see!" cries the sniper.

Teska jumps the wall and rushes him. He detects an approach and starts wildly shooting in the general direction of Teska's footsteps. Blind, his efforts are fruitless. Teska gets within thirty feet of him and unloads half her magazine clip. The getaway car screeches away, fishtailing as it peels out.

We inspect the body. Look for clues. We find his wallet. His driver's license places him as a resident of California, named Nicholas Kurtz. He has several credit cards, a gym membership to LA Fitness and a few hundred dollars in cash. Some keys. A cell phone. Teska holds it to the corpse's face and the phone unlocks. She changes the password and pockets it.

There's no other information on this guy. If we leave him like this with no ID, he'll be John Doe'd by the coroner, and in very little time he'll be identified with his fingerprints, then his home in Cali will be sealed off as a crime scene.

We might want to use his place as a base of operation. We know his address and have his keys. It's best we delay things. I'll hide the body.

The night remains silent. It's 0345. This part of Phoenix isn't awake.

I say, "I'll take care of this guy. You listen to their conversation."

Teska grabs the phone from me and places it against her ear.

I look for a hidey-hole. I find a storm gutter with a sizable opening. I drag his body and shove it down in. It'll be days or weeks until they find him, if ever.

We head back to the van. We've pilfered his equipment, sniper rifle and personals. We catch our breath, hydrate and assess.

Teska says, "They're headed back to LA. They're scared and pissed. They want to call Alistair, but it's too early in the morning."

I say, "Okay. When they talk, we listen. The QuadFilium Suburban remains in place. We haven't located their helicopter, but they'll access it in the morning."

Teska says, "We track the Suburban in the morning. It'll take us to the chopper. Don't know how, but we have to plant a device in it. Then we GPS-track Tweedledee and Tweedledum to LA and see if they lead us to Alistair."

I nod.

"Those guys will be in LA by 0900 if they go straight through," I add. "We'll have their destination. Now, your turn to rest. You need to call Jeffrey before we leave."

We get back to the van. Teska rests. I watch the GPS for the

Suburban. I charge the devices. I listen to the thugs on my phone and hear another phone ring in their car.

Thug one says, "Shit, shit, shit! It's Alistair!"

"It's too fucking early. What time does this geezer get up?"

"No shit. Answer it."

"Hello, sir. It's RJ and MK."

"Where is Ryan?" asks Alistair, in his classical, diabolical English accent.

"Sir, he is dead."

"And Mike?"

"Dead also, sir."

"What happened?" asks Alistair.

One guy clears his throat, "We found the car with the make, model and license plate you gave us. We scoped the scene, circled the block a couple times. The car was in a dark suburb and appeared abandoned. We did a heat sensor check. There was nothing. Hadn't been driven, no live bodies inside. Before approach, Ryan did a recon for any ambush. He checked every car, looked behind every building, wall or bush within 200 feet of the car. Mike checked the upper levels... the rooftops, the parking garages. He also reported nothing. He set up a sniper spot to pick off targets if they appeared. Nothing.

"Next thing we know Ryan comes tumbling into the street, right in front of us, and gets half his head blown off."

Alistair says, "Cocky asshole, this Wade. An expositional brag. Kills a skilled bounty hunter exhibiting his clumsy demise. Like a toy. Bold and cold. An alpha move."

"We went to pick up Mike after he rappeled down the building. A flashbang blinded him and a pile of bullets shredded him. We bolted. We're eighty miles west of Phoenix on our way to LA."

"This Wade is formidable. Too formidable for you, I dare say. Evades every sortie. He has GPS chips installed in his head and yet his own people fail to track him down."

How does he know that?

"… he's good... his own people?"

"Yes. I've got them on the job as well, and they're good. The best. The prize goes to the one who gets him." *He has QF on the job of hunting me? Alistair does?*

"…right…"

"Be at Operations by 0930. I want to see you in person. We will need to come up with something that will actually work, even if there is considerable collateral damage involved."

"I'm following, sir."

"No… you're not…"

"Okay… sir."

Alistair hangs up.

They are silent for a moment.

"You hear what happened to Johnny on that so called high-collateral incident?"

"I heard something about it, what happened?"

"Some unkillable fuck, messing with Alistair's business. He had background in military or something, whatever. This fuck dodged every fucking hit. Alistair took his mercenaries, at least the ones left over. He does a lottery."

"A lottery…?"

"Yeah. Johnny lost. He was sent with dynamite packed under his jacket, to do a mass killing. The unkillable fuck was there. Just to hit this one guy."

"You're fucking kidding me!"

"Times Square a couple years ago, came out with guns in both arms? Unloaded into the crowd and blew himself up. Got,

I don't know, thirty-five people or something. Was all over the news. They said it was Isis. Had evidence the guy was some jihad type, whatever you call it. That was planted. Isis was happy to cooperate… all-powerful, strike anywhere, any time. They love that shit."

"Jesus! So did kamikaze dude smoke the target?"

"Yeah. It was the only way."

"How the fuck Alistair get that asshole to kill himself?"

"Tortured him for days, drugs, found out who his family was and his girlfriend and his mother and promised to give them all a ticket to see the Titanic firsthand or something."

"How do you know this shit?"

"Ryan told me."

"How'd he know?"

"Cuz he pulled the right lottery ticket. He was there."

"You think Alistair's going to do the same with us?

"It sure as fuck sounds it."

"Oh man, we're fucked?"

"We could run. Be hunted down in cold blood. One day, sitting in a café enjoying a scone when your head blows up into a cloud of pink mist, mid sip. You'd have better chances playing rock, paper, scissors with these other guys than you do running."

"Fuck!"

"It's the life we lead, my friend. Yo, ho, ho, ho, a pirate's life for me."

"Seriously? You're singing that shit?"

"Only way to live, my friend."

They banter more.

They are going to lead us straight to Alistair. If QuadFilium doesn't stop us first. Now I know that Alistair has some serious leverage on Jean Jacques. He knows about QF. He must have Jean Jacques family. That's the only thing that would explain this all. *How did he find out about us? How did he get to the family?*

Chapter 58

Jean Jacques

A lone and helpless. Everything I try fails. In one week, my family, my organization, my closest friends, losing it all.

A punishment? God's wrath?

I need to braze up. Be the leader I am.

Its 0600 in Phoenix. My team, what's left of it, rests.

I walk out of my office. It's 1403 here. I walk down the hall. The walls look watery, milky. Sound echoes. Jagged thoughts dart and make me flinch. Dissonance is my cloak. I'm losing it. I feel like I'm sedated.

A QF crew member walks by, smiles and nods. I mimic her like a robot. I'm dizzy but hide it. My smile disappears the moment I pass her. At the refreshment bay, I tap the coffee machine button. It drains into a mug. I sip. The scald on my tongue and throat jars me out of my haze a little. The caffeine makes its way to my brain and ignites what neurons survive. My heart stops tapping my ribs and hulks up a bit, playing a small rhythm.

I walk over to the Mind Booth and open the door. Ashkay leans in close to his computer screen. He stares at images from security cameras and tries to find Wade or Teska. His hair is clumpy, unkempt. Snack particles litter near his feet. Kris talks to Heidi. Heidi takes notes. They stop and look up when I enter.

Weary, I ask, "What the fuck's the plan?"

Heidi answers, "There's been no leads or signals from Ashkay's recognition software. Wade and Teska have adapted.

Probably covered his tattoo."

She continues, "They have not called Jeffrey. If they do, we only need them on the phone for thirty seconds to triangulate their position, burner phone or not."

"Good. Let's hope they call. What's the status on our downed agent in Austin?"

Kris answers, "Kevin's stable but has a ways to go. Recon says the doctors diagnosed him with amnesia. Smart move on his part. He's had a couple of surgeries to sort out hemorrhaging. His crushed ribs are braced to hold them together while they heal. He'll live, but he won't walk out of the hospital tomorrow."

I say, "Understood."

"Alistair has given us twenty-four hours to solve Wade. If we don't, he starts in on my family. He informed me of this three hours ago. We have twenty-one left." They look at me with solemn faces.

I continue: "Ashkay, is there any other way we can isolate them?"

"Tough, boss, cuz right now they're in a vehicle that has no connection to their aliases. I've tapped into the stolen car bulletins, but the chance that Wade forgot to change license plates is slim to none. Not likely they get pulled over.

"I have every tappable camera locked into my facial and tattoo recognition software. I looked through photos of Wade and Teska. Found nothing new to track.

"We are still tapped into Jeffrey's phone. He also has a burner. I have the remaining agent in Austin on him. He managed to get hold of the burner and its number. We tapped it. Jeffrey and Teska don't know. Nor does Wade. Wade will suspect it. But it's our best angle at the moment. If they contact

Jeffrey, we triangulate their position."

"Excellent. Do it. Keep thinking. More ideas. Anticipate..."

I walk to the head of the conference table.

"Heidi, I deputize you QuadFilium commander and mission leader. I have to go to Los Angeles."

"...okay, sir."

I leave and go back to my office. I announce on the PA that Heidi is the acting commander. I pack.

Chapter 59
Teska

It's 0600. The Suburban is moving. We fire up the old Ford van and follow, using the GPS to track them rather than visual surveillance. Too risky.

The Suburban goes down three streets and makes two turns. We are two blocks away. It parks and the guys jump out in front of a building that looks like an old hospital. Hospitals have helipads. Chopper's on top.

"You know helicopters. Where do we attach the phone and battery pack?" asks Wade.

"Choppers have landing skids, pylons, all sorts of doohickeys to stick it on. You have the duct tape?" I ask.

"Yeah. I'll get to the top of the building and see what I can do. I need to beat them there," Wade says.

It's a three-story building with a fire escape and drainpipes running down the walls. Wade jumps onto a dumpster and leaps to the first landing of the fire escape. He runs up like a monkey, fast and silent.

I watch and listen. A minute later, I see Wade come down the stairs with his agile gusto. He jumps to the pavement and says, "Done. Let's go."

We get back into the van and drive away. I look at the phone connected to the one I put on the chopper and ensure the GPS is working.

"Call Jeffrey now," says Wade, as he drives towards the highway on ramp heading east.

"Why are you headed east?" I thought we were going to LA?" I ask.

We are. But if QuadFilium or any assassins tapped Jeffrey's burner, they'll spot our location. If they see us going east, they'll assume we're heading back to Austin. We want that. I'm getting sick of all the excitement," says Wade.

"What do I say to Jeffrey?" I say. Butterflies build in my stomach.

"Tell him we are being attacked from every direction. We don't want him in the crosshairs. We'll take care of all the noise and return, so you guys can sort out everything," says Wade.

"Okay. Calling now." Wade gets onto the highway headed east on Interstate 10.

"Hello, Teska?" asks Jeffrey.

"Jeffrey. Hello."

"My God. This has been the craziest week of my life. So excited to see you, then terrified you were in danger. I've been sitting here trying to figure out..."

"I'm fine Jeffrey. I'm travelling with Wade and we are going to get all of this dangerous shit taken care of. Then I'll come back and we can sort everything out."

Jeffrey says, "I don't trust Wade. If he can hear me, I don't care. The guys from the unit you guys are from showed me footage of Wade doing some seriously outlandish shit. I know he has contracts on him from world-class assassins. I don't want you with him. It's *dangerous!*"

"Jeffrey. I understand how you feel, I don't blame you. But there's an enormous amount you need to understand. And know I'm the safest I could be right now. Trust me."

"It's not you I'm worried about. That footage really fucking shows Wade's a fucking psycho—"

"What footage?"

Wade whispers, "Put him on speaker."

I do.

Jeffrey continues, "Wade was throwing knives into some helpless guy's body and loving it. It was sick Teska. Sick!"

"Jeffrey," says Wade.

Silence.

"I'm going to tell you exactly what you saw. And you're going to listen to every word I say and make your own judgment.

"That guy had purchased sixteen kidnapped girls between the ages of ten to sixteen and abused each one of them sexually, one or two at a time, until they were used up and he didn't like them anymore. Then he traded them in for upgrades. The used ones got sold for less or harvested for organs, or simply discarded into a processing plant that turns living matter into fuel for engines.

"I did that painful demonstration under strict orders from the very guys showing you how sick I was. I vomited between each knife throw. It was disgusting to have to do. We did that to send a copy of the video to every single client that had purchased slaves for sex, and get them to... reconsider their habits. It worked. The operation lost over 3000 clients which resulted in 20,000 fewer young girls and boys enslaved. That's why the video was made. It's true. I kill people. I don't enjoy it. I only kill people actively involved, profiting and engaged in the irreversible destruction of others. And I try to do it in a humane way, except in the video you saw. I did it to save the lives of 20,000 kids and was forced to do it."

Long pause.

Jeffrey says, "Uh.... okay, okay, I... I..."

"It's 100% true. You know we got along. We bonded, right?" asks Wade.

"Yeah. Until I saw the video. Then I freaked out and was worried about Teska."

"As anyone would," says Wade.

"I... I... I told them where you guys were meeting."

"I figured. But, I don't blame you. In the animal kingdom, the most powerful, vicious identity is Protector. A mother with her cubs. I understand."

"...yeah"

I jump back in, "Jeffrey. I vouch for Wade 100%. Do you believe us?"

"...I mean... I trust you... so... I guess... yeah."

"I'll come back when this is done. And we can talk about everything. Okay?"

"Okay. Be safe please."

"We probably will," I say.

Wade chimes in, "I don't intend to let anything harm her, Jeffrey."

"Thanks... Wade."

"Cheers," says Wade.

We end off the phone call and Wade pulls up next to a brown pickup in the neighboring lane and says, "Throw the phone into the bed of that truck."

"Why?"

"Listen," he says.

The faint sound of a helicopter gets louder. I look at the burner phone that has the GPS of the chopper's position. It's heading towards us. I should have been paying more attention.

I throw the phone. Bullseye. Wade exits the highway and stops under an overpass. Sound of the helicopter intensifies from the west. QuadFilium agents are on the move. They had Jeffrey's burner tapped and triangulated us. They'll follow the pickup truck, hopefully for a long while.

We get back onto the highway and head west. No one knows where we are, what we drive or where we're headed. We have trackers on the helicopter, the Suburban, and the thug car and 360 degrees of cameras on this van.

I check the GPS on the thugs. It is 0720. They are ninety-five miles outside of LA. We are three hours behind them. The Suburban's still in Phoenix. The helicopter looks like it landed near a hotel. Interesting.

"You're not going to believe what I heard last night," says Wade.

"What?"

"Alistair has Jean Jacques in his grip."

"What?!"

"He knows we're chipped and he told the thugs that he has QF hunting me."

"How on God's green Earth could he have accomplished that?"

"Since he specializes in using kids as currency, I can only imagine he found out about QF, Jean Jacques, Madame Girard, and Carmen, and kidnapped them. Now he's getting Jean Jacques to do his bidding."

"How could he have figured that out?"

"Lord only knows."

"He's in LA. I suspect the kidnapped family are as well. Let's go save them."

"How?"

"We'll figure it out."

We argue a bit. I like to plan out every scenario, every

detail. He, on the other hand, says, "She'll be awright," or "I don't know yet." Maddening.

After an hour and half of driving on a very straight road through desert, I see the thugs on the GPS tracker navigate the city of LA. They exit the 405 freeway at Wilshire and turn east.

"Wade, they exited the freeway and are now on the streets," I say.

"Okay. When they stop, get the exact address," he says.

The GPS shows the thugs plod along Wilshire for a few miles and then turn left up into the regal part of Beverly Hills, where stately mansions stand on display to the world. They wind through the neighborhood and pull into a driveway. I screenshot it for reference. The GPS shows the car enter and then disappear. The app says, "Signal Lost."

"They went underground," I say. "Signal's gone. I got the property."

"Okay great. How far away are we now?" he asks.

"Two and a half hours."

Chapter 60
Wade

The ride goes fast. We trade off taking power naps and enter LA on the 10 freeway.

We tracked the helicopter and saw it finally stop moving after two hours, then take off ten minutes later. They realized they were chasing a red herring. The chopper lifted and is headed west.

It's early, just after sunrise.

I say, "Let's go to Nick Kurtz's place and set ourselves up for the next leg of this adventure."

"The sniper we snuffed?"

"Yeah."

"What's his address again?"

I look through his stuff.

"He's got a place in Brentwood, close to where the 405 meets the 10. Close enough to Beverly Hills."

"Let's do it," says Teska.

We go north on the 405, on the west side of Los Angeles. We exit at Sunset Blvd. A couple blocks away, off a side street, we pull into Nick's driveway. A couple of expensive cars bejewel a beautiful dark-stone driveway.

"This pickle tickler is... was... well paid," I say.

"Looks to be empty."

We get out and knock on the door and wait two minutes.

"No one's home, let's go inside," says Teska.

We use his key and enter. Vaulted ceilings frame a

triangular wall of glass opposite the entrance and across a span of well-placed designer furniture.

"Bloody beauty of a place." I say.

We hear a beeping sound and look over to a plastic box on the wall with a red flashing light. It says "Home Alarm" on it.

"We didn't think about the code," says Teska.

"Hand me his phone," I say.

I punch in the new password Teska set up and go the *notes* section and type in the search bar, "Passwords."

A note appears that shows a hand-typed list of passwords this Nick guy kept. I scroll down and find "Home Security System" and note the five-digit code, walk over to the plastic box and punch it in, followed by "Disarm."

The beeping stops.

We look around and admire the fashionable life this man led. The fine leather furniture, the ornate décor, the fine crystal, California coastal fixtures and art. The far glass wall looks out to a small but nice back yard. Looks like some sort of Japanese garden or something.

"Let's find some gear," I say.

We look through closets, cubbies, pantry, home office and find a cabinet where rappelling equipment is stowed.

"We need one of these grappling hooks and some of the rapelling line," says Teska.

"True. Grab it. Any weapons?"

"No."

"Okay. Well... let's make ourselves a hearty brekky. Sleep for a couple of hours and then fuck off."

"Sounds great."

We head over to the kitchen and throw together a nice egg and bacon brekky.

"I will say, American bacon shits all over Aussie bacon. That's one thing the Americans really fucking aced," I say.

"Don't you think we've aced hamburgers and pizza?"

"Pizza, yes, hamburgers? I like the Aussie ones better. Americans don't even put beetroot on their burgers."

"What the fuck you talking about?"

"Yeah, how come you guys don't put beetroot on your burgers? That's how every self-respecting Aussie does it. Always have."

"That's so random. I doubt that any American, since 1776, has ever put a piece of fucking random-ass beetroot on a burger. You guys made that shit up. I can't even think with that."

"We don't think with it. We eat it. And it's good."

"It's random."

We polish off the nourishing food and hit the sack. We fall asleep fast and wake up two hours later. Ready for action. We head back out to the Scooby-Doo van and jump inside. We look over the details of the whole scene.

The Suburban left Phoenix, went straight to LA and parked itself in Los Angeles's San Fernando Valley. The thug car never left the Beverly Hills estate it entered, our destination. We head down the 405 south, pull off on Wilshire and go east towards Beverly Hills.

I say, "Let's drive by the property wearing our caps and sunnies and get a looksee."

We turn left on Santa Monica Blvd, lined with yoga-pants-wearing dog enthusiasts, some sculptures that are pretty modern, stately mansions and huge manicured lawns. We turn left on Camden and head up into a more shaded and secluded part of the town. We drive past several gated driveways and on the right is the estate we spotted. It has twenty-foot walls covered in ivy, a large solid metal gate with a guard booth and no way to see inside. We circle around and note the property takes up the entire block.

We park on a dead-end side street. I say, "The plan is we get inside, kill Alistair and anyone who gets in our way, and rescue the captives."

"How?" asks Teska.

"I still haven't figured that part out yet. But we know our objective."

"Right," she says.

"How many nanny cams do we have?" I ask.

"Five and three more if you count the ones on the car," she says.

"Okay. Get all of them. We'll throw them over the walls and see if we can get any intel. First, we locate their property cameras," I say. "Let's take a walk."

We walk around the property as if we are just neighborhood passersby. The cap and sunnies don't stand out. It's noon and sunny. Besides, it's standard attire for Beverly Hills elites.

They have PTZ cameras on every corner and bend on the property. Pan, Tilt, Zoom. Security loves this shit. Gives the blokes in the control room the ability to zoom in on any cockroach, walkers or us. Most of these security blokes are bored. I know just the thing.

I say, "What kind of bra you wearing?"

"Excuse me?" she asks.

"Does it look like a bikini top? Or is it lacey?" I ask.

"It's not lacey. I guess it could pass for a bikini," she says.

"I'm sorry to have to do this, but can you take off your shirt and walk over there and stand on the sidewalk and soak up the sun, facing that PTZ camera?" I ask. "The guard in the control room will zoom in on you rather than keep the camera in pan mode. I need a blind spot to pitch some nanny cams over and get an idea of the lay out of the place."

"All in the name of saving people's lives," she says as she sighs, and pulls off her shirt. I can't help but notice the beauty that God has created. Hope the guards can't either.

She walks over to the spot. Within ten seconds, the camera tilts down, points at her. These guys are fast on the draw. Vigilante wankers. Really on the ball.

I walk over to the blind spot and chuck a couple of the nanny cams over the wall. I look at my phone to see the views. One is black. Must have landed in a bush. The other is angled partly towards the house and partly towards the yard. A fountain. A guard walking. A colonnade. Ivy grows up everything including a gazebo. Nice joint. Fancy shit made of marble and limestone and other pricey materials.

I throw a couple more cameras over. One shows another angle. A more direct line to the house. The other is blacked out, probably face down in dirt. I glance over at Teska. She's definitely putting on a show for the randy guards. The camera doesn't budge. I see in the nanny cam another guard not far from the first. Looks like Alistair favors a heavy use of guards as his security solution. I don't see any other manmade measures like barbed-wire or towers, besides the gate and high walls. If the guards were out of the way, we'd have free reign. I calculate two platoons in and throughout the building and estate. All well-paid, experienced killers. Like in his last compound. Maybe better.

I study the wall. In walking around the block earlier, I saw no other entrances but the front gate. So, it's either jump the wall or break through the front. Our only two options. I suppose parachuting in is an option but not super feasible without a plane or a chopper… or a parachute.

I signal Teska over. The camera moves to pan position. We get back into our van and look over our supplies. Mostly stuff I got at Target in Phoenix or that Harold gave me as part of his Armageddon bug-out bag. And the rope and grappling hook we got from Nicholas Kurtz. Three handguns. Forty bullets. A couple more nanny cams. Four lighters. Two cans of hairspray. Duct tape. And some magnets. And a backpack. It's too bad I don't have Dimitri's fancy catapult shoebox thing.

I dress in shield skin battledress and put civilian clothes over them. Teska doesn't have hers. She stays in civvies. We remove our caps and glasses. At this point, I don't mind if QuadFilium identifies us with facial recognition. Their agents coming to this barbeque would be fine.

I set up the lighters to have them on continuous streaming gas by popping off the caps and taking off the regulator clips. I tape them to a can of hairspray along with the magnets. I keep the other hairspray can accessible in the backpack. We load our guns and waistband them. Two for her and one for me. Twenty bullets each.

We walk up the street on the other side of the road, outside view of the front gate and cameras. I keep an eye on the PTZ cam, to make sure it doesn't point towards us. We're in the shadows of overgrown trees.

We wait a good thirty minutes. The gate opens and a car drives out. Not the thug car we rigged with the GPS. We wait another forty-five minutes, and a van pulls up to the gate. I set the lighters on continuous stream of butane. They hiss. We walk towards the van, like strollers on the sidewalk. We veer around the van as any walker would. I light the lighters on the hairspray can. The flames are continuous and tilted, heating up the can's contents. I stick the contraption under the van's back bumper, held by the magnets, and walk with Teska. It all took three seconds.

We walk back to the part of the wall that looks easiest to throw a grappling hook over. We stand there and wait for the can of hairspray and its explosive, pressurized chemicals, to blow. And the chaos that will ensue.

Chapter 61
Jean Jacques

M y plane descends into the Santa Monica Airport. Before we touch down, Ashkay calls.

"Sir, we just tagged Wade and Teska on facial rec. They're in Beverly Hills."

"Get me their exact location and send the closest operatives there. How far?"

"Operatives in Encino. Twenty-three minutes away. About the same distance you are from Beverly Hills."

"Good, I'll head straight there."

With my bag of gear, I jump out of my plane onto the jetway. A car waits. I pile in. It was a long flight. I slept, but I'm groggy from jet lag. Then the adrenaline kicks in and washes it away.

Ashkay calls again, "Okay sir, the helicopter unit is on the way, thirty minutes out. The vehicular squad is twenty minutes to target. Sir, how'd you know to go to LA?"

"I knew they'd follow Alistair's men. Alistair only calls me on Pacific time. When Wade eliminated half his mercenaries, it was the logical choice.

"We have one hour left until Alistair's twenty-four-hour time clock chimes. Tell the operatives to step on it. They don't wait or hesitate—they take Wade out. I *cannot* let anything happen to my family!"

"Yes, sir."

My phone rings. It's Alistair.

"Hello," I say.

"Hello. How is our little expedition going with the ever-talented Wade? I'm having second thoughts. Your wife and daughter are so alluring... tick tock, tick tock..." says Alistair.

"We spotted him and we're less than twenty minutes away," I say.

"Splendid. A photo finish—" the call is interrupted by a loud bang I can hear in Alistair's phone. "I have to go!" Alistair hangs up.

"Step on it!" I say to the driver.

Chapter 62
Wade

Explosion. I hurl the grappling hook up towards the top of the ivy-covered wall and tug. It latches first try. I clamber up the rope and roll onto the top of the wall. It's heavily covered by tree branches and stems of ivy plants with buds and flowers.

Three guards sprint towards the van that brought the explosive device. All wearing sunnies, off-white blazers, black ties and white shirts. Slicked hair. None notice me.

Teska is on her way up the rope. I roll off sideways and land on some mulchy ground next to ferns and rose bushes.

I draw my sidearm. Teska lands behind me. Then we hear barking. Dogs smell us. Two snarly German Shepherds approach. If I shoot them, I blow our location and my diversion.

I reach into my bag and pull out the hairspray can and tilt it upside down. The first canine lunges at me. I spray his face with the upside down can. It freezes his moist nose. He yelps, jumps back and runs. The second one meets the same fate. Both run to their dog pen. One shakes and yelps. The other, frantic, rubs his nose and muzzle in the grass.

Teska and I scan the scene. A back patio, pool, a bar, a jacuzzi, a ping pong table. Two skimpily clad girls float on inflatable lounges in the pool, sitting up and looking in the direction of the bang.

I look up to a balcony. Its size says it's attached to a master bedroom. Leaning outside the sliding glass door, ever so slightly, is Alistair himself. I can tell it's the right one this time. No decoy. The last Alistair I killed was goofy. I knew it right away. I explained it away... the wine... the intoxicating women... he was witless. No. This is the real guy. Posture, predatory stance. He's a killer. Greed, lust, envy, wealth, debauchery, immorality, selfishness, gluttony and every other deadly sin.

Alistair's flanked by two hard-ass mother fuckers. These guys look like they could punch through a wall with their faces, and they have, judging by their scars. They scan the scene. Teska and I freeze behind a bush. One pauses, stares right at us. He steps forward on the balcony, removes his glasses, and squints. His eyebrows are so angular they form a V above his eyes. The seconds seem long. I hold my breath. If he sees us, a troupe of troops will run at us with machine guns and bullets we can't dodge. Luckily, we are seventy feet away. Alistair grabs the man's shoulder, turns him around, and points, assigns him a task. He missed us.

I lead Teska along the wall shrouded by trees, away from the commotion. The van's rear caught fire when the hairspray can exploded, and launched fiery shrapnel into the undercarriage and the back doors. It pops and fizzles, bringing all attention. We run along the wall. The pool girls paddle over to the edge and get out, and dry themselves off, eyes fixed on the burning van.

We crouch low and dart. We make our way to the back of the mansion behind a couple of hedges. Back of the house has a wide flat lawn with an adjacent tennis court and pool house. Across the lawn is a guest house, probably 3000 square feet, its own luxury home.

A patio extends from sliding glass doors. Behind them

looks like a dining room. I make out a stream of light coming from above. A sunlight. Roof-top entry.

I whisper to Teska, "If we're spotted, any hostages are dead. If it's Carmen and Madame Girard, they're gone if we twitch wrong."

"Ten-four," says Teska, "We get to them first. Alistair would already suspect a diversion. In minutes, guards will comb the whole perimeter."

I respond, "I'd say we have a minute. If captives, they're probably in the basement. Guards. No windows."

Every house I've been in like this one has internal basement doors. Wider than bedroom or bath doors. They won't be visible to living areas... dining room... living room.

I say to Teska, "Laundry or back kitchen. Let's go."

Chapter 63
Jean Jacques

"Sir, we're three minutes from the Beverly Hills target. Where do we meet?" asks the team leader in the Suburban. He has three other agents with him. Experienced and skilled.

"Will Rogers Park. Parking Lot," I say.

The helicopter team leader asks, "Sir, fifteen minutes out. Three of us geared and ready. Advise on touch down."

"Beverly Hills Country Club. Land on the golf course. Fuck the golfers. We need all-hands on deck."

"Ten-four."

My driver enters Will Rogers Park and heads to the back of the parking lot, away from the few cars parked close to the entrance. We stop. I get out and look in the direction of where we spotted Wade's location.

Above the trees, I see a small puff of grey smoke. Not black smoke like a barbecue. Or white smoke like a factory. Grey. Bad flames. I remember the bang I heard through Alistair's phone earlier.

Is Wade going to blow it? Reveal himself and trigger the execution of my family? That evil English fuck is true-blue psycho. He'd do it.

The chopper touches down a couple blocks away at the country club. The soldiers high-tail it to us.

"Everyone gear up for maximum tact, but look civilian," I say.

The group dons full battledress garb, and covers it in baggy sweatshirts and sweat pants. Not Beverly Hills chic, but it will do. They jam as many weapons as they can into their outfits and regroup. I point above the trees.

"We'll follow that smoke and assess on arrival. Tac options 3, 7, 9. You know the drill. Hostage sit probable," I say.

They respond in the affirmative. We speed-walk towards the smoke. A gaggle of stiff-postured, athletic men scanning streets and houses.

We reach the street. Grey smoke rises over a large estate. Smoke billows are less. Fire extinguished? Ashkay chimes in on feed, "The camera we caught Wade on is the neighbor's. You just walked past it." Ashkay sees us through the camera. We walk out of the frame to the far corner, behind an ivy-covered wall on the opposite side of the street.

"This must be Alistair's place. I suspect Wade is inside. So are my wife and daughter." Rage overtakes mind and body. "I want to ram the door down and light the place up," I say. My operatives share glances. They detect the strain in my voice and face. A voice in the back of my head tells me to use logic and intelligence, not emotion.

The place is a fortress. Twenty-foot walls. A twenty-foot-high gate. One way in. PTZ cameras along the walls. A guard booth. This screams 'dozens of bodyguards inside.' Twenty-five minutes to Alistair's deadline.

I talk to the Mind Booth.

"Heidi. Talk to me!"

She says, "Ashkay has the blueprints. Basic mansion template with four or five common rooms, eight bedrooms, two kitchens, a guest house, pool. There are a series of underground rooms. Likely for 'business operations' and captives."

I ask, "Is there any way in besides the wall or through the

gate?"

Ashkay answers, "No, sir."

"Merde!" I say aloud. "No time! Kris, Heidi, *talk to me!*

Kris says, "Bring chopper in at 600 feet and rappel. Team penetrates the manor, takes out the bad guys, kill Wade, and saves the family."

I answer, "The guards will skeet-shoot us out of the sky as we drift down."

Heidi says, "After the bang and smoke they're not going to let anyone on the property even if they had scheduled servicemen to fix something. Wait until the last minute, C4 the gate, and storm in as a Hail Mary."

When faced with an unsolvable impasse, historical generals challenged each team member for solutions. Brilliant ideas emerged. At this point, I and the strategists have zero.

I answer, "That Hail Mary is our last resort." I turn to my squad and say, "In the next minute, I need everyone to come up with their own idea. Don't discuss it. How *you* would do it. Outside the box, whatever it takes. We use the best idea."

Chapter 64

Wade

On the roof are two riflemen, perched in their stations, in beige-coat guard uniforms. I see one long-barrel rifle point at the sky. He holds it like a staff. Long range. Scope.

One of the trophy, pool-lounging ladies stays by the pool, unaffected by all the commotion. Probably high. Teska sneaks up on her from behind, grabs her around the mouth, puts her arm around her body, and pulls her into the bushes. The squirming girl's efforts are futile against Teska's battle-hardened musculature. I pull off a piece of duct tape and place it over the woman's mouth. She's terrified.

Teska says, "Hold her."

I grab her arms and Teska removes the woman's bikini top and bottom, apologizing and promising we won't hurt her. The poor girl calms but cries. Teska undresses. Two naked sheilas that look this good could be the last sight I see before I die. My luck seems to affect all aspects. *Focus, Wade.*

Teska puts on the bikini and uses her discarded shirt to cover the woman. We place her against a nearby tree. She sits, faced away from the house. We tie her.

Teska walks to the pool area, in the woman's shades, and fits right in.

I scamper up the drainpipe on the back of the house and onto the back patio's overhang. Crouched, I look over at my two targets. These guys are much bigger up close. At least 225 each and young enough to be recent ex-military, special forces if sniper-trained. The bang and the commotion have them doped up on adrenaline, ready for action. That makes them five times more deadly than a sitting, daydreaming, bored guard.

I pick up a pebble and creep towards the waist-high wall that separates us. I flick it to the opposite side of the small square area they stand in. It clinks against metal flashing. They both turn away from me in the direction of the sound.

I jump over and cat-land behind the closest guy. His head and neck are a solid stump out of the thick mass of his back. His hair is covered in glistening sweat droplets coming through a light-haired military cut. I choose the pressure point behind his right ear and swing my elbow. I keep my hand open to prevent the muscles of my forearm from enveloping the ulna, the bladelike bone that runs through the forearm. This makes the sharpest and hardest blow deliverable by the human body. I pivot my core and keep my thumb against my chest as I land it. The pole-stroking primate didn't know what hit him. The knockout sounded like a two-by-four hitting a telephone pole. His body goes limp and collapses left.

The other guy is quick on the draw, like Billy the Kid from the wild west. He spins and pulls his sidearm in one smooth, practiced motion. Hollywood would have used that take.

I can't let him pull the trigger. The gunshot will alert the whole estate and trigger a full lockdown.

I'm eight feet away as he turns towards me. My eye catches that his finger's not on the trigger yet as he snagged the firearm out of his holster. That extra tenth of a second is all I have.

Sergeant Crutcher once trained me how to prevent an assailant from pulling the trigger. You can knock the gun sideways, towards the inside of his palm, before the trigger is depressed. The gun won't go off. Follow it with a kick downwards on the barrel and the gun flies out of his hand. He made me practice over and over until I was lightning fast.

I leap forward off my right leg and bring my left foot around, toes outstretched. I kick the barrel right as his finger squeezes. The gun doesn't go off. I land on my right side and bring the left leg down on the barrel. It clangs out of his hand. He reaches to grab it, opening up his legs in the process. I punch him straight in the nuggets, with an upward angle. Irreparable damage. Crutcher would be proud.

The bestial part of his brain sounds an alarm and his whole body gives one hard involuntary convulsion, and deactivates his motor controls and dexterity. A suffocated gurgle of pain squeezes out of his noosed voice box as his face turns bright red. He crumples into a fetal position and I deliver a knockout strike to the back of his neck, Out cold, probably thankfully. *You're welcome.*

I take his uniform and put it on, sunnies and all.

Chapter 65
Teska

There were enough random bikini-clad females here a minute ago, I don't look out of place. The others ran inside. I enter through the sliding doors and go to the kitchen. I turn on all the stove burners but no flames. Gas leaks out. I blow out the pilot light on the oven and do the same, turn it up to max and open the oven door. Gas hisses. I grab two knives and head to the back kitchen where hired help prepares meals. With the knives behind my back, I enter and see two workers in chef hats, preparing food.

I walk to the first man, who stands surprised and confused as I approach. He isn't looking at my eyes. I swing my fist and connect at his chin with enough force to cause his brain to bounce back and forth in its cerebrospinal fluid, rendering him unconscious. He topples over. The other guy makes a run for it. I throw a knife into his back thigh; he screams and falls forward. I walk over and grab his hair on the back of his head and pop his head into the ground. Knockout number two. I drag their bodies to the walk-in fridge and close and lock the door.

I walk over to all the stoves and ovens and stream the gas out of them as well. I run out to the living room just in time to hear a loud crack and see shattered glass rain down, glistening and glittering. Two guards shield the falling glass with their arms as Wade drops from the high ceiling. Halfway down, he unloads two bullets into them. Both men fall as Wade lands in the middle of the room, one knee down, a sniper rifle across his back.

I run to the girls gathered in the study and scream, "The house is going to fucking blow up! Get into the pool. *now* !"

I say it so aggressively, terror ignites their fight-or-flight autonomic system protocols and they scramble out of the room towards the pool. Wade has already darted towards the door under the grand staircase, hopefully leading downstairs.

I head back to the kitchen and grab a spray can of olive oil and put it in the microwave set for ten minutes. I run outside to the backyard and untie the girl behind the tree. I drag her to the pool and get both of us in.

Chapter 66
Wade

I'm dressed as a guard. And there's enough here to require more than double-take to realize I'm not the real deal.

I open the door under the stairs. A stairway leads down. I march down confidently, looking down so my face doesn't register with whoever is on guard. I get to the bottom and see three guards standing in front of a door. They glance up and I neutralize them. But just before I shot them, all three flicked their eyes slightly to my right. Human instinct finds a last hope of survival. There must be a guard there just behind me. I jump to my left as the bullets I loosed enter their bodies. A gun goes off and misses me by a bee's dick length. A guard from under the stairs had popped out.

Their eye flicks saved my life.

He starts firing wildly. He's close but behind the stairs.

Next to me there's a wine barrel. Probably wine. It's heavy. I tip it over and roll it across the floor. The distraction gives me half a second. I slide across the stairs headfirst and poke him right in the cheek with the barrel of my gun as he turns back towards me.

"Drop it!" I yell.

He does and throws his hands up. He isn't paid enough to commit suicide.

"Where are the ladies?" I yell. His hesitation tells me he thinks I'll kill him once he tells. And, if he does survive, he's dead for telling me.

"This place is rigged to blow up in one minute! Tell me and get the fuck out of here! Everyone is going to die!"

This curtails his balk. He offers a key and says, "They're in that room!" and points to the door the three guards were manning.

I push his face away with the barrel of my gun. *"Get out of here!"* I yell. He runs up the stairs on all fours like an eager puppy.

I unlock the door and fling it open. Both women are there. Disheveled, make up smeared down their faces. Unclean.

"Madame Girard! Carmen! Come with me!" The guard uniform throws them off. "I'm with Jean Jacques. I'm saving you!" I say. Madame Girard recognizes me.

They follow me out the door and up the stairs. I estimate we have twenty seconds.

We run into the larger kitchen and open the walk-in fridge door. On the floor lie two unconscious men. One has blood running down the back of his leg. I shove the women inside. I pull the door closed behind me.

Chapter 67
Jean Jacques

The minute of thinking up ideas is up.

"Who's got a….?"

An immense *boom*. The heat of the flames from the estate hits us and we turn away. Shrapnel and debris rain down. The entire house is alight. *My family is in there.*

The magnitude of that explosion was unsurvivable. *What has Wade done? Has his brashness killed my wife and child?* I fall to my knees. The high walls hide any view of the place. A large oak on the property smolders, and pops into flames.

The team's crouched to avoid the shower of sparks around us.

"Ashkay! Tell me?" I ask.

Ashkay says, "Satellite view has the whole place on fire, boss. The Beverly Hills fire department isn't far. I'm glad you weren't in there."

I'd rather have died with honor trying to save my wife and daughter, than live the rest of my life knowing I didn't. I kneel in shock. The sound of a distant siren stirs me out of my trance. We're going to look guilty when the authorities arrive. I stand.

"All crew, stagger positions and wait for instructions!" I say.

They break off, hide their weapons, and blend into the neighborhood, spreading along the sidewalk. A couple of them gather with other onlookers. Others walk away from the disaster site. I stand on the far corner and watch flames devour the mansion. The ivy-covered perimeter walls are in flames. The breeze blows cinders into neighborhood trees. Some smolder. This could get worse.

The distant shrill of sirens is louder.

Three fire trucks arrive and the workmen-like team plug their hoses into hydrants and begin the fight. The other two engines attack the mansion from other sides.

They crash the front gate and move into the property. No sign of life. I see the guard from the booth carried out on a stretcher. I can't tell if he is alive or dead.

After ten minutes, multiple other departments arrive. Police, ambulances and more fire trucks. Stretchers with bodies carried out by the minute. The fire's finally contained and rising black smoke is all that remains. The firemen lead bikini clad women in blankets to awaiting ambulances. They look soaking wet. I look for my wife and daughter amongst them. Nothing. One of the women is Teska! She glances at me from fifty feet away and we lock eyes. I can't tell. *Is it hate? Disgust?* No. It's simple observation, clean and direct. I want to talk to her. But the place swarms in paramedics, police and firemen. I'm an onlooker.

Then Alistair, flanked by two firemen, walks out of the disaster zone. Like he's a fucking celebrity, being escorted by his personal entourage. I feel an irresistible urge to kill.

He is fifty feet away.

I do it.

I run in an accelerated sprint.

He notices me. I draw my sidearm like a berserker, aim it at his face and fire. The first man I've ever shot. I've ordered many men killed. Never with my own hands.

Alistair's head recoils as one bullet hits its mark. His

muscles twitch from chaotic neurological commands firing through his synapses. He flops limp to the ground. I empty my gun into his twitching body.

The fireman to his right already has a gun drawn. I turn look at him. *Why would a fireman carry a gun?* I see his face as he lifts the gun in my direction. It's a face identical to the man I shot.

He aims.

I'm a dead man.

His chest explodes outwards, towards me. Wet body parts shower my face and torso.

The jolt knocked the helmet off his head, and I see him even more clearly. The real Alistair. Not the decoy being led out by firemen. The dying Alistair falls.

I turn. The fireman to my left pulls a gun and points it at my head. *What did they do with the real firemen?* Honest hard-working men with families, now dead. All so Alistair could march out unharmed. *How'd he survive the blast?* I can see his finger squeeze the trigger as I look down the barrel of the gun.

So, this is how it ends.

My life's work has brought death to me and my family. My mistakes have killed not only the people I most love, not only me, but also the captives I could have saved.

My mind reels in flashes: my grandmother tells me stories of Nazi concentration camps... friends and family die, like pieces of meat or animals... piles of bodies stacked... school friends I had... Frances and I find love in California. The montage stops. I muse about the life we created together, and how I've destroyed her greatness by my unscrupulous behavior. Carmen. Raising her. I have no peace with God. I deserve to burn in hell. I accept my fate. The gun goes off.

Time stops. I'm not dead. The man's head disappears into pink mist. I'm still alive. The two imposter fireman are dead. One, Alistair. The other, his guard. Alistair's decoy is dead. I look down at the real Alistair. His blank eyes stare right at me. Still arrogant and condescending in death.

I stand with a loaded weapon. All of this commotion took less than three seconds. *Who shot them?*

On top of the guest house, 200 feet away, in standard sniper pose, lies Wade Maley.

He just saved my life and killed Alistair. And gives me hope my family is still alive.

Five policemen draw their sidearms. The point man yells to me, "Freeze! Drop your weapon!"

I do. I'm marched to a police car and read my rights. Four of my team rush the policemen, tackle them, and cuff them with their own handcuffs. They grab me and we run towards Will Rogers Park.

We board the chopper and take off.

I still don't know if my wife and daughter are alive, or burned to a crisp, like my dignity and worthless soul.

I wipe misted blood off my face and Alistair's body bits off my clothes. I look at the estate below. Smoke still vapors above the mansion. From this height it looks like the end of a campfire, a small trail of smoke billowing upwards. I stare forward, giving no directions or orders. Agent Alex Gonzales runs the show, talking, dishing out instructions.

Two operatives remain on the ground in the neighborhood. Police choppers will take up chase with us any minute. We need to touch down and ditch the chopper.

I look out at LA, an endless city. Most cities have limits, encircled by rural zones. Not LA. Every inch, city or dense suburb, in every direction. I see the coastline that separates LA from the Pacific. Where can we hide a chopper?

We land it in the middle of the so-called LA river. A cement structure that veins through the city and mocks all real rivers. Blatant. Unapologetic. Artificial. Thirty-degree angle banks, a thin trickle of water in the middle channel. The river symbolizes LA. Blatantant falseness. Unexcused. This city pretends to be lush, though a desert. It pretends to be glamorous but is unsightly or even slum. It hosts the largest pornification and sex trafficking in the country. It pretends to be romantic, a place of dreams. It calls itself a city of angels....

The top of the embankment is prime real estate for the tented un-homed. An entire village caps the angled banks around us. We abandon our chopper, run up the bank and out a gate, and are swallowed by the city of LA.

We check into a hotel and get several rooms. Alex remains with me and fills me in.

"Sir, we have no news on your family. The two operatives on the ground have not seen them. Twenty-six zipped body bags have been brought out of the property. We can check morgues.

A knock on the door. Alex frowns. Could be room service or the concierge. He checks the peephole. His head whips towards me and he says, "It's Wade." Alex draws his firearm.

"Wait! Let him in," I say.

Alex opens the door and I stand up and turn to Wade.

Wade enters, Teska behind, in a bikini. Wade knows what happened to my family. Alex brings a robe to Teska, and she puts it on.

"My wife and daughter were in that explosion, weren't they?" I ask.

"Yes," says Wade. My heart stops and my vision goes tunnel. My worst fears—

"They survived. I shoved them into a walk-in fridge in the kitchen and joined them. We watched the flames through the small window in the fridge door. We waited until the fire subsided. I had them stay in there while I neutralized Alistair. He tried to pull a fast one and sneak out like some fucking hero fireman. I foresaw that this time."

"They're alive?" I yell. Tears begin running down my face. "Where are they?"

Teska answers, "In the hospital, routine for injuries and smoke inhalation. Luckily the fridge was airtight. They're completely unharmed."

"Oh my God," I say as I fall to my knees and clasp my face and head in my hands, and cry uncontrollably.

I look up in shame.

I can hear Carmen's voice in my head, "Lying leads to crying and dying."

The man I was trying to kill, in order to save my family and hide my iniquities, saved them. Saved me. Saved… everything

Chapter 68
Wade

Jean Jacques gets us separate rooms in the hotel. He leaves for the hospital with the fat-guy mask and plans to walk past the police who are looking for him.

I go over to Teska's hotel room and knock on the door. She opens it and we sit down at the table. The room is white, with off-white furniture. Open windows allow a breeze in. It's a fresh and open layout. Luxurious. She looks refreshed, having eaten, showered and napped. I did the same, and am feeling replenished.

I say, "We need to talk about the Jeffrey thing."

She says, "Yes, we do."

"We should set it up to go and see him. And the two of you alone, talk and come to terms with the craziness of the last two years of your lives," I say.

"Yes, we should and will. But I need to tell you something, Wade."

"Yes?"

"That experience with Jeffrey was unfair to him, me and us. It ruined the best thing that ever happened to me up to that point in my life. It ruined a great life where we could flourish, build a family and grow together. It was destructive and dishonest of Jean Jacques to do that.

"I've been away from Jeffrey for the last year and a half. I don't love him the way I did anymore. It would be fake for me to rebuild a life with him. I'm not who I was. I'm who I am now:

a trained, special-forces-level assassin. I'm not going to be happy flying a helicopter for rich dudes going from Austin to Dallas and back, or for the traffic channel.

"As bad as what Jean Jacques did, I'm a lot happier than I ever have been, in my whole life.

"And a major part of that happiness, is you.

"I love you, Wade Maley."

...

I can't talk.

A feeling ripples from my stomach to the top of my head, slowly, as if lowered into a bath of warm happiness. Butterflies, excitement. Childish giddiness. My ears feel hot.

I calmly say, "I love you, too."

She leans in and kisses me. We press our mouths together and patiently feel one another's lips. It gets more passionate and my heart jumps another ten or twenty beats. Teska leans forward, pushes me back onto the couch on top. We kiss more. We rush to get in all the kisses we denied ourselves in the past in as little time as possible. A frenzy builds. She sits up and pulls her shirt and bra off over her head in one motion. I lean up and do the same.

The next hour is concentrated ecstasy, rapture, pleasure, thrill, satisfaction. The panting contemplation of it all, afterwards, lying in bed and staring at the ceiling.

After fifteen minutes of silent rest, Teska says, "I still want to talk to Jeffrey. But first we need to talk to Jean Jacques. He's got some things to sort out."

"Indeed," I say.

We get up and dress, then head over to Jean Jacques' hotel room. I knock and Agent Alex opens the door. In a circle, in the middle of the living room area, sits the Girard family full of weeps and hugs.

They look up and see us. Madame Girard looks up and stands. "You saved our lives, Wade and Teska. Thank you."

"My pleasure, ma'am," I say. Teska nods.

Jean Jacques looks down. He can't look me in the eyes. Carmen gets up and walks over and hugs me, and says, "Thank you."

I lightly and respectfully reciprocate.

My look to Teska says, "We'll do this later." She nods. We leave.

Chapter 69
Madame Girard

We have some food and tea, and then we all shower. Jean Jacques comes out of the bedroom into the room's living area. His face clouded in deep shame. I've never seen this face. He sits down, completing a triangle of Carmen, himself and me.

I break the silence, "Tell us everything. Beginning to end."

"I owe you that."

"Yes, you do, dad," says Carmen.

"I told Carmen everything about QuadFilium."

"Okay."

Jean Jacques tells us how he started using dishonest scopulus tactics. He'd force vulnerable prospects into a state of shock to recruit them. He tells of letting himself be fascinated with Teska and how it impaired his ethics and sense of judgment and it ill-affected all his behavior in every area. It became worse and worse. I took solace when he claimed he never touched Teska, said it was no excuse.

"Frances. Almost losing you was the coldest ice-water dip I'd ever had. You have always been the most important person to me. You are the love of my life. When you were ripped away it was even more apparent. I will always love you and will always remain loyal, and never stray ever again. That is, if you can find it in yourself to ever have me back as your husband."

Jean Jacques continues to explain how things went downhill fast: Wade departing, Alistair threatening, Teska going AWOL and his attempts to eliminate Wade to save his family.

"Dad. I can't believe you did that. You tried to kill Wade by lying to your own crew? Making them all believe he was the bad guy, when he really was the best of the good guys?"

"I did, dear. I won't blame you if you hate me forever. If there's any way I can make this better, I'll do that."

"You'll have to be very clever. For now, you are on indefinite probation as my husband," I say.

"Yes. No matter what or how long it takes, I will make it good again."

Chapter 70

Teska

I visited Jeffrey on my way back to QuadFilium in France. We made peace with everything, including providing him a gift from the Girard family of ten million dollars to for the pain and suffering he endured through the dishonest setup Jean Jacques had perpetrated in my recruitment, that mangled Jeffrey's life as he knew it.

We closed the book on our future romance. Jeffrey was sad, but felt it coming. He had already been mourning my death for almost two years by this point. And had started to finally take interest in the woman next door.

He was very thankful for the payment. We left on great terms and vowed to stay in touch at all times. I thanked him for pulling me out of a life of depression and an irreversible succumb. I told him I would always love him for everything he had done for me and for the life he gave to me, and I was sorry for ever believing he was unfaithful.

NOW
QUADFILIUM HEADQUARTERS

Jean Jacques invites Wade and me to his steel and glass office, a few hours after we arrive back at the base. We enter, and Jean Jacques stands. His eyes beam remorse. He gestures towards the chairs across the desk.

Wade goes first, "You spared no effort trying to kill me."

"I know. Then you saved my life. And my family's. By my

own book, I deserve the death penalty."

"A standard tribunal is in order. You should be treated the way any other QuadFilium member is treated. You have offenses. That's the method we use here."

"I fully agree. For what it is worth, I'm sorry, Wade, and Teska. I'm sorry. And... thank you for... everything.

"I step down as the leader of QuadFilium and turn it over to someone who's ethics are befitting of a leader of this group. Of course, I will go through the full tribunal and live by whatever penalty I am handed."

I say, "Agreed."

Wade says, "Yeah, you fucked up, bad. You deserve twenty-five years in prison, and serious ass kicking. But the type of pressure you were under, I can understand. Your family. It's inconceivable. Aside from all this, I know you as a man of honor. And the only way you are going to live free and happy is to confront the dishonesties, in detail, and those affected. Every one of them. Your wife, your team, us. Come clean on everything. Figure it out and communicate to each person affected by your dishonesty. Anyone you lied to. Any dishonest setup you had. Any scandalous arrangement you partook in. Make a list. Leave one stone unturned, it will sink you. Take your time. Soul-search and do it.

"Then give it all to the tribunal. It will give you a fair trial. You'll be penalized for things you deserve and acquitted for those you're innocent of.

"You came up with our justice system from your study of ancient Buddhist jurisprudence. It works. It's worked for twenty-four years. You are not above it. It is based on human behavior. It is brilliant. It will also weigh your overall value against your offenses, and that will play a role in the judicial body's findings."

"Wade, I will do that."

I ask, "One other thing. How did Alistair discover QuadFilium and kidnap your wife and daughter?"

"...I asked my wife, on the flight over here, if she had told anyone about QF. It was the only possible leak I could think of. She had. She admitted that in her therapy sessions with Dr. Garnier, her psychiatrist, she told him everything. He's the the only outsider that knows about QuadFilium, and of course, Carmen now knows about it. She also knows that it was incredible good luck in surviving that hell in the shipping container that inspired both the founding of QF and the policy on recruiting those with that gift."

Wade looks over at me.

I say, "Seems like we need to pay Dr. Garnier a visit before he takes off to the West Indies or looks to profit even more from the information."

Epilogue

The tribunal found Jean Jacques guilty of attempted murder and high treason as a trusted leader and of setting up Wade and Teska's scopulus. Jean Jacques also admitted to three other setups.

He wrote out a full confession, explaining that his motive with Teska was not just professional, and that he had violated his sacred rule of non-invasion of privacy with regards her visual feed.

The tribunal assigned him to the galley as a dishwasher for ten years, with no days off unless Madame Girard or Carmen specifically request time with him. He was also assigned to train through all the Special Forces, and other regimens the rest of the group were required to undergo—three times through from beginning to end. He was outfitted with the same devices the rest of QuadFilium crew wear, ocular and phonic.

Jean Jacques gave a full briefing to the crew, confessed everything and officially removed himself from his post as Commanding Officer, and placed himself at the mercy of the justice system he developed. One he had placed himself above.

Wade and Teska were each awarded ten million dollars in damages and were granted a leave of absence to visit Peyton in Australia and see the world on a two-month vacation. They told Peyton the truth and of course secured her pledge to keep it a secret.

Jean Jacques personally paid Peyton ten million dollars for her fake kidnapping and attendant stress. This saved her family from total desolation— they were just weeks away from becoming homeless.

QuadFilium voted in a new Commanding Officer, John Crutcher. Dimitri was asked to be a nominee but declined. He felt his extant position was the best one for him. He retained his capacity as the Director of the Science Division, but accepted the assignment of lead strategist. Brett retained his lead position as John Crutcher's advisor.

Jean Jacques humbly and gratefully accepted these terms.

The tribunal weighed his overall contributions to mankind against his offenses. His offenses were proven factual. As were his humanitarian accomplishments: building an effective anti-slaver group, reducing the global slave count by over two million, dedicating his life to the freeing of victims of the sex and organ trade by the eradication of monstrous criminals. All mitigated his crimes. His honesty at the end was also considered a welcomed reform. It saved him.

Before going on vacation, Wade and Teska paid Doctor Garnier a visit. They extracted how much he received for the intel he sold to Alistair: thirty million dollars. He was "encouraged" to wire the entire quantity in his bank accounts into an encrypted QuadFilium account. Forty-five million. After which, when Wade and Teska were deciding what to do with him, the doctor took his own life. He swallowed something and flopped to the floor moments later.

Ashkay, Heidi, Kris, and all accessory operatives were given tribunals for attempting to execute Jean Jacques's illegal orders to kill Wade. They each received appropriate individual sentences and were removed from any positions of power they had enjoyed.

Wade and Teska visited the restaurant owner in Grenoble that housed Teska during her escape and gave him a thank you gift of 100,000 US dollars. They did the same with Harold and Maude. They gave $20,000 to the family in Montana that helped Wade when he fell from the sky. They found Dolly and gave her an award of $250,000 for her heroism in the LA Distribution center.

After their trip, Wade and Teska resumed their posts as field operatives, and Wade moved in with Teska and Spider.

John Crutcher took the bull by the horns as the new Commanding Officer, and QuadFilium is poised to scale up and change the world, as it has always done and will always do.

Carmen joined QuadFilium and is now in training.

Made in the USA
Las Vegas, NV
27 February 2023